PRAISE FOR THE NOVELS OF SHAYLA BLACK

"Scorching, wrenching, suspenseful, Shayla Black's books are a must-read." —Lora Leigh, #1 *New York Times* bestselling author

"Wickedly seductive from start to finish." —Jaci Burton, *New York Times* bestselling author

"If you like BDSM-themed ménage with strong, dominant males, you will enjoy this book." —*USA Today*

"Ms. Black is the master at writing a steamy, smokin'-hot, can-I-have-more-please sex scene." —Fiction Vixen

"The perfect combination of excitement, adventure, romance, and really hot sex . . . this book has it all!" —Smexy Books

"To die for. [A] fabulous read!" —Fresh Fiction

"This one is a scorcher." —The Romance Readers Connection

Wicked for You

SHAYLA BLACK

BERKLEY BOOKS, NEW YORK

BERKLEY

An imprint of Penguin Random House LLC
375 Hudson Street, New York, New York 10014

Library of Congress Cataloging-in-Publication Data

Black, Shayla.
Wicked for you / Shayla Black. — Berkley Trade paperback edition.
p.   cm
ISBN 978-0-425-27546-7
I. Title.
PS3602.L325245W52   2015   2015016230
813'.6—dc23

PUBLISHING HISTORY
Berkley trade paperback edition / October 2015

PRINTED IN THE UNITED STATES OF AMERICA

10 9 8 7 6 5 4 3 2 1

Cover photograph © Karina Simonsen / Arcangel Images.

Penguin
Random
House

Wicked for You

Chapter One

MYSTERY Mullins had finally had enough. After six and a half years of carrying this burning torch, she intended to snuff it out tonight.

The door to the run-down beer bar creaked when she opened it. As soon as she looked inside, she truly wished she hadn't. The late-afternoon sunlight cast rays into the dark room, highlighting dingy checkerboard floors, a crack in the plastic face of the old jukebox, and a faded wooden bar. Pictures of beaches, bikini babes, and motorcycles lined the walls. In faded aqua paint on driftwood, a framed piece of "art" proclaimed IT'S FIVE O'CLOCK SOMEWHERE.

In front of her, a bank of TVs hung from the ceiling, some facing the door, others away to serve the patrons on the far side of the U-shaped bar. She scanned the room, glancing over the two dozen loners, mostly male, nursing their beers. Between the dimness and the obstruction of the various flat-screens, she couldn't see all their faces.

She'd never stepped foot in a place like this. Trendy hot spots where one's name had to be on the list, sure—when someone twisted her arm. But a dive? She winced. The reality was, if she wanted to scratch her itch for the one man she couldn't seem to purge from her system so she could move on, this was where she needed to be.

Because *he* was here.

A gust of hot wind assaulted her through the still-open door. The heat already felt like the worst of a London summer, despite the fact that May in Dallas had barely begun. Or maybe she was just flushed and nervous.

An ineffectual swamp cooler clattered as it tried to adjust the temperature inside to something bearable but failed. Mystery wiped at the fine film of perspiration at her temple, flipped the faux hair out of her face, and hoped like hell this scheme worked.

The patrons in the bar were beginning to stare, not as if they recognized her, thank goodness. But what if he did? Utter, humiliating disaster. She'd planned this disguise so he'd never know her identity. The auburn wig with bangs cloaked her dark hair. Color contacts morphed hazel eyes into a stunning blue. A makeup artist Mystery knew from one of her father's previous movies had worked his magic to make her cheekbones appear rounder, her jaw softer. During her brief time with her crush, she'd never had the luxury of wearing a shred of makeup. If he'd seen pictures of her since they'd gone their separate ways, he knew she usually dolled up and wore Chanel or Prada for the cameras. Today, she'd donned ratty jeans left over from her few days in college, a tight Hooters tank top, and a pair of wedged flip flops. The press had never photographed her this dressed down. Everything about her should appear different. He couldn't possibly recognize her now.

But what if he did?

Mystery shook her head and told herself to stop dithering. She hadn't stepped foot on U.S. soil in over a half dozen years, and he had no reason to suspect she'd come to his home turf now. Appointments back in London meant she could only be here for a week. The private investigator she'd hired had sworn he was still single and had just entered the bar alone a few minutes ago. It was now or never.

Because she'd never moved on from her teenage crush. She'd ten times rather write off her feelings as gratitude and stupid hero worship. After all, he'd saved her life. But if that's all she felt, the ache for him should have worn off long before now. She would have stopped comparing him to other men she dated. Since he wasn't going to fall desperately in love with her, she simply had to get him out of her system and move on, leaving him none the wiser.

"You need some help or you just want to let all the hot air in?" As she stood frozen in the doorway, the young bartender looked at her as if she must be on the stupid side.

"Sorry," Mystery murmured, easing farther into the joint and scanning the room once more.

A couple of *Duck Dynasty* wannabes occupied the booth in the corner. A woman in a skimpy halter top sat with them, pouring tequila into a shot glass shoved into her artificially enhanced cleavage. More than one dived for the booze. Mystery halted in her tracks.

This place certainly underscored the fact that she and the man she yearned for hailed from different walks of life. But that didn't matter. She'd only have him for a night.

She prayed that was all she needed.

Mystery's stomach knotted. Though she hadn't seen him since that last fateful night years ago, her nerves seriously annoyed her. She tried not to allow anything to faze her anymore. Not paparazzi, not walking the red carpet at the BAFTA awards with her A-list father, not even appearing on TV.

But Axel Dillon . . . Even the thought of him turned her inside out.

Mystery glanced around again, easing farther inside. Some biker types in the far corner playing pool eyed her. The bartender still stared down his pierced nose at her. Three cops huddled together all turned and focused on her. Did they think she was casing the place for a robbery? She had to stop standing in the middle of the room like an idiot. *Take a seat and order a drink.*

Finally, her head forced her body to obey, and she eased into a little booth near the back. Once she'd seated herself, everyone around her started talking again. And from her new vantage point, she could see the back half of the bar, previously obscured by the wall of televisions.

There he sat, absently staring at ESPN and sipping a beer, his profile strong. As usual, his rugged face was unreadable. He still kept his dark-blond hair military short. And he still looked like the side of a mountain. Somewhere around six foot five, he'd always been built big, but in the last few years, she'd swear he'd put on another slab of muscle. His tight black T-shirt hugged every hard swell and lean dip, tapering past a flat belly to narrow hips. She had to hold in a sigh. Even a single glance of him made her heart knock against her ribs and everything below her waist tingle. Mystery swallowed.

He didn't once look her way. Somehow, she'd hoped their stares would lock. He would approach her, want her, and whisk her away for a spectacular night of unbridled sex that would blow away both her panties and her mind. But right now, he clearly had no idea she existed.

On shaky knees, she stood again and headed in his direction. She tried not to stare. A glance up at the television proved he watched a recap of a pro basketball game. With a grunt, he glanced down into the neck of his beer bottle as she slid onto the empty stool beside him.

Now that he was so near, Mystery could feel his body heat, smell him—rugged earth, cut wood, musk. Damn, being this close made her feel both safe and weak.

"Something on your mind?" He turned to her, his stare expectant.

She searched his expression and didn't see a hint of recognition on his large, blunt face. What a relief. But the cleft in his chin and his bright blue eyes still made her feel weak and wanting. The instant chemical attraction she'd felt years ago hadn't waned in the least.

"There is." She mimicked the British accents she'd been surrounded with since she'd fled the U.S.—and him—over six years ago.

Her assertion obviously surprised him. Though he narrowed his eyes, they pierced her.

"I'll bite. Lay it on me."

The bartender chose that moment to come around and plunk a napkin in front of her. "Now that you found a seat, you want a drink?"

A glass of vino sounded heavenly. "Do you have a wine list, please?"

He snorted. "No. I got three types: red, white, and pink."

Mystery paused. She hadn't expected anything private label, but surely more of a selection than that.

"Is the white a pinot grigio?"

The bartender looked as if he was losing patience. "I don't know what kind that is, but the jug of white I have is as close as I've got. You want some or not?"

That could be seriously terrible.

"Then I'll have a glass of water, please." Better to keep a clear head, anyway. "Thank you."

As he turned and grabbed a glass, the bartender shook his head and muttered something to himself. Mystery really didn't want to know what.

"I'm not sure what threw him off more, your accent or your request." The corner of Axel's mouth lifted in amusement, giving her a flash of dimples.

She'd forgotten the way his smile could soften his harsh face. She grinned back. "He seemed quite ruffled."

A moment later, the young, pierced guy set a glass in front of her with lots of ice and a bit of water, sans lemon. She blinked, and her colored contacts jabbed her eyes with a reminder of their existence. Or maybe it was a warning that her plan would fail spectacularly.

"So do you," Axel said. "I won't point out that I've never seen you here, but I'll guess you've never been to a place like this."

"Never," she admitted. "What gave me away?"

He chuffed. "Leaving the door open so you could gape with barely disguised horror was a start. I particularly liked the way you turned slightly green when you stared at the guys about to do body shots with Trina." He nodded to the corner where the bearded men and the woman in the halter top all laughed. "So why are you here?"

She'd forgotten how observant he could be and how accurately he could draw conclusions. He did it in an instant, as if nothing in the world shocked him anymore. The world still shocked her all the time.

She hadn't, however, forgotten how direct he was.

"Curious," she lied and held in a wince at her lame answer.

He shrugged. "Let me try another way: The place is more than half empty, so why did you sit next to me?"

Brutally direct, she mentally corrected.

Mystery gaped for an answer. "Why not?"

In retrospect, she could have been a little less obvious and a little more coy in choosing a seat. Maybe she should have sat a few stools away, ordered some terrible wine, and seen if he struck up a conversation. But she'd taken one look at him, and any thought of careful or logical had flown out the window.

He leveled her with a disbelieving stare. "That's all you've got? You couldn't even have come up with a good lie?"

Not really. She could have gone the "You look familiar" route, but that would have been too close to the truth. As far as she could see, that only left her one tactic.

"You're very attractive. Pardon me for being interested."

A little smile lit up his eyes before he took another swig of beer. "I didn't say you being close upset me. You're attractive yourself." He stared a moment longer, then glanced down at his empty beer before he shifted his attention to her untouched glass. "You sure I can't get you something stronger to drink? I can't believe a girl like you would risk life and limb to come to this dive for a swig of water."

Truth was, drinking didn't hold a lot of appeal for her. In the past, she'd pretended otherwise, but . . . "While I appreciate the offer, I'm actually not interested in alcohol." She forced herself to meet his inquisitive stare. "Would you like to find somewhere more private to . . ."

"Talk?" He gave her an ironic curl of his lips.

"No." She sucked in a shaking breath. "To fuck. Would you be interested?"

* * *

AXEL sat back in his stool. Surprise pinged through him—which didn't happen often. He'd thought she'd strike up a conversation, maybe flirt. He certainly hadn't expected a sex invite. It happened, but he hadn't seen it coming from little Miss Prim. Sure, she'd dressed sexy and vamped herself up, but he'd bet his right nut the woman didn't know much about sex. And that she'd enjoyed even less of it.

Interesting turn of events . . .

Why would she proposition a complete stranger? Though he didn't know a stacked redhead like her or even a British female, something about her looked slightly familiar. He couldn't put his finger on it.

The one fact that was obvious? She was decidedly nervous. And she'd zeroed in on him immediately. If he had anything worth stealing, he'd worry she was a scam artist. But she would have to be a different sort of woman for that, one with a less perfect manicure, who picked up a stranger with ease.

But offering sex to a man she'd just met in a bar was something she'd clearly never done.

The whole situation begged him to question *why*, but he didn't want to kill the mood and pry the information out of her . . . yet. A beautiful woman wanted to get naked with him. Normally, he didn't do one-night stands. Casual fucks didn't go well with his kink of choice, which required more than passing trust. Vanilla sex usually wasn't his thing, either. But this woman was the first to raise more than mild interest in a long time. There was something about her . . . At this point, everything, really. She was not only one gorgeous package but an interesting riddle he'd like to solve. She had a reason for lowering herself to come to his favorite dive and pick him up. In an hour or two, he'd figure her out.

"Never mind." She scrambled out of her stool, looking at the floor. "You're not interested. I understand. It was foolish. I'm sorry."

"Sit," he barked automatically, then bit back a curse.

She wasn't a sub at Club Dominion, had no idea he was a Dominant who expected to be obeyed and would paddle her lovely ass if she didn't.

Axel opened his mouth to apologize, but she'd already complied. Suddenly, more than his interest rose. "I didn't say I wanted you to leave. You just surprised me."

A pretty little flush crawled up her cheeks. "I suppose I was a bit forward."

"Do you regularly proposition men?" He couldn't resist baiting her.

She cast her gaze down at her lap, and he drew in a steadying breath, beating back a sudden jolt of lust. Did she have any idea how many submissive signals she was giving off? His cock was every bit as piqued as his interest.

"No," she mumbled.

Though he probably should, Axel didn't stop himself from curling his finger under her chin and lifting her gaze to meet his. Vivid blue eyes with thick, black lashes. A full, bowed mouth. An air of unawakened sensuality he hadn't seen in years.

She wasn't the sort of woman he usually went for. He liked brunettes, especially if they sucked cock well and craved bondage. This red was absolutely the sort who would have sex with more than her hormones. She'd bring her heart and get it all tangled up in the man who gave her pleasure. Definitely, he should walk away.

"Where do you want to go?" Axel asked.

"I—I . . ." She blinked as if she hadn't thought this part through. Or maybe she was just nervous. Either way, she really was terrible at casual hookups. Axel found that oddly endearing.

"My place?" he offered. "Or would you rather have a hotel?"

"Y-your place." She frowned. "You're saying yes?"

"I'm saying yes." He took her hand. "Let's get out of here."

With his free hand, he slapped a ten-dollar bill down for his beer and guided her toward the door.

"What's your name?" he asked as they approached the exit.

"It's, um . . ."

"Bye, Ax," the trio of cops in the corner called.

He waved in greeting. "See you. And enjoy your beers with the boys now, Matt. As soon as that baby comes, it's going to be dirty diapers and exhaustion for you."

The other regulars laughed while Matt flipped him the finger.

With a hearty grin, Axel opened the door. As soon as they stepped out to the surprising spring heat, he stopped on the sidewalk and raised a brow at her. "Name?"

"I'm . . . Elise."

So Elise wasn't her name. He didn't know what it actually was and he didn't like being lied to, but there was some reason she'd chosen this bar and him with casual sex on her mind. In good time, he'd unravel the why and learn the truth, along with her real name. Maybe he shouldn't take someone unwilling to be honest to bed, but he'd already mentally undressed and started fucking her in his head. He wanted to do more than imagine.

"And you're Ax? That's unusual."

"Axel." He nodded. "It's not my given name, but it's what everyone calls me, so we'll leave it at that. You come here in your car?"

"No. I was in the area and saw this bar and . . . popped in."

The joint was off a side street, halfway down an alley, in a grungy part of town. No one just "popped in" unexpectedly, especially someone like her. Though her approach wasn't practiced, it had definitely been premeditated. *Hmm.* And how had she gotten here without a car? How had she expected to leave without transportation of her own?

Axel scowled. Two and two wasn't adding up. But he was a big boy. She wasn't going to roll him. Not that she gave off the vibe that she planned to. No doubt, however, that she wanted him for something.

Not-Elise was getting more interesting by the minute. Not only was she the first woman he'd wanted in a while, but she'd be the first he'd take to bed in way too long strictly because *he* wanted her, not because she needed him.

The thought nagged him with a sludge of guilt, and he shoved it away.

"Popped in, huh?" he drawled.

Her flush deepened. "Shall we call a taxi?"

Like it would be simple getting one in this part of town? "My bike is over there, if that works for you."

She followed his gaze and found his gleaming silver and black Ducati. "Can we?"

Had she never been on a motorcycle? Axel couldn't figure this woman out and he kind of liked that. The way her face lit up made him eager to explore her. The thought that he'd be able to see her climb to orgasm in those pretty eyes turned him on even more.

"Let's go."

Within minutes, they were settled on the bike. He'd fastened his too-big helmet on her head and given her a few basic instructions. She seemed fascinated, excited for this clearly new experience. As he started the bike and she settled behind him, wrapping her arms around his waist, he smiled. If new experiences turned her on, he had all kinds he could unleash on his little enigma.

* * *

AS the wind whipped around her, Mystery clung to Axel's lean waist, actually able to feel the muscles of his abdomen and back as she pressed herself against him and held on for dear life. After thirty seconds, she decided that she needed one of these when she got home. Her father—if he wasn't on location somewhere—would have a conniption. But wow, the freedom of feeling the air on her skin and the motor beneath her body exhilarated her.

She looked up, her gaze snared by the back of Axel's thick neck. Maybe she should resist the urge . . . but she didn't. Instead, she straightened a bit and braced her hands on his waist. It was a reach, but she pressed her lips to his skin. The moment she did, Mystery tasted a mild tang of salt, smelled clean soap blending with his rich, manly scent. Her head swam. Her body tightened.

God, this was going to be the best night of her life.

When she moaned and nipped at his nape, he tensed slightly, but she didn't get the impression he disliked what she'd done. On the contrary, he shuddered and reached back with one hand to grip her thigh.

She gasped and found Axel glancing at her over his shoulder, his blue eyes penetrating. The look he shot her told her that she was in for something fiery, fast, and irresistible. Mystery flashed hot all over. Finally, she'd know what he felt like as a lover. The years of fantasizing had only left her wanting.

A few turns later, he pulled up to an older house, something faintly art deco that had probably been built in the thirties, given the purity of the big rectangular windows, the flat roof, and the huge trees lining the quiet street. The rest of the elements looked traditional— brick accents and flagstone walkways. The landscape was sparse but healthy. Everything looked meticulously maintained. But that didn't surprise her. He'd always been methodical and precise.

"It's beautiful," she murmured as she lifted his helmet away, thanking the heavens it was way too big to pull her wig off.

He took it from her outstretched hand and hung it on the rearview mirror. "Thanks. It's peaceful. I like it here. Let me put this away." He reached into a saddlebag attached to the side and pulled out a garage door opener. With a press of a button, the big door raised, and he pushed the gleaming bike into the garage that, aside from a few organized tools, was otherwise empty.

Task completed, he hit the button to close the garage door and jumped over the sensor before returning to her side and taking her hand. "You sure about this?"

"Yes." Mystery didn't hesitate.

A smile broke out across his face, the kind of grin that told her that she was in way over her head. She knew all too well that she was—and she didn't care. Her pulse skittered. Breathing took a backseat to staring at him. He'd never know how long she'd waited for him to do his worst.

"Then come with me."

He unlocked the front door and opened it for her. She stepped over the threshold, into a gorgeous space with tall ceilings, pale honey floors, and a beautifully restored antique art deco dining room table. Through a big opening that likely wasn't original to the house, she peeked into the expansive kitchen. Their gray cabinets, white quartz counters, and a whole wall of windows invited her in. She could picture him cooking in here, sipping beer, and relaxing.

"It's lovely."

"Thanks." He led her into the domestic space. "I restored it myself. Drink?"

It seemed a bit odd to be pondering seduction late in the afternoon, as sunlight slanted through the bare windows. She'd pictured nightfall and champagne and elegance. But this was somehow quieter, more intimate. Perfect.

"No, thank you."

Axel prowled toward her, so big and intent, so male that she instinctively retreated a step. Her belly tightened. Her back met the kitchen counter. He kept coming, and her stare tangled with his. The wry smile he wore revved her heart.

"I might have better wine than the bar."

She wanted a completely clear head for this, wanted to remember every moment—and not dull her wits or risk blowing her cover. He'd been the first to teach her that booze had a time and a place, but not when one had a purpose. Her goal was to have incredible, orgasmic sex with the man she'd pined after and leave before he figured out exactly who he'd hit the sheets with.

"I'm sure you do, but no, thank you."

Nodding slowly, he leaned in to brace his hands on the counter, on either side of her body. The last few inches he left between them tortured her. Her ache to erase the distance between them writhed like a physical thing. The years of fantasies about him collided in her head and zoomed down to converge between her legs until she throbbed.

And Axel hadn't even touched her yet.

"Something to eat?"

Mystery got the distinct impression that he had no intention of cooking for her. He just toyed with her because he knew she wanted him so badly. If he'd figured that out and had no idea who she was, why not be brazen and ask for exactly what she wanted?

"I appreciate the offer, but if you're taking requests, I'd rather you show me to your bedroom and take off your clothes." Mystery didn't demand; she knew better.

He chuckled. "Eager, aren't you?"

"Yes." Why hide the truth?

He cocked his head and studied her. "I owe you some torment for kissing the back of my neck on my bike. And truthfully, once I get you to my bedroom, I'm going to be all over you and so far inside you, I'm likely to shock your sheltered sensibilities."

Her entire body jolted at his words. With a sharp gasp, she sucked in her next breath. "I want that."

"In good time. Let's . . . make our way to the couch."

More waiting sounded awful. More waiting would make her go mad.

Mystery surged forward, planting herself against his chest and bracing her hands on his massive shoulders. He didn't move as she brushed her lips over his and stole a kiss.

At first contact, fire sparked through her body. Another wave of heat zipped through her. She moaned and wrapped her arms around him.

Until she realized that, other than puckering up, Axel wasn't participating.

Horrified, she leaned back. "I'm sorry. I . . ." *Am mortified that I can't seem to control myself.*

She tried to duck out of his embrace, but he kept her caged between his body and the slab of quartz, then eased her back against the counter.

Mystery couldn't meet his gaze. "Please don't. I'm embarrassed enough."

He shook his head. "You shouldn't be. It's not that I don't want you kissing me, so if you're feeding yourself a ration of insecurity about that, you can stop. You're new at this whole seduction business, and I'm flattered you chose me."

God, he had her pegged, and Mystery wanted to crawl into a hole because she could hear the "but" in his speech. She'd heard him give her such a speech before.

"It's all right. You don't have to explain. If you've decided you're not interested, I can call a taxi and—"

Axel cut her off by wrapping his beefy hands around her waist and lifting her onto the counter. He used his big body to pry her knees apart and stepped between them. As he wrapped thick arms around her, he yanked her flush against him. "Look at me."

Hot and cold, bewilderment and need, shock and excitement—everything clashed in her bloodstream. Scarcely daring to breathe, she peeked up at him, lashes fluttering, until she found the gumption to meet his stare head-on. "What?"

"You're misunderstanding. I just want our first kiss to be something you remember, so scratch that last peck from your memory bank."

Their first kiss *had* been unforgettable. Not a day since had gone by that Mystery hadn't thought of it—and him—with longing. No man had ever made her ache more with his whole body than Axel had with just his mouth.

"Let's do it right," he murmured, cupping her face in his big hands.

All too eager to experience him again, Mystery met him halfway as he swooped down and captured her lips in a hard press. Instantly, the jolt of need she'd only ever experienced with him shocked her entire system. Every cell turned electric, glowed, pinging and lighting up. After the initial spark went through her, she threw her arms around him, more than happy to lose herself in the burn of his passion.

He was everything she'd waited to feel for six and a half long, lonely years.

As he pulled back and stared down at her, his big chest rising and falling faster than before, she lost herself in his blue eyes and remembered the first time she'd seen him.

Chapter Two

Six and a half years earlier

So *cold.* Mystery huddled into her blinged-out crop jacket and curled into the corner of the run-down shack. Her shoulders ached. She felt as if a furry creature had taken up residence in her mouth.

The wind howled, and she was thankful for the rickety wooden structure around her. As gusty as the weather had become, she worried the little hut—her only shelter—would blow over.

Closing her eyes, she tried to still her throbbing head. As groggy as she was, as much as sleep lured her to blissful oblivion, every time Mystery closed her eyes, she kept remembering the moments she'd walked out of the bar that she'd bribed and blustered her way into. At nineteen, she shouldn't have been there—and she wished now that she'd gone home, as she'd promised her father. But no. A few of her friends had had luck at this swanky, A-list bar with both booze and hot guys, so she'd decided to be daring and give it a try.

Being *the* Marshall Mullins's daughter had gotten her in immediately, no questions asked. No one in Hollywood hadn't heard of the Oscar-winning actor-director. He was as famous for his epic talent as he was for his romantic exploits over the last two decades.

But the scene in the bar hadn't been her thing. Loud. Lots of drugs and random hookups and pretty, heartless people. At just before midnight, she'd pleaded a headache and let herself outside, fishing in her purse for her car keys and thinking of things she could tell her father about where she'd been.

Mystery absolutely hadn't been expecting the burlap hood over her head or the rough hands pulling her into a vehicle, then speeding off into the night.

She hadn't struggled for long before she'd felt a needle in her arm. When she'd awakened, the hood had been removed. It looked like midmorning. Her purse, car keys, and cell phone were gone. She'd been handcuffed but was blessedly alone. A glance out a grungy window revealed nothing but miles and miles of desert.

It still seemed surreal that she'd been kidnapped. Did someone mean to ransom her? Rape her? Kill her? Mystery had no idea, and the not knowing sent panic skittering through her system. It was one of the few things keeping her awake.

She wished she could open her eyes and find this had been a nightmare, that she'd made different choices, that she could just run to her father's open arms and that he'd make everything all right again. But none of that was going to happen. She'd have to find her own way out of this mess.

The door to the shack opened, and a man wearing a ski mask and head-to-toe black entered, heading straight for her. She tried to shrink back, scanning the shack for another door. Nothing.

The masked man grabbed her by her arm and hauled her roughly to her feet. Mystery thought of kicking him and running but he was twice her size. Menace rolled off him like a thundercloud. He wore some sort of assault rifle strapped over his shoulder and a hideously large knife from a sheath, attached to his belt . . . right near his hand. She shrank back. *Please, God, don't let him use either on me.*

He grabbed the edges of her light jacket and shoved it down her arms.

"Don't," she pleaded—and hated herself for doing it. But she'd never been in danger. Hell, she'd hardly ever been out of Beverly

Hills. She didn't want to die here now. She had so much life in front of her.

And after her mother's high-profile death, if she died violently, it would kill her father.

He didn't acknowledge her pleading, just whirled her around until she faced the wall. "Hold still."

A moment later, he reached for her wrists and gripped one tightly.

Mystery stared at the dilapidated wood, her thoughts racing. What was he doing? Waiting for? Did he plan on stabbing her? Strangling her?

A second later, she felt a prick at her wrist, like a needle penetrating her skin, invasive in her vein.

"No!" She couldn't handle more drugs. Already she felt weak and shaky, vaguely sick to her stomach. Another round of that . . . The thought made her dry heave.

"Shut up!" he commanded. "Hold the fuck still."

"What are you doing?" She wanted to struggle but didn't dare, especially with the needle still stuck in her skin. She just wanted to get out alive, see her father again, be a normal teenager. If she could, she'd be so good, never do anything wrong again. "Stop!"

"I told you to shut up. I'm not hurting you, but if you keep flapping your mouth, it will be my pleasure."

Mystery pressed her lips together tightly. Long, terrible seconds passed as she waited for the drowsy lethargy to overpower her again. Instead, nothing broke the terrible silence except his rough breathing. God, she hoped that holding her captive wasn't sexually exciting him.

Finally, he withdrew the needle from her vein. He slapped something over the spot, then she heard a clanking sound, a bit like small gears grinding.

Suddenly, her arms were free. Mystery stretched them at her

sides, then crossed them in front of her as she whirled to face her attacker. He'd already stepped away and now hovered by the door.

"There's a bathroom in the next room. I left food and water in the sack on the workbench." He nodded in the direction of the rickety table shoved against the wall. Sure enough, a paper sack sat there, bulging with what she hoped would be edible. She was starving and no doubt dehydrated. At least it seemed he didn't mean for her to die right this instant. Later . . . she had no idea.

"The sun will be setting in the next two hours. There are over ten thousand square miles of virtually uninhabited desert all around us. It's over ninety degrees now. It will be in the thirties tonight. I don't think you'll get far in stilettos, a mini dress, and that flimsy jacket. But you're welcome to try. You might be saving me something messy in the future."

When he turned for the door, Mystery panicked. "Wait! What do you want? Why am I here?"

He scoffed. "Now you ask, you stupid bitch . . ." He fingered the knife at his belt, silently reminding her that he held the power. "I'm just following orders. Someone wanted you here. I don't ask questions; I just do jobs. I don't really give a shit what happens next."

Then he was gone, slamming the wobbly door behind him. Mystery stared out the window, watching him go. He walked away with a purposeful stride, toward an ATV. He mounted it, sent her a mocking salute, then disappeared.

The moment he rolled out of sight, she released the breath she'd been holding. Adrenaline bled out. She shook all over. What was she going to do? Her pampered life hadn't prepared her for this. She knew how to shop, how to play hostess for a party, how to pose when the paparazzi showed up. She didn't have a single survival skill. Did she want to run through the desert with no footwear, huddled in a coat meant purely for decoration, and carrying limited water, hoping she'd encounter a Good Samaritan? It didn't sound like a fantastic idea. Then again, hanging around here, waiting for that asshole to come back and end her didn't sound smart, either.

The probably slow death or the almost-certain quick one?

The quandary filled Mystery with icy-sharp dread.

She paced over to the food and ate every bite of the ham sandwich and the accompanying apple, then she downed one of her two bottles of water. God knew how long she'd been without hydration.

The sustenance helped her to think, to realize that she'd be best off to set out shortly before sunrise and walk all day, even if she'd do it barefoot, and try to find civilization. She'd hang onto this second bottle of water. It might be all she had to see her through a hot day.

She found the little bathroom next. It was tiny and disgusting and she refused to actually sit on the toilet, but it flushed. The dilapidated shower worked, but on second thought, did she really want to get naked when her captor could come back at any moment?

Then it became a waiting game. A couple of hours slid by. The sun brushed the horizon, and Mystery realized there wasn't a single light in this little shack. She'd pass the whole night in utter darkness, unable to see if dangerous critters—or the asshole who'd taken her—sneaked up on her. The thought added a whole different layer of fear.

Just before darkness fell, the door opened again, and Mr. Ski Mask appeared.

"What?" she demanded. Had he come to kill her now? Who's orders was he following?

"Change of plans. Boss doesn't want you going anywhere." He grabbed her and jabbed another needle in her arm. "Nighty night."

The last sound she heard was his chuckle as he shut the door and the world went black.

* * *

FOR the next two days, her routine fell into exactly the same pattern. By day three, Mystery knew she'd have to break it. Her captor didn't touch her—thank goodness for small miracles—but he liked to scare her with knives. When he'd brought her yesterday's meal, he'd hinted that he should soon know her fate. Every attempt to question him about why he'd drawn her blood and why he was holding her hostage he countered with threats or silence. She didn't know who was paying him or if they'd even made a ransom demand to her father. Poor Daddy had to be going insane, wondering where she was and if she was alive. She almost hated her captor as much for worrying her parent as she did for scaring the hell out of her.

Mystery watched out the window for her nemesis. He'd soon be coming with her food and hydration for the day. She'd consumed the water he'd given her and saved the bottles, refilling them in the bathroom sink. Amongst the junk in this little shack, she'd found an old duffel bag. It was small enough that she could fashion it into a backpack of sorts. She still wasn't sure what to do about shoes—a must in the desert—but she'd rather take her chances with the elements.

Finally, as the sun began heading for the horizon, Mystery saw the asshole who kept her prisoner climb off his ATV and stroll toward the shack. With a jaunty step, he opened the door and let himself in, plunking the paper bag with her usual sandwich, fruit, and water on the table.

"Well, the boss wants to see me when I'm done here. Maybe that means our 'special' time together is over." He sidled closer, leering in her direction. "If he tells me to end you, I promise I'll give you a wild fuck before I do."

When he cupped her breast and pinned her to the wall, Mystery screamed and struggled, kicking him. He just laughed and adjusted the bulge in his crotch before heading out and slamming the door behind him. She watched out the little window, waiting for him to straddle his ATV and roll away so she could make her final preparations to start her trek through the desert.

Suddenly, the sound of gunshots exploded through the air. Her captor froze, then ran for the ATV, rolling to the ground and using the big metal frame to shield his body. He poked his head up and aimed over the vehicle, shooting toward a target Mystery couldn't see. More bullets flew, some ricocheting off the metal of the four-wheeler, others kicking up sand.

Someone was shooting at her captor. Who would be out here in the middle of nowhere, trying to kill him? Had his enemies hunted him down? Or was she being rescued? Her head raced. She didn't know what to think and didn't want to reveal her presence in the event the guys shooting now were badder than the criminal who'd taken her. Still, she had to be prepared in case they killed her captor and she was forced to walk through the desert to find civilization.

She gathered the duffel with water bottles and a canvas she'd found on the old vinyl floor yesterday, hoping the scrap of sturdy cloth could serve as footwear or covering for her head as needed, since she didn't have any sunscreen, either.

After looping her arms through the handles, she peeked out the window to see two men in camo running toward the ATV, guns blazing. One of them ducked behind the vehicle, then inched up to shoot at her assailant at the other end of the rolling tin can. That was all the time her captor needed. He shot one of the new arrivals, and the man jolted, jerking with the impact before crumpling to the ground, unmoving.

Mystery gasped, then slapped a hand to her mouth. She doubted anyone would hear her over the wind and the din of the shots being exchanged, but if they did . . . she wouldn't come out of this alive.

The second of the two combatants she'd seen grabbed a big rifle from his fallen comrade's back, shoved in a new magazine, then quietly sneaked toward the front of the ATV.

Her captor obviously didn't trust the silence. He leaned around the front of the vehicle, and when he spotted the enemy, they exchanged another hail of gunfire.

To her right, the door to the shack burst open. The wood slammed against the wall, making the whole structure shake.

Then a big, dark shadow fell across the threshold, blocking most of the sun slanting behind his huge form. Mystery shrieked and scrambled back, looking for a way to escape whatever he'd come to do to her. But she already knew from her days of captivity here that no other path to freedom existed. The shack had only two small windows, which he obstructed, and no other doors.

The huge man stepped into the beams of light streaming through the window, gripping an assault rifle, ready to shoot. A small pack hung around his beefy shoulders. A tight khaki T-shirt stretched over a powerful chest. His hair was so short, she could barely discern the color, but it was something with a golden tint, glinting under the waning sun. His sharp blue gaze zeroed in on her immediately. She shrank back.

"Don't be afraid. We're here to rescue you. Your father hired us."

Jubilant relief poured through Mystery. She trembled so hard, she couldn't quite stand steady. She'd known that Marshall Mullins wouldn't wait for the police to rescue her. Doing nothing had never been his style. On the other hand, this man was a total stranger. Why should she believe him?

"Wh-who are you?"

"Axel Dillon. I served two tours of duty in Afghanistan and now I'm private hire. Your father contacted my CO day before yesterday. We've been looking for you since. Are you hurt?"

Mystery wasn't one hundred percent sure she believed him. And she could still hear gunshots pinging outside at a furious, fatal rate.

"For fuck's sake," Axel roared. "Stay here and hidden. I'm going to end this son of a bitch."

He turned around and marched out of the shack. She watched the retreat of his wide shoulders and narrow hips. Everything about him shouted that he was a soldier, just as he'd claimed. But did that mean he was her father's soldier-for-hire? Mystery didn't know, and after being abducted, then threatened with murder and rape, her trust was admittedly thin. Exhaustion and hunger were wreaking havoc with her logic.

She ran to the window again, watching as he raised his rifle, peered through the scope, and fired. Her captor feinted just as he pulled the trigger, but the shot still managed to hit the asshole. He slapped a hand to his side and tried to climb the hood of the ATV and scramble into the driver's seat.

Axel's sidekick leapt onto the vehicle and fired his handgun. Her assailant must have seen or sensed trouble coming because he rolled out, back to the hard sand, then took off on foot, heading away from the shack. He fired off a shot every few steps over his shoulder at the other man in camo.

Where did her captor think he was going? He'd said himself there was nothing but desert for miles. Had that been a lie? Or was he simply hoping to escape into the expansive landscape as night fell, then limp his way to safety?

Axel darted toward the dueling pair, but the other soldier was closer, scrambling into the driver's seat of the vehicle so he could head off in hot pursuit of her captor.

Mystery watched, her stomach twisting. The bastard who'd ripped apart her world . . . he wouldn't get far. She wasn't a mean or violent person, but sudden death was too good for that thug. She kind of wanted to watch someone beat the shit out of him or drive the ATV over him again and again until the life left his body.

As the other soldier started the mini four-wheeler, it leapt forward, kicking up sand behind it. Her captor looked over his shoulder, then tried to run faster. But he was no match at all.

As if he'd figured that out, he stopped dead in his tracks and faced the oncoming vehicle as it ate up ground, on a collision course to run him over in seconds. Instead of fleeing in another direction, he reached into his pocket and withdrew something, then aimed it at the vehicle, almost like a remote control.

The ATV and Axel's fellow soldier burst into a big orange ball of flames, instantly consumed in a conflagration. She gasped in horror.

Her captor laughed beneath his ski mask as he palmed his gun again and pointed it at Axel, now running toward the killer who had already murdered his two brothers in arms. Both Axel and her captor aimed and pulled the trigger, but the bastard who had abducted her didn't have a weapon made for long shots. The handgun was no match for the high-powered rifle at that distance.

The asshole who had taken and tormented her jackknifed back, then fell to the ground. He didn't move again.

Now she was alone with Axel, a man who could save her life— or end it.

She swallowed, her heart racing, her veins running with pure adrenaline, as he jogged toward the first of his fallen peers. He checked the pulse at the man's neck, then sighed heavily and rose to his feet. Bypassing the burning remains of the ATV, he aimed his rifle at the unmoving form of her captor, cautiously approaching as he checked for signs of life. Apparently, he found none because he began searching the asshole's pockets.

Slinging his rifle onto his back, Axel turned and made his way toward her, his gaze sharp and focused.

Mystery trembled. God, she hoped he was one of the good guys, sent by her father, as he claimed. Because if it was a lie to win her trust, he could do whatever he wanted to her out in this godforsaken desert. Cut her, rape her, strangle her . . . Snapshots of all the hideous ways he could murder her flashed through her brain. He could leave her bones to bleach out in the potent sun and walk away without anyone the wiser. This gun battle certainly had no other survivors who might rescue her—if they'd ever intended to.

Tears rolled down her cheeks. On the one hand, she realized that she was probably being overly dramatic and the odds of three men hunting down someone else's captive to brutally murder her made very little sense. Why would he try to trick her into trusting him just for that? On the other hand, some small part of her mind realized that after everything she'd been through in the last few days, she wasn't exactly prepared to be rational. Thoughts raced. Terror clung.

She just wanted to go home, feel her father's arms around her, get back to normalcy, which seemed a million miles away right now.

Axel turned and headed her way. She screamed.

He took off at a dead run for her. Mystery panicked and sprinted out of the shack. The wind whipped through her hair, kicking dust onto her skin. The sand felt hot on the bare soles of her feet, and she knew right away that days of being undernourished and afraid to sleep would catch up with her quickly. Axel's pounding footsteps behind her drew closer and closer, and she felt powerless to keep him from capturing her.

It seemed as if mere seconds had passed before his arm snaked around her waist and he hauled her against his big, solid body.

"Don't run. I've got you. I know you're scared, but I'm going to save you."

He panted against her neck, and she felt his chest rising and falling with every breath. She couldn't seem to suck in enough air, either. Her heart beat furiously. Fear spiked her veins.

"Let me go. I just want to go home."

"I know," he assured, his voice surprisingly soft for someone who looked—and felt—all soldier. "I'll take care of you. But you can't charge through the desert without shoes. It may look dead around here, but I assure you, the land is very much alive, and you'd be no match."

In her head, Mystery knew that. At the age of nine, she'd been with her dad on their way to Palm Springs for some celebrity event when their car had broken down. Even being stranded on the roadside for a few hours had been hot and harrowing. She'd never been so aware of the harsh elements and her inability to survive them.

Until now.

The fight left her muscles, and she nodded miserably.

Gently, Axel set her back on her feet and turned her to face him. She was almost afraid to look at him, worried she'd see cruel glee on his face just before he ended her. Instead, she saw a well of patience.

He knew she'd had it tough and he empathized. The human kindness Axel showed her was the first she'd seen in seemingly forever.

Mystery burst into tears again.

"Hey. Hey!" He cupped her face and thumbed tears from her cheeks. "Shh. I know you're on emotional overload, but we can't do this now. Breathe with me." He fused her gaze to his and demonstrated by dragging in a long breath, then letting it out. He did it again, waiting patiently until she followed suit.

Calm slowly made its way through her panic. With each breath and every second she looked into his eyes, she relaxed a bit more. Her mind wasn't a constant explosion of chaos and terror.

As soon as the adrenaline dissipated, she felt incredibly weak. Her muscles no longer seemed able to support her, and she sagged against his chest.

"That's it," he crooned. "Nothing to be afraid of. I need some quick information, all right? Tell me if the man holding you hostage had any help? Anyone else who assisted him in keeping you captive?"

She shook her head. "H-he talked about someone who hired him, but I . . . I never saw him."

"So it was just the two of you?"

Mystery nodded.

"Good. That gives us some breathing room. Come with me. We'll go back to the shack and map out a plan."

Plan? "I don't want to go back. He kept me there. He—"

"I know." Axel took her hand and slowly led her back to the place of her captivity.

She tried to dig in her heels, but he was far stronger. In fact, her legs gave out from under her, and without breaking stride, he bent and carried her against his chest, taking huge, ground-eating steps until the shade of the little outbuilding sheltered them again.

Gingerly, he set her on her feet, then kicked the door shut. "There. Now, another deep breath. Let's talk this out rationally, okay?"

His deep voice soothed her. Mystery felt herself sliding slowly off the pinnacle of panic. She nodded at him.

"Listen to me. I was an army medic, sent as part of this rescue crew in case you need medical attention. But you have to be honest with me. I can't help you to the best of my ability if you're not. Understand?"

Again, she nodded.

"I need you to be verbal with me. We don't have room for misunderstanding here. Say 'Yes, Axel.'"

She swallowed and stared at a spot of smudged dirt on his T-shirt. "Yes, Axel."

"Good. Did your captor beat you? Tie you, restrain you, or otherwise put you in any position that might have caused injury?"

"I was cuffed with my hands behind my back when he first brought me here. My shoulders ached for a bit. I'm all right now. He never struck me or restrained me again."

Axel nodded. "Did you hurt your feet running outside barefoot just now?"

Her soles smarted, but nothing more serious than when she'd played barefoot in the backyard as a kid. "No."

"When did you last drink water? Eat? Did he feed you regularly?"

"He gave me one meal and two bottles of water a day. I haven't eaten yet today."

"So he provided enough to keep you alive but not well hydrated." Axel cursed, then let out a deep breath. "We can work with that."

"Well, I drank the bottles then refilled them in the little bathroom sink. It's disgusting, but I knew that if I tried to escape alone through the desert that I'd need to stay hydrated."

He grabbed her shoulders. "Good thinking. You have to use your head to survive this climate."

She nodded, every muscle in her body weak, even those in her neck. She felt like a bobble head. Then she remembered that he wanted a verbal response. "Yes, Axel."

"Anything else?"

"He drugged me every night so I couldn't escape."

Axel tensed. "Any idea what he gave you?"

"No. He injected it. It made me sleep for half the day, sometimes more."

"Any side effects?"

It wasn't what he said or even how he said it, but something about the tight set of his mouth told her that everything her captor had done to her had really pissed him off. That made her feel better. If he was indignant on her behalf and concerned about her health, maybe he really was one of the good guys.

"No. I mean, I'd wake up groggy, but it would wear off eventually."

"No drug cravings?"

That hadn't occurred to Mystery, but she was damn glad the asshole hadn't given her anything she might become addicted to. She shook her head. "No."

"I don't want to hurt or scare you, but I need to give you a quick medical exam."

She frowned. "Why wouldn't we just call the authorities now? Get away from here and let them take me to the hospital?"

"I wish it were that simple. Let me check you over, then I'll explain."

There wasn't a hospital, some police, an explanation—and her father—in her immediate future? Based on what he'd said, she didn't think so. That filled her with anxiety again. "What do you mean, not that simple?"

"Hey, no need to worry. Let's tackle one issue at a time. The first thing I need to know is if you're all right."

"I'm conscious. I'm talking. I'm walking. And I want to go home."

"I know, Mystery. I'd love to take you there. But with my two teammates dead, that presents some complications."

Oh, wow. She hadn't stopped to think of that. And what must Axel be feeling, losing two people he considered his . . . what? Co-workers? Friends? To help a woman he didn't even know. "I'm sorry. W-were you close?"

His jaw tightened and he looked away. "It's not important right this minute. I need to focus on you."

Her father had once starred in and directed a military film about soldiers in Vietnam in a harrowing situation, against almost impossible odds. He'd actually interviewed a bunch of soldiers at her house, and she'd eavesdropped. She remembered them talking about the necessity of compartmentalizing until they dealt with the situation that needed immediate attention. Once everything was secure and they were alone, they would deal with whatever they'd shoved to the recesses of their mind . . . hopefully. Some never did; they simply locked their grief or stress away in a mental box tightly and threw away the key. It was why things like PTSD and suicides cropped up in the military community so often. Even those who dealt with it or got help sometimes still found it too over-whelming and couldn't cope.

"If you were close to them and you're upset, I . . . I know you don't know me, but I'm willing to listen and help."

Something in his face changed. A faint surprise registered. Apparently, he was used to being the hero. Didn't anyone ever try to save him?

"That's very kind, but the first thing I need to do is my job. You're my primary responsibility. The other two soldiers were both my backup and provided essential elements to the rescue. Carr, the one in the exploding ATV, was our comm officer. When everything went up in flames, so did our ability to communicate with the outside world."

Meaning that he didn't have a way to just call the police to come out and whisk them back to Beverly Hills? He didn't have a way to ask her father to come get her?

"You don't have a cell phone?"

"Sure, I do. But there isn't a nearby town or even a highway. In terms of mobile communication, this is all a dead zone."

"So . . . I guess we're walking to your jeep or chopper or whatever you came here in?"

His entire body tightened as he shook his head. Mystery got the distinct impression that he was doing his best to remain calm and not show any fear. That worried her more than anything.

"Alvarez, Carr, and I came in on a HALO jump. We didn't leave behind a vehicle in case it could be detected."

Sure, she'd heard the word, but she had no idea what it meant. "HALO?"

"High altitude, low opening." When she frowned at him in confusion, he rubbed at the back of his neck. "We jumped out of a plane at thirty thousand feet. A plane at that altitude mimics a jetliner. By keeping the opening low, we don't make waves on the radar. So just in case anyone is monitoring the airspace around here, it wouldn't look out of the ordinary."

She'd never thought of that. It had never occurred to her they wouldn't just drive in with a small cache of weapons and do their thing. "Oh."

"So the downside is, we have no vehicle. And since we lost our comm gear in the explosion, we're going to have to hike our way to civilization."

"The asshole holding me prisoner told me we're surrounded by miles and miles of desert."

"We're smack in the middle of the Mojave. This is Death Valley."

It was some of the most unforgiving land in all of North America. She remembered learning that in school after one of her classmates in high school had gone on a camping trip with some buddies and their rock climbing equipment had given out, leaving him stranded in a ravine. He'd dehydrated in the desert in less than twenty-four hours.

She tried to swallow back panic. "Do you know the fastest way to civilization?"

"Yeah. We're looking at a fifteen- or twenty-mile trek southwest. But we have to be prepared for the conditions of the desert and to climb a few mountains. So the first thing I need to do is to examine you." He took her hand. "Because I've got to be honest. Your skin is a little clammy." He pressed two fingers to her carotid artery. "And your pulse is a little fast and weak. I need to make sure you're just emotionally distraught rather than going into shock because of an injury. Will you let me check you out?"

Mystery understood clearly that if she wanted to see her father and home again, she was going to have to walk her way out. "Yes, Axel."

He shrugged the pack off his back and took out a stethoscope, taking a quick listen to her heart and lungs. After a moment, he nodded as if satisfied before checking her blood pressure.

"One-forty over ninety-five. It's high."

Was he actually surprised by that? He stared as if he expected a reply. She just shrugged.

With quick efficiency, he attached a little device to her finger next.

"What is that?" Mystery frowned.

"A pulse oximeter, which measures the saturation of the oxygen level in your blood. I can also see your pulse rate." He held her wrist in his enormous hand and stared down at the device. A frown wrinkled his brow before he smoothed it away. "Your oxygenation is on the low side, your pulse a bit high."

"I'm more than a little freaked out."

"Fair enough. I'll check you again in a few minutes. Have you come into contact with any rusty metal or anything that might cause tetanus?"

"I don't think so."

"Any deep cuts that might need stitching or scrapes that need dressing? Infection isn't your friend in the wild."

In silence, she showed him a scrape on her elbow and one on her thigh, just above the hemline of her fraying dress. Without a word, he doctored them with some antibiotic ointment and covered them with gauze, his hands surprisingly gentle, despite their size. Then he paused and looked directly into her eyes. "The police equipped me with a rape kit. I need you to be honest with me. Should I administer it?"

"No." She swallowed and shook her head. "Thank God, no. H-he threatened but didn't . . ."

"That's good," he said in a soothing voice. "That's really good. So you've prepared bottles of water?"

She showed him the canvas duffel and the eight full bottles she'd stashed inside. "Two of these are fresh."

"That's good thinking. Any food?"

"Just before you came, he left me a ham sandwich and an apple in a paper bag."

"We'll grab it. Do you have any shoes?"

"Stilettos." She winced, then looked to the shoes she'd long ago discarded in the corner. Prada wasn't doing her any good in the desert. "But I found this." She held up the scrap of burlap. "I thought if I could find a rope, maybe I could rip this in half somehow and tie one around each of my ankles and—"

"It's a good thought, but that's not enough protection. Stay here."

Axel stood and grabbed his rifle, positioning it for action as he slipped out the door of the shack. On shaking legs, Mystery stood and watched him creep across the desert to the body of his first fallen comrade. He knelt, keeping the rifle directly beside him, and snagged the man's backpack, slinging it over one shoulder. Moments later, he lifted Alvarez in a fireman's carry and headed back for the shack.

What was he doing?

She had her answer moments later when Axel stepped through

the front door and eased the body of the fallen soldier onto the floor. Blood stained the man's T-shirt around the fatal wound open in his chest. Axel's face looked tight, his jaw clenched. Mystery's heart went out to him.

With methodical precision, he stripped off his friend's boots and tossed them her direction. The man's socks came off next and followed in an arc across the shack. "Put them on."

"They'll be too big," she blurted.

He zipped a stare in her direction, his blue eyes cool and demanding. "They'll protect you from the hot sand and possible snake bite."

Mystery hadn't even thought of that possibility and she felt so stupid. She'd been completely unprepared to survive in the desert. Maybe not a surprise since she'd been dressed for nightclubbing, not roughing it. But the fact that she didn't have the first clue how to take care of herself out here, that she had to rely so totally on this stranger who had just lost two of his fellow soldiers, that she had no idea how to shoulder some of his burden, disturbed her.

Rather than argue or squirm at putting on boots that had just come off a dead man, she drew the socks over her bare feet. They were still warm.

Beside her, Axel removed Alvarez's jacket and set it aside, then grabbed the old duffel she'd stuffed. He dragged out the burlap scrap and gripped both ends in his meaty hands. His biceps bulged and his chest bunched, his strength obvious. The heavy fabric tore in half. She swallowed. Her heart skipped at the realization he could squash her like a bug. Again, she had to hope that in her desperation to be rescued, she wasn't trusting the wrong man. But her instincts said he'd do what it took to get her to safety.

Without missing a beat, he tore one of the scraps in half again and shoved a piece in the toe of each boot. "Now put them on. They'll still be too big, but walking through the sand will be exhausting enough. The more easily you're able to walk, the less taxing it will be."

She nodded, then remembered his request. "Yes, Axel."

"Good." He watched her, his gaze hawkish, missing nothing.

No doubt he saw her hands shaking because as soon as she'd slipped her foot into the first boot, he took her ankle in his big hands and straightened her leg, lacing it up with a few twists of his fingers and a couple of firm tugs. Mystery watched, fascinated. He moved so quickly and economically for such a huge man. No lumbering or fumbling. Axel was incredibly proficient, and she was so grateful in that moment.

He repeated the process with the other boot, then looked her way. "How do those feel?"

"Fine," she said hoarsely.

With a satisfied nod, he got to his feet and offered her his hand. "Stand for me."

Mystery stared, looking up his forearms roped with muscle, his strong biceps, his huge chest, up to a face that could have looked so harsh. But the understanding there made her tear up again.

She brushed the wetness from her chapped cheeks, sniffed her reaction away, then took his hand. "Sorry."

"Don't be. Adrenaline crash. We've all done it. That's probably why you're shaking, too. If you feel faint, let me know."

"I'll be fine." She had to be. Mystery was determined not to let him down.

Without another word, he helped her to her feet. Her legs shook, and she felt as if she stood on wet noodles. But she drew in a deep breath. She'd suck it up and pull her weight. If they wanted to survive, she didn't have a choice. Two innocent men had already died to save her, and she'd carry that guilt forever. She didn't want Axel to suffer any more.

After another check of her blood pressure, pulse-ox, and pupils, he nodded. "Better. You good to go?"

"Yes."

He re-stashed his medical equipment, then picked up Alvarez's pack, shoving in the water bottles she'd saved before he tested its weight in his hand. With a frown, he drew his own off and handed it to her. "This one is lighter. Carry this as long as you can. If it gets to be too much, I'll take it back. Let's go."

Mystery gaped at him, looked back to Alvarez's fallen body, then out the shack's little window. "We're not . . ." Burying him? Where? With what shovel? Yeah, stupid question, so she swallowed it down. "Shouldn't we wait until morning?"

"You said your captor worked alone, but he admitted that someone hired him?"

She nodded. "He never said who."

"If he doesn't check in with his boss soon, someone else might come out here to find you. I'd like to be long gone before that happens. As it is, we're only going to have an hour or so before dark and we're going to leave tracks in the sand. If we can be a few miles from here by nightfall, I'll rest easier, knowing that we'll be harder to find."

Right. Again, he'd thought of things she should have. If she hadn't been terrified and exhausted, if she'd had time to consider their quandary, she might have come to the same conclusion. But extenuating circumstances aside, Mystery felt as if what she didn't know was holding them back.

"I understand. I'm ready. I'm strong. I can walk all night if we need to."

"We might have to," he said grimly. "I don't love that idea, but I'd rather take my chances against the coyotes and mountain lions than the direct sunlight. My sunscreen is limited. We'll use less water and energy if we sleep during the day and walk at night."

Mystery understood. She wanted to ask how they'd know where they were going in the dark, but for the foreseeable future they'd just be walking in a general direction, she supposed. Maybe he'd been trained to follow the stars or something.

"That makes sense."

Axel nodded, then knelt to his fallen friend, bending to close his unblinking eyes for the final time. "Bye, buddy. I'm sure as hell going to miss you." He lifted Alvarez's hand and drew off his wedding ring. "I know you'd want Rose and the baby to have this."

Her heart sank. This man had been married and had a child. And he'd never see them again because she'd been stupid enough to be out at night where she shouldn't have been, then unable to escape the man who'd held her prisoner.

"I'm so sorry . . ." She could barely get the words out past her broken voice.

Axel stood again, clearing his throat. He pocketed the ring, his expression locked up tight. "Let's go."

Chapter Three

THEY seemed to trek for miles . . . and miles. Endless sand and desert, dotted only by brittle brush, even as snowcapped mountains surrounded them. Mystery felt as if they'd be lost out here forever. The thought of never seeing her father again chilled her veins with icy panic. The weather didn't help. The desert at night was freezing.

Axel had long ago ordered her to eat the sandwich her captor had left. He also put on his jacket and made her wear Alvarez's. He had to be exhausted, too, but he just kept putting one foot in front of the other, looking up at the sky periodically, then checking an old-fashioned compass he'd pulled from his pack.

"How are you doing?" he asked suddenly in the silence broken only by the sound of footfalls on the never-ending sand.

Ready to fall over. Beyond exhausted. "Fine."

He smiled grimly. "Anyone ever tell you you're a terrible liar?"

Despite everything, she smiled. "My dad. Apparently, I'm not as good as the professional liars he works with. That's what he calls actors. He stays behind the camera—rather than in front of it—more often now, but over the years, he says he'd heard every lie ever told."

"I'm sure. You sound fond of your dad."

She smiled up at Axel. "He's really fabulous. The press isn't always kind, and I know he's had a well-documented love life, but as a father, I couldn't ask for more. What about you?"

"My dad did the single-parent thing, too. I'm the third of four boys, so he always had his hands full. But he tried to do right by us."

Mystery nodded. She didn't want to pry, but she'd be lying if she said she wasn't deeply curious about this soldier who'd saved her life. "Where's your mom?"

"Who knows?" He shrugged. "She wanted more excitement than a small town could give, so she left."

His conversational tone stunned her. That was it? "Do you miss her?"

"It wouldn't do me any good. Besides, it was a long time ago. You still miss yours?"

Everyone knew about her mother's death. It had been the stuff of tabloids since the police still classified it as "unsolved." Some believed her mother had committed suicide. Others were convinced her father had murdered the wife he hadn't wanted and couldn't afford to divorce. But the DA had never been able to gather enough evidence to indict him—or anyone. Mystery wished she had someone to blame and hate for taking away the woman who had birthed and loved her. Her father had many faults—an eye for the ladies and a wandering dick among them. But he wasn't a killer.

"All the time. Maybe . . . it's different for me. Mine didn't leave; she was taken. I know if she'd had a choice, she would have stayed."

"Sounds like it." He paused, sending her a direct stare full of honesty . . . and a surprising dose of concern. She wouldn't have been able to see it out in the desert except the moon was full and bright tonight. "You know there will be a media fervor when we make it back, right?"

She felt every pound of that pack on her back with each step, but she refused to wince. "I'm used to that. I was three when Dad won his first Oscar. It hasn't slowed down since. The spotlight is all I've ever known."

Granted, she usually stood just outside its bright light, but the glare caught her every so often.

"Interesting life."

"It's whatever you get used to, I think." She shrugged. "Everything is a trade-off. I'm not that fond of the limelight, but being the only child of Marshall Mullins opens doors."

"You going to follow in your dad's footsteps?"

People asked that a lot. She shook her head. "I'm not much for the whole . . . Hollywood scene. I prefer books. My dad thinks it's funny, but I like mysteries."

He sent her a speculative glance. "So why were you at a night-club when you were taken?"

"I let some of my friends talk me into it." And wasn't she annoyed with herself? "I was also leaving. I'm sure they stayed for hours. Was my dad all right when you saw him?"

Axel's mouth flattened into a grim line. "He's really worried; I won't lie. Your disappearance shook him. He kept waiting for a ransom note."

"He never got one?" That surprised her.

"Unless he's received one in the last eighteen hours, no."

Mystery shook her head. "That makes no sense. I mean, none of this does. My captor didn't say much, just kept me isolated. He didn't mention any demands he or his boss planned to make. The weirdest part is, the morning I arrived, the bastard holding me drew blood."

Axel frowned. "He cut you?"

"No. He took out a syringe and physically drew my blood like a phlebotomist, then said something about waiting a couple of days. I have no idea why or what that's supposed to mean."

That frown of his became a downright scowl. "I don't know, either, but I'm sure once your father hears this, he'll look into it."

He would, but Mystery just wanted this incident behind her. She wanted to be away from Hollywood, the club scene, the press. She certainly didn't want to fixate on some freak's motives and try to find logic.

"Yeah. Sure." She tried to send him a wobbly smile.

He continued his strong, sure cadence through the desert. Something about his face fascinated her. Big, kind of square, not at all refined . . . and she still couldn't stop staring. He wasn't so much handsome as rugged. Mystery had grown up knowing many of the most gorgeous men on the planet. *People* had labeled her as one of the most beautiful celebrity children, which kind of creeped her out. Suri Cruise and those Jolie-Pitt kids qualified. She had her mom's hourglass figure, a fall of dark hair that in no way resembled the sea of California blondes around her, and a wide mouth some Internet sites speculated would look great giving blow jobs. The individual parts of her didn't add up to the most stunning sum, in her opinion, but whatever. What mattered was that she was alive.

"We've gone five or six miles. Let's stop for a water break." He paused near an outcropping of rocks and sat his pack down, extracting her half full bottle.

"I'm not thirsty. I can conserve awhile longer."

"No. It may be cold and dry tonight, but you're still working up a sweat. You have to replace your fluids." He thrust the bottle at her with a demanding stare.

She sighed and took it. "Anyone ever tell you you're bossy?"

A faint grin crept across his face. "All the time. Some people actually like it, princess."

Mystery suspected that he alone understood the punch line to his joke, but she was too tired to care what it might be. Instead, she washed the taste of sand out of her mouth with a couple of swigs of water. He'd put a water purification tablet in the bottle before he'd let her drink it, and it had a strange chemical taste, but she could stomach it if that meant not getting sick.

She handed the bottle back to him.

He just shook his head. "Finish it."

Then he lifted his own bottle and polished it off in four long swallows. She watched his thick neck working, the Adam's apple bobbing in his throat as he gripped the plastic with his large hand. Then the reason for her fascination with him hit.

Besides being her hero, he was a *man*.

Yes, she'd been surrounded all her life by members of the opposite sex, some even very attractive in that polished, Hollywood, metrosexual way. But Axel was a walking, talking billboard for testosterone. He oozed it, gave it off as easily as others exhaled carbon dioxide. It hung around him like a pheromone. He would never worry about whether his hair looked just right or if his pants weren't perfectly fashionable. He wouldn't care if he was seen at the right restaurants or what anyone thought of him. Axel was one hundred percent secure in himself and his masculinity.

Mystery had never seen anything more attractive in her life.

She swallowed against the sudden surge of awareness as he shoved his empty bottle back in his pack, then gave her an expectant look. Dutifully, she swallowed the rest down, wondering all the while what, if anything, he thought of her. Stupid, spoiled little rich girl?

Wasn't she?

Refusing to let the thought defeat her, she handed her bottle back to him. "How long until the sun comes up?"

"About three hours. You hanging in there?"

"I told you I would."

"You're not used to this, so if you need a longer break . . ."

She shook her head. "I'm good."

His expression turned somewhere between amused and impressed. "Then let's do it."

Axel led. She followed. But for all her big talk, Mystery was exhausted and nearing her limit. Every step made her feet ache, jarred her very bones, made her back cramp. Not for anything in the world would she confess that. Adrenaline and lingering terror had gotten her through the first couple of hours. After that, just talking to him had melted her discomfort. Maybe she could distract herself again.

"The stars out here seem so bright." She looked up at the night sky, stunned anew by the stark beauty. "It seems as if there are a million more here than in the city."

"No other light to dilute their appearance." A small smile curled his lips. "It's one reason I don't mind the desert. Just me and that bright sky. No trees to obscure it. The colors are unlike anything else. This kind of landscape has a haunting beauty."

She'd never thought about it before, never really noticed. But Axel had a point. Yes, they were in a dangerous situation, hiking toward freedom. But it didn't look as if they'd been followed. They hadn't seen any scavengers or snakes. Out here, she could pretend for a little while that they were the only two people in the world. She could fantasize for just a moment that Axel could be interested in her.

"Yeah, I can see that," she murmured. "Did you grow up in the desert?"

"Nah. I'm originally from Tennessee. I joined the Army and shipped out to Afghanistan. I saw a lot of desert over there. You learn to appreciate it or you go insane."

Mystery felt her gaze cling to him. She should probably stop staring and embarrassing herself, but she enjoyed the view of him too much. But he wasn't just attractive. She really liked the way he rolled with the punches, accepted what was, and learned how to embrace the moment. Most of the men she knew, other than her dad, were creative folks with the artistic temperament to match. Very high-maintenance. Nothing seemed to faze Axel. He'd lost at least one friend today, yet that hadn't sent him into a rage, a drinking binge, or a catatonic frenzy.

"I never gave it much thought, but I suppose you're right." She bit her lip and hesitated asking the next question on the tip of her tongue, but couldn't help herself. "Is Axel really your name?"

"Nope. Troy." He shrugged. "It's a family name."

"Do you like it?"

"No one has called me that since I was about nine, so I don't really think about it. Once I started working on cars, my dad gave me the nickname and it stuck."

"Troy doesn't sound like you." She frowned. "Sorry. That didn't come out right."

"No offense taken." He scanned the empty horizon, seemingly always on alert. His sharp profile fascinated her. "What about you? Mystery is a very unusual name. Where did that come from?"

She grinned. "Well, besides the fact that celebrities always give their kids weird names, my mom told this story about how my father did three movies on location in different parts of the world shortly after they married. It wasn't really planned that way, but he didn't get to come home much. She joked that it was a mystery how she got pregnant, and it stuck."

That made him laugh, a rich, deep rumble out of his chest. "I'm assuming she eventually figured it out."

Mystery rolled her eyes. "I suspect."

A few more minutes passed in silence. Axel's hand swung right next to hers. Their knuckles brushed. She wished she had the courage and the right to tangle her fingers in his. Instead, she just watched him. He hovered protectively, constantly surveying her, their surroundings, the conditions. He made her feel secure. Nothing that had happened, nothing she'd said, nothing about her life freaked him out.

People made movies about men like him. Actors fought to play his character. But as soon as the director cut the scene, Axel didn't head for his trailer, which he'd demanded to be stocked with a cool-mist humidifier, Casablanca lilies, and a case of Red Bull. He just kept right on being exactly who he was.

Mystery watched him—not the landscape—when she managed to stumble over a rock directly under her left toe. As she fell forward, Axel wrapped his strong arm around her middle. His other hand clamped around her wrist and dragged her upright, against his chest, so hard she felt every moment of his years of physical exertion.

Mystery dashed a glance over her shoulder, blinking up at him. "Thank you."

He nodded. "You all right?"

Getting her feet back under her, she nodded. "Yeah."

Though her breathing still felt a bit uneven. Then again, he had that effect on her.

"You're tired. And you didn't tell me." He looked disapproving.

She eased out of his embrace. Not that she wanted to, but leaning on him didn't help them or prove that she could stand on her own two feet.

Hoisting the backpack higher on her shoulders, she shook her head. "It's just dark and I didn't see the rock. We need to keep going, right?"

"I've also promised to bring you back healthy. Tomorrow will be more difficult. Let's rest."

But they had hours of cool darkness left. "No, I promised that I'd keep pace. I will."

He sighed. "Now you're just being a stubborn brat."

Because she wanted to pull her weight? "This is me being re-solved."

"At the risk of your well-being. I'm not having it."

Mystery wanted to ask him why he thought he was the boss of her, but she knew the answer. Without him, she'd very likely be dead. With a heavy breath, she shook her head. "Fine."

"Good. I'll scout for a good place to sleep."

She looked around the expansive, open landscape. The moonlight put a silvery glow on everything, and it almost looked magical.

"What about over there?" She pointed to a small trail just off to her left. "That looks like a dried-up riverbed."

He shook his head before she even stopped speaking, looking up to a cropping of rocks on the right. "See the grooves through the rock leading straight down into that gully? That's the path from past flash floods. It runs off the stone and down to the low point."

She scoffed. "I don't see flash flooding being a big problem here."

"It is," he corrected. "In a good storm, it can rain six inches or more in an hour. All the water will race down the surrounding hills and collect right here in the old riverbed. People can wash away and drown like that in minutes."

"In a place as dry as this, doesn't the soil soak up all the water before it can flood the low spots?"

"This earth gets baked until it's nearly as hard a concrete. Gravity rolls the water down. It happens really fast. If you're asleep, you won't see it coming. You'll just be overcome by water and die."

As serious as he sounded, she believed him. "Okay, where do we camp, then?"

"Up higher. Stand right here for a minute. Let me do a little climbing." He dropped his pack and kept his rifle slung over his shoulder. Then, as if he hadn't been walking in near-freezing temperatures for the last few hours, she watched Axel grip a rock, then put his foot on the one directly below and climb the side of a hill with the same ease he'd ascend a ladder.

He was so physical and capable. She couldn't help but admire everything he was and had accomplished. He was probably in his mid-twenties, but had already served two tours on one of the most dangerous battlefields in the world. His mother had left. He lived away from his family. He'd lost a friend today. Nothing broke him. And Mystery admired his courage so much. She wanted to be that brave.

He disappeared up the rock face, then when he reached a ledge, he walked into some opening she couldn't quite see.

A few moments later, he reappeared and bounded his way back to her side. "This will work. It's high so that if the bastard who paid for your abduction sends a search party, we won't be immediately visible. There's a little bit of an overhang to protect us from the wind.

We'll still have to watch for things like scorpions and mountain lions, but we were going to have to be cautious about those wherever we stopped."

Some protective rock sounded great, but . . . "How do you expect me to get up there?"

He crossed his arms over his chest as if this point was nonnegotiable. "You're going to climb."

Automatically, she shook her head. Yeah, she wanted to be brave, but she knew her limitations. That wasn't happening. "I can't. I've never climbed a rock like that in my life. I don't know how, especially in the dark. Isn't there something else closer to the ground?"

"There might be, but I'm not wasting more time searching for it. We need to eat something, drink more water, get settled, then catch some sleep. You might find that harder as the sun and the temperature come up."

And he wouldn't? Then again, she knew from that military film of her father's that hard-core soldiers like him could close their eyes and sleep just about anywhere. They trained themselves to grab a few minutes of shut-eye here or there, never knowing when the opportunity would come again.

Mystery looked up the face of the rock again. It wasn't a sheer vertical climb, but it still looked steep and daunting. She tried the honest approach. "I'm not trying to be difficult. I'm scared."

His body language relaxed, losing the stiff and authoritative stance. Instead, he bent to her and clasped her shoulders. "I'll be with you every step of the way. The man who abducted you didn't defeat you. The desert hasn't gotten the best of you. A few rocks won't, either. I'll take your pack up with me. You'll do great, princess."

It had to be the trauma of the last few days, coupled with lack of sleep. She teared up. His encouragement was some of the nicest words anyone had ever said to her. He believed she could do it—whatever she set her mind to. No one expected her to be capable of anything. Her father had always indulged her and told her to do whatever she enjoyed. So she'd shopped a lot, read, hung out with friends, and had done just enough to slide by in school. College had been more for show than anything. Daddy was an implacable, driven man. Kind of like Axel. Suddenly, she was a little ashamed that she hadn't developed more drive or more spine as she'd grown from a child into a young adult. Maybe Axel was right; maybe she could do this.

"I'll try."

"You'll succeed," he promised. "You watch."

She gave him a shaky nod.

He bent a little lower and put his face directly in front of hers. "Be verbal. We'll need to communicate as we climb."

She'd forgotten. "Yes, Axel."

He picked up his pack and slung it over his beefy shoulder beside the rifle, then took Alvarez's pack, stuffed with a canteen and most of the food, in his hand. "Now grab that rock just above your head. When you set your fingers back deep enough, you'll find there's a little dip that will make a nice ledge for your grip."

He eased the strap of her pack up his arm, to rest in the crook of his elbow, then anchored both of his hands around her hips. As he touched her, pure lightning heat zipped through her body, flashing to her extremities, then conflagrating inward, centering between her legs. She gasped. That had never happened to her. Ever. The few boys she'd had sex with in high school had been ultimately uninteresting and forgettable.

Somehow, she already knew she'd never erase Axel from her thoughts.

"Something wrong?" he asked, releasing her middle from his grip.

"No." She swallowed and tried to think of a plausible lie. "I just can't believe I'm going to do this."

"Believe, princess. You've got too much spark to let a rock defeat you. Put your right foot on the jutting section of that stone at knee level. Yes," he coached as she did what he asked. "Now just use your hands and the muscles in your legs to pull yourself up. It's not much different than climbing a tree."

Mystery refrained from mentioning that she'd never climbed trees as a kid. There weren't many in Beverly Hills not manicured within an inch of their lives. Besides, the nannies her parents had hired when she'd been younger would have had a heart attack if she'd tried to shimmy up some bark to hang out on a limb.

"Sure."

Axel gripped her hips again, and as she hoisted herself up, he gave her a push, his thumbs so, so close to cupping her butt. Did he think of her as a child? Or had he noticed that she was a woman? The thought distracted her from all worries of falling and breaking half the bones in her body. Suddenly, she stood on the little outcropping and had a better view of the vast landscape all around them, along with Axel smiling up at her with something like pride.

"I did it!" Mystery knew she wore a cheesy grin that TMZ and the tabloid press would make fun of, but she didn't care.

"Told you. Wait for me there. I'll coach you through the next level." He reached for her pack, tossed it up to her, then headed up the face of the cliff again, climbing as if he'd been doing it forever.

She watched in fascination, then felt her body ping when he stood beside her again. The ledge was narrow. They had to stand close. Axel didn't touch her, but she wished he would.

She sent a smile up his way before she felt heat rush through her, and she pretended to look up as if studying the next part of the climb. "Now what?"

"This part is a bit trickier . . ."

But like before, he coached her up, holding her by the hips and lifting her when the rocks beneath her felt a little crumbly and unstable. They repeated that twice more before she stood at the top of the hill and glanced at the outcropping as he pulled himself up beside her, slinging the last pack onto the ledge below her feet.

"Here we are. You did great."

She loved the way he encouraged and praised. It seemed unusual for a soldier to be so good at what her father would call touchy-feely stuff. Even his communication skills were amazing. Mystery wondered where he'd learned and gotten so much practice that it seemed as natural as breathing to him.

"With a lot of help from you, thanks. The rescue was harrowing, but the journey since could have been grueling and terrible. You've made it really . . . all right."

He nodded her way, pretending to tip his imaginary hat at her. "Just doing my job, ma'am."

She giggled. "That is the worst cowboy accent."

"We all have our limitations." He shrugged.

In her estimation, he didn't have many. He'd make a great husband and father someday—if he wasn't already. OMG, she hadn't even considered that. She'd been mooning over him and crushing hard, and he might already have a significant other in his life. The thought deflated her. He was too awesome to be alone, and imagining him with a wife or girlfriend tugged her into a sad little exhaustion.

"Here's our home sweet home for the night." He pointed to an alcove under an overhang of rock. Another outcropping protected them from the fierce oncoming wind swiping at them up this high.

It didn't look like much, but it certainly beat dropping onto the sand and trying to drift off, she supposed. She ducked under the overhang and started to lower herself to the cold rock below.

"Wait." He fished through his pack and extracted a flashlight, quickly scanning the area. Seemingly satisfied, he flipped it off, then pulled out a thin, khaki blanket with a tinfoil-looking lining. "We're clear. I needed to check for scorpions and any other venomous creatures that like warmer, dark spaces."

Yikes, she hadn't even thought of that. "I'm glad we're alone. I don't like pinchers."

"It's not just the bite, but the venom. Bark scorpions lurk around here. I know a guy who got stung once. He said it was the most painful seventy-two hours of his life. They're hard to see because they're about a third of the size of the desert hairy variety, but those suckers can be lethal. We'll start a fire to keep them away. They burrow. They like warmth but not flames. So now we just need to be careful of rattlers doing their equivalent of hibernating. They're too sluggish to move this time of year because they've already hunkered down against the cold, so if you disrupt them, they're more likely to strike."

He knew everything about the landscape and the wilderness. Again, he filled her with total awe. Kind, smart, built, manly . . . "Is there anything you don't know and can't accomplish?"

Axel looked taken aback. "I don't think I'd do too well if you tried to put me in a ballet."

Mystery tried to picture him in a tutu and burst out laughing. "Probably not."

"But I cook a lot, sew when I have to, keep things tidy because I don't like clutter."

"The woman in your life is really lucky. My dad can't boil water. And he won't pick up after himself. I'm constantly moving his stuff out of my way."

He shrugged, and she held her breath to see what his answer would be. The whole fishing expedition was a little silly. He probably had no interest in her, but that didn't stop her from wishing.

"I probably have it easier since I live alone," he said. "I only have to keep up with myself."

He sounded single. That made her sizzle. He might not consider nineteen grown up . . . but she was pretty mature by virtue of being an only child and having grown up in Hollywood. Dad tried to shelter her but she'd experienced more than a few adult vices. She wasn't an innocent kid. Maybe if Axel saw that, he'd see her as woman enough for him.

"Let's get settled," he suggested before she could continue their conversation.

That would probably be best. She felt a bit tongue-tied, and the wind was picking up. Alvarez's jacket blocked some of the cold, but her exposed legs were freezing.

Axel spread out his blanket, then crawled in and bunched his jacket into a makeshift pillow. He set it against the rock behind him and eased his head back. Then he patted the spot beside him on the odd silvery material. "C'mon, princess."

Sleep curled up with him? She flushed hot. No, it wasn't exactly a sex invite, but lying beside him, sharing blankets barely big enough for two, entwined together all night . . . it seemed so intimate. She wasn't a virgin but she'd never actually shared a place to sleep with anyone of the opposite sex. Her heart stuttered.

"Something wrong?"

Mystery wished she could have a minute to herself, but where? The little ledge on which they slept wasn't big. Two steps in any direction and she'd be falling down the mountain, probably to great injury or death.

"No. I'm good," she lied, then dropped to her knees beside him. She couldn't stop herself from looking into his eyes as she slid under the blanket. It was a buffer from the wind, but Axel was far warmer. Being against him was like cozying up to a blast furnace. After hours of feeling her hands stiff and tingly from the chill, she breathed a contented sigh.

He dragged his pack into his lap and unzipped a bulging pouch. It tipped over and into her lap. Holy cow, that sucker was heavy. And he'd been carrying it all day? Slinging it around like it weighed nothing?

"Sorry," he muttered, then righted it again, delving inside.

"It's fine. I guess we're going to be really close up here. Not a lot of space."

"Roger that." Moments later, he withdrew two brownish plastic pouches from his backpack and handed one to her, along with another bottle of water. "I want it all gone."

Mystery held the little package and tried to read the black writing in the dark. She didn't have a lot of luck. "What is this?"

"MRE. I think you've got the meatballs in marinara sauce."

She tried not to wince. How was that going to work without a microwave? But she knew soldiers survived on these all the time. It fueled them while they defended the country, so she could swallow it down and just thank God she was still alive. "Good. What about you?"

"Scalloped potatoes with ham." He smiled at her in the darkness. "They all suck. You get used to it." He bumped his MRE with hers. "Bon appétit."

"Bon appétit."

As she pulled her meal open, a little glow warmed her inside. They felt a bit like a couple on a camping trip, having an adventure for the hell of it. With Axel, she could almost forget that someone had gone to a lot of trouble to abduct and keep her hidden from her father and the world. Beside Axel, she felt safe again.

Oh, she had it for him bad.

In silence, they ate. The dehydrated meals tasted like cardboard, and she'd be damn glad to get back to some of her favorite restaurants. She'd certainly never look at a ham sandwich again without thinking about her terrifying days at the shack.

"How did you find me in the middle of nowhere?"

Axel swallowed a bite and washed it down with some water. "The club had a parking lot cam that captured footage of your abduction. We noted the license plate of the van. Whoever pulled the job either didn't know he was being taped or didn't care if we caught the plate number. We managed to pick up that same plate number on freeway cams on Highway 14 heading north out of Palmdale, so we knew the general direction he'd headed. The last place we picked him up on camera was on the 395 junction with 190, and he headed east. From there, we worked with the Inyo County Sheriff's Office. We did a thermal sweep of the area, and they were able to tell us where the heat signatures from towns and settlements should be. We started investigating anything that didn't belong, which led us to you."

"Wow, you made quick work of finding me."

"We got a couple of lucky breaks, and your father moved mountains to make it happen."

Money talked. It always had, and Dad was never afraid to throw it around if he believed in the cause. "I'm so grateful to everyone involved. I'm particularly sorry for Carr's and Alvarez's families. I feel awful that my stupidity caused their deaths."

He took her hand in his. "You weren't stupid, and nothing you did caused their casualties. You were being a teenager, Mystery. Which meant you were sneaking away to do typical stuff teenagers do. You didn't ask to be kidnapped. When Carr, Alvarez, and I took the job, we knew the risks. We plan as much as we can for every eventuality and all do our best not to get dead. Not every mission goes our way. It's something you accept as a soldier."

"Carr and Alvarez did something for me I can never even thank them for. I feel terrible for the wives and children they left behind."

"Carr only had a mutt I'll probably inherit. His parents passed away last year. He never married or had kids. Alvarez's wife, Rose, will take it hard. They've only been married two years. Their son is six months old."

Hearing that was like a stab in the heart. She had to talk to her father when she got home, see if he could do anything to help the poor woman who'd just lost her husband and become a single parent.

"But if I hadn't gone to that awful club . . ." she choked out.

"If the asswipe who took you hadn't accepted that job, if someone with cash and a nefarious purpose hadn't contracted your abduction . . . Mystery, it's really not your fault. Don't beat yourself up."

"Do we have any way of knowing whether the guy you killed outside the shack is the same one who took me?"

Axel nodded. "Yeah. That's him. I pulled off his ski mask and saw the same prince charming who appeared on the traffic cams. I got a good look at his face on some footage from a gas station where he stopped to fuel up."

That was a terrible relief, to know that the bastard who'd forced her into the van and taken her away couldn't do that to anyone else ever again. But that presented another problem. "Do we have any idea who hired him?"

Axel looked reluctant to answer. "No. It will take a little longer to identify this guy and comb through his finances, see if we can track the mastermind that way. Your captor was a pro, though. Whoever hired him wasn't an idiot. I'm not expecting to find anything but a dead trail."

Anxiety seized her. "So that means whoever wanted me kidnapped in the first place could do it again. He could hire someone else to—"

"Maybe. But you're more aware now. You know better than to have your head in your purse while you're walking through a dark parking lot. When I get you home, you need to take self-defense classes. When you go out, observe some basic safety precautions—go out in groups, always be aware of where you are and who's around you."

"My dad will hire a bodyguard, I'm sure." The idea depressed her a bit. This whole incident smacked her again. It represented the end of childhood, freedom, and in an odd way, innocence.

She'd grown used to the idea of her father being so public and everyone wanting to talk to him. Mystery had always regarded herself as a mere curiosity in the white-hot realm of his spotlight. But the paparazzi had never focused on her as an individual. Axel had warned her the abduction would change that. He was probably right.

"I know it's inconvenient, but it's not a bad idea. I'd rather have you safe and slightly annoyed than fighting for your life again."

He was right about that, too. She nodded. "Do you have any idea why all this happened? I'd thought it was to extract money from my dad, but the fact that he never received a ransom note makes me wonder."

Axel shook his head, directing a concerned gaze down at her. "Sorry. You might find out as the investigation continues. But if you don't learn who engineered your kidnapping, you may never know."

That would be a bitter pill to swallow. And she had to believe that if her father had managed to pull the right strings to find her, then he'd find out this madman's reason for taking her in the first place.

The wind picked up, whistled past her as if singing an eerie tune. In the distance, a coyote howled. Mystery curled her arms around her knees and froze.

Axel slung his arm around her. "It's okay. The wind is normal. The coyote sounds miles away."

"Everything makes me jumpy right now, I guess."

His face softened. "That's normal, too. Close your eyes and try to relax."

Their faces were so close. His body was plastered against hers from shoulder to knee. Her heart thumped. Desire was probably the wrong response to this situation, but she couldn't deny it existed as she blinked up into his face.

"Go on," he urged.

She was still wearing Alvarez's jacket to ward off the cold, so she had no pillow. Axel made up for that by cradling the side of her face in one of his large hands and leading her cheek down to the slab of his chest. Mystery went willingly, her eyes sliding shut. His heart beat a steady rhythm in her ear.

He wrapped her tighter in his arms. "You're safe, princess."

Yes, she felt that. "I can't thank you enough for all you've done."

"You don't have to thank me. Just close your eyes and rest."

She was never going to sleep on a rock, against an unfamiliar man, with the wind whipping around her. She wasn't comfortable and wasn't sure she could get tired enough to stop the terrible abduction from playing in her head over and over like a bad horror film. The drugs her captor had given her left her in a groggy waking state for the most part. She hadn't really slept, just been out of it. When she had drifted off, nightmares had plagued her. Terror crept in and disturbed her. She wouldn't sleep tonight, but Axel had done so much. She would humor him.

"Sure," she murmured and closed her eyes to play along. "I'll try not to hog the bed."

He chuckled in her ear. "If you do, that's all right. I'm just happy you're safe."

* * *

HEAT overwhelmed her. Suddenly, Mystery felt sweltering. Sweat broke out along her hairline, between her breasts, along her back. Sleep dragged her back down, but the need for cooler air and a bathroom brought her back.

She cracked her eyes open. Sunlight sliced at them like a pickaxe. She gasped. Where was she? What time was it?

The last few days came rushing back to her, then she realized that the rock at her back was moving gently, a rise and fall that emulated breathing.

"Hold still," he muttered in her ear.

Axel—beside her with his arm around her waist, holding her against a body that felt hard everywhere. But something in his voice warned her.

"What's wrong?"

"I heard a helicopter fly overhead. It could be one of the good guys or nothing to do with us at all, but . . ."

It could also be whoever had paid for her kidnapping wondering where his investment had escaped to. She swallowed. "What do we do?"

"We wait. When daylight wanes, looking for us on the desert floor will be like looking for a needle in a haystack. Whoever it is seems to be flying pretty low, which tells me it's either a search-and-rescue mission or someone determined not to let you get away. The less we move now, the more we look like part of the scenery. The more likely they simply fly over us and away."

That made sense, but her heart beat a hundred miles an hour. The distant sound of chopper blades seemed to get closer, closer. Axel tensed.

"Son of a bitch," he breathed. "That's the third time I've heard them fly overhead. I'd hoped the wind would blow away some of our tracks in the sand, but I'm guessing not enough."

What if the helicopter landed? What if someone got out with guns and hunted them down? Axel was good, but he was still one man with one gun against people who would be better rested and prepared . . . It sounded like a recipe for death.

To her right, the helicopter swerved and headed straight toward them.

Chapter Four

WHAT are we going to do?" she asked. "Tell me how I can help."

Axel pulled the desert camo blanket over their heads and tightened his hold around her waist. "Right now, we're just laying low and hoping they go away. It's about noon, maybe a little after. We might be hanging here for a while. It depends on how determined they are."

That wasn't good news. She wasn't sure she could lie in this same position for the next five hours and wait for night to fall. For starters, her bladder was full. Worse, fear spiked her bloodstream. She wasn't ready to face danger again. She certainly didn't want to die.

And somehow, above all that, being pressed up against Axel aroused her.

Beside him, she breathed hard, trying to steady herself.

"You're shaking," he murmured. "Slow your breathing down. I'm going to do everything in my power to keep you safe."

Mystery didn't doubt that for a minute. She gave him a little nod. "What if they land? What if they come looking for us? What if—"

He shifted slightly, cupping her cheek. "I'll handle it. I'm armed. I'm trained."

But these ruthless people chasing her had already eliminated two of his comrades. How did Axel expect to take out whoever was in the helicopter by himself?

He pried open one of the Velcro pockets in his fatigue pants and thrust a gun in her hands. Mystery shrank back as if it was an enormous hairy spider come to eat her.

"Take it," he demanded. "The safety is on. To turn it off, you flip this switch down." He demonstrated, then quickly flipped the lever back in place. "Once the safety is off, squeeze the trigger hard. The gun will kick you back good, so be ready or it will knock you on your ass."

He was preparing her to defend herself in case he couldn't. And she could only think of one reason he'd be unable to keep her safe.

Panic surged. She rolled closer and lunged, throwing herself against his chest. "No."

He grabbed her chin. "You have to be ready. If that chopper lands, there are anywhere between two and four men on board. They will split up and search for us. If your abductor sent them, I'm extraneous. They'll simply kill me. What happens to you depends on their orders."

"Meaning?" Her voice shook.

"Either they'll take you to a new location to finish what your captor started or they'll end you. In either event, you need to be prepared to defend yourself."

"I don't know how to use this." She didn't even want to touch the gun but it was sandwiched between them, sitting on her chest, seeming to weigh a thousand pounds.

"I'm telling you," he bit out.

The helicopter drew closer, hovered not far from their location. She risked a peek over the top of the blanket and saw the vehicle make a slow sweep over the landscape.

Then it drew closer to the ground, kicking up sand and spewing it everywhere. Mystery gasped, tensed. They were coming for her.

Beside her, Axel clenched his jaw. When he turned to her, his expression looked bleak. "Listen to me. We're going to get off this rock. You're going to run ahead of me. I'll stay and fend them off."

"No!" Splitting from him terrified her.

She could get lost. She could die. Funny that her biggest fear was never seeing him again.

He went on as if he hadn't heard her objection at all. "Go west southwest." He pointed that direction. "Keep walking. I've told you about some of the dangers around the landscape. Take your pack. I'm going to give you the water. Keep walking as long and as fast as you can. You should come to a town named Keeler. Not many people there, but find someone who has a phone. Call 911."

"I'm staying with you."

The helicopter went vertical, setting down beyond the next ridge, just out of sight. As soon as the sound of the blades slowed, Axel took that as his cue to stand. "You're going. That's final."

He grabbed her pack, took the water bottles from his and shoved them into hers. Then he wadded up the blanket and jammed it into one of the pack's side pockets. It wouldn't zip but he deemed that good enough because he dragged her to her feet, thrust the gun on top of the pack, shoved it into her hands, then gave her a jerk of his head. "Go."

Mystery froze for a moment. "What will you do?"

He reached for his rifle, then withdrew a scope from his pack, along with extra ammunition. He slithered to his belly along the top of the flat rock. "I also went to sniper school."

As he started assembling his weapon and lining up shots, he completely tuned her out. His breathing evened. He looked utterly focused on the ridge ahead.

She couldn't fall apart. It wouldn't help either of them.

Dragging the overstuffed pack onto her back, she sucked back a groan at the additional weight. Already, her feet hurt from yesterday's trek and were protesting now. But she heard the helicopter's engine cut off. Adrenaline shot through her, and she welcomed the chemical. It staved off pain, made her sharp, gave her courage.

She slid off the rock just as Axel began wrapping his finger around the trigger.

On her trek down the first tier of rocks, she scraped her leg. Damn dress. The silvery sequin fabric had looked awesome catching the light in the club she'd gone to. It hadn't held up at all in a survival situation. It certainly hadn't protected her skin as she'd slid down the stone facing.

As Mystery brushed the debris from her thigh, her hand came back slightly wet. Blood. She winced, remembering what Axel had said about injury, but infection wasn't her biggest threat now.

She moved on and clawed her way down the next face of the rocks, holding on by her fingernails. As she dangled, she looked down—and gulped. The ground seemed too far away, like she might hurt her leg or break an ankle if she simply let go. Shaking, scared, she forced herself to study the stone in front of her for any foot or handholds. Nothing.

If she remained hanging here, she was easy bait. Dead meat. Closing her eyes and saying a prayer, she released her hold. The ground rushed up to meet her with a thud. Thankfully, the soil just around the rock seemed a bit more sandy than the hard-baked soil of the dried-up riverbed. Though the landing still jarred every bone in her body, the loamy quality of the dirt immediately below cushioned her fall enough. Juggling her pack on her back again, she darted away from the outcropping, hugging the sides of the hill, clinging to what was left of the shadows.

She'd barely taken five steps before Axel's first shot rang out above her.

Mystery tensed. That would certainly give away their position and send whoever was in that chopper running after them. What if they were another search-and-rescue sent by her father? Then again, if Axel was shooting, he must have reason to believe they weren't.

A second shot rang out less than twenty seconds later. She swallowed, paused. He'd told her to go, run to the nearest town.

But she couldn't leave him.

Mystery took the gun from her pack and headed back to Axel. This weapon would be far more useful in his hands.

Just as she reached the outcropping again, she saw him sliding down the facing of the rock as if his ass was on fire. The second he landed, he turned to find her. He barely had time for a glower before he rushed over and grabbed her arm, staying her.

"I picked two of them off. There were two others. The first headed back to the chopper before I even fired a shot. The second scrambled down the hill. I expect him to try to hunt us down."

She put her hand in his and tugged in the direction he'd told her to trek. "Let's go."

Axel yanked on her hand and shook his head. "This way."

Mystery frowned. She hadn't misunderstood what he told her previously. When he turned and pulled on her hand, she got the picture immediately. "Toward the helicopter?"

And the bad guys? Was he crazy?

"With one guy searching the valley for us, we might be able to sneak our way past the other and either radio for help or get the hell to civilization. Walking through this valley without anywhere to hide or adequate camouflage isn't my first choice. But if we run toward civilization, they head back to the chopper and find us in five minutes. We don't have better options."

The idea filled her with fear. Dashing across the valley was risky, probably close to insane. But Axel knew far more about staying alive in a combat situation than she did. He'd gotten her this far. She trusted him with her life.

"All right."

Nodding, he pulled her along as he hugged the outcropping of rock. Before he rounded the corner, he grabbed his rifle, at the ready, and peeked at the vast expanse beyond.

Her heart thrummed as she waited for him to say something—anything. The interminable seconds slid by in silence.

"We're going to make a dash across the long stretch of nothing between us and that hill. They'll probably see us and give chase. Or shoot. Keep running, no matter what. Got it?"

She nodded frantically.

"Answer me," he demanded.

"Yes, Axel."

He let out a sound that was a cross between a sigh and a curse. "Follow me."

They stepped out from behind the stone facing. Instantly, sun beat directly on them. Intense heat shimmered up from the hard-baked ground. Mystery didn't bother wishing she had sunglasses or a hat, but she blessed Axel for insisting they cover as much ground as possible at night.

"Any idea where they are now?" she murmured.

"Nope. One will probably head in our direction but climb that northern ridge to get above us for a better shot." He pointed. "The other will probably stay by the helicopter. He's likely the pilot. They'll have some comm device going between them to keep tabs on us. We have to stay alert for surprises. Ready?"

No. "Yes, Axel."

He grabbed her hand. "Go!"

They set off across the dusty, brush-dotted landscape at a full run. Mystery gazed frantically between the rocks littering the ground beneath her feet and the endless desert in front of her, shielding the men likely trying to kill them. Her breath rushed out of her chest. Terror crowded every part of her body. And she clung to Axel, knowing he was the only way she'd possibly survive this.

As they ran, time had no meaning. A few seconds? A few minutes? Then a shot rang out, skipping the dirt directly in front of Axel. She yelped.

He jerked on her arm and sent them running in a random zigzag pattern. Not a single hill, tree, bush, or rock to shield them in this low, brush-scrubbed valley. A few hundred yards in any direction would take them to some sort of shelter, but that might as well have been a million miles. As another shot rang out and kicked up the soil less than a foot from her, she wondered if there was any chance they'd make it to safety alive.

"Keep running!" he called over his shoulder.

It was either that or die. "I'm with you."

More shots echoed through the canyon, sounding as if they came from above and to their left. Mystery tried not to scream. Axel didn't let up, just kept charging toward the ridge in the distance. He dragged her to an angle slightly right but still toward the rise in the distance—their only chance at freedom.

As another bullet dive-bombed the ground just behind them, she kept chugging, one foot in front of the other, the impact of each step booming through her body. The watery mirage of the landscape in front of her began to come into sharper focus. A stitch ticced in her side. Her lungs felt ready to burst. But she didn't stop, wouldn't drag Axel down.

They sprinted closer to the ridge, still taking a slight angle to the right. The shots behind them sounded farther away, missed them by a wider margin.

"Almost there," he shouted.

Mystery hoped she made it that long. And that no violent gunmen awaited her.

Finally, they reached the base of the hills flanking the valley on the right, and he dragged her into shadow. He slowed their pace to a jog. She had a thousand questions, but now wasn't the time. Besides, she was panting too hard to talk.

He took a path between two hills, rounded behind one, then began ascending, staying out of sight of anyone in the valley.

"We're going to use the cover of these ridges to creep closer to the chopper. Stay right behind me."

Compared to her, he didn't sound winded at all, but like he'd simply been taking a leisurely stroll. If she made it out of this, she would get in better shape and learn to use a freaking gun. And she'd thank Axel profusely.

The ascent up the hill wasn't necessarily easier than the sprint across the valley. Her thighs ached and her lungs burned by the time they reached the last hill. The pilot sat in the chopper, walkie-talkie in hand, looking around nervously.

Axel knelt on the uneven ground and tried to get a steady stance as he lifted his rifle and aimed, but not toward the pilot. Mystery looked in the direction Axel pointed his barrel—and caught sight of the man who'd been shooting at them earlier. Or rather, she saw the business end of his rifle. He'd set up behind a rock, his weapon peeking over the top as he waited for them to come into view so he could pick them off.

"Stay here," he demanded. "I'm going up."

He'd be visible and vulnerable on top of the next rise. Mystery hated that she had no idea how to help him. "Be careful."

"If something happens to me, you know what to do and where to go." Then he grabbed his weapon, shirked his pack, checked the ammo in his pockets. Then he was gone.

In less than a minute, she heard multiple shots ring out. The reverberation of some were really close. Axel's rifle, she supposed. Others echoed around the valley.

The two exchanged gunfire for tense minutes. Worry gripped her. What was going on?

Mystery crept up the hill just a bit, enough to see the bottom of Axel's boots, toes down.

"I hear you." He didn't sound pleased.

"I'm worried about you."

"I do my job better when I'm not worried about you. Get back down."

Mystery crouched, staying where she could just see the heels of his boots. The air around them went still. As far as she could tell, Axel didn't move. She tensed. The waiting was killing her.

Suddenly, more gunfire erupted, a rapid *tat-tat-tat* of bullets. The sound came from a different angle, one higher up.

Axel scrambled off the hill and came barreling down, wrapping an arm around her. "Let's go."

She didn't have the chance to ask where, just picked up their packs and did her best to run beside him as he shuttled her down the hill and around the back, still closer to the helicopter.

Once it came into view, she saw the pilot sitting inside, still on the walkie-talkie as he scanned his surroundings. They were a bit behind him and to his left. He hadn't seen them yet, but it wouldn't be long.

Axel grabbed her arm and brought her up short. "We're going to make a run for it. When we get close to the chopper, hurry around the back, to the other side. Dive in. Keep your head down. Wait for me. Got it?"

"Yes, Axel." She wouldn't let him down.

"Go!" he urged in her ear.

Together, they ran, his big body on her left, blocking her from the last known position of the gunman, his arm around her protectively, keeping her crouched low.

Mystery saw the moment the pilot spotted them. His eyes widened. Thankfully, he didn't appear to have a gun. But he spoke animatedly into the little handheld communication device.

When he noticed the rifle in Axel's hand, he scrambled from the vehicle, shaking hands held in the air. He looked close to fifty, dark hair slicked back, showing off his clearly Italian genes. "I'm just a hired pilot. I don't want anyone else hurt."

Axel gave her a little nudge toward the back of the helicopter. She took that as her cue to dart to the far side of the flying contraption, like he'd instructed.

She glanced inside the cockpit for anything that obviously resembled a radio, but saw so many buttons, dials, levers, and switches. She had no idea if any of them would allow her to communicate with the outside world.

Quickly, she flung herself and the packs inside, then leaned forward and stared out the window. Axel was bearing down on the pilot, who backed away. That wasn't happening. Axel grabbed the pilot by his arm and—

Another round of shots ricocheted around them. Axel slammed the pilot to the dirt. A bullet struck the helicopter. Mystery heard the metallic ping of the impact. Feeling like a sitting duck, she scrambled out and onto the hard ground.

Another shot struck the vehicle. Then another. She heard a *thump*, a grunt, then . . .

"You okay?" Axel called.

"I don't know," she called back.

Tears stabbed her eyes. Damn it, now wasn't the time to fall apart. Later, when she was safe—or dead—she could freak out. Right now, she had to pull her shit together.

"Are you hit?" he asked.

"No. Just scared. I'll be fine."

Axel darted around the back of the chopper's tail and clapped eyes on her. The hard warrior stamped all over his face softened for a moment. "I know. I'm going to get you out of here."

He squeezed her arm, then scooted past her, toward the front of the aircraft, and raised his rifle.

Seconds ticked by in silence. She watched Axel, his wide shoulders set, barely rising and falling, though his heart rate had to be sky-high and adrenaline shooting through his system. His seeming calm set her at ease. Maybe he knew where the shooter was. Maybe he had a plan. No, probably. She hadn't known Axel long, but he'd do everything to keep them safe. No one would be better in a life-or-death situation.

Finally, he gave an almost imperceptible movement in his right arm. She leaned around to get a better view. He pulled the trigger.

The shot arrowed across the valley.

Seconds slipped past, punctuated by a silence that made her want to crawl out of her skin, her pulse race. She didn't hear any return fire from the other gunman.

When nearly a full, still minute had passed, Axel glanced at her over his shoulder. "Get in."

Before she could comply, he disappeared around the front of the aircraft again. Mystery wrenched open the door—and found a bullet hole in her seat where she'd been sitting only minutes ago.

On the other side, Axel opened the chopper door and zeroed in on her. He must have seen her frozen because he followed the direction of her gaze. And cursed. "It's okay, princess. He's gone. He's not coming back. Get in so we can get you home."

Mystery started trembling. His words pinged around her brain before she finally nodded. "Okay."

Closing her eyes, she hoisted herself into the seat. No way would she look at the hole in the leather and think about the fact that if she hadn't followed her instinct and gotten out, she'd be dead now.

Pushing the packs into the back of the vehicle, she tried to bring her shaking under control as Axel got in after her and started the helicopter. It started up, the whirring of the blades a jarring sound that ultimately soothed her. She could go home.

"You shot the guy trying to kill us?"

Axel hesitated and looked her over. Getting a read on her mental state?

Finally, he nodded. "He got impatient. When he couldn't find me to get a good shot from his previous location, he poked his head up to look. I was waiting."

Mystery swallowed hard. "And the pilot?"

"He wasn't armed. I hit him over the head. He'll be conscious in a few minutes."

Small comfort. Six people dead in the last twenty-four hours just to keep her alive. All but his two buddies had been criminals, but she still felt oddly guilty for being the one to survive. "I'm sorry."

Axel shook his head, his blue eyes completely reassuring. "You didn't ask for this."

But if she'd followed her father's rules, none of this would have happened. She and Axel had already had this argument, so she wasn't going to waste her breath or his time having it again.

Then she noticed him fiddling with something in the aircraft's complicated console. "I looked for the radio, but I couldn't figure it out."

He pointed to a few wires sticking out. "I'm betting the pilot disabled it on the gunman's instructions when it didn't look like they'd end up on the winning side."

Crap. "So we can't alert the police or tell anyone we're coming?"

"I'm afraid not." He flipped a few more switches and turned some knobs.

"Then what are you doing?"

Was this the helicopter equivalent of hot-wiring a car?

"Disabling the IFF transponder." He focused on the buttons in front of him, studying.

"What's that? Some sort of GPS?"

"It stands for 'Identify Friend or Foe.' It transmits a four-digit octal identification code with the aircraft's tail numbers. If I don't disable this, local air traffic control might be able to identify me. Until we know whose side they're on . . ." He yanked it free. "Better to be safe than sorry."

Mystery was so grateful he'd thought of all that. Without him, no doubt she'd already be dead.

He grabbed the controller, and the helicopter began to rise off the ground. Now probably wasn't a good time to mention that she'd always been deathly afraid of them. She tensed and clenched her eyes shut. Better not to look.

Then it hit her. She really was going home—to her father, to everything familiar.

To life without Axel.

He lifted the chopper off the ground. It surged back, then he pulled on the controller. They gained altitude before they lunged forward. The brown of the brush-scrubbed hills rose up in front of them, the obstacles she hadn't been sure how they'd cross to get out of this blasted valley. But suddenly they were flying above them. A sense of euphoria gripped her.

They were going to live. They were saved.

Suddenly, Axel cursed and gave a mighty yank on the controller. Despite that, as soon as they crested the rise of the hill, the nose of the aircraft leaned down. Mystery braced her hands and feet anywhere in the cabin she could find so she didn't splat face first into the windshield.

"Put on your seatbelt," he demanded. Beads of sweat popped out along his forehead, at his temples.

A terrible thought occurred to her. "You don't know how to fly this thing?"

That would be bad. So, so bad . . . She scrambled to buckle her restraint. It wouldn't save her if they crashed and went up in flames, but she'd hope for a better outcome. She hadn't come this far to die in some mechanical contraption designed to get her the hell out of danger.

"I do," he assured as the aircraft started spinning in circles. "But I think we've lost the manifold pressure in the engine. It probably got damaged by gunfire. I can't control the chopper anymore."

That made Mystery's heart stop. She did her best not to panic or scream, especially when they seemed to be losing altitude fast. The nose of the craft tilted down even more. She tried to reach across the space and grab the steering contraption and give a mighty tug.

The fact that he didn't object told her they might be in serious trouble.

"I don't think I can recover." He swallowed.

And the ground raced up toward them as the aircraft itself started spinning faster and faster.

"Oh, God . . ."

"Now might be a good time to say your prayers."

Mystery's heart stopped. "Can we do anything?"

He hesitated only a split second to look at the complicated dash of dials and indicators. "On my count, pull on the yoke as hard as you can. We'll see if we can even this up. We're still going to autorotate down. Get ready for a bumpy landing. One . . . two . . ." He gritted his teeth. "Pull!"

Bracing her feet on the floor, she wrapped her fists around the yoke and used every ounce of her strength to bring it back up. Axel did the same, the tendons in his neck standing out, his biceps bulging.

Mystery tugged with all her might, but it was like pulling a pole through concrete. The thing just wasn't budging. They began to spin around faster and faster, the landscape coming at her in dizzying speeds, disorienting her. She wanted to close her eyes to cut down on the nausea. She didn't dare.

The one bright spot was that it appeared they'd made it over the hill and stood a decent chance of putting this thing down on level ground. She only hoped that they didn't burst into a ball of flame the moment they did.

"Get ready for impact," he barked.

How was she supposed to do that? But they didn't have time for questions. "Got it."

Axel took in deep breaths and kept trying to steady the yoke. The blades stirred up the dust around them. She choked as it invaded her nostrils and clogged her throat. The tail of the craft kept whirling around, adding to the dizzying spin. God, she hoped they made it out of this alive. If she did, Mystery swore she'd do so many things differently.

The back of the aircraft hit the ground below, pushing them forward and destabilizing the entire aircraft. The legs at the front hit with a jarring thud. Her head snapped back as her body slammed to the seat. Like a teeter-totter, the little craft ambled back and forth, rocking in place, before finally settling on the ground.

Axel killed the engine, then panted a few deep breaths, obviously trying to bring his adrenaline under control. "You all right?"

Other than her heart racing like a mad thing and being scared half to death? "Yeah."

And, damn it, she still had to pee.

He turned to her, stared, said nothing for long moments. He curled his fingers into fists. Sweat poured down his face. He looked taut, as if holding himself back.

Mystery frowned. "You?"

Her question seemed to jolt him. "Fine."

She wasn't sure she believed him.

He reached behind them and grabbed the packs from the back. "Can you carry yours?"

Testing her fingers, wrists, arms, and legs, she was relieved to find that nothing felt broken or even hurt. "I should be able to."

"Let's go. We'll have to walk again. Getting over that range of hills was a big help. It saved us hours of hiking. We might find some shelter ahead before nightfall."

But their water supply was running low. He didn't have to tell her that, even if they made it through today, they'd likely be empty by tomorrow. Then what? She didn't need an expert like him to tell her that they wouldn't last long in the desert without hydration.

That was tomorrow, though. Today they'd dodged another bullet. She was lucky to be alive.

Axel bailed out of the side of the helicopter and slung his pack on his shoulder, then jogged around the front of the vehicle to her side. She spilled out into his waiting arms. Axel scooped her up and held her tightly against his body. She felt his racing heart against her own. He smelled like man and sweat and life.

Mystery blinked up, looking into his eyes. His expression, so sharp and aware, made her catch her breath. She dropped her gaze to his lips, aching to know what they felt like.

He grabbed a fistful of her hair and tugged, his stare sliding over her, fused to her. Then his lips crashed down onto her own. She gave a cry at the impact.

Axel took her mouth, possessed it. God, she'd been kissed before but not by anyone who could make her feel his touch through her entire body. The drugging relief she'd been feeling just after the crash mixed with a pure sexual thrill to give her a zing that soon had her climbing his big body, wrapping her legs around his waist, desperate for more.

Axel lifted his head, panted harshly in her face, then swooped in for another blistering kiss. This time, he drilled his tongue into her mouth and tangled it with his own, sweeping deep, scorching her all the way to her soul. His addictive flavor filled her. It wasn't like artificial breath spray or toothpaste. It wasn't whatever he'd been eating or drinking. It was just him. She tightened her legs around him and struggled for her next breath, not really caring if she found it.

He pulled at her scalp as he slanted his mouth across her lips at another angle, then dived deep into her a third time. Aching for him everywhere, Mystery wriggled on him and . . . Oh, did she find him hard and ready and so big. Yes. She wanted that. She wanted him. She yearned for more of his fingers tangled in her hair, his kiss taking absolute command of her body. She yearned to find out what it felt like to be filled by a guy who wasn't simply trying to score.

She whimpered and tightened her arms around his neck. He

gave a groan as he filled his hands with her ass and ground her against his raging erection.

He hit her right against the most sensitive spot. Mystery couldn't stop herself from breaking the kiss and tossing her head back in pleasure. "Axel . . ."

Drawing in deep draughts of air, he set her back on her feet and jerked his hands from her as if he'd been burned. "Jesus, I didn't mean to do that. I'm sorry."

"Don't be. I'm fine. I—"

"Grab your pack." Axel gritted his teeth, then gave a jerk of his head toward the expansive distance in front of them. "Let's go."

She frowned but did as he asked. Once she had it on her back, she fell into step beside him as he headed west, into the sun beginning its fall from its midday zenith. "What's wrong?"

He refused to look at her. "I feel like an asshole. That was totally inappropriate."

Mystery frowned up at him. "I liked it. A lot."

That admission only seemed to turn his expression grimmer. "We'll walk away from the crash site. With the transponder disabled, it should take whoever sent those guys a while to find their chopper."

"So you don't think my dad sent them?"

Axel shook his head. "If he had, they shouldn't have been shooting at us. I waited to see if they'd fire first. When they started lining up their first shot, I acted accordingly."

So whoever had paid for her abduction already knew she'd been rescued and was coming after her. "How long do we have?"

"Before they come after us again?" He shrugged, looking like he didn't want to answer.

"Sheltering me doesn't do us any good."

"I know." Axel squinted against the sun. "You've already been through a lot and . . ."

He didn't want to put her through more. She appreciated that, but that didn't help them. "It's not over, so I can't be a spoiled little rich girl and sit around waiting for someone else to solve my problems if I'd like to live. And the last thing I want to do is drag you down with me."

"If he's got another team on standby, an hour. Maybe two. If not, we might have a few hours more."

The temperature sweltered. In order to reach the nearest town, they had to walk in the direct, blazing sun. They'd probably leave tracks in the sand that a blind man could follow.

"So we either find a place to hide nearby or make a run for it?"

"Yeah. And neither option is particularly good."

Mystery understood that, but she hadn't come this far for nothing. If she'd survived an abduction, a bullet-ridden rescue, a trek across unforgiving landscape, and busted out of her comfort zone so she wouldn't be a burden, all of that couldn't be for nothing. She wouldn't let herself, her father, or Axel down.

"It seems to me that the closer we get to civilization, the better off we'll be. Once we can tell someone I'm still alive and where to find me, they'll have to give up. Or at least regroup."

He nodded, then sent her a look filled with pride. "Hanging here makes us sitting ducks."

"Then let's keep going. If it doesn't work out . . . we'll know we did our best."

"Good call." He tilted his head at her. "Now drink water."

"You're bossy."

Despite the gravity of the situation, a smile tugged at his lips. "That's never going to change."

Probably not, but she liked that about him. In fact, she liked everything about him. And if they survived this ordeal, Mystery didn't think she could go back to her life without telling him exactly how she felt.

Chapter Five

THEY walked the better part of the day, skirting hills, rock formations, tall shrubs—anything that provided cover. The sun blazed, and they used up the last of their sunscreen. Axel donned a hat to protect his scalp from the rays. Mystery fought with her long hair until Axel found a length of string in his pack. She tied it on top of her head and kept putting one foot in front of the other. As afternoon waned, their water supply dwindled dangerously low, and she wondered what they'd do if they ran out altogether. Die within a few miles of civilization?

Axel glanced her way and frowned. "You look exhausted."

She was. "It doesn't matter right now. Are we walking until night falls?"

He studied the landscape, then turned back to her. "I'm thinking we need to make our way to that outcropping of rocks." He pointed to a spot in the near distance. "We should rest there, soak up a little shade. We haven't been followed yet, which tells me that whoever wants you is regrouping. When night falls, we'll set out again. If we walk then, we'll have to endure the cold, but it will preserve water."

Right now, Mystery couldn't imagine being not sweltering but she knew from experience that once the sun set, the wind often picked up and the temperature plummeted. Then the dry chill would whip at her bones.

She nodded, and they walked to the designated spot in silence. Neither of them said a word about the kiss. Had he just been damn glad to be alive and willing to lock lips with anyone to celebrate that? Or did he feel something for her that he'd written off as either unprofessional or a distraction to his mission? The question gnawed at her brain.

Once they reached the outcropping, Axel gestured to the shade wedged between two of the boulders. "Set your stuff here for a minute and take a load off. Make sure nothing is crawling around before you do. I'm going to climb up here and see if we can spot anything that might resemble dinner. MREs are running low."

That struck further disquiet inside her. She and Axel could survive maybe another twenty-four hours. Thirty-six if they really conserved. What if no one rescued them before then? Or would her abductor's goons materialize again even sooner to finish what they'd started?

If she thought about the possibility of either dehydrating or bleeding to death, she'd only start panicking.

"Can I help?" she asked as he tugged his big body onto the rock and stood to his ridiculous height on top, surveying the area.

Suddenly, he froze, then squinted toward the bright, falling sun. He checked his compass, then seemed to do some mental math, dissecting a problem in his head.

"What is it? Do you see something?" Had they been saved?

"A few buildings. They look rickety, though. Maybe it was once a town."

A bit of hope filled her. At the very least, maybe the structures would provide reliable shade. If she and Axel were lucky, maybe they would find water, food . . . something to sustain them, maybe more. "The desert is littered with ghost towns. My dad scouted a few for a movie about eight years ago, and I went with him. Some have been renovated for use as sets or for tourist adventures that show what mining in the old west must have been like."

He whipped his gaze down to her. "You mean, some of these buildings could be habitable or have access to the outside world?"

She shrugged. "Maybe. I don't know which ghost town this might be, but we've at least got a shot."

Axel jumped down with renewed vigor. "Then let's go. It's less than a half mile, just beyond that little rise in front of us."

The smile he wore was infectious and showed off not only the cleft in his chin but the dimples in both cheeks. He wasn't slick or polished or pretty, but when happiness lit up his face, he looked completely irresistible.

He ignored her stare and pressed on. "This could be good. We'll approach cautiously in case your abductor is holed up here, but it looks deserted."

"The whole ordeal might be over? That would make me so happy." *But I wish I could take you home as a souvenir.* "Lead the way."

As the big ball of the sun dipped toward the horizon and seared their faces, they hoisted their packs on their backs and hauled ass across the desert.

When they reached the outskirts of the little abandoned town, they found a big rock with a bronze plate just off the side of a dirt road. The town, Cerro Gordo, had once been the county's wealthiest producer of minerals like silver, lead, and zinc. They'd sent water and other supplies by mule train, tram, or boat across the Owens Lake to build the pueblo of Los Angeles.

"Wow," she murmured. "I'd heard that L.A. owed its roots to some of these old mining towns."

Despite being hungry, sore, tired, and wrung out, Mystery wanted to see more of the place. If she could remake this nightmare into an adventure, even temporarily, maybe that would help her to cope with all the other stuff she couldn't deal with yet.

Cautiously, they approached, Axel insisting she stay behind him just in case they encountered anyone out to kill them. With weapon drawn, he walked almost soundlessly, keeping her close behind.

Part of the town appeared at the base of a hill, while a few buildings perched on top. One of the first buildings they approached was a two-story structure made entirely out of wood. A wide porch stretched across the front, leading to a door flanked by two murky windows. A green and white sign proclaimed it the AMERICAN HOTEL. A balcony above boasted three windows and a railing no one should lean on. But overall, the building was in one piece and gave Mystery hope.

They tried the front door and found it locked. But one of the glass panes above the knob had been broken, leaving a gaping hole Axel stuck his hand through. With a turn of his wrist, he reached the lock and turned it.

They ducked inside the building to find it utterly deserted by anything except dust. People had been here, probably within the last few months. Dark hardwood floors, original to the structure, led to a long wooden check-in desk. Someone had painted the ceiling green, but left the exposed beams a cedar color. On one side of the room sat a massive woodstove. What might have once been an ornate copper wall behind it now looked green. Behind the counter, shelves of old-timey, empty bottles stood in a haphazard arrangement.

Around the corner, the theme continued as the room segued into a large bar/saloon area with an adjoining restaurant. The bar had been ravaged by time, then restored to something rustic yet polished. Above it hung a painting of a blonde in a white dress holding something that looked like an apple. A few bottles of modern beer sat on the corner, empty. Shot glasses lay upside down on a nearby tray, gathering dust.

"Do you think anyone is here?" she asked him.

He shook his head. "Maybe someone fixed this up and tried to make a go at drawing in tourists, then gave up recently."

"Or they closed up for the winter. It snows around here sometimes."

He nodded. "Let's keep looking quickly. We're losing light."

A glance out one of the windows proved him right. They had maybe twenty minutes before everything went black.

"Any chance your phone works here? That someone installed a cell tower or something nearby?" she asked.

He pulled it from his pack and shook his head. "Nothing. Sorry."

His reply disappointed her—mostly. Some small part of her rejoiced at the idea they'd get to stay together and alone just a bit longer. Which she knew was stupid.

She shrugged. "It was worth a shot."

The bar led back to a restaurant. Despite the old cast-iron stove and the cabinets that looked as if they'd been built in the late nineteenth century, the place had a modern refrigerator, a microwave, and a ceiling fan with lights. Pots and pans hung from hooks in the ceiling.

Mystery flipped on a switch beside the doorway, hoping . . . But nothing. The refrigerator wasn't humming, either. *Damn.*

Axel checked behind a little curtain set back in one wall. "Hey, I found some canned food here—beans, soup, veggies."

At least they wouldn't starve. She opened the refrigerator. A gust of hot air rushed her face, and the smell of plastic almost made her choke. Inside, sat a case of unopened bottled water.

"Axel!" she shrieked.

He rushed over and stopped short, then laughed. "That's a welcome sight. Hot damn."

A smile stretched across her face. Despite chapped, sunburned cheeks, blistered feet, and a layer of grime on her skin two inches thick, the sight of Axel happy made her grin. "Right?"

"Gather all that up. I saw some lanterns out in the restaurant. Hunt around for matches. I'm going to hope this hotel has a generator somewhere nearby.

She hadn't even thought of that. "I'll also see if, by chance, we have running water."

"If not, I'll look for a well or pump out back. Stay alert, just in case we're not alone. I'll be back by dark."

As Axel eased out of the kitchen, she tried to turn on the sink. Nothing, damn it. With a sigh, she gathered up a few cans of food, then rifled through the drawers until she found a manual can opener and spoons. She wrenched one of the bottles of water from the pack and began sucking it down gratefully as she hustled back into the restaurant, grabbed a few lanterns, then searched the bar until she found a book of matches. Lighting a couple of the little lamps, Mystery grabbed one and decided now might be the best time to explore the upstairs.

Each step creaked as she made her way to the second floor. Hot, stagnant air lingered up on the landing, but she could see sunlight eeking through the cracks in the log cabin walls. She had no doubt that as the temperature fell outside, it would do the same in here.

She found five closed doors upstairs. All but one were locked. The one she could open revealed what looked like the suite. It consumed the area at the front of the hotel with a big, old-fashioned wrought-iron bed, homemade-looking quilts, a honey-colored dresser and basin, complete with an old porcelain pitcher and bowl. An old-fashioned plush chair in a fussy beige damask with a skirt covering its squatty legs took up one corner. Outside the window, she glimpsed a sweeping view of the desert they'd just traveled and the mountains beyond.

Everything in the room was quaint and charming, and the idea of sleeping in any bed at all was beyond welcome. Cozying up with Axel . . . The thought made her shiver and flush.

A door in the corner led to a bathroom with a pedestal sink and an old claw-foot tub. And a toilet with a pump handle to flush. After making use of it, she snooped around. Someone had left behind a few new toothbrushes and a tube of toothpaste, a comb, a bar of soap, a bottle of shampoo, a razor, and a spray can of deodorant. Mystery thanked her lucky stars.

Back in the bedroom, she opened the dresser drawers and hit pay dirt. A woman had obviously been here and left behind a pair of jeans. They'd be two sizes too big, but way more practical than her skimpy dress. Not only that, but she found a few shirts, some clean socks, and tennis shoes close to her size.

Lantern in hand, she searched the rest of the hotel. The office that had obviously been shuttered a while ago had an old phone, but it didn't work. The rest of the hotel held a parlor with an aging piano, a storage room empty of everything except a few rusted antiques, and not much more. By Beverly Hills standards, she was totally roughing it. But if she stacked it up against last night's accommodations, this was the freaking Ritz.

Mystery returned to the kitchen as the sun edged behind the mountains. Outside, the sky turned dark fast. Inside, too. Axel busted through the back door, carrying a bucket of water in each hand. "I found a well. I've got more where this came from. Does that stove work?"

She hadn't thought to check and shrugged.

"Matches?" he barked.

Mystery grabbed the rest of the book and handed them over. Axel set the buckets down and took them, gesturing to her. "Bring the lantern over here."

She followed him across the kitchen, then watched as he lit the match and turned the knob to release the gas from the stove. It hissed and sputtered, then the burner flared to life.

"That antique works?"

"It's a replica. I found the old wooden stove in a storage shed, along with a couple of propane tanks. I guessed this one was rigged up to heat like a barbeque since the gas company probably didn't run lines out this far. Grab some of those pans. Let's heat up this chow. The rest of the town is empty, by the way."

She'd suspected as much.

Together, they grabbed pans from the ceiling and wiped them out with clean dish towels while Mystery filled him in on everything she'd found upstairs. He looked pleased.

Within minutes, they were shoveling in beans and soup, then washing it down with the bottled water. As they did, Axel heated the well water from his buckets in two big pots. He ate more than a few cans, shoveling food in at a rate that amazed her. Where did he put all the calories? After a can of stew and half a can of green beans, Mystery was stuffed.

As the water in the pots began boiling, he carried one across the room. "Can you lug that other bucket of water upstairs?"

Mystery retrieved it from its resting spot near the back door. It seemed to weigh a hundred pounds, and she grabbed it with both hands. "Probably. What are we doing with this?"

"Getting you clean."

"Like . . . in the bathtub?"

"Originally, I was going to suggest sponge baths in the kitchen, but since you found an actual bathtub, lead the way." He gestured to her with a nod of his head.

For that, she'd carry this bucket up a mountain. The muscles of her shoulders strained, and the brittle plastic of the handle threatened to break, but she kept on, leading him in the shadowy dark to the bedroom, then the small bathroom beyond.

He set the bucket on the floor behind her. "Stay here. I'll bring one of the lanterns."

Mystery groped her way to the old tub and shivered in the dark.

It wasn't cold but the air around her felt a bit creepy. She supposed this was known as a ghost town for a reason. History lingered, and she almost felt as if she could close her eyes and picture the people who had once stayed here, when this mining town had been in its heyday.

Axel returned a moment later, shedding soft, golden light on the situation. He set one of the lanterns in the little pedestal sink and gripped the other as he edged past her to shove the old rubber stopper in the drain. After, he dumped the bucket of hot water inside the tub. Steam rose in a billowing cloud, fogging up the old mirror hanging in its wooden frame above the sink. Mystery looked at herself and nearly shrieked. She didn't look anything like the cool, sophisticated girl who'd gone out for a night on the town a few days ago. Now she looked bedraggled and filthy . . . and haunted, as if she'd seen more of the seedy underbelly of life than she'd been ready for.

She managed to bite her tongue, then catalog what she needed to do to get clean. At least the dirt on her cheeks and her rat's-nest hairdo would be gone soon. As for the emotional turmoil from her ordeal, she couldn't do anything about that now so she locked it away in a mental box for later.

"Put your hand in the tub," Axel instructed. "Too hot for you?"

Mystery dipped her fingers in. Together, they worked to add some of the cool water from the bucket she'd brought upstairs until the temperature felt just right. The tub didn't even fill halfway, but she could work with it.

"You'll rinse with the rest of this water." He pointed to the bucket. "Let me see if I can find one more thing . . ." He left the little room and after opening and closing some doors and drawers, he returned with a blessedly clean and big towel. "Here you go. When you're out, I'll do my thing. Until then, I'll keep guard in the hall, just in case unexpected company comes."

Then he closed the door behind him, leaving her alone with the glow of the lantern. Mystery stripped and stepped into the tub. *Just like heaven* ... She shampooed her hair twice, then soaped down and shaved, rinsing with the final bucket of icy water. She was shivering as she stepped out, but she was blissfully clean.

She dried off, tossed on some of the clothes she'd seen in the dresser, braided her hair over one shoulder, brushed her teeth—and felt incredibly human again. When she emerged from the bedroom, Axel stood in the hall with a pan of steaming water and another bucket from the well.

"You done?"

"Yeah. I found soap, shampoo, clean toothbrushes, a comb . . . It's all in there. Do you need anything else?"

"Good job." He slid past her with the pan of hot water.

She dragged in the cold after him. "We make a good team."

Mystery cringed the second the words left her mouth. Ugh, that sounded stupid. Axel knew how to survive. She'd just done her best to keep up and follow his directions.

"Sure," he tossed back.

But he didn't mean it.

"Here's your cold water," she blurted, bucket in hand.

With a nod, he stopped up the tub, then turned to her like he was waiting for her to shut the door so he could get started. And there she stood, gaping at him like an idiot. *Awesome.*

In the hallway, she heard water sloshing, imagined him taking off his shirt, his boots, his pants . . . Did he go commando? Was he big all over?

Mystery's breath caught, and she pushed away from the wall, heading downstairs. Mooning over him was totally embarrassing, yet she couldn't seem to stop. Everything about him appealed to her. Yes, he was handsome, but that didn't impress her. He was smart and funny, of course, but she'd met guys like that before, too. What made Axel so special was that, on top of his other qualities, he protected. He cared. He'd made sure she ate, drank, covered her feet, kept her face from burning. Hell, he'd even given her a place to pillow her head on his chest. Okay, so that might be part of his job, but he could have been an ass about it. He could have treated her like a thorn in his side or like a kid. Instead, he'd encouraged her, talked to her, actually listened.

He was special. With civilization and the bad guys so close, Mystery wasn't under any illusion; they'd either be rescued or dead by tomorrow. Tonight was it.

Downstairs, she rifled around behind the bar and found an unopened bottle of tequila and a shaker of salt. Not her first drink of choice, but better than nothing. She set them out, then selected a glass from the tray and waited.

Axel emerged a few minutes later with a towel wrapped around his waist. He carried his clean, dripping clothes in one hand, a lantern in the other. Mystery nearly swallowed her tongue.

Muscles covered his enormous chest in slabs. His wide shoulders bulged. The ridges of his abs led toward narrow hips with the beginnings of a treasure trail visible just above the towel. Then he turned for the kitchen, and she drank in the view from the back. More muscles everywhere. Shoulders, triceps, upper back, lining his spine. Beneath the towel, Axel clearly had a really fine ass. *Holy crap* . . .

He emerged from the kitchen a moment later with his lantern and sidled up to the bar beside her, smelling of soap and toothpaste and something so manly it nearly dropped her to her knees. "I hung my clean clothes from the hooks above the kitchen sink, where the pots were. Hopefully, they'll dry soon. I didn't see anything of yours worth washing except the bra and panties. They're drying, too."

Mystery's eyes flew wide. He'd washed her undergarments, the expensive French variety she'd worn to the club that night in case she got lucky? The lacy, silky gray sheer panties and matching wisp of a bra? Heat rushed up her face.

"Thanks," she managed to bluster out. "They'll be good in a few hours, I guess."

He nodded, then directed his attention to the bottle. "You found tequila, huh? Legally, you're too young to drink."

"Do you think I've never been drunk?" She slanted him a stare that begged him to get real.

"Oh, I know you have. Mystery Grace Mullins, age nineteen. Attended Beverly Hills High, class rank one hundred three out of six forty two. Accepted to USC with an undeclared major, but you dropped out after a semester. The apple of your Oscar-winning father's eye and his only child with his late wife, Julia, whose homicide remains unsolved over a decade and a half later. Listed as one of the most beautiful celebrity kids, you've got a reputation as a wild child, but I think that's overrated. Because you no longer have your mother and your father is busy, you'd rather have attention than a party. That explains why you let yourself be arrested at fifteen for joyriding with your then-boyfriend, and why you keep sneaking into bars. You have a lot of friends, none terribly close. You spend most of your time with your books and computer. You're not sure what you want to do with your life, and the last few days have been more 'adventure' than you bargained for."

God, with every word, he stripped her bare, reducing her life to a few lines that, even to her, sounded pathetic. How had he realized so quickly that she'd been trying for years to get her father's attention? She loved him more than anyone . . . but sometimes she resented how much Hollywood demanded of him and how little he had left for her.

"Well, you have me all figured out," she quipped and poured a shot of tequila. "Congrats."

She licked her hand, shook the salt, and sucked it off, then downed the booze. It burned her throat, and she missed the lime to cut through that. Her eyes watered, but she refused to choke and look like an amateur. This wasn't her first rodeo, after all.

He took the bottle and salt, then followed her lead, downing the shot in one quick toss. "I didn't mean to upset you. Just point-

ing out that I'm not a total stranger, even if it feels that way sometimes."

Blue eyes could seem so cold sometimes, but never his. They held
a warmth, a humor, an understanding that drew her. Yes, she was
stupidly crushing on him and had been since shortly after he'd rescued her. Was anything so wrong with something happening between them? They were both adults.

Mystery poured another shot, her stare meeting his as she licked
the back of her hand slowly. He drew in a sharp breath, his gaze fixed
on her. Those blue eyes darkened. Good, she had his attention. Her
body sizzled hot. As she poured the salt, the thought made her tingle
all over.

She tongued off the tart sprinkles, then knocked back the tequila. His stare clung to her mouth as she swallowed and licked her
lips. He didn't even blink as she set the shot glass on the bar. His gaze
followed her hand, then landed on the slope of her breasts under the
overlarge shirt.

The tingle inside her became full-fledged arousal.

The warmth of the booze spread through her, making her mel-
low and a bit hazy. She leaned forward, bracing her elbows on the bar
and wondered if he could see down the front of the large, slightly
gaping tee enough to get a peek at her cleavage.

"So Troy-who-goes-by-Axel from Tennessee, where do you live
when you're between missions or whatever?"

"Dallas." He grabbed the bottle again. This time, he drank
straight from it, then reached for the cap and began screwing it on.

"Give it back! I wasn't done with that."

"Yeah, you are. I can't drink any more if I'm going to stay alert,
and we have to cut out of here in a few hours, so you don't need the
dehydration or the hangover. We've still got about eight miles to
walk."

"I'll be fine. I can hold a little more liquor than that before I
feel it."

His face lost all hint of friendly. "I said you're done."

She sent him an annoyed tsk. "You're not my father, you know."

"I'm fully aware of that."

She narrowed her eyes at him. "You're not my boyfriend, either."

"I am not. If I were, I'd be taking you over my knee about now."

Mystery gaped at him. "Y-you'd *spank* me?"

"Yep," he answered without pause or apology. "Do you understand what I'm saying, little girl?"

She only had the murkiest idea what he meant, but no way would she admit that. She'd heard of men who liked to tie women down and sensually torture them. In fact, her father had been given a script for a thriller about a sexual Dominant accused of murdering his sub with a huge twist at the end, but he'd declined the film. The whole BDSM scene had sounded shadowy and kinky to her . . . but admittedly intriguing. What would it be like to turn herself entirely over to a man like Axel? He'd already earned her trust, so she knew he wouldn't do anything to truly risk or hurt her. The idea of being his singular focus really turned her on, in fact.

"I know what you're saying." Her voice shook as the image of her tied to his bed while he loomed over her, strumming her naked body with his big fingers, played in her head.

"Then you understand that I'd curb and punish self-destructive behavior. But being your Dom isn't my role. Being your rescuer is. I intend to get you home to your father in one piece—without you being wasted."

"It was just a drink," she objected.

"A potent one. With so little food in your belly and so much exposure to the sun, your system will be more susceptible to the alcohol." He grabbed her chin and brought her face close. "Your eyes are a bit unfocused and dilated. You're already half drunk."

So what if she was? "For the first time since we left that rundown shack, I'm not terrified out of my mind. Thanks for being a buzzkill."

He crossed his arms over his huge chest and gave her a disapproving glare. It crawled up her back and ignited her temper. But another part of her realized that it also lit the fuse on her arousal. *If I grab the bottle and drink from it again, what will he do?* The question whispered through her head as if the devil sitting on her shoulder prodded her.

"Booze isn't the way to escape your fear," he pointed out, his voice deep and firm.

Mystery shivered at his tone. God, she wanted to hear more of that—a whole lot more as he pumped his big cock inside her and made her scream.

The devil on her shoulder poked her again. She grabbed the bottle and stepped out of his reach, staring at him defiantly as she unscrewed the cap and poured a big gulp into her mouth.

She swallowed and smacked her lips. "Now what are you going to do, big man?"

For a long moment, he did nothing but stare at her as if she'd made some grievous error she would come to deeply regret. Slowly, he uncrossed his arms, then sighed, sizing her up like an animal considering its prey, waiting for the perfect moment to pounce.

Her heart pounded. Her nipples beaded. Her whole body lit up. Not once had any of the admittedly stupid string of boyfriends she'd had made her feel this much like a woman. Her breathing speeded up. She swayed a bit closer. Would he touch her? Would he lay his lips over hers and claim her mouth before he delved into her body?

She exhaled a ragged little sigh. "Axel . . ."

Her whispered entreaty put him in motion. His eyes went dark as he skirted the bar, sidled closer—and kept coming at her.

A dizzying wave of desire swept through her as he reached for her. His fingers brushed her waist. She swayed. Her back hit the wall. She gasped. He pinned her with his big body, his hands braced on either side of her head. Heat seeped into her. His erection pressed hard and massive into her belly. She closed her eyes, her head falling back as she offered him her vulnerable throat.

"Princess . . ." he murmured low and soft in her ear.

Her entire body trembled. "Yes."

When he didn't say anything right away, she opened her eyes to find him staring at her. He hovered right over her, his face so close. Lust ripped across his expression, darkening his eyes, firming his lips. She couldn't wait to feel him . . .

"Yes." Mystery positioned her lips just under his.

But he didn't kiss her.

Instead, he swallowed hard, body taut. His nostrils flared. He clenched his jaw. "Wait here."

He turned on his heel and left the bar, marched through the kitchen, and out the back door.

Wait? If he was a Dom, maybe he needed rope or some way to restrain her. Or maybe he looked for some other instrument with which to give her pleasure or pain. The thought made her breathless.

Axel slammed back in a moment later, returning to the bar with a bucket in his hand. She frowned. *What the hell?*

After he set it on the floor beside him, he returned to cage her body against the wall with his own. If anything, his face loomed closer, his lips an aching breath away. Mystery tried to inch closer and seal her lips over his. Before she could even blink, he grabbed her wrists and held her against the wall. She gripped the neck of the bottle, kind of wishing he'd pour it all over her body and lick it off.

"You're saying yes?" he asked in a rough whisper.

"Yes."

"Whatever I want?"

To all the erotic ways he could take her currently spinning in her head? "Yes."

He grabbed the bottle from her grip and took a step back. "I'm saying no, Mystery." Before she could sputter a reply, he turned the bottle upside down and poured the tequila into the bucket, onto a mound of dirt he'd scooped inside.

"What the hell are you doing?" she screeched.

Axel shook the bottle a couple of times to make sure every last drop emptied out. "No, Mystery. I don't think you've heard that word enough in your life. No, you cannot get wasted. No, you cannot check out when you're in the middle of danger. And no, you cannot have sex with me just because you want it."

He dumped the empty bottle into the bucket and turned his back on her.

Shock pelted her, then quickly morphed to anger. She charged after him. When he whirled to face her, she poked a finger into his steely chest. "You wanted me. I felt it." She stared pointedly at his tented towel. "I still see it."

He stiffened. "I'm just a man. You're a pretty girl. But I don't need to fuck someone every time I have an itch to scratch. Do you?"

"No. I just thought—"

"I was a novelty? I'd thank my lucky stars that you'd grant me use of your famous pussy for an hour or two so you could wrap me around your little finger?"

"No!" That he'd even imagined she felt that way horrified her.

He narrowed his eyes, and she felt chastened. "Then what did you think, girl?"

Tears welled. Her mouth turned down, and she knew an ugly cry was coming. She couldn't stop it to save her life. "That I liked you and wanted you. I hoped you liked and wanted me, too."

Something in his face softened, but his stance didn't. "I like you just fine. You're easy to talk to. You learn fast. You've got backbone and a tender heart—an appealing combination."

"Then why—"

"You need to finish growing up. And you can't handle what I'd demand from you in bed, especially after the trauma you've just been through. Besides, you're too damn young for sex."

"I'm not fucking five. I'm a legal adult."

"So you think that means you should exercise your right to spread your legs?"

"You don't have to be an ass about it." She swiped away the un-wanted tears scalding her cheeks. "What's your hang-up, anyway? It's not like I'm a virgin."

His expression became a fortress, the windows to his soul slam-ming shut and cutting her off from his every thought. "So you think I should corrupt you more?" He raised a brow at her. "The absence of a hymen doesn't make you a woman. We're done here. Take your lantern, get in bed, and try to sleep."

With just a few sentences, he'd turned her down cold, embar-rassed the hell out of her, and dismissed her utterly. A part of her wanted to call him names, argue and rail. The other part felt too humiliated and just wanted to escape.

But she couldn't resist a parting shot. "Fine. Just don't talk to me anymore. Don't act nice or pretend you give a shit. Just do what my father paid you to do and get me home."

Chapter Six

Present day

"EARTH to Elise." Axel snapped his fingers.

His words didn't jar her back to the present, but the sharp sound following did. Mystery started and blinked at him. Crap, how long had she been drifting into the past?

"Sorry. I . . ." What did she say now? She didn't really have an excuse other than a trip down memory lane in which he'd been the star. Not that she could tell him that. He'd turned her down flat once. Despite their promising exchange at the bar, Mystery feared he'd do it again.

"You having second thoughts?"

"No." *Hell no.* "Last I recall, I asked you if we could hit your bedroom and you could lose some clothes."

"We were kissing. You in some hurry?"

He couldn't begin to imagine how done she was waiting for him. Just being in the same room with him excited her beyond belief—unlike the last time they'd shared space.

After he'd rejected her in the old hotel's bar, Mystery had felt two inches tall. She didn't think he'd intended to hurt her feelings as much as he'd wanted to put distance between them. In retrospect, she would have turned herself down, too. She'd been a stupid kid playing adult games. And she hadn't been in the right mind-set for sex. He'd known that. But his rebuff had dented her pride and wounded her heart. She'd stomped up the stairs to bed, expecting to spend a few hours alone to cry out her confusion and heartache. Instead, he'd followed right behind her and plopped himself onto the chair in the corner, then spread his big-ass gun across his lap.

She'd been so pissed off that he'd denied her the privacy of a good cry.

A couple of hours later, he'd awakened her fully dressed. He'd handed her the bra and panties he'd washed for her and instructed her to get her clothes on. Ten minutes later, they'd been walking through the desert, lit only by the moonlight, neither saying a word.

As dawn broke, they'd walked into Keeler and were spotted by an elderly man, who kindly let them borrow his phone. Fifteen minutes later, the Inyo County Sheriff's Department showed up, sirens blaring, and took her back to her father. She hadn't seen Axel much during questioning, just long enough for him to ask her to keep his name out of the press and to wish her well.

A media circus ensued afterward. Her picture had been plastered everywhere. She'd hidden in her house for weeks, waiting for the frenzy to die down. Her father had hired her a publicist and an agent . . . then drowned himself in a new starlet. She'd been approached to write her story for millions of dollars by publishers and TV producers. Mystery had refused them. She didn't want to recount for the world how stupid she'd been.

And she'd never heard from Axel again.

The other dark cloud hanging over her memory? Her abduction had never been solved. Her captor had been identified as a thug for hire with a record a mile long, but they'd never managed to figure out who had paid him to kidnap her or why. Her father had freaked out, convinced that his celebrity had been to blame, that someone wanting to extort money or kick-start their fifteen minutes of fame had taken her. In the absence of a better theory, it made sense. He'd insisted they move elsewhere, and had been prepping to shoot a film in London. Mystery had tagged along, and they'd never left.

In the ensuing six and a half years, she'd put the incident behind her, stopped having nightmares, and managed to move forward again. She'd finished university, three cozy mysteries with a hip flair, the most recent of which would be published in June. She'd learned self-defense, taken up yoga, and begun to live with purpose. She'd succeeded at everything she attempted—except having a full love life.

She'd never, ever been able to forget Axel or stop wondering what if things had been different . . .

"I might be in a bit of a hurry," she admitted, glancing at Axel from beneath her lashes. "But I suspect you'll be worth the wait."

He grinned, flashing his dimples. "You're an interesting little flirt."

Interesting? Mystery wasn't sure if that was a rebuke or a compliment. "Surely you didn't bring me here simply to figure me out."

"Maybe I did. You intrigue me." He cocked his head. "And you look somewhat familiar."

Fear struck to the bottom of her heart, but she plastered on her best poker face and tried to laugh it off. "You don't have to feed me a pick-up line. I'm already here."

Before he could respond, she wriggled off the counter and landed on her feet, brushing up against him. She knew Axel preferred to be in charge, but damn it, she couldn't give him too much time to think. And she didn't want to wait anymore.

Mystery reached for the hem of her tank top, then pulled it over her head in one fluid move. As she flung the cotton onto the counter behind her, she heard him suck in a sharp breath and found him staring at her plump mounds spilling from her underwire lingerie.

Yeah, if you like this lacy black bra, wait until you see the matching thong.

"You look . . . edible."

If that was true, why wouldn't he take a bite out of her? She cupped her breasts in offering and leaned closer. Instead of grabbing her by the hand and hauling her to his bedroom to promptly strip her down and plunge inside her, he grabbed her shoulders and drilled his stare into her.

"I'm going to take you so hard, baby. But in my time and in my way. Come with me. Leave your shirt there."

When he clasped her hand and hauled her out of the kitchen, she wondered where they were headed. It didn't take long before she realized he really did want to cuddle on the couch. He sat on a sleek gray sectional and pulled her into his lap. On the bright side, she felt his very insistent erection against her hip. The huge drawback? He wanted to talk. The longer they chatted, the more time he had to figure out who she truly was.

"Call me old-fashioned, but I like to know a little something about a woman before we share skin."

"Not much to say. I'm boring unless I'm horizontal."

He tossed his head back and laughed. "Somehow, I doubt that. And the more you push me, the more I'm going to drag this out. So give over and tell me all about you."

Mystery believed him. He hadn't hopped into bed with her simply because he could years ago. Apparently, nothing had changed. "I'm twentysomething and single, educated, and tired of European men. I'm here on vacation and fascinated by you."

"Why? You don't know me."

More than one flippant answer streamed through her head, but she'd been mostly stupid and impatient today. If she wanted him, she had to put a hold on her hormones and her heart. She had to use her damn head.

"You look . . . comfortable in your skin. You seem the sort of man who lives life robustly. You can relax, as you were when I saw you at the bar, drinking your ale. But you quickly caught on to my intent, and I like people with brains and wit. I can't deny that I found you quite sexy. Does attraction require more explanation than that?"

He raised a brow at her as his hand slid down her waist, over her hip, caressed her thigh. Mystery didn't feel just a shiver roll over her skin; his touch shook her whole body.

"I suppose not," he admitted. "But you've given it more than a little thought."

If he only knew . . .

"Why did you say yes?"

She probably shouldn't ask because he'd start dissecting his reasons and replay their meet in his head. Who knew where that would take his thoughts? But she was too desperate for the answer to keep her mouth shut.

"I like a straightforward girl who can tell me what she wants but doesn't always expect to get it. You intrigued me since you obviously didn't belong in that bar and felt more than a bit of trepidation going in. But you put your big girl panties on and did it, anyway. I'm still not sure why, and your attempt to order wine made me smile. I haven't been amused in a long time."

She let out a slow breath. Intriguing and amusing she could handle. Him guessing her identity would make this whole evening go south. Mystery felt somewhat guilty for tricking him. He didn't want her then, and if he knew who she was, she doubted he'd want her now. But she honestly didn't know how else to move on with her life. She no longer had any taste for vain actors, party-hardy musicians, or "regular" but starstruck men. Mystery seemed completely stuck on Axel.

"I'd like the chance to amuse you more." She leaned forward and layered her lips over his.

He let her, cupping her nape to bring her closer. He sank past her lips with a groan, his tongue seeking hers for a sensual slide as his palm found its way up her abdomen, then paused just below her breast. Soon—finally—Axel Dillon would actually be more intimate with her than a kiss. Mystery wanted to arch into his hand until he palmed her breast, but she knew he wouldn't give her what she wanted simply because she wanted it. So she waited, hoping, unable to catch her breath. Even the thought of his touch made her light-headed.

Instead, he leaned back and stared into her face, as if trying to figure her out. No, as if trying to figure out who she was.

Time to distract him—fast.

She repositioned herself on his lap until she straddled him and pressed her sex against the ridge of his hard cock. Gyrating over his erection, she arched her back and thrust her breasts closer to his mouth. He braced his big hands around her waist and ground her onto his thick staff with a groan. As a thrill reverberated through her body, she reached behind her back and unclasped her bra. Her breasts bounced free, and she brushed one of her nipples across his lips.

"You're pushing me," he warned.

"I want you to see what I'm dying to give you."

Axel took her face in his big hands. "You want to show me?"

She nodded too quickly, aware that she was making the same mistake she had more than once—throwing herself at him. But damn it, this man made her lose all self-control. "Please tell me you want to see me."

"Oh, yeah. But we're going to do this my way. Stand."

Mystery wasn't at all surprised when he took control. She'd expected it, hoped for it. Since he'd divulged the fact that he was Dominant, she'd done some reading and talking to people in the lifestyle. She probably only knew enough to be dangerous, but what she'd learned had prepared her to roll with his commands.

On shaking legs, she backed off his lap and rose to her feet in front of him, wearing her jeans and sandals and not much else.

"You listen well and you take direction nicely. Have you strolled down this path before?"

She knew he asked if she'd ever dabbled in BDSM. After the lies she'd already told him, she wanted to stick with as much of the truth as possible. "Not personally. I know something about it, though."

He sat up straighter with a long, slow smile. "Looks like my afternoon just got more interesting. You wearing panties?"

She nodded, then remembered he liked verbal responses. "Yes, Axel."

Mystery nearly bit her tongue after that. Crap, she didn't need to jog his memory about their days together in Death Valley. On the other hand, how many women since then had given him their assent to do his worst using just those words? She tried not to answer herself.

He cocked his head again. "Compliant. But I still see your head working. Interesting . . . Strip off everything but the panties."

She probably should have thought of it sooner, but he didn't have a single drape covering the windows, and the blinds had been opened all the way to their casings, leaving the glass bare. Houses surrounded him. Could any of his neighbors see inside his place?

"You're hesitating," he observed. "Tell me the problem."

"I'm eager to show you what you asked to see." She cast her gaze along the back wall of windows again. "I don't really want to show anyone else."

"While you're with me, it's my job to keep you safe and protected. I realize you don't know me, and I'm asking for a lot of trust, so I'm going to be lenient. My neighbors on the left don't have any windows facing this direction. My neighbors on the right are in Cabo all week. I've intentionally grown the trees in my backyard tall enough to block the sight line between the second story windows of the house behind me and my own. Any other questions?"

In short, no one would be able to sneak a cheap peek—or snapshot—of her. Mystery dragged in a steadying breath and thought the situation through once more. "I don't think so."

"Good. Now take off everything but your panties."

Mystery didn't make a striptease out of his command. After all, she wanted to make love with him, not give him a lap dance.

After she kicked off her shoes, she found unbuttoning her pants, lowering the zipper, and peeling the denim down her hips a little unnerving. He watched her with that intent, almost unblinking stare, as if nothing in the world could break his concentration. After she'd overheard a woman in a pub just last week complain that a guy she'd picked up had actually been texting his boss while pumping inside her, Mystery found Axel's single-mindedness so sexy.

The jeans fell past her knees, and she stepped out of them. She trembled all over, and he could have no illusions that she was cold, not with these warm temperatures. She felt almost naked, and his stare raked every inch of her. Had he noticed that her panties were sheer? That she'd waxed bare?

He scooted to the edge of the sofa and leaned forward, his face less than a foot from her pussy. "Come closer."

Her knees nearly knocked together as she inched toward him. He kept gesturing her in his direction, and she shuffled nearer until he curled a hand around her thigh to stay her.

Axel didn't speak right away. He hadn't done anything more than kiss and look at her, so his thumb sliding across the thin, transparent fabric over the pad of her pussy made her gasp.

"Wet," he remarked. "I like that."

He lifted his thumb, and since he'd pressed the panties to her flesh, Mystery couldn't miss the way the soaking cloth clung. "I am."

"My doing?"

"Totally."

His smile widened. "I like that even more."

And when he raised his thumb to his mouth and licked it, she felt absolutely faint. *Oh, holy crap . . .*

"Sweet. I'll enjoy spreading you wide and getting my mouth on your cunt. Will you trust me enough to spread your pretty legs and tie them down so you're nice and helpless?"

His words ripped an almost visceral arousal through her. For a shocking moment, she couldn't speak. She wanted this man so much. In the past, sex had been mostly about curiosity or combating boredom or because she hoped she'd find someone who flipped her switch more than Axel.

Now she knew better.

"I-Is that what you want?"

He gripped her hips and tugged her closer, then lapped his tongue directly against the filmy mesh shielding her pussy.

"To start. Will you be a good girl and let me?"

* * *

"YES." She couldn't seem to say the word fast enough.

Axel didn't bother to hold in his satisfied smile. He had more than a few reasons to be suspicious of not-Elise. She'd singled him out in a bar that obviously wasn't her type of joint with seduction on her mind. He didn't worry for his safety, his "fortune," or any blackmail opportunities. The vibe she gave off was more eager than nefarious.

Originally, he'd taken her up on her offer because she was a beautiful woman with all the right curves who looked in desperate need of corrupting. And she'd be an interesting riddle to solve. Axel knew himself too well. If he'd let her go without exploring who she was and what she wanted, it would bug him to no end.

Time to see what the hell she was up to. Then he'd find out what she knew about submission and exactly how much of herself she was willing to give him.

"Turn around." He motioned with his fingers.

She complied right away, stopping after a one-eighty turn and presenting him a view of her backside, covered only by the tiniest triangle of fabric at the small of her back. If her ass wasn't the most luscious he'd ever seen in his entire fucking life, it was in the top two. High, firm, round . . . Lust dropped another dose of desire into his already saturated system. The dainty bow perched on each hip only accentuated her tiny waist above the womanly flare of her hips. He already knew her natural breasts would be damn close to a perfect handful—a shock since he was a man with big hands.

The woman flipped a nervous stare over her shoulder. "Axel?"

"You're beautiful," he assured her. He wanted her off-base enough to spill the truth about her name and why she'd sought him, but he didn't want her self-conscious. "Back that pretty ass up and bring it to me."

Once he touched and kissed it . . . Hell, once he paddled and fucked it, he'd be a happy man.

She shuffled back to him, and he wanted to drown in that un-tapped sexuality she dripped. Her body looked ripe for satisfaction but everything about her told him she hadn't really ever found it. For some reason, he loved the thought of being the man to give her all she craved.

But he also couldn't shut off the analytical side of his brain. Why did she look familiar? She was in her mid-twenties, give or take a couple of years. Her British accent was almost flawless, but every once in a while, she'd slip up with an *ah* sound in place of an *o* vowel—a distinctly American quality. Her skin was unlike a fair English rose's. The olive of her complexion suited the pretty oval of her face and the smooth satin covering her body, all the way down to that perfect ass. She wore too much makeup, and he'd like it gone so he could really see *her*. And he'd bet her hair wasn't any shade of red, but something darker, glossier. Brunettes turned him on, always had.

Most every guy he knew would ask him why the fuck he bothered questioning a beauty so willing to go to bed with him. Axel didn't like unanswered questions. His gut told him to keep digging.

Finally, the woman reached him, and he dragged his knuckles

across the firm globes of her backside. Arousal gripped his chest, tightened his groin. He cupped her butt in his hands, thumbs brushing from the insides of her thighs and up her soft crease.

Maybe he should fuck her now and ask questions later.

She jumped, seemingly rattled by his soft caress.

"Easy . . ." he murmured, then leaned in and placed his lips on her right cheek, nipping it lightly with his teeth.

Her little gasp went straight to his dick. He did it again. This time, he watched her squirm, shifting her weight from one foot to the other, as if trying to create a little friction in her pussy to ease the ache.

Axel gripped her hips. "Don't be a bad girl. Stand still. Spread your legs."

She gave him a whimper that told him she clearly understood giving in meant the end of any possible relief, but she still did it.

With his hands on her hips, well . . . that touchable ass just begged for his fingers and palms. How could he turn that down?

Axel plucked at the bow over her left hip. The barely there wisp of black cloth fell, revealing one hip completely, along with more of her succulent butt. As he caressed the skin he'd just exposed with one hand, he tugged on the bow over her other hip. Instantly, her thong fell into a heap between her feet. His first view of her bare ass made him suck in an oh-holy-fuck breath.

Rounder than he'd originally thought, her cheeks protruded, juicy and ripe and ready for his plucking. No doubt about it, he intended to bend her over the nearest piece of furniture and have his wicked way with her before the night ended.

He adjusted his stiff cock in his jeans. His hormones seemed to be having a temper tantrum that he wasn't balls deep inside her yet. He'd fix that right quick—as soon as they got a few other things out of the way.

"Face me," he demanded.

She turned and looked down at him. Her blue eyes seemed

almost too brilliant . . . not quite real. Another glance at her face told him that red definitely wasn't her natural color. When the color of the drapes had been altered, he could usually tell what nature had given her by checking the carpet. Axel stared at her bare pussy for the first time. Plump, a deep flushed rosy that pouted for his attention, like the side of a ripe peach. He could see every pore and every goose bump because she'd removed all hint of the carpet here. And she hadn't simply shaved. No stubble to impede the flow of his tongue or reveal the coloring nature had given her. But Axel didn't worry. The night was young. He'd figure her out.

He dragged a finger from her navel down to her cleft. Her entire body jolted. She shuddered. Moisture coated his finger. Her clit was already hard.

Why would a woman as gorgeous as this one be so hungry for sex? Certainly, she could get any heterosexual man to fuck her just by crooking her finger. For that matter, he'd found over the years that women tended to be more responsive with men they knew, trusted, cared for. Was that why she hadn't found anyone to satisfy her? But then, why choose him? She didn't know the first fucking thing about him beyond his name and address. Hell, he'd had more intimate verbal exchanges with his insurance agent, and yet not-Elise seemed incredibly eager to slide between his sheets. She just got more intriguing, and Axel wanted to solve her. But with every second, his hunger rose. He definitely had to fuck her and relieve some of this crazy tension she'd built inside him first.

He stood, steadying her against him with a firm grip on her hips. He looked down at her, and that pleading look in her eyes went straight to his cock. He could imagine her on her knees, at his mercy, begging him with that stare. Everything about her revved his libido, but that expression . . . *Shit.*

"Let's go," he demanded.

"To your bedroom?" She sounded breathless.

"Yeah."

He took her hand and led her out of the TV room, down the hall, stopping only when they'd reached the side of his sleigh bed. He hadn't made it this morning, and his beige sheets were tangled up with his chocolate comforter. Not-Elise didn't seem to give a shit about his décor or his lack of tidiness.

Instead, she inched in front of him and fingered the hem of his T-shirt, her fingertips brushing his abdomen. God, she really did have some of the most delectable breasts. He'd been so busy looking at her ass that he'd missed out on something special. Wow.

"Please," she asked softly, tugging up on his tee.

At once, he had two thoughts. First, she'd learned already that demanding would get her nowhere with him. And second, that if he didn't get naked with her soon, he'd fucking explode.

Axel grabbed the hem and yanked the black cotton from his chest, tossing it across the room. He took hold of her wrists and fastened them onto his pecs. He wanted her touch, needed to feel her skin, her desire.

The beauty curled her fingers into his flesh, urgent, seeking. Her mouth fell open. Her face filled with something like wonder, and Axel couldn't figure out for the life of him why something so basic should seem so new to her. No freaking way she could be a virgin.

He tucked a finger under her chin. "I need you to be honest with me. You'll do that, yes?"

She flinched, then tried to cover it with a faint smile. "I'll do my best."

Not a perfect reply, and certainly not the one he wanted, but she didn't understand the rules—yet.

"Good. That's all I ask. Tell me the last time you had sex."

She recoiled. "Why?"

"You look pretty damn nervous."

"It's been a few months," she admitted. "And it's always nerve-racking getting naked for a new lover."

Her answer made sense, but Axel still wanted to press her for details. She insisted she had sexual experience, but her jumpiness seemed like more than typical nerves. All these incongruities just kept mounting in his head . . .

He tried being brutally honest with her. "I seriously don't think I've ever met a woman who intrigued me as much as you. And you've got the most beautiful body I've ever touched."

She wrinkled her nose in disagreement.

"You do," he insisted. "And the most kissable mouth. Give it to me."

Without hesitation, she tilted her face up to him, her expression wide open in offering. Her desire to give to him was absolute, so pure it reached inside his chest and tugged.

He'd spent so long helping Sweet Pea, Club Dominion's submissive receptionist, scaling the walls of her defenses so he could tear them down. No matter how much she wanted to submit her all so she'd be ready for the day she met her One, he always hit her hard emotional limit well before her physical one. It frustrated him. It frustrated her. He often wondered if he couldn't reach her because they were friends—lovers on those rare occasions she needed to be held—but they weren't *in* love.

Never had Sweet Pea offered him the sort of complete, unvarnished sincerity this woman presented right now. She might be lying to him about her name and why she'd come to his favorite beer dive. But her expression gave him a glimpse inside the gates to her soul.

Why?

Her thumb flicked across his nipple as she explored every bulge and ridge of his torso. She caressed his shoulders, skated her fingertips down his ribs, bisected his abs with one nail, and flirted dangerously close with the screaming head of his cock, trying to make its way out of his jeans.

His every muscle went taut as she continued with her casual touches. The innocent way she attempted to learn his body, as if being with him was a wonder and the moment they shared felt reverent to her. He'd agreed to a one-night stand . . . but she wasn't treating it as a throwaway at all. On some level being with this woman whose name he didn't actually know felt important, which made no sense at all.

He grabbed her wrist before desire overwhelmed his better sense and he threw her onto the bed and fucked her senseless. They'd get there soon; he'd make sure of it.

Axel lifted her hand to his neck. As if she'd read his mind, she curled her slender fingers around him, caressed her way over his shoulder and eased closer, that lush mouth falling just under his. She parted her rosy lips, and her lids slid shut. At once, she managed to look both eager and beautiful. When she rose up on her tiptoes, his patience ended.

Gripping her shoulders, Axel swooped down and claimed her mouth. He took more than a brush of lips, wouldn't be satisfied with a simple caress. No, he lifted one hand to cup her jaw and apply just enough pressure to force her mouth open for him. He delved deep, fascinated by her taste—complex and addicting. Just being this near her made his head swim, his blood tingle. Some instinct kicked him in the gut, telling him this moment was significant and he'd better drink it in.

He could analyze that to death and probably would—later. Right now, the most fascinating, willing woman stood naked in his bedroom, melting against him. Jesus, she had the softest skin, too. Her proposition had been one hell of a turn-on, but the minute he'd touched her, she'd downshifted and put herself in his hands.

As he slanted his mouth the other way for deeper penetration, her flavor assailed him again. She groaned into their kiss as his tongue tangled with hers. At the sound, his knees went the way of his head—suddenly unstable, floating, not quite functioning.

He groped for the nearby bed, then toppled her onto it. He didn't bother lying beside her. Fuck that. He settled her against him, then rolled her directly under him, spreading her legs with a shove of his thighs. She didn't give him a single iota of fight.

The few seconds his lips had been away from hers seemed like a torturous decade, and he sent his mouth crashing onto hers again. She yielded in welcome, which both soothed and baited the hungry beast inside him. What was it about this woman that lit his body on fire? That had his libido doing a happy dance?

As if he could only find the answer inside her, Axel thrust his way into her mouth again and gripped her hips, arching the length of his weeping cock against her bare pussy, cursing the denim keeping them apart. Some distant part of his brain calculated how long it would take him to rip open his fly and find a condom. Before he could compute the answer, his beauty arched into him, pressing her hard nipples to his chest, rubbing her sex against his own as if desperate for relief. And the freaking little whimpers she made in her throat short-circuited his brain. His restraint died a quick death.

"If you don't want me inside you in the next sixty seconds, say so now."

She panted, her eyes wide and clinging. "Can you make it less than thirty?"

Oh, fuck. "I'll go for ten."

He stumbled to his feet, shoving his jeans and underwear off, then kicking them aside. In his nightstand, he fumbled for a condom and wondered why the hell he was as excited as a teenager with his first girlfriend. The urgency ripped fire through him like an aphrodisiac, sizzling his skin.

Axel had no doubt this woman was about to rock his world—and he wasn't even sure why.

He tore open the foil and rolled the condom down his length. His gorgeous supplicant wasn't helping when she sat up and ran her fingers down his abdomen, his thighs, then his buttocks as she leaned in, kissing and nipping at his hips, his thighs. When she laved his balls with a low little moan, he fucking lost his mind.

Axel pushed her to her back and spread her legs. "You want to play dirty?"

"I want you inside me."

His urge to dominate warred with his need to be buried balls deep. He gritted his teeth, then pushed her farther across the bed and fell to the mattress between her spread legs, his mouth hovering just over her cunt.

Her breath caught. "What happened to ten seconds? Those are up."

"I can't let the opportunity to tease this pretty pussy pass me by." He dragged his fingers across the smooth skin. Like a baby's butt. Not a bump or a hair to flaw the perfectly silken pad.

At his touch, her entire body tensed. When she tried to lift her hips to him, he held her down.

"You can't throw it at me. I'll take it when I'm ready." He gave her an evil smile. "When I know you're beyond ready . . ."

She tossed her head back, melting into his mattress. "Please, Axel. Don't make me wait. It already feels as if I've waited forever."

Perversely, that only made him want to torture her more. "Poor baby. Patience a problem for you?"

She cupped her breasts, pinching her nipples. "I ache. Everywhere."

Her high, thready voice slammed his libido. But the visual of her fondling her own flesh in a desperate search for relief rocketed his desire to soaring, new heights. Holy hell, if he'd ever wanted a woman so badly he was damn near ready to climb out of his skin and crawl over jagged glass to have her, he didn't remember it.

Still, she didn't get to control the tempo and timing of their sex. She especially didn't get to control him. He grabbed her hands and forced them to her sides, holding each beside her corresponding hip.

She protested with a wail and spread her legs wider. "Please. Don't make me wait. I've never felt this way. I don't know how to ..."

"Yeah," he grunted. "Join the party."

Surprise widened her eyes. She hadn't thought he'd want her the same way in return? Had some douchebag belittled her in the past? Refused her harshly? That dude's loss was his precious gain.

Then her scent wafted up to him and brain function shut down. He had to have her flavor on his tongue now or he'd go in-fucking-sane.

Pinning her wrists beside her, he bent and raked his tongue through her slit, through her swollen folds, all the way from the soft, juicy opening he couldn't wait to sink his cock into, up to the candy clit so sweetly hard for him, it jolted another spark of need through his system.

Under him, she twisted. He repeated the motion, this time more slowly, lingering on the needy bud of her nerves and toying with it, using the tip of his tongue, the edge of his teeth, the suction of his mouth. She cried out, thrashing, but he kept her immobile under his bigger body, holding her still for his pleasure.

"Axel ..."

Something about the way she said his name in that pleading, high-pitched keen had his blood boiling. It wasn't about power or a need to control. With most any woman, he could hold a part of himself away and almost clinically determine a tactical plan to dismantle her defenses and take her body apart before systematically implementing his strategy and enjoying the victory of conquering her with orgasms. This woman dragged him into a need that sucked him under like quicksand. The more he fought for control, the less he had. Yes, he wanted her pleasure. Hell, he wanted her screaming as she dug her nails in his back and shattered for him. But planning a sensual conquering was the farthest thing from his mind. Right now, he couldn't manage much more than lapping at her pussy like a starving man at an ambrosia buffet.

The soft, sweet perfection of her filled his mouth. Everything about her—every texture, flavor, sensation—addicted him. He'd been interested in the bar, intrigued as they made their way to his house and kissed in the kitchen, but now he'd fucking die if he didn't have her frantic and clawing and taking every inch of him.

Under his hungry mouth, her flesh swelled even more. She tensed. Her fists flailed, grabbed at the sheets. A series of gasps, each higher-pitched than the last, juiced his need and melted his resolve.

He shoved a finger inside her, groaning as her tight flesh parted for his invasion like slick silk, then sucked at him in a silent plea. Jesus, she was going to dismantle him with this pussy, and he couldn't wait.

"You're close," he managed to growl out.

"Yes. Oh . . ." She writhed, then opened her eyes to spear him with a needy, almost panicked look. When he curled his finger against the one spot designed to send her soaring, she cried out and thrashed again. "*So* close. It's right there. Please."

Axel wanted to be inside her when he gave her this first orgasm. And he damn well knew it wouldn't be the last.

With one last lave of her twitching clit, he climbed up her body, anchoring his hips between her thighs. Elbows on either side of her head, he took her mouth and probed her pussy with his searching cock. She spread even wider for him, lifted up, helpful and welcoming, silently begging. Dizziness swarmed his head. Jesus, she was headier than the best buzz.

His heart pounded, his blood surged as Axel pushed at her opening, insistently trying to bury himself in the juicy heat. But her cunt felt tighter than a vise. He'd barely managed to wedge more than the head inside her when the grip of her flesh impeded him from submerging deeper.

"Open up to me. I'll make you feel so good once you let me."

"I know." She pushed up at him, and he sank in another inch.

It wasn't enough. In that moment, he wondered if he'd ever get enough of her.

The thought had barely finished blindsiding him before she exhaled and forced her body to relax. He sank in a bit more, then retracted, coating his stiff length with more of her delicious essence before he pushed in again—and again.

Slowly, her body yielded to him. Her thoughts and her desire had given way to him long ago. Now he merely fought the head-spinning clutch of her cunt grabbing at his stiff length. She made him work for every inch she ceded. She milked his flesh, squirming all over his cock, before her body seized up again. The incredible struggle only dragged him closer to the edge of his own pleasure, and he could see the giant chasm of ecstasy right before him.

Damn it, he had to fuck her first. Good and hard, in some way leaving his mark on her so she could never forget that he'd been here and taken her thoroughly. He liked the hell out of that idea.

As Axel surged forward again, determined to plant every aching inch of his cock inside her, she surrendered a bit more. Everything about her made him need to conquer her, to say he'd filled, claimed, taken. Made her give him absolutely every bit of herself to him.

She arched, keened again. She'd be a screamer, he'd bet, and he couldn't wait to hear her cries in his ear as she burst into ecstasy around his cock.

"Just a little more. Almost there . . . Breathe with me." He dragged a lungful of air, then released it audibly, gratified when she joined him. "Spread just a little wider and—" He couldn't swallow back his groan when she finally opened enough to take the last inch of his erection deep in her hungry cunt. "Oh, fuck yeah."

She panted and opened her eyes, staring up at him with a wonder that damn near stopped his heart. She wasn't a virgin. Despite her tightness, he could attest to that fact. But her expression told him that, in some way, she was experiencing pleasure for the very first time.

That yanked him off the chain so fucking fast, Axel didn't even have time to tell himself to slow down before he grabbed her nape, holding her gaze captive, and began pounding into her relentlessly.

She lit him up like a live wire, as if, through her, he'd begun superconducting enough electricity to light up the Dallas skyline. Energy sizzled over his skin and shuddered down his spine before settling into every stiff inch he'd buried inside her. And with each thrust, her eyes widened, finally taking on a stunned, dazed quality. But she never looked away from him.

Damn it, he'd love to see her without the wig, the contacts, the makeup. Axel had a feeling he was fucking the most beautiful woman of his life, and he really had no idea what she truly looked like.

Before round two—which they'd definitely get to—he'd whittle away all the artificial crap and see the real her.

For now, he settled into the most heavenly pussy in his memory, feeling the gentle bounce of her breasts as he drilled her without pause. He'd ask her if it was too much, too hard, too fast, but given her unbridled response, everything he did with her felt more than all right. Under him, she rocked with every stroke. A rosy flush stole up her cheeks. Gasps and groans sounded from those sweet lips, slowly turning more guttural. And she gripped his cock like she wouldn't last more than a few moments without falling into orgasm.

Axel couldn't stop himself from seizing her mouth and devouring her. Fuck, he was inside of her in every way, and somehow it still wasn't enough. He had to hear her, see her, feel her climax for him.

"You're going to come." He didn't bother asking because he knew. Primal pleasure filled him at the thought that he could drive this beauty to that pleasure so quickly and completely.

"Yes!" She struggled against his hold on her wrists. "Let me touch you."

Normally, he'd prefer to stay in control. He dictated when and where he allowed a partner to put a hand on him at all. This one? He wanted everything she would give him—desire, affection, screaming orgasm.

Axel released her wrists. His beauty flung her arms around him and gripped his hips with her legs, clasping him close—not like a woman merely chasing ecstasy. No, she drank in the experience and clutched him, almost as if he *was* the experience. He'd often been valued for his control, his Domination, even his prowess. He wasn't sure he'd actually had a lover who wanted more than what he could do for her when she fell under his command and into his bed. Something about the way she welcomed him into her body said she also wanted the man under the Dom.

He pinned her with a delving stare. In a distant part of his brain, he wished to fuck he could figure her out. At this moment, most of his concentration centered around holding back long enough to make her come first. The tight grip of her sex threatened to blow the top off his head, and he couldn't wait to feel her explode around him and shoot him into the stratosphere.

"Axel!" She dug her nails into his shoulder. Her mouth fell open. Her eyes slid shut.

No fucking way. "Look at me."

Her lashes fluttered, drifting open again, revealing her artificial blue eyes. But colored contacts couldn't mask the way she melted under his body, dissolved for his touch. He shuttled in and out of her pussy at a breakneck pace, seating himself deeper with every stroke. She was right on the edge, so close, he could almost see her toppling into the abyss.

Axel intended to help her along ASAP.

He slid his hands under her world-class ass and lifted her up. Now he applied friction to her clit with his body, back and forth in a burn of skin that coiled her even tighter and ratcheted up the tension between them. It brewed, built, escalating, climbing faster and harder and higher.

Until she clamped down on him so tightly he couldn't move even a fraction. And she screamed.

Her cry rang in his ear, in his head. Something about it—about her—absolutely flipped his switch. Knowing he'd given her the sort of pleasure that made her rake his back with her nails and cling to him as if he were the only man on the planet did everything for him. It shot him off into the kind of mind-jarring, soul-shifting ecstasy he'd heard guys like Mitchell Thorpe and Logan Edgington talk about sharing with their women but had always quietly suspected was bullshit.

The need gathered low in his belly. Blood rushed. Tingling began at the base of his cock and began working its way upward. He couldn't breathe, couldn't think or control his movements or care about a damn thing except this woman in his arms whose name he didn't really know. But she gave to him so completely and honestly that, as the prickling pleasure shot up his dick, he groaned out, sank his fingers into the firm flesh of her ass, pulled her as close to him as possible, then released everything he had to give inside her in a fireworks of unparalleled bliss.

He slowed his strokes, then stopped. She panted in his ear, still gripping him as if her life depended on it. Axel realized that he'd buried his nose in her neck somewhere along the way, so he nuzzled her, kissed her jaw, meandered with his lips over to her mouth and pressed his own to hers for a long, worshipful breath. His head spun. And even as his blood slowed, he still felt the impact of her through his system like a fucking seismic event.

What the hell had just happened?

Her eyes watered. A tear slipped from the corner and rolled down her temple.

"Hey . . ." He wiped the droplet away with his thumb. "What's wrong?"

She smiled, something tremulous and almost sad. "Nothing.

This was everything I wanted. I'm just emotional, I guess. No worries. I'm sure I'll get myself in order shortly."

Axel wasn't sure he actually wanted her to. He liked knowing he could reach her on a level beyond sex. He liked the way he felt something beyond desire and satisfaction with her, too.

He caressed her cheek with his knuckles and kissed her forehead softly. "No rush. At all. Just like you, this was everything I wanted." He gave her a sly grin. "I can only imagine how much more amazing the next time will be."

If she hadn't been under him, he might not have noticed her tense, yet she gave him a smile. "I can't wait." Then she winced and squirmed a little. "But right now, I can't breathe."

Axel had no illusions about his size, especially in relation to the fairer sex. For that reason, he rarely had sex on top of a woman, even though he loved the hell out of it. Despite the fact that his beauty was taller than average, she was still slight, and he still towered over her.

"Sure. Sorry." Reluctantly, he eased from the warm glove of her pussy and sat back on wobbling knees. His world tilted, his head still spun. His legs felt like jelly. Satisfaction seeped down into his bones.

She rolled away and darted to her feet, grabbing the sheet for covering. He frowned. *Now* she decided to be shy?

"Um . . ." She cleared her throat. "Do you mind if I grab some water from the kitchen? My throat is dry."

Maybe, but his bullshit meter was flaring like a motherfucker. She was up to something. He'd give her a little rope and see if she used it to hang herself . . . or bind herself to him. "Go ahead. Glasses are in the cabinet to the right of the fridge."

Raising up on tiptoe, she kissed him for a long, lingering moment, then sent him a smile. Her heart all but bled out of her eyes, and he wished to fuck he understood the sadness lurking there.

"Are you all right?" he asked, cupping her cheek.

She looked ready to cry. "Never better. Be right back."

Wrapping the sheet around her a bit like a toga, she hightailed it out of the bedroom and padded down the hall. Frowning, Axel shook his head and made his way to the bathroom. He disposed of the condom, splashed some water on his face, then returned to the bedroom to wriggle into his jeans.

As he made his way to the kitchen, he didn't hear a sound. Night had fallen, and she hadn't turned on a single light, so he flipped the switch on the wall. Her shirt was gone from the kitchen counter. He dashed over to the sectional, only to see the rest of her clothing was gone, too. She'd left the sheet pooled on the floor.

"Elise!" he called. No, it wasn't her name, but he didn't know what it was and he hoped to fuck she'd answer to it.

She didn't. Had she gone?

A panic he didn't understand began to pump through his veins as he ran to the front door, only to find it suddenly unlocked and barely pulled to. A stiff wind would have blown it open.

Axel pulled it wide and jogged down his porch, out onto the street just quickly enough to see a sleek black car he hadn't noticed before pull away from his curb.

Chapter Seven

MYSTERY shook as she slammed the door of the town car and huddled in the backseat. The car lurched forward, and she had to force herself not to look back at his house one last time.

She'd done it; she'd conquered Mount Axel. Well, that wasn't precisely true. He'd conquered her just by being his amazing, fabulous self. Again. In fact, she wondered if she'd ever be the same.

She let out a shuddering breath and struggled into her shoes. The simple action gave her purpose and focused her. Inside, she was a raving mess.

His taste still lingered on her tongue. His scent still filled her nostrils. She still felt him hard and massive and insistent between her legs. Every flash of memory—the way he'd tasted her, touched her, filled her—crowded her head. Before today, she'd only believed that she'd had sex. Certainly, she'd thought so before she had carelessly plotted to experience the man she'd been hung up on since the end of adolescence. She hadn't actually considered that he might overwhelm her, that once would never be enough to ease the craving she'd long had for him.

"Are you all right?" Heath, her longtime driver and bodyguard, asked from the front seat, sending her a concerned stare in the rear-view mirror.

No. "Fine. Can you take me back to the hotel?"

He knew her too well to believe her, and his frown deepened. "Of course. No other stops along the way?"

When she looked tousled and shaken, probably wore whisker burns on her cheeks? If the tabloids figured out she was in town and intercepted her on her way into the hotel, wouldn't they have a field day with those pictures?

"No. I'll order room service." Despite how well meaning Heath was and how much she usually liked his company, she wanted desperately to be alone.

"You father has called twice, inquiring after you. I told him you were visiting a . . . friend."

Mystery's eyes slid shut. She couldn't miss the hint of disapproval in Heath's tone. Obviously, he'd caught on to her fuck-and-run routine. Of course, it must be hard to miss now since she was doing the early evening equivalent of the walk of shame. Still, he didn't say a word, simply slipped a tiny hint of censure into his tone.

She felt it like a yawning abyss of guilt. "I'll call him as soon as I reach my room."

"Very good," he said in his crisp British voice. "Don't forget the six-hour time difference."

A glance at the clock in the car told her it was already after midnight in London. Damn it.

"Got it. Thanks."

They rode the rest of the way in silence back to the Hotel Crescent Court. The journey took less than fifteen minutes—not really enough time for her to get her head together. She avoided Heath's blue-eyed stare of concern in the rearview mirror.

Her father had sent him along to both bodyguard and babysit her, keep her out of trouble. Her driver would never cross the line and question her actions—but he'd sure as hell tell her father. Marshall Mullins had never stopped being panicked and overprotective after her abduction. He had to be completely fraying at the edges with her traveling to another continent.

Just one more worry . . . but certainly not her biggest.

She gnawed on her lip as the valet attendant from the hotel approached to collect the car. Had she been clandestine enough to keep her identity a secret from Axel? She didn't want to hurt or deceive him, and she felt more than vaguely ashamed that she'd flat-out lied to seduce him. She'd rationalized it by telling herself that she was saving them both the embarrassment of Axel refusing her again because of their past and her name.

In the hush of evening, that felt a lot like excuses.

Heath opened her door and helped her from the car as the valet attendant slid behind the wheel. Curling an arm protectively around her, Heath placed his body between hers and the street.

"Duck," he warned in her ear. "In case we encounter press."

Mystery tried to relax. After all, how could the press possibly have known she'd come here? Mystery hadn't told anyone other than her father, Heath, and her mother's sister, Aunt Gail, that she intended to visit the States.

"In this disguise, they won't recognize me." After all, Axel hadn't. The fact that she'd emerged from a town car and not a limo was a point in the favor of discretion. But having what amounted to a bodyguard curl himself around her would, no doubt, draw attention.

"Hold my hand, just in case." She put distance between them and shoved her palm against his, interlocking their fingers. "We'll be less conspicuous if we look like lovers."

Heath hesitated, then relaxed at her side. "I'm afraid that's wishful thinking."

Why? It wasn't unheard of for a woman in her mid-twenties to date an attractive man pushing forty. Thankfully, she didn't have to argue her point. He humored her, folding her hand against his own.

They walked from the car and approached the hotel's entrance without incident. Mystery clutched Heath and released a long breath as they neared the entrance.

As he opened the door to the hotel, a woman her age wearing blingy jeans and an NYU T-shirt sprang to her feet from a plush sofa in the lobby. "Mystery Mullins! Why have you returned to the States after all these years?"

She hadn't braced herself for press *inside* the hotel. Stupid and probably naïve. She really didn't deal with this much in the UK and had forgotten how aggressive some tabloid reporters could be.

"I—"

"No comment," Heath said beside her, motioning to one of the hotel's security agents as he hustled her toward the elevator.

He pressed the button to bring the car to the lobby. As they waited, the security guard rushed forward to intercept the young reporter.

The woman protested, shouting across the cavernous interior of the hotel. "Our readers want to know about your sudden visit to the States, Ms. Mullins. I just need five minutes—"

The security guard must have cut her off because Mystery didn't hear another word from the reporter. Instead, she clutched Heath's hand, feeling rattled, anxious, and vaguely contrite about everything that had happened today. Maybe she should have bypassed the Dallas portion of her trip and left Axel in peace, simply flown to her aunt's place and retrieved the effects her mother had left to her on her eighteenth birthday, as she'd been promising to do for years.

"Hurry up . . ." Heath growled at the elevator, willing it to reach the lobby and whisk her away.

Before it did, a young man she hadn't previously noticed jumped out from behind a tall potted palm with a camera and snapped her picture repeatedly, the flash popping in her eyes.

"Get the devil away." Heath stiff-armed the man.

"Why are you back in the U.S.?" the photographer demanded, looking over the top of Heath's head to clap eyes on her.

When he tucked the camera under his arm and held up his phone as if rolling video, she closed her eyes and looked away. "No comment."

Since the security guard was tied up with the reporter who'd approached her earlier, a female desk clerk bustled over and latched a firm grip around the photographer's elbow. "You're harassing our valued guests. I'm going to have to ask you to leave."

The photographer shook off the hotel employee and darted past Heath, rolling more video as he got in Mystery's face. "Are you here to figure out how and why your mother died? Was that the reason for your Tweet last night about looking forward to revisiting some of your mother's effects?"

"No comment," she choked.

God, she didn't need these sleazebags to remind her that the anniversary of her mother's death fast approached. She thought about it every spring and often sorted through pictures to remember the woman who'd given her life. She should stop Tweeting when she did that shit. She'd meant it more as a memorial than a "look at me." Of course, these assholes who made a living scamming off people in the public light could care less.

"Is this your secret lover? Is he married? Is that the reason for your disguise?" the photographer demanded. "Did he give you the love bites on your neck? What's your name?" he shouted at Heath before turning back to Mystery. "Would your father approve of you dating an older man?"

Another employee of the hotel, this one a slight male in an impeccable suit, approached the slouchy photographer and grabbed his arm. The desk clerk grabbed the other.

"We've called the police. If you don't want to be arrested, leave before they arrive. You have less than two minutes."

That finally got the photographer's attention. He looked at Mystery, then flipped off the video on his phone, and took off running with a curse.

Mystery released the breath she hadn't realized she'd been holding. Why in the hell didn't these people just leave her alone? She wasn't an actress or a singer. She'd done nothing to warrant their attention—except be the daughter of one of the most infamous men in Hollywood. She certainly didn't try to live her life in the public eye. She simply wrote books and worked to forget the past. Was a little peace too much to ask?

"Please allow me to express my deepest apologies," the man in the suit offered. "We respect the privacy of all our guests and value your—"

"Thank you." Heath interrupted as the elevator finally dinged its arrival. "Now keep these people away from Ms. Mullins. And bugger off."

They ran into the elevator, and the hotel's employee gaped after them as the yawning doors snapped shut, encasing her in silence with Heath. He still didn't release her hand, but his grip loosened, becoming a gesture of comfort. "Are you all right?"

"Any idea how they found out I'm here?"

"None." Heath shook his head grimly as they ascended to her suite. "I presume a hotel employee thought to make a quick dollar or a fellow guest recognized you when we checked in yesterday. I wish I knew."

Mystery wished she did, too.

As the elevator doors opened at the top, Heath urged her out, his arm curled around her protectively, scanning the hallways for other potential threats. Thankfully, the concierge floor was quiet, almost unnervingly so. But she supposed that observation had more to do with her jittery mood and the knowledge she'd soon be alone with her thoughts . . . and her regrets.

If Axel realized that she'd deceived and seduced him, would he ever forgive her? It probably didn't matter. It wasn't as if she would ever see or speak to him again. But damn it to hell, she valued his opinion. The last thing she wanted to do was upset him. Yeah, she probably should have thought more about that before she'd lied to worm her way into his bed.

As they reached the door, Mystery fished her card key from the pocket of her jeans. All she wanted now was a long, hot shower and a bite of food before she curled up in bed with a mind-numbing sitcom and drifted off.

"Ring me if you need anything. I'll just be down the hall," Heath advised softly.

"I know." She set gentle fingers on his arm. "Thank you."

"I'm sorry I couldn't do more to keep the press away. Vultures."

"Well, I'm low on the totem pole. Maybe a Kardashian will do something crazy tonight and no one will give a shit about me tomorrow."

He sent her a wry smile that wished her good luck with that. Yeah, she needed it.

Mystery sighed. "Night."

"Good night." He stepped away. "I'll wait to leave until you're safely in your room. Unless you'd like me to come in to ensure no one is here waiting to bother you and nothing has been disturbed?"

Heath would. He'd done it more than once during their six years together. But she'd already had a long day. An even longer night stretched out in front of her. She really just wanted to be alone and figure out how, now that she was intimately familiar with Axel's touch and already ached for more, she could possibly move on and find a future without him.

"I'll be fine. I'll text you in the morning when I'm up. What time is our flight to Kansas City?"

"About noon. We should leave here around nine thirty. Have a good sleep in and enjoy a leisurely breakfast. We'll take you out via the parking garage to ensure we don't have any more unwelcome pests chasing you as you depart. I'll work with their security."

"Thanks. I don't know what I'd do without you." She smiled as she opened the door to her room.

He caressed her shoulder. Then, as she slipped into her room, he headed down the hall. The door shut behind her.

Inside the room, Mystery raced for the desk against the left wall. Nothing lay on the walnut surface except a small task light, a pad of paper with the hotel's logo, a pen, and her charging phone. She reached for the device and texted her father that she'd returned to her room, and after a little encounter with the press, she was fine. He quickly replied that he was glad she was safe. He loved her, and they'd talk tomorrow.

Relieved to finally be alone, she wandered into the bathroom, shedding the dark auburn strands of her wig. The bob had brushed her jaw and chafed her nape for hours. She felt a ridiculous urge to scratch her scalp.

She tossed the wig on the counter and removed all the pins before fluffing her own long, dark hair back into its usual tousled waves. She removed the evil blue contacts sticking to her eyes and ditched them in a case with some saline. Hazel orbs blinked back at her in the mirror. The clothes came next, and she exchanged them for a robe to peruse the room service menu. Once she'd made her selections and called, she glanced at the clock. She'd have plenty of time to shower before the food came.

By the time she emerged from the steaming tile box all clean and her face freshly scrubbed, Mystery felt her tummy rumble. She tossed on her exotic garden tank nightie with its admittedly girly cheetah trim and shrugged into the robe she'd strewn across the bed earlier.

In the last thirty minutes, night had become a black chasm with only the Dallas skyline to her south to light up the world. At least the view was pretty. She flicked the switch on a table lamp to its dimmest setting, softly illuminating the elegant space, and meandered over to the desk to retrieve her phone. A quick text to let Heath know she was all right might be in order. He worried, bless him.

But when she sashayed that way, she found a photograph on the gleaming surface. It hadn't been there before her shower.

The image was of her blindfolded, hands bound, and wearing the little sparkly dress she'd been kidnapped in more than six years ago. It had been taken in the shack that had been her prison.

Mystery stared at the picture in horror. Her blood ran cold. Who the hell would have left this in her room? How had they sneaked in during her shower? The only person who could possibly possess this image was the captor who'd paid for her abduction.

With trembling fingers, Mystery lifted the photo, blinking, staring. Holy hell . . . She needed to do something. Say something. Call the police.

Almost automatically, she flipped the picture over, looking for hints or clues. Her blood froze. In big black letters on the back of the image sat five chilling words.

RETURN TO ENGLAND OR DIE.

* * *

AXEL cursed himself up and down as he slammed through the house, combing it from head to toe, inside and out. Nearly thirty minutes later, he was still scratching his head. How the hell could she have gotten dressed and out of the house in the time it took him to peel off a condom, wash up, and throw on his jeans?

But that's exactly what had happened. He'd looked high and low—kitchen, TV room, bedroom. Nothing. His mysterious lover had fled, taking every shred of her existence with her.

"Fuck."

No, he hadn't expected to spend a lifetime with her, but he'd also thought he'd at least get to learn her real name, peer into the true color of her eyes, run his fingers through her natural hair, and find out why the hell she'd completely rocked his world. Before he let her do it again.

Besides the great sex—pretty much the best he'd ever had—something about her kept tugging at his memory. She'd looked familiar, and he couldn't figure out why. He didn't like unsolved problems and surprises. Too often they ended badly.

With a sigh, Axel slammed the door to his bedroom and headed back to the kitchen. At his side, his cell rang with a special tone he'd know anywhere.

He tensed. "Hello, Misty."

On the other end, she hesitated. He usually only called her by her given name when she'd disappointed him. In every other situation, he—and everyone else at Club Dominion—called her Sweet Pea.

"Have I displeased you, Axel?" Her naturally high-pitched voice sounded even more Betty Boop than normal.

No doubt, his irritable attitude had put her on guard. He already had enough problems trying to keep her from hiding behind her walls. She didn't need his attitude to shove her behind them even more.

"No, little one. I'm just in a craptastic mood. It has nothing to do with you," he assured her. "I'm sorry."

Dom 101: Hold a tight leash on your emotions. Control yourself and your sub. Keep your shit together.

He'd barely spoken to Sweet Pea and he was already doing a shitty job.

"It's entirely my fault. I'll behave. Well, as much as I'm capable." He forced himself to joke with her. "Do you need something?"

"I just wondered if you'd seen her since she's in town."

"Who?" Axel mentally sorted through the possibilities. Callie had returned from her honeymoon with Sean and Thorpe recently. Gia Denning was still away with her husband, Jason, probably beaching somewhere exotic. None of the female club members he could think of had recently been away. Who the hell else would Sweet Pea be talking about? "Since I haven't seen any of my female friends today, I'll go with no."

Sweet Pea sighed with a hint of annoyance. The woman had a huge heart, even if she was a bit naïve. And she usually had almost unlimited patience . . . unless orgasm depravation was involved. Other than that, he could think of very few subjects that pushed her beyond her usual placid smile. "Okay, what pop culture reference am I missing?"

"It's all over TMZ. Mystery Mullins arrived in Dallas last night."

Axel dismissed the gossip at first. She'd been a beautiful girl when he'd rescued her, and he was glad that he'd been able to prevent someone from snuffing out her bright light. They hadn't spoken more than a few words after their awkward night in Cerro Gordo. So it wasn't as if he expected her to look him up for a meal or a drink just because she'd jetted to the city.

A drink. Hold up there . . . Mentally, he tripped over the thought again. Then his world tilted.

A beauty with fake hair, hiding her real eye color, and masking her face behind a shit ton of cosmetics had picked him up in a bar, seeming as if she couldn't wait to be with him. Why would someone go out of their way to proposition him, yet hide everything about herself?

Suddenly, Axel thought he had the answer.

"Did TMZ post any pictures of her?" he barked.

"Yeah, and video, too."

Axel raced back to his bedroom and shoved the door open. Fuck, the place still smelled like the sex he'd had with her, and that made him hard all over again. He hadn't been done with the woman. Once more wouldn't have been enough. Probably not even a hundred times more. He'd been dying to restrain her, spank her, explore every inch of her skin, clamp her nipples, and hear her scream for him again.

If she'd been Mystery Mullins, then his desire for more didn't surprise him at all.

He grabbed his tablet off his nightstand and quickly surfed to TMZ. Tapping his toe while the site took its sweet time loading, he let out a mental string of curses that would have made a sailor blush.

"She looks great. I'd love to have her boobs. And her hips," Sweet Pea lamented. "She looks like a woman, not a girl still waiting for puberty."

"You're small but mighty. Don't demean yourself, Misty. We've had this conversation."

"And you've given me the spanking to go with it. I know . . ." She sighed. "But when you see her, you'll know what I mean. I almost didn't recognize her, but she looks stunning."

About that time, the website popped up. Front and center, he caught a still photo of Mystery wearing the same wig and clothes she had when he'd first seen her at the bar. In this picture, she held the hand of an older man who hovered protectively. The caption snagged Axel's attention. It sent his temper—and his desire to get his hands on her again—soaring.

MULLINS IN DALLAS FOR MYSTERY LOVER?

He scanned the accompanying "story." Blah, blah, blah . . . Staying at the Hotel Crescent Court.

Bingo!

Had she really run from his bed as if her ass was on fire so she could crawl into this man's? The thought chilled him to the core. No way. No fucking way. Axel didn't question why he felt possessive. He hadn't thought of Mystery except fleetingly in years. Okay, that wasn't entirely true. Days might be more accurate. She was never too far from his thoughts, but he hadn't succumbed to the urge to look her up and reminisce about old times, even if he'd wondered more than once what would have happened if he'd taken her up on her unspoken offer in the desert. Right now, he'd love to remind her exactly who had given her the pleasure that had urged her to leave half-moon marks from her nails deep in his back as he fucked her again.

"Is that her boyfriend?" he growled at Sweet Pea.

"I don't think so. Let me . . ." His friend and submissive tapped away on the keyboard he heard in the background. "Nothing on Google about a boyfriend since she briefly dated one of those British boy-band dudes, but that was a good year ago, according to what I can find."

If she'd finally returned to the U.S. to see this other man she posed with in the photos tonight, why would she have picked him up in a bar earlier today? Curiosity? Had she hoped to scratch the itch lurking under her skin since that night in the ghost town? Axel wasn't sure what rolled around in the seductive Hollywood princess's head, but he vowed to get to the bottom of it—and get another taste of her. He'd turned her down at nineteen, despite how badly he'd wanted her, because she'd been young, traumatized, and out of her element. Now that he knew she was all woman who could take every inch of the hard dick he had for her?

It was *so* on.

He went in search of his shoes. "I have to go."

"What? Now? I'd hoped we could . . . you know, hang out tonight."

In other words, she wanted him to scene with her. Their schedules hadn't matched up since Thorpe's birthday weeks ago. It had been far longer than that since she'd asked for sex. Lately, he'd sensed the pressure cooker of her emotions churning, building. It wouldn't be much longer now until she caved to her turmoil and asked him to unravel her.

"When was the last time you cried, Misty?"

She hesitated. "I tried."

"Good to hear it. Answer the question."

Sighing, she hemmed and hawed, then gave in. "It's been a while."

Exactly as he suspected. With a grim press of his lips, Axel shoved on his shoes and went in search of his keys, then stormed into the garage, pressing the button to lift the door.

"We'll have to talk about this tomorrow. Because, yes, I've seen

Mystery. And I need to go ask her some pointed questions right now. Will you be all right?"

"I will." But she sounded disappointed. "Callie has been having morning sickness, so she's laying low. She invited me over for some movies tonight."

Axel would feel better if Sweet Pea stayed with the other woman—and under Thorpe's and Sean's watchful eyes. "Do that. We'll talk tomorrow."

The second he hung up, he scrolled through the other contacts on his phone, wondering who the hell could help him with this last hurdle . . . He knew in which hotel he'd find Mystery but that information would only take him so far.

Finally, he found just the number he was looking for. The man answered on the first ring. "Your dime. Shoot."

"Hey, Stone," he greeted Jack Cole's new super-hacker, particularly glad the man was one of few words. "I need a favor. Can you dig through a specific hotel's guest records and give me a room number?"

"Technically, it's illegal." Stone sounded as if that amused him, too.

"It's also pretty damn important." Because there was zero way Axel intended to let Mystery slide out of his life again without finding out just why the hell she'd fucked him and run off. He had his suspicions, but he wanted to make her say them aloud, to his face—while he was buried deep inside her.

"What's it worth to you?"

So they were bartering today, huh? It made sense. He and Stone were hardly bosom buddies. In fact, he'd only met the guy a handful of times while trying to help Kata's brother, Joaquin, save his bride-to-be, Bailey.

"What do you want?"

"You have something exclusive with that hot little thing everyone calls Sweet Pea?"

Axel recoiled in surprise. He hadn't even been aware that Stone and Misty had met, much less that the man had a hard-on for her.

"Nope. Never have. I'm a friend doing her a favor. That's it. But I'll warn you now, if you just want to fuck and chuck, she's not your girl."

Stone chuckled. "Okay. Understood. Agree to set up a meet-and-greet between us, and I'll find out whatever you want to know. Hell, I'll give you the target's blood type and what they like for breakfast."

As he backed out of the driveway in neutral, Axel paused. Sweet Pea was emotionally fragile, and he wasn't sure if Stone had any interest in her beyond sexual. It was on the tip of his tongue to spill some of the girl's secrets. He didn't. She'd resent the shit out of him for it. In fact, it had taken months of talking and a lot of trust-building between them before she'd divulged anything about her past. He'd sworn to keep her secrets, some of which even Thorpe, her boss and mentor, didn't know.

"I'll do it," he told Stone finally. "But I can't promise she'll have any interest. If you hurt her, I'll beat the shit out of you."

"I've been duly warned. I want to see her this week."

"I can make it happen tomorrow."

"Even better." Satisfaction rang from Stone's voice. "What do you want me to find out?"

"Mystery Mullins is staying at the Hotel Crescent Court in Dallas. I want her room number."

Stone didn't sound surprised—or as if he even cared. "Give me a few. I'll have it. Any chance she's staying there under an assumed name?"

"Yeah. She probably checked in yesterday. That's all I've got."

"It should be enough," Stone said.

Axel breathed a sigh of relief. "I'll call you in fifteen."

"I'll have an answer even sooner, but whatever floats your boat."

Before he could say anything else, Stone hung up. Axel debated the wisdom of introducing the brash man to shy little Misty, but she should branch out. She needed a man who made her feel something other than safe. Axel knew it wasn't him.

Starting and revving his bike, he tore out of the driveway and headed into the night. He could think himself to death about why Mystery had hidden her identity to trick him into bed. It either had a lot to do with a bottle of tequila, a ghost town, and his rejection . . . or she'd wanted to see how the trailer half fucked.

As soon as he arrived, he parked his motorcycle. If he had his way, he'd be staying far longer than ten minutes.

Inside the lobby, he pulled out his phone. Again, Stone answered almost immediately.

"What do you have for me?" Axel asked.

"You'll like this. She's registered as Elise Rattlebottom. I searched the name. She's the lead character in Mystery's series of novels."

Axel remembered reading when she'd signed her first publishing deal four years ago. At least he understood the name she'd given him at the bar now. "Rattlebottom?"

"Yeah. She's a vegan cat burglar from London who hates her name. She steals precious items from their current keepers and returns them to the rightful owner. You know, rare dogs, paintings stolen from Jews by the Nazis—that kind of stuff. The character is known by the alias Robin Plunder."

Despite his annoyance, he grinned at that. "Room number?"

Stone rattled it off, then didn't wait a second before barking a question back at him. "What time tomorrow?"

"Plan on six at Club Dominion. I'll let you know if there's a change."

Axel hung up before the man could comment or protest, then stepped into the elevator.

Time to unravel his Mystery.

Chapter Eight

SHAKING from head to toe, Mystery snatched up her phone to call Heath. She shouldn't be alone now, not after someone had just sneaked into her room. He would handle hotel security and the police. She would try to calm her father and keep her fears in check.

Because it looked as if her past was coming back to haunt her. Once upon a time, whoever had paid for her abduction had wanted her for something terrible, maybe even deadly. God forbid if they wanted her again, this time to finish what they'd started.

Mystery punched in her security code to unlock the phone, then flipped through her recent calls. She'd just spotted Heath's number when someone began pounding on her door.

With a shriek, she dropped the phone and lurched back against the wall. "Who is it?"

She cursed her trembling voice, her racing thoughts. Maybe room service had merely arrived. Maybe the hotel management intended to check on her after the incident in the lobby. Or maybe someone lethal had come to finish her off.

"Open the damn door," a man growled on the other side.

Yeah, after some psycho had forced his way into her room and left her a threatening photo, she wasn't inclined to comply. "Go away."

"Like hell. Open up."

"I'm calling the police," she shouted.

"Damn it, I need to talk to you, Mystery."

Something about his voice cut through her panic and sparked her memory. It was familiar, evoked safety. It wasn't Heath, but . . . Axel?

With relief flooding through her veins, she darted to the door and peeked through the peephole. Sure enough, there stood the mountain of a man who'd once rescued her. The man she'd seduced earlier. He would understand the threat she'd just received.

With shaking hands, she pressed down on the lever and opened the door. The sight of him in her portal, a huge sentry keeping out all the bad, rushed over her.

It was probably stupid, but she didn't care. Mystery threw herself into his arms. "Thank God you're here."

Axel propelled her back into the room. The door slammed behind them. He reared back, wearing a thunderously furious expression.

"What the fuck kind of games are you playing with me, princess? You disguise yourself to seduce me, tell me a bunch of lies, then the bed is barely cold before you're gone—"

She wrenched free and ran to the desk, retrieving the picture. "This just happened."

When she thrust it at him, he grabbed it but didn't look, just scowled. She trembled. As he studied her, his anger melted into concern. "You're afraid. Of me?"

"No," she assured. "Look at the picture, front and back."

He gritted his teeth at her, then jerked his gaze down to the photo in his hand. After a long stare, he flipped it over. His glower of epic proportions turned to absolute ice.

"Tell me how you got this," he demanded.

She drew in a shaking breath, the voice in her head screaming that she needed to keep herself together. "I left your house and came back here. Once in my room, I hopped in the shower. When I got out, I found this."

"You're sure it wasn't here before then? That someone didn't bring it in while you were out of the room?"

"P-positive," she assured. "My phone was on that desk, so I texted my father before the shower to tell him I was all right and to sleep well. When I came out, I'd planned to send Heath a text—"

"Who is that? The man I saw on TMZ holding your hand in the lobby?"

Mystery recoiled. Anger seethed from him when he asked the question.

She swallowed. "Yeah. He's my driver and bodyguard. My father hired him shortly after we moved to London. He's been with me since."

"Does he have a key to your room?"

"No. We don't have . . . I mean, he's not, like, my lover or boyfriend or anything. He has no reason—"

"If I were your bodyguard, I would have a key to your room, regardless of our relationship—which we're going to discuss eventually. Right now, we need to be clear that whoever left you this picture knows about your abduction. Maybe he was even in on it."

"Or responsible for it. I'd already thought of that."

"Have you swept the room?"

"What?" Mystery didn't understand, not with her heart racing, her fear spiking. "Searched it, you mean?"

Axel nodded. "Did you?"

"No." Stupidly, she'd assumed that whoever had left her the picture had simply dropped it off and stolen out again, not wanting to be seen. In retrospect, if someone plotted to leave her a death threat, they were likely serious about killing her and might have hung around to do the job.

His head snapped up. He looked around the room. "Sit in that chair." He pointed to the elegant piece with curved legs, upholstered in white damask, until she followed directions. "Phone in hand. Dial 9-1-1 and keep your finger hovered over the call button. If you hear or see anything out of the ordinary, hit it. I'll be nearby."

Mystery did as he demanded. Her finger shook as she stabbed at the buttons on her screen and waited. She followed him with her stare, feeling so much safer with him near. Axel alone understood where she'd been held, the harrowing ordeal of her kidnapping and rescue. She hadn't had to explain why that photograph had terrified her or what it meant. He knew.

Around her, he opened the closet, checked behind the drapes before he pulled each one closed. Then he searched under every stick of furniture, including the bed—anywhere a person might lie in wait.

Finally, he emerged from the bathroom, its mirror still steamy from her shower. "The coast is clear." He sat on the edge of the bed and dragged her chair closer to him. "Did you ever find out who paid for your abduction and why?"

"No." She swallowed hard. "When we moved to London, I focused on putting it all behind me. My father swore that was the best course of action. I refused the tell-all book and movie deals. A lot of conspiracy theorists and crackpots wrote my dad and I about why they thought it had happened. I read the first few, but . . . I know I wasn't abducted by aliens or the mafia or a super-secret sect of the government."

"Of course not," he agreed, looking around. "You didn't know this Heath guy before your move to the UK?"

"No. He's former MI5. He's a good guy. His wife died. Um, I think he considers himself an unofficial uncle, if I had to guess. If you're thinking he would ever hurt me, then no."

Axel sat back. "I'm going to have you involve Heath in what happens next only because if I don't, I suspect your father will freak out and hop on the next plane here."

He'd figured her father out quickly. Despite the grim situation, she gave him a faint smile. "To say the least."

"Call Heath, then. I'm going to reach out to some people myself. We're going to figure this out. And once we do, you're going to answer a whole lot of questions about why you lied, why you fucked me, and why you left without a word."

* * *

RAKING a palm over the top of his shorn hair, Axel paced the room, watching Mystery have a trembling conversation with Heath. He'd check this guy out himself shortly because anyone who could look at Mystery and feel like her uncle had to be dead below the waist—or lying like a motherfucker.

Despite the danger, Axel's desire to wrap his hand in her dark hair and watch her hazel eyes widen just before he captured her parting lips rode him hard. The need to have a long talk with her about the whys of her seduction today and all the reasons he found her deceit unacceptable needled him, too. But he'd handle those items once she'd calmed and he'd ensured her safety.

Cursing, he pulled his own phone from his belt, trying to decide who could best help with this situation. He needed Stone's hacking ability again. But that would only get him so far. To keep Mystery safe, he needed to figure out who had abducted her years ago and why. He could count on one hand the number of men he thought capable of hunting down a ghost from someone's past—but at least he knew that many. One in particular jumped out at him.

He hit the contact button and connected the call.

"Axel?" said the man on the other end with obvious surprise.

Yeah, they hadn't exactly started off as the best of friends—accusing the guy of abduction and rape tended to make one unpopular with a new acquaintance—but they'd come to an understanding.

"Joaquin. Hey." He winced. "I'd, um . . . start with some small talk and ask how you and Bailey are doing in Lafayette and how the wedding plans are coming—"

"But you need something."

"Badly. You were able to solve Bailey's past and get to the bottom of the threat that hung over her for years. I'm protecting a woman who needs the same."

"She's in danger?"

"Imminent."

"I'll do what I can."

Axel breathed a sigh of relief. "I owe you."

Joaquin snorted. "Hunter and Logan will probably send you a bill. They're beasts on the shooting range and in the weight room. But holy shit, they are meticulous about billable hours."

If the situation weren't so dire, Axel might have laughed. He'd bet that taking over his retired stepfather's security firm with his new stepbrothers, both former Navy SEALs, had been interesting.

"Whatever it takes," he found himself saying.

Axel didn't know why Mystery and her safety were so important to him. He could tell himself that he'd worked hard to rescue her once and refused to see her die now. He could say that she'd been through enough and didn't need to endure more. He might even bullshit himself and claim he was only helping her because he didn't like the idea of any woman in peril.

But Axel knew it was because of this sense of possession brewing deep in his gut. Right now, she was *his*. He wasn't done with her—not by a long shot.

"What do you need?" Joaquin asked.

Axel filled the man in on today's incidents. "Can you peek into Mystery Mullins's past? See if you can find anyone who might have wanted to harm her then or now. I don't have a lot to go on."

"Fair enough," Joaquin shot back. "I'll start digging. You involving the police?"

"I don't think there's a way around it, but they won't investigate the reason behind tonight's incident. They'll treat it as a simple B and E and move on."

"Yep. I'll let you know when I've got something."

"Thanks a bunch. I'm, um . . . sorry I accused you of hurting Bailey when we met."

"I was an asshole and probably deserved it."

They laughed, and Axel hung up.

He had one more person to phone, but Mystery's driver/ bodyguard wrapped her in his arms. Axel watched, not at all happy. She might believe Heath saw her as his sweet surrogate niece. Axel snorted. No chance in hell.

She introduced them, and they sized one another up with a wary handshake.

Finally, Heath turned to Mystery. "You're not hurt?"

"No," she assured. "Scared, but whoever it was had come and gone before I even knew they'd been here."

"When did you arrive on the scene?" Heath grilled him, his proper British accent unmistakable.

Axel didn't like the man's intimation. "If you're asking whether I left this photo in her room to upset her enough to send her into my arms, the answer is no. I rescued her from that abduction years ago. Until earlier today, I hadn't seen her since then. But didn't you drive her here from my house? Haven't you been just down the hall all this time? You have a key to her room, I'll bet."

Heath bristled. "Yes, I drove her here and I've been down the hall. And I do have a key. It's my job to watch over her. Why would I try to frighten her this way?"

Axel shrugged. "Job security. As long as she thinks you're ne- cessary, Mr. Mullins will keep signing your paychecks."

Or more likely the stiff Brit just wanted to fuck her. He under- stood that need completely.

"Axel . . ." She sighed, then turned to the other man. "Heath. This is silly. I refuse to believe either of you had anything to do with this."

"I'm merely pointing out that he had opportunity and motive." Axel stared at the other man.

Heath crossed his arms over his chest. "I suspect you had opportunity as well, since you 'happened' to arrive just after she found this photo in her room. I don't know your motive yet. Maybe you were angry that she left your house quite suddenly today?"

"Stop it, both of you," Mystery insisted. "Honestly, wouldn't it be more productive to look for the real perpetrator instead of you two circling one another like rabid dogs?"

As much as Axel's temper didn't like it, his head knew she had a point. "All right. Since her kidnapping is unsolved, we'll have to work that angle separately. For now, we need to contact the hotel's security and see if they can find the video surveillance from the stairwells, elevators, and hallways leading to Mystery's door."

"Agreed. I'd like them to tell us whose key card was used to access the room."

"Absolutely." Axel nodded and turned to Mystery. "If you're ever in a hotel room alone again . . ." Not that she would be for the foreseeable future. "Always throw the dead bolt home. You never know how good a hotel's security is or the character of the people on their staff who have a master key to all the rooms."

Heath cupped her shoulder. "He's right. You must be careful, sweetheart."

The sight of him touching her, even casually, rubbed Axel the wrong way. It took everything he had not to be a fidiot caveman and threaten to rip the man's hands off.

"I know," she murmured. "I forgot. I was . . . distracted. I feel so stupid now."

"Never." Heath sent her a searching smile. "Why don't you sit again? I'll call hotel security."

"Do you think if I wait until morning to call my father—"

"He'll hear about it before then," Heath told her.

She sighed again. "Right. I'll handle it."

The other two both made their respective calls. Axel watched Heath warily. He didn't trust the guy. Or maybe he just didn't like the idea that another grown, heterosexual man got to spend so much time alone with Mystery. Axel doubted they'd slept together. But maybe that ugly truth just pissed Heath off.

Axel also wondered why it mattered so much. This morning, Mystery hadn't been on his radar. Well . . . much. Now, he didn't want any other man's hands on her.

Filing that truth away as something to explore later, he made his way to a quiet corner of the room and scrolled through the recent calls on his phone again and hit Stone's number once more.

"Twice in one day?" Stone asked. "Can't get enough of me?"

"Maybe you should give up hacking and go into stand-up if you're so fucking funny."

Stone laughed. "No, I'd suck at it. But you give as good as you get. I like that. What's up?"

"I need more information."

"Since I've already got a date to meet the girl I'm interested in, I'm not sure what more you can offer me."

Axel didn't hesitate. "I'm her protector. She doesn't say shit to anyone without my permission. If you want conversation, I suggest you help me."

"You're a sly bastard," Stone groused.

"What's it going to be?"

Stone cursed. "Tell me what you need."

Axel smiled into the phone. "The hotel we discussed earlier? I need to see if you can hack into their security systems. I need camera footage of the top floor, leading to the room number you gave me. I also need to see if you can give me a list of everyone whose key card accessed the door to her room. We're asking hotel security for these same records, but if someone on staff is involved, they could easily tamper with the evidence."

"No sweat. Give me a few hours. It may not take that long. But I'll give you some answers."

"Thanks."

"Hopefully, Sweet Pea will thank me on your behalf," Stone said suggestively.

Axel rolled his eyes, and he realized that he didn't mind another man touching the woman he'd shared scenes and sex with for the last two years. Across the room, Heath had his arm around Mystery, the woman he'd taken to bed exactly once, and Axel felt murderous.

He needed to get a fucking grip.

"Don't hold your breath. Trust doesn't come easy for Sweet Pea. She's a kind soul and she'll be polite as hell. I wouldn't expect more than that for now."

"You control who fucks her, too?"

Axel didn't think Misty had been to bed with anyone else since they'd settled into their arrangement, but he could be wrong. And it wouldn't bother him. As long as she found someone good to her, he was cool. "I'm not her pimp, asshole. I look out for her."

"I don't think that's all you do to her, but I'll put a lid on it, get you an answer, and call back soon." Stone hung up.

Prick.

Axel watched across the room as Heath caressed Mystery's back. She'd grown tense as she talked into the phone. She winced, shook her head, and looked like she fought back tears. Axel approached the two.

"Daddy, no. I'm fine," she assured. "Between Axel and Heath, I'm perfectly safe. We'll figure this out. I need to see Aunt Gail. I keep promising her I'll come get some of these things Mom left for me, and I . . . just haven't wanted to deal with it. She's going on a mission trip in a few days, so it's now or never. Besides, none of us ever knows how long we have left, and it's been too many years since I spent time with her. I'll be home soon."

That perked Axel up. He remembered from Mystery's bio information that her mother's sister, Gail, was a spinster who lived in rural Kansas. Was that the reason Mystery had come to the States in the first place? If so, why had she stopped to spend a night or two in Dallas?

Heath gave her one more comforting pat, then sauntered his way. "I talked to the hotel's security director. He said he'll have the video feed and key card records for us by morning."

"Morning? I was thinking more like an hour or two."

"I was, as well," Heath admitted. "Unfortunately, he says all those records are kept at a facility off-site, and they're closed until tomorrow."

Well, Stone would have answers much faster. Maybe he'd tell Heath that later. But until he trusted the guy, Axel refused to divulge much.

"So we'll work around it for now. Did you call the police?"

"Hotel security said they would. They have a protocol for these things." Heath clearly didn't like the bureaucracy.

Axel seconded that. "We don't need the red tape."

"Exactly. But I suspect it's a dead end, anyway. The police won't know who left her that picture, and even if they could figure out the perpetrator's identity, I'm sure it would be a greedy maid or a hired thug."

Maybe. But someone far more nefarious had given the intruder that picture.

Axel paced. Joaquin couldn't get to the bottom of Mystery's past soon enough. He had to start figuring out who wanted to hurt her and why.

"You know, whoever left this picture for her tonight . . . what's the motive? Why remind her of her abduction after all these years? Why now? What set this person off?" Heath asked.

Good question. "Well, judging from the message on the back, this person doesn't want her on U.S. soil. She's supposedly safer back in the UK. Has she encountered any threat there?"

"No." Then Heath reconsidered. "Well, someone broke into their London flat not long after they moved in, probably five years ago. It was trashed. Some of Mystery's jewelry was taken. But I think we were dealing with a petty thief, not the sort of animal who would threaten the life of a young woman."

He didn't have enough facts to say for certain. Axel filed that incident away and moved forward. "Who knew she intended to fly to the States, besides you and her father?"

Heath rolled his eyes. "Everyone who reads her Twitter feed. I've advised her to deactivate it, but she insists it's one of the ways she keeps in touch with fans and friends."

"She put on her Twitter that she was coming to Dallas?"

"Not precisely. Look." Heath pulled out his phone and launched Twitter. "This is her feed for the last week. Four days ago, she posted a picture of her suitcase."

Axel read the caption that said she was excited she'd be visiting her aunt soon. "Shit."

Heath scrolled and came to another picture of a plate of Mexican food posted two days ago. The accompanying verbiage indicated she was so happy to be getting some of the cheesy-gooey goodness, which was hard to find in London. The picture seemed harmless enough, but the menu with the restaurant's name and location stood up on the table in the background.

He looked up at the other man with accusing eyes. "Why aren't you preventing her from posting this?"

"I've tried." Heath winced. "I can suggest all the reasons it's a terrible idea, but I'm not her father, and he hasn't seen fit to forbid her to use social media. He claims it's good for her career, that she needs to be visible."

"Not if it's going to get her killed," Axel grumbled.

"That's where I come in. I'm simply supposed to be more vigilant, you see," he said wryly. "Perhaps after this incident, he'll grasp the scope of the danger."

Heath scrolled again, revealing the next post. No picture, just one hundred forty characters or less explaining that she was curled up in her hotel room and looking forward to receiving some new personal effects of her mother's.

When he would have scrolled again, Axel grabbed Heath's wrist. "Wait. Read that again."

The other man did and shrugged.

"Does she often post things about her mother?" Axel asked.

"No . . . but, of course, it tends to cross her mind more as we approach May twelfth."

The anniversary of her mother's death. Less than a week away. "That's natural. I'm wondering if that has anything to do with the reason Mystery has been targeted. After all, it's an unsolved case."

"I've looked into it extensively. Personally, I think Julia Mullins was intentionally pushed off that mountain. Perhaps I'm wrong, but—"

"I don't think so. I've thought it, too," Axel said. "Just like I've considered that Mystery's kidnapping might have something to do with her mother's murder. I might be wrong, and proving it would be a long shot, but no other violence has befallen the family. I know Mullins believes the abduction had something to do with his celebrity, but why didn't someone send him a ransom demand when Mystery was held captive?"

"Or flash this picture to the world to show off what they'd done if they were so bloody proud of their 'accomplishment'?"

Axel nodded. "Whoever took her prisoner has been damn quiet these last six and a half years."

"Precisely."

"So why would this douche suddenly start making noise again? What else is on her Twitter feed?"

"Very little." Heath scrolled and paused over another picture, this one of the Dallas skyline, probably from her hotel room. She'd posted it this morning. "Bloody hell. I hadn't seen this yet."

"She might as well draw everyone a fucking map and tell them how to find her." Axel shook his head.

"If I weren't a gentleman, the things I would say and do . . ."

Yep. She needed a damn good spanking, and when she wasn't so upset and scared, Axel intended to give it to her and make it clear that, until they'd solved this shit, her social media was off limits.

"Assuming the police will find nothing about who broke into her room—which is what I'm anticipating—what are our next steps?" Heath asked.

Axel didn't really like his attention to Mystery, but he also couldn't disagree with the way the man thought. "She can't stay here tonight."

"Of course not. Everyone knows where to find her."

"I'll bet you haven't seen all the shit on TMZ yet, either."

Heath just closed his eyes and shook his head. "Well, pardon my French, but what a fucking debacle. And if I can't keep her safe, her father will have my balls."

"Mullins is intense, for sure, especially where his daughter is concerned. I know where we can hide Mystery for a few days while we figure out what's going on and how to stop it."

"But Aunt Gail is expecting me tomorrow," Mystery cut in, clearly finished talking to her father. "She's leaving on that mission trip to Indonesia on Saturday. I can't miss seeing her. I'd like that stuff my mom left for me, and I don't know when I'll be back in the country."

"I don't think a jaunt to Kansas wise," Heath began. "You can visit her when she returns from Indonesia. But go home now."

Axel snorted. "He's being polite. At this point, you've told everyone—including the people coming after you—that you're planning to visit her. Go the fuck back to London."

"You're assuming these people read my Twitter feed," she protested. "I only have fifty thousand followers. Maybe whoever is threatening me found out some other—"

"That's fifty thousand potential whack-jobs you're telling what you're doing and where you're going. Have you put this information anywhere else?"

"Everything I post to Twitter loads to Facebook. I also have an Instagram account. I don't use it much."

"Shuttle them all," Axel demanded.

Instantly, she balked. "I have a book releasing in six weeks. I use my social media accounts to promote—"

"You won't be doing that if you're not alive to use them, Mystery."

"Wait. Perhaps we shouldn't change her patterns so abruptly," Heath suggested. "If she suddenly closes everything down, not only do we alert this bastard that we're onto him, but we also lose our means of communicating any message that might help us."

Axel opened his mouth to argue, then shut it. "You're right. We should be using the accounts to misdirect this asshole and take the heat off her."

"Precisely." Heath nodded.

"I like that idea," Axel admitted. "Post now that you've had a change of plans and you'll be returning to London tomorrow."

"But my aunt—"

"You can call her and tell her privately that you're still coming." He held up a hand to ward off her protest. "But to the rest of the world, you've had a great if short visit, but you need to get home."

Heath shook his head. "People will see her at the airport tomorrow if she boards a flight not heading to London. And it's not as if she's going to New York or Chicago, where she might be catching a flight to the UK from there."

"Good point. Can you cancel her Kansas City flight?" Axel asked the other man.

"On it." He took his phone back from Axel's grip.

Mystery put a hand on her hip. "So how are we getting to Aunt Gail's?"

"Normally, I'd say we could drive, but it's not as if you can stop at McDonald's for a restroom break and lunch without potentially being spotted," Axel pointed out.

Heath muted his phone. "Private charter."

Axel pointed at the Brit. "That's the ticket."

"I'll find one for the two of us as soon as I finish with the airline," her bodyguard supplied.

"I know who can arrange one." Thorpe could get anything handled. And as far as Axel was concerned, the smaller the paper trail that led back to Mystery, the better. "And all three of us are going."

"No." Heath looked decidedly pissed off at that suggestion.

Too fucking bad.

Axel crossed his arms over his chest. "I've evaded this son of a bitch before. I know more about how he thinks. If we play this right, I might even be able to figure out what he wants. So I should stay with her."

Heath hesitated, then looked at Mystery. "Sweetheart?"

She bit her lip, indecision all over her face. Likely, she was weighing her sense of personal safety when she had him nearby versus the tongue-lashing he intended to give her as soon as they were alone.

As she strolled into the nearby bathroom, she flipped on a light, then reached for a little elastic band. She gathered her damp hair over her shoulder and returned, braiding the mass. Axel watched in fascination as her nimble fingers worked at the tresses covering her neck, falling softly over her breast, hanging around her waist. He imagined that sleek, soft mass all around him, caressing his skin, as she straddled him and rode his cock. Or him gathering all those strands in his fist as he took her from behind, her ass deliciously pink from the slap of his bare palm over and over . . .

"Is that okay?" she asked.

Fuck, what was the question? He'd been fantasizing about her and missed every word she'd said. "Repeat that."

Mystery loosed a frustrated sigh. "I said my father indicated he'd feel better if you could stay close to me." She hesitated, and her cheeks flushed. "I'd like it, too."

Given the way she'd left his house as if her ass were on fire, that surprised Axel a little. But he'd proven once that he could keep her safe. She knew he could, and that was a point in his favor now. If that fact gave him opportunity to spend time with her? Done.

"Then I'll be coming with you. Now post to your Twitter that you're flying back to London ASAP."

Mystery reached for her phone and tapped out a quick post. "All right. I did."

She no sooner spoke the words when someone knocked on the door. Automatically, Axel shoved her behind him. Heath waited until she was out of sight before he approached the door and peeked through the hole.

"The police," he muttered.

"Let them in," Axel replied.

Heath did, along with the hotel's security director. Room service rolled up, too, clearly never having received the memo that shit had gone down.

The next hour was filled with questions about what she'd seen or heard. After a grilling from the cops and the security director, they all left, promising to follow up. The hotel's manager also stopped in and offered Mystery a different suite.

"That would be great," Axel answered, sending the man in his shiny gray suit and wingtips away to make the arrangements.

As soon as Heath closed the door after them all, he stared at Axel. "Have you gone mental? We agreed she can't stay here."

"Of course she can't." Axel nodded. "But until we know if someone associated with the hotel is helping the enemy, it's in her best interest to keep the employees here guessing."

"True." But Heath didn't look as if he liked it.

"Pack up your things, princess. Be ready soon. We'll concoct a story, then get you out. I rode my motorcycle here, and we can't all leave on that. They'll be watching for your town car. A taxi will be too easy to trace . . ." Axel ran through the possibilities. How could he get Mystery out of the hotel with no one the wiser?

"What about my bags? I can't leave them here. I have some jewelry of my mother's. Some of her pictures and—"

"Okay. I'll think of a way to sneak the bags out, too. Just give me some time to work on a plan. You should probably pack up, too," he told Heath. "We'll need to be ready to pull out at a moment's notice."

Heath hesitated, clearly not liking Axel's suggestion, however rational.

"I'll return in five," he finally said, shutting the door behind him, leaving Axel and Mystery alone.

Chapter Nine

For a long moment, silence prevailed in the cozy hotel suite.

"Thanks for stepping in to help," Mystery finally offered. "You didn't have to, but—"

"You're welcome. Now explain what happened between us this afternoon."

She didn't even try to misunderstand, just grimaced. "I tricked you into bed. I know you must be angry."

Mystery looked genuinely contrite. And so beautiful, Axel gritted his teeth. He was pretty damn sure she wasn't wearing a bra, and the whole time Heath and the police had been here, every male in the room seemed to be sneaking a peek at the lush mounds of her breasts, barely concealed by the pink flowery fabric.

"Confused," he admitted, prowling closer to her. If he only had five minutes to figure this out before her bodyguard returned, he wanted to get a few things straight. "Why did you leave without saying good-bye?"

She crossed her arms over her chest. "I figured you were done with me. Why linger and make things awkward? Especially when you weren't supposed to know I was the woman in your bed."

"Ever? Because of our past? Or because, in your head, the trailer park guy is only good for some afternoon delight?"

Mystery blinked back in horror, frantically shaking her head. "No. Ohmigod, that's not it! You'd turned me down once. Your first rejection crushed me. I couldn't give you the chance to turn *me* down again. If you refused whoever I'd disguised myself as . . ." She shrugged. "I guess I thought it wouldn't hurt as much. And I cringed at the thought that, if you knew I still wanted you, you'd laugh or think I was pathetic or—"

Axel cupped her face, gathered her closer, and cut her off with a scorching kiss. He seized her lips and lay them under his own before he spread them wide and dove in. She was safe and warm and alive in his arms. She wanted him and didn't seem to give a shit that he'd grown up a hick from the sticks. And damn, she felt so fucking good.

Instantly, Mystery stiffened, dragged in a breath. He braced for her to push him away. Instead, she latched onto his shoulders, fingers digging into his flesh, and lashed his tongue with her own.

Electricity rolled up his spine, shot down through his veins. She revved his system like nothing he'd ever experienced. More than she had even a few hours ago. And damn far more than she had six and a half years ago. He'd been harsh with her then, knowing he couldn't take sexual advantage of a traumatized young woman, even if he'd found her attractive as hell. Nor had he wanted to betray her father's trust or cloud his head while they were potentially still in danger.

Now? Maybe he should leave her alone, but fuck holding back. He wanted her.

For the last half dozen crappy years, he'd looked for something more in his life, some*one* to fill the odd void he hadn't understood. With Mystery pressed against him, he totally understood what he'd been missing.

She moaned into their kiss and all but climbed up his body to get closer.

Axel growled and grabbed her lush ass in both palms, all but lifting her against his aching cock. "Am I laughing? Does this feel like I think you're pathetic?"

"No," she whispered, her gaze melded with his own.

"No," he confirmed. "When you left my house, I wasn't done with you."

Mystery swallowed hard. "And now that you know I was the girl you slept with earlier?"

"I don't remember a lot of sleeping, princess. But I'm thinking we should do it again, just to make sure I remember right."

She sent him a relieved smile, coupled with a little laugh. "I'd like that. But with so much happening now . . ."

"I'll handle it." He kissed his way up her neck, reveling in her soft skin, her clean soapy-vanilla scent, the little love bite he'd left on her neck. He ached to leave them on her breasts, hips, thighs, smooth pussy. "But don't you doubt that I intend to get you naked and under me again."

Her breath hitched. "Please."

Axel couldn't stand it another moment; he had to touch her. He caressed his way down her shoulder, then skated his palm toward her breast, cupping the mound covered only by thin cotton. Her nipple tightened.

He brushed his thumb over the sensitive peak, his whole body tensing with need when it hardened even more. "I want this in my mouth."

With a little moan, she slid her head back, as if granting him access to her neck, her chest. Hell, giving her whole body to him. She was the most gorgeous creature. He'd tried like hell not to notice it when he'd rescued her from Death Valley. She'd still looked a bit like a girl then. Now that she was clearly all woman . . . Jesus, this need was eviscerating his restraint.

"Axel," she pleaded.

"We don't have time now, damn it. But soon," he muttered, his voice thick. "I just need to know one more thing . . ."

He shouldn't do this now, not with Heath returning soon. But Axel intended to take every opportunity possible to touch Mystery.

So he dropped his hand down her body again, gliding his palm over the curve of her hip until he reached the hem of her short nightgown. Tucking his fingers under the frilly trim, he skated his knuckle up the soft skin of her thigh until he reached her pussy and burrowed between her folds. Sweet, bare, and so damn wet for him.

Axel let out a low groan. "I can't wait to get this off you and shove my aching cock into you again . . ."

A clinking noise at the door alerted him that they wouldn't be alone for long. With a frustrated curse, Axel pulled his fingers away from her cunt. After the sound of a retracting door handle, Heath barged inside and looked at them as if he knew exactly what had been going on.

Someone get the genius a prize.

"Now that everyone is gone, we should discuss our exit strategy," Heath said, not taking his eyes off the two of them.

Axel couldn't seem to stop himself from wrapping an arm around her waist. Heath glared his way.

"On the way out, we'll tell the hotel manager we've had a change of heart about that suite, and Mystery will be flying back to London right away. It's the same story we're floating on Twitter," Axel pointed out. "If whoever is threatening her thinks they've won for now, it should buy us some time to get her to safety." And figure out who the fuck kept ripping her sense of security to shreds. "I'll walk the two of you to the parking garage with your luggage, then you'll follow me. I'll be on my bike. I have a location in mind. If someone tries to follow you, we'll do our best to lose them."

Heath didn't look as if he liked the plan—or maybe just Axel—but he conceded. "You live in this city and know it better, so I'll let you lead on this. How long?"

"Can we head out in ten?"

Heath nodded. The gray just beginning to lace his dark hair, along with the impeccable dark suit, made him look somewhere between distinguished and dangerous. After an hour or two with him, Axel wanted to believe the man had Mystery's best interests at heart. But he was pretty sure Heath's concept of her ideal future didn't include Axel at all.

"Great." Still, he hedged his bets. "If you don't stay with the plan, if you put her in any sort of danger, there won't be a hole small enough for you to climb in. I will find you. And I will kill you."

* * *

AFTER walking Mystery and Heath to the parking garage, Axel hopped on his bike and waited on the side street for her bodyguard to bring the car around. The Brit better not stab him in the back. The warning he'd given in the suite might have been overkill, but he'd bet it was effective.

He plucked his phone from his pocket and texted Stone, advising that if he wanted to meet Sweet Pea, it had to be tonight and to get his ass moving since the drive would take about five hours. The man replied with a quick affirmative.

Then Axel sighed. He had to make a call he really didn't want to, but he didn't see a way around it.

Mitchell Thorpe, Club Dominion's owner, answered on the third ring. "What part of 'a day off' isn't computing for you?"

"Pretty much all of it. I've got a . . . situation. I need your help."

Thorpe sobered instantly. "What's up?"

Axel explained Mystery's danger, then hesitated. "I want to bring her to the club, to keep her safe until we get her to her aunt's house."

"Is letting her visit the woman at all wise?"

"No, but she won't be talked out of it. She's argued with her father, Heath, and me. Apparently, she promised the woman, and I get that. I don't love Mystery's insistence, but it's not my decision to make." *Yet.*

"She's a grown woman, and you can only direct her so much. I know someone else very much like that. Yes, I'm talking to you, pet." Thorpe obviously teased Callie. She was the only one he spoke to in that voice filled with love, affection, and pride.

"They are a lot alike. They're definitely both survivors. I know with Callie's pregnancy you probably don't want me to bring danger to your door. But it's the safest place I can think of for Mystery until we arrange a charter to take her to Kansas tomorrow."

Thorpe paused. "I'm not thrilled, but you're right that Ms. Mullins can't stay at the hotel. I'll make sure Sean takes our girl home and away from any potential threat."

"Thanks. I appreciate it."

"You helped me a lot with Sean and Callie. I owe you."

Axel hadn't done much more than track down the former fed's place and threaten to beat the shit out of him when Thorpe had believed Sean was a threat to Callie, but if the club owner wanted to consider this calling in a favor, fine. "We should be there in less than thirty minutes."

"Good. I'll get everything here moving accordingly. Have any of you had dinner?"

Mystery had never gotten to eat her room service with the police and hotel security crawling everywhere. Axel hadn't even thought of food. "No."

"I'll ask Callie to order something good before she leaves." Thorpe hesitated. "Does Ms. Mullins know where you're bringing her?"

"I haven't mentioned it." He should probably tell her she would be staying in an active BDSM club where, almost every night, Doms and subs pushed themselves to their mental, physical, and emotional limits. But he lacked the privacy to have a personal conversation with her now. Besides, the perverse side of him wanted to see her undoctored reaction to Club Dominion. He ached to know now if she could fit into his life.

Then, maybe, he could try to figure out if he fit into hers, because right now, trailer park upbringing and all, he didn't see himself letting her go.

* * *

BESIDE Mystery, Heath remained quiet as they raced down dark Dallas side streets, winding their way toward their destination.

"Do you know where we're going?" she asked.

Heath's mouth tightened. "I don't."

And he didn't like it. That went without saying. She'd sensed the tension between the two men, and it worried her. They were supposed to be on the same team, wanting the same outcome. Why wouldn't they get along?

"He's actually a really wonderful guy," she began.

"Pardon me, but from where I'm standing, he was paid handsomely to rescue you, then abandoned you the minute you reached safety. He didn't call you to follow up or check in to find out if you were all right, did he?"

"No, but—"

"He earned his paycheck. Nothing more. He clearly didn't care a whit about you. If he had, he would never have turned his back on you after that terrible abduction."

"I propositioned him before we were rescued." She felt heat flare across her cheeks. "He turned me down flat."

Heath gripped the steering wheel until his knuckles turned white. "You were barely more than a child and had been through a terrible ordeal. I would hope he was a gentleman and refused. But the fact that you felt the need to disguise yourself so utterly in order to persuade him to appreciate your beauty, inside and out, chafes me. And you're continuing to let him touch you, even though you had to deceive him to catch his attention. He doesn't want you for *you*, sweetheart. I don't know what he wants precisely. More money probably, and I can't—"

"Disguising myself was my choice. The moment he realized who he'd spent the afternoon with, he came to find me. He hasn't left my side since," she argued.

But deep down, she wondered if Heath was right. Not about Axel wanting money, but about him not wanting the real her. Maybe he'd just enjoyed their fuck and wanted another.

"Watch yourself with him. I believe he'll keep you physically safe. Emotionally . . . I worry. I think he's a player."

Mystery didn't have a comeback. She'd had Axel all to herself in the desert years ago. They'd been blessedly alone together at his house. She didn't know everything about Axel and his life. They'd had absolutely spectacular sex—fireworks, ballads—the works. She wasn't ready to let him go. Of course, when she'd seduced him, she hadn't been thinking of a future with him, but rather a full one without him. Now, her heart felt tangled in him, full of him. They didn't even live in the same country, and she was sounding crazy. But she wasn't sure how she'd live the rest of her life without him.

They pulled up in front of an industrial building with a well-lit parking lot and a brightly colored door. Axel parked his bike and took off his helmet, stowing it on a peg, then coming toward her.

He helped her from the car. "This is where I work."

"Club Dominion?" she asked, shutting the door behind her. She'd learned about his job from the private investigator. She knew what sort of club this was. Her stomach knotted.

Heath stepped out on the other side of the car.

"You knew?" Axel asked, clearly surprised.

"I hired someone to find out where you were and what you were doing these days, yes." She nodded.

He cocked his head. "You're resourceful and a step ahead of me."

From Axel, that was almost a compliment. "Why did you bring me here?"

"It's secure. I can keep you on lockdown. Unless someone at the hotel is being bribed, almost no one can tie me to you in any way except your rescue years ago. As far as anyone knows, you're heading back to London. We should be safe here tonight." He took her elbow and escorted her across the lot.

Mystery sensed Heath behind them, could almost feel his disapproving scowl. "How secure?"

"Cameras, top-of-the-line system, lots of eyes and ears. Nothing will happen here." Axel dismissed Heath and turned to her. "Just tell me whatever you need to be comfortable. I'll make it happen."

"Thanks."

Instead of entering through the front, Axel skirted the side of the cavernous building and led her around back. He pulled out a key card, then settled his thumb over a biometric reader. The door buzzed open.

"That's pretty high tech," she remarked.

"Some of our members are city and state officials. We've got cops, billionaires, former SEALs—people who either need to keep a low profile or rely on unbreachable security before they get their freak on."

Mystery didn't say anything more. She wanted to see Axel in his environment. She wanted to experience this place for herself. As she thought of that, a shiver zipped up her spine.

They made their way down a long hallway with concrete floors and doors on either side, then Axel led her to one and knocked. He briefly introduced her and Heath to the owner, Mitchell Thorpe. Mystery remembered hearing about him on the news, harboring runaway heiress Callindra Howe for years. Rumors swirled that, though the woman had married the FBI agent tasked with tracking her down when she'd been a fugitive, Thorpe was also involved romantically with the beauty.

The distinguished man in the suit welcomed her. "Axel will keep you comfortable. If you need anything, he'll take care of you. Callie ordered you three a bunch of Italian. It's in the kitchen. The action up front will be in full swing in another couple of hours, so . . ."

"I'll keep her away from there," Axel finished.

Thorpe nodded. "Good call. If anything happens, you know the drill."

Axel gave him a thumbs-up. "I'm set. Sean texted me and said he'll be on standby."

With a faint grin, Thorpe turned her way. "You're in good hands. I'll leave you to them. Callie wants both Sean and I home so we can"—he winked—"rub her feet."

With that, he was gone. Axel led her down the hall again, toward the back of the building and showed her into a purely masculine suite with a king-sized bed, attached bath, and a window seat that looked cozy for reading.

"I'll grab your bags from the car, then we can eat. You must be starving."

She nodded. "I'll need to call my aunt, too."

"I'll leave you to it." Axel turned to Heath. "Follow me. I have a separate room for you."

The door shut, enclosing her in silence. So far, this wasn't what she'd pictured when she'd thought of a BDSM club, and Thorpe certainly didn't seem like the sort of man to own one. But this room felt comfortable, so she relaxed and dialed her aunt. The woman's voice mail picked up. *Unusual.*

With a frown, Mystery hung up without leaving a message. What if the danger had somehow already reached Aunt Gail?

A moment later, she heard a knock, then Axel breezed in, carting her luggage. Every muscle of his arms and shoulders bulged, the veins in his hands and forearms popping. Mystery's mouth suddenly felt dry.

"Everything all right?" he asked, setting her bags down.

Mystery managed to string her thoughts together enough to explain the call. "Maybe I'm paranoid. Maybe my aunt is still at Bible study."

"We have no reason to suspect she's in danger. Relax. You're safe here. And your aunt is probably fine, too."

She sincerely hoped so. "Thanks."

"Let's go eat. I'll give you a quick tour. Then . . . we're going to talk."

About earlier today. He didn't say that, but she heard it in his voice, in the disapproval lacing his tone. Before she could broach the subject, he left the room. She followed, watching him pound a fist on the door of the room next to hers.

Heath wrenched the door open. "What is it?"

"Italian food?"

"Please." He sounded less stiff—barely.

Ten minutes later, the three of them sat in the small kitchen, forking in lasagna and salad with a decent bottle of wine. Axel chugged back a beer, watching them carefully.

"So what's next?" she asked to break the uncomfortable silence.

"Thorpe put a call into some friends of his, the Santiago brothers."

Mystery blinked. "The guys who own the defense contracting business?"

"Yeah. Them." Axel nodded. "They're happy to let us borrow their corporate jet. Their wife, London, just gave birth to a little girl a few days ago, so they won't need the plane for a while."

"*Their* wife?" Heath asked.

Axel scowled. "Yeah. Don't judge. It's not what my ideal marriage looks like, but it works well for them."

"Sounds like Callie, Thorpe, and Sean share a similar relationship?" she ventured.

"They aren't public about it, but yeah. And now they're expecting a baby in November. It's good to see them happy, but all kinds walk through our doors. Hell, we once had a member who bought a mannequin at a department store closing because, according to him, it held the soul of the love of his life—and his perfect sub." Axel shrugged. "As long as it's legal and consensual, whatever floats your boat, I say."

Mystery snickered. "But a mannequin is kind of funny."

The conversation dropped away again. The silence grew thicker with each passing moment. Heath stared at Axel with thinly disguised distaste. Axel glared back.

Desperate to end this tension, she pushed her half-eaten meal away. "How about that tour?"

Axel glanced at his plate, then at her face. He rose and held out his hand. "Let's do it."

She laced her fingers with his, allowing him to lead her down a long hall. Heath followed, silent and seething. She wished he would go back to his room if he didn't want to peek into the part of the club where people played, but he kept on behind them, seemingly determined not to let her out of his sight for longer than he must.

With a swipe of a key card, Axel opened a heavy door and gestured her into a darkened room. He flipped on a few switches, and the space illuminated in sections. A bar to the right, a few tables beyond, then a front door and foyer about fifty feet in front of her. So far, she didn't see much out of the ordinary, just an industrial-looking hangout.

He hesitated, then flipped the last switch. Then the view got really interesting. She knew what most of the items were called from pictures and descriptions, but she'd never seen a spanking bench or a St. Andrew's Cross in person. She could just imagine Axel cuffing her to a piece of equipment and touching her, giving her both pain and pleasure. Of course anytime he touched her she melted, but imagining him sending her into the intriguing void of subspace made her shiver.

"Wow," she breathed, squirming as her imagination went wild. "I'm a little . . ."

"Speechless," he teased.

She laughed. "Obviously."

"Intrigued?" he asked—and seemed to hold his breath.

Because her opinion on the subject mattered?

"Yeah," she admitted with a flush. "After you said you were into

BDSM when we were in the desert, I looked into it. So intrigued is a good way to put it."

He squeezed her hand. "I like that answer." He leaned down to whisper in her ear. "I'd love to give you a more personal tour."

Behind them, Heath cleared his throat. "Escape routes?"

Axel gritted his teeth and turned. "Front and back entrance. There's a side door from the kitchen you probably noticed."

"I did," Heath assured.

"A few interior doors in the building are steel and lock from both inside and out. Thorpe's office, for one. The bedroom you're in, Mystery. If something happens or you feel threatened, and no one you trust can get to you, throw the dead bolt from the inside and call the police."

She nodded. "Got it."

"But we'll see someone coming long before then. I've got cams all over the parking lot, covering the street out front, and the alley beside us. No one can even reach the door without appearing on film."

"Thank you for the explanation," Heath said stiffly.

"You're welcome. Now if you don't mind, Mystery and I have some unfinished business."

Heath squared his shoulders. "Actually, I do mind. I'm her bodyguard, and I stay with her until she's ready to retire for the night."

Mystery really didn't know why Heath was being somewhere between a stick-in-the-mud and an ass. She'd always found him polite and accepting and easy to talk to—until today.

Was he . . . jealous?

When he took her by the arm and led her down the hall, just out of Axel's earshot, she gaped at him. "What is up with you?"

"Have you gone mad?" Heath hissed, then glanced back over his shoulder at Axel. With legs planted wide and fists on his hips, he looked utterly unyielding. "Do you know the terrible things he wants to do to you? Tie you up."

Imagining herself strapped to Axel's bed, helpless as he spread her legs and did anything and everything he wanted to her . . . Her breath caught. Would he make her beg? Spank her until the rest of the world melted away? Force orgasms on her? Demand she kneel before him and suck his cock?

Desire, thick and hot, rolled through her.

Heath looked down at her breasts. Mystery followed suit and found her insistent nipples stabbing the front of her shirt.

Flustered, she crossed her arms over her chest and concealed them. "I'm an adult. I know what I want from a lover. Not that it's any of your business."

"Your father made it my business. Do you really want a man who will paddle your butt like you're a child? Who will discipline you? What if he's the sort who likes needles or knives or to control your breath?"

Mystery recoiled. "Ohmigod, what are you . . . No. That's not—"

"I've seen the seedy side of the underworld. Normally, I'm a gentleman and I don't speak of such things, but I'm concerned for you. Have you fallen for him so hard that you'd allow him to whip you until you bleed? Give you to a stranger?"

She shook her head. "He would never hurt me or put me at risk. I'd insist on a safe word, but I'm sure he'd ask me for one first. I know you don't know him. But I do. He rescued me. We survived together. I've had a thing for him ever since. Please don't get in the middle of this."

Heath sidled closer, his expression a cross between incredulity and anger. "A thing for him? You've known him a total of three days, and you trust him enough to give him complete control of your body?"

When he put it like that, the concept sounded ridiculous. But her gut told her Axel wasn't the sort of Dom Heath described. She couldn't picture him as a sadist. Besides, she'd heard that people in a D/s relationship should discuss their limits with each other and negotiate what happened in a scene before they got too busy. Axel was responsible. That's what he would do.

"Actually, I do."

Heath gripped her arm and loomed over her, shaking his head. "You don't understand what you're inviting. I did a turn undercover in a club in London, and the things I saw . . ."

"Problem, Mystery?" Axel sauntered down the hall with a practiced nonchalance. But every muscle in his body looked tense.

Heath turned and stepped forward, putting himself between her and Axel. "I object."

"I don't give a shit," Axel shot back.

"Her father would not approve." Heath crossed his arms over his chest.

Mortification rolled through Mystery. "My father still wishes I wore ribbons in my pigtails, too. He doesn't always get his way where I'm concerned. I don't think we have anything left to say on this subject. Good night." She stepped around Heath and approached Axel.

He took her hand in his. "Let's go."

Axel led her back to her bedroom, and she tried to ignore Heath sputtering behind her. She didn't like to upset or hurt him. He'd been nothing but protective and supportive for years. But tonight, he'd crossed a line.

Once inside the bedroom, Axel shut the door and dead-bolted it for good measure. "Are you all right?"

"Sure." But Heath's words rang in her ears. "He's just protective. It's his job."

"And he thinks I'm going to hurt you."

She shrugged. "He doesn't know you."

Axel sat on the edge of the bed. "Well, you and I have some catching up to do as well. We need to get a few things straight."

He'd dropped just enough disapproval into his tone to make her tummy tighten. Mystery tried not to notice that her palms suddenly turned damp. "I know. I explained and said I was sorry, but . . ."

"You did." He nodded. "I understood and appreciated that. But that doesn't make everything all right."

Axel looked calm. He almost always wore an impenetrable ve-
neer of calm, like nothing really got to him. Now, she saw a chink in
that—and got the feeling he'd been holding this rebuke in for hours,
just waiting for the chance to make his point.

She thought about backing up a step. "I didn't think so, I just . . ."
He motioned her closer.

Mystery shuffled forward. She wasn't afraid of him physically,
but he definitely had the power to hurt her with his words.

"You really think it's all right to deceive someone in order to
have sex with them? If our roles had been reversed, and I'd pretended to be someone I wasn't so that I could wheedle my way into
your bed, how would you feel?"

Confused. Used. Wretched.

Mystery winced. "You're right I guess . . . I figured if you were
saying yes to a stranger, did it really matter if I was a woman you'd
never met or one you'd known a long time ago? The point was to
exchange pleasure, which we did."

"But what if that wasn't the only point for me?"

He'd wanted something besides sex? "What else . . . ?"

"What if I'd let you pick me up in the bar because I thought you
were interesting, witty, and beautiful, and I'd hoped to use the evening
to get to know you more, maybe see if we could start a relationship?"

"That never crossed my mind. I'm sorry." Guilt lashed her. "I
thought I'd spend a few hours with you and get you out of my system
so I could move on because I'd never forgotten you. I've never, ever
wanted anyone else so badly." When he raised a sharp brow, she
looked down, feeling chastened. "I didn't think you wanted me so I
tried to be someone else, thinking we'd both get what we wanted
and . . . then we'd be done."

"You made a whole lot of assumptions, little girl. I never wanted
you?"

"You turned me down," she pointed out, her voice rising as her
guilt did. "What else was I supposed to think?"

"That I was trying to be responsible and respectful of you after what you'd been through. Did you think I wanted you this afternoon?"

"Yes." Together, they'd been incendiary, insatiable, unstoppable. She'd never imagined sex being that intense, ever feeling so much pleasure.

"Damn straight," he reiterated. "I wanted you that much in the desert years ago. It took every ounce of my restraint to walk away from you that night in the ghost town. I'm sorry if my rebuff was harsher than it needed to be. But I knew if I didn't eliminate the tequila and ensure you didn't tempt me again, you wouldn't stop until I was balls deep inside you, right?"

Mystery wished she could refute him, but no. She'd been so happy to be alive another day. She'd been so grateful to him for making that happen. Her hero worship, the booze, his incredible body and spirit . . . She'd been so drawn to him. He'd done about the only thing possible in that scenario to stop the inevitable.

"Maybe if you had kissed me and said that, later—"

"When I kissed you after the chopper crash, I barely managed to stop myself from laying you down in the sand and fucking you. I knew if I kissed you again at that old hotel, I wouldn't be able to stop. You needed comfort, not sex, and I didn't have a single condom with me."

Birth control hadn't even crossed her mind that night. How stupid and irresponsible did that realization make her feel?

"And I didn't look you up later because I knew you'd be going through some PTSD," he continued. "You needed time to recover and readjust, to finish growing up." He looked between his feet. "Being totally honest, I worried that your attraction to me wouldn't hold up in the real world. Even if your father had let you date me— which I highly doubt—once you returned home, you had a glitzy world at your fingertips, and I didn't fit in. What the fuck do I know about designer labels or country clubs?"

"I don't care about that crap." Why did he imagine that mattered at all?

He shrugged. "Maybe not, but I didn't see us working, so I backed away. I never forgot you, but I was doing all right. Until you seduced me and took my sanity from me."

God, she'd had no idea he'd given them even half that much thought. Mystery slumped her shoulders, looking around for a chair. There really wasn't one close to Axel. She needed to curl up, think this through, maybe have a righteous little cry about how badly she'd screwed this up.

"Wherever you think you're going, no. Come closer." He waved her near.

She owed it to him to comply. After all, she'd royally muffed everything.

As she closed the distance between them, Axel wrapped his fingers around her wrist. "For the record, if you'd approached me as yourself today, I would have jumped all over you. See, what you felt back then—the breathless attraction, the inexplicable pull, the undeniable attachment—I felt them, too. If you'd come to me today and asked me to be your friend, your lover, your whatever, I would have said yes. Even with the disguise, I was already fascinated by you. I was already thinking beyond the sex. The man in me didn't like that you'd deceived me or run out."

"I know." God, she felt stupid and small. "I'm sorry."

He put a finger under her chin and lifted her gaze back to him. "You understand what I've said?"

"Yes. I never meant to hurt you."

He nodded. "Now that you understand how the man in me reacted, let's talk about what you don't understand. Let's discuss how the Dom in me reacted." He pointed to his thighs. "Put yourself over my lap. Now."

Chapter Ten

SOON he'd take this choking chain off its leash. Now he'd find out if all the submissive signals Mystery had been putting out were real. Nearly everything else about her fit him perfectly. Damn it if he didn't want their kinks to match, too.

"What?" She blinked at him, her stare bouncing from his face to his thighs and back.

"Did you *not* hear me?"

"I think I did, but—"

"Is there any part of the instruction you don't understand?"

Her stare fell to his lap again, and she couldn't possibly miss the eyeful of hard cock there under his jeans. He adjusted himself, trying to find a position that didn't strangle his erection, then patted his thigh.

She frowned. "Like lie across . . ."

"Face down, ass in the air. Yes."

"Oh." Still, she hesitated, as if she tried to make sense of his command in her head.

"Questions? Problems?"

"I don't know." She shifted nervously. "I've never done this."

But Axel suspected the idea turned her on. She sounded breathless. She fidgeted. Her nipples looked hard again. She stared, lips parted, sucking in a raspy draught of air.

His cock stiffened even more.

"There's a first time for everything, Mystery. Somehow, I doubt it will be our last. You've got three seconds, or I'm adding a count of ten."

Which wouldn't hurt his feelings in the least. He knew exactly how beautiful her ass was. Having the opportunity to touch it again, this time to spank and discipline it? Fuck, yeah.

Mystery scrambled toward him, casting another uncertain gaze his way, before she lowered herself awkwardly over his thighs. She towered over an average girl by six inches or so, but he still dwarfed her. Axel appreciated that folding long legs in an unfamiliar position wasn't easy, but he was beyond impatient to get this punishment rolling so they could get back to pleasure.

She wriggled and scooted, bracing herself to slide this way or that over his lap. Again and again, she brushed his sensitive cock. His body tightened, and he'd love to just fuck her every which way. But if he wanted any future with her, he had to set the expectation now.

Finally, he palmed her hips and stilled her, dragging in a long breath before he moved her body up a fraction, sending her long braid spilling, ends brushing the floor. "Don't move."

"A-all right."

"Nope. I expect a polite 'Yes, Axel' or 'Yes, Sir.' Either is acceptable." Later, he'd be more exacting, because if this relationship went where he wanted it to, she'd be calling him Master. For now, he simply waited, reaching down to give a gentle tug on her braid.

"Yes, Axel," she gasped.

"Better." He cast his gaze over her body, still except for her harsh breathing. The yoga pants she'd tossed on just before they'd left the hotel hugged the curves of her ass and lovingly outlined her thighs. Not a line or a bump marred the black cotton surface.

"You're not wearing underwear," he observed.

"No, Axel."

"Perfect." He dragged his fingers up the crease between her cheeks, and the fabric clung inside the crevice, stretching even tighter across her ass, further defining its shape. "Beautiful."

As Mystery splayed over his lap, he felt the rise and fall of her body, heard her long shuddering sigh. She lifted her butt to him, seeking more.

He smiled, then trailed his fingers from the crease of her backside toward her pussy. With barely a brush of his fingers over her cotton-covered folds, he realized she was damp. No, soaking wet. The longer he rubbed lazy circles over the mound of her cunt, the more her moisture wet his palm.

Mystery Mullins liked submitting. To him. That realization jacked up his desire, and Axel had to leash his need to fuck her, at least until he made a few things clear.

When she began to whimper and press her hips toward his playful fingers, he pulled away. "Does my touch feel good?"

"Yes, Axel." Her words were high-pitched, spoken somewhere on the cusp of orgasm.

"Good." He intended to have fun with her now. "Pull your pants down to the tops of your thighs."

Without hesitation, Mystery complied, loosening the tie at her waist and wriggling as she shoved the garment over her hips. When the waistband fell, exposing her gorgeous, perfect ass, Axel couldn't keep his hands off her. He palmed it instantly, kneading, pinching, and gripping it. She gasped and raised her butt, seeking more of his touch.

Oh, she was about to get it.

Axel raised his arm and slammed it down, hitting her bare ass with an unforgiving smack. "One."

She yelped, froze, then gasped and struggled to get away.

He pinned her with a heavy arm across her body. "Stay still."

"What are you doing?"

"You've heard of punishment, I presume." He rubbed his wide palm over her bronze backside, the same sun-kissed shade as her back. Knowing she sunbathed in the nude just turned him on more.

She moaned as he spread the heat under her skin. "Yes."

"To start, I'm going to make sure you understand I won't tolerate any more lies. I expect you to be honest with me from now on. Do you understand?"

"I didn't know how else to get close to you," she replied.

"So, in order to protect your feelings, you decided mine didn't matter?"

The starch went right out of her spine. "No."

"What I didn't know wouldn't hurt me?" he challenged.

"I guess I thought if you never knew . . . yeah." The contrite posture, without an ounce of fight, told him that she now grasped his point.

"I understand why you were afraid and uncertain. You could have tried to e-mail or call. I even have a Facebook account. Did it cross your mind to open a conversation, ask me if I was interested, and see what happened? I'm going to guess no because you'd already decided what my answer would be. Isn't that right?"

"Yes, Axel." She sobbed the words.

Sometimes, Mystery had so much moxie, he forgot she could be fragile. She'd been raised with privilege, but she'd also been through way more than her peers. He had to tread carefully as he reached her. She would only associate the pain of a harsh spanking with rejection. As soon as he'd finished making his point, he would start rebuilding her again.

Axel lifted his palm and struck her backside once more, watching her flesh give and bounce with his touch. More red bloomed across her cheeks, and he rubbed her skin to distribute the heat even more. "Two."

As she moaned, he smacked her again, more to keep her

attention and awaken the submissive inside her than to cause pain. "Three."

She squirmed on his lap. "That feels . . ."

"I know," he crooned. "Hold still, Mystery. No more manipulation. You will communicate openly and tell me even the painful truths." He spanked her other cheek. "Four." Then he waited for the impact to sink in.

She whimpered. "Axel . . ."

"Yes. I can give you more of that—and so many other sensations that will send your body soaring. I want to introduce you to a whole new realm of pleasure. You want that?" He stroked her from nape to ass, following the sleek line of her spine.

"More than anything," she rasped out.

"I want to give it to you. God knows, I've wanted to for years. I even hate to admit how long and how often I've taken a temporary withdrawal of you from my spank bank." He let his fingers drift between her thighs.

Despite the waistband, she managed to spread a bit wider, and he appreciated her effort to open herself for him by caressing her slick folds and skating his fingertips over her hard clit.

"That's so good," she gasped out.

"The way I'm touching you?"

"Yes." She grabbed his shin and rubbed her face against his calf, despite his jeans, as if she needed to touch him. "But also knowing you stroked yourself while thinking about me turns me on so much. I—I touched myself thinking about you, too."

He circled her clit again, bringing her closer to the edge of ecstasy. "That was beautifully honest. Let's have more of that between us, not lies or topping from the bottom."

Mystery didn't answer him. Her body language told Axel that desire rumbled through her body, thundered in her head, and clouded her hearing. He removed his fingers.

"No," she protested breathlessly.

"Yes. We're not done talking." He swatted her ass softly, delivering a blow that should sting sweetly. "That's five."

She jolted, but the whack did its job, bringing her back to attention.

Now he could say his piece. "You trying to force me to give you your way, removing my choices? That's unacceptable. I'm the Dom, so I'm in control. I can't be in any sort of relationship with someone who can't respect my needs. I'll always do my best to respect yours. I know right off the top of my head that you need affection, attention, and understanding. I'm sure you require more, and I'll find out what as we get to know each other more. I will always do my damnedest to satisfy you. But if you try to manipulate me like that again, it's a deal breaker. Do you understand?"

"Yes, Axel." She sounded almost solemn, and he hoped he'd actually reached her.

"Good." He helped her rise on unsteady legs between his feet and gripped her thighs to balance her. When he looked into her slightly dazed eyes, so yearning for approval, his heart clutched. "Kneel here."

He helped her down, and she wasn't graceful—not that he gave a shit now. She was willing and open and wanted more. Nothing else mattered.

Axel cupped her face and leaned in to kiss her, a gentle clasp of lips at first. But damn it, Mystery was so fucking sweet, and he'd been fantasizing of having her—as her—for way too long to hold back.

He parted her lips with a nudge of his own, and she acquiesced instantly, rolling out the welcome mat with an enthusiastic passion that made his desire skyrocket and tilted his world on end.

Jerking away, Axel looked down at her, his stare following the trail of her body, her rosy lips, the little bites on her neck, the T-shirt stretched just a bit too tight across her breasts, then the pants banding around her thighs with that sweet bare pussy almost hidden between.

He grabbed her chin and looked right into her eyes. "I'm going to fuck you."

His words made her jerk as if they'd impacted her chest. "Yes, Axel."

"It wasn't a question. And I wasn't asking for permission. I'm telling you what will happen, unless you're giving me your safe word. That clear?"

"Very."

"Good. Do you have a word in mind?"

"I—I don't know. I've never . . ." She shrugged, looking a little lost. "What's your recommendation?"

"Let's use the traffic light system for now. It's something you'll remember." He gave her a wry grin. "I want to try a million perverse acts on you and watch you respond. If I'm hurting you too much or doing something you absolutely don't want, call 'red.' If I'm approaching the edge of your comfort zone, say 'yellow.' Make sense?"

She nodded, looking at him with eager eyes that glowed green and needy. Knowing he'd put that expression on her face revved him up even more.

As much as Axel wanted to tear through her clothes and shove his cock into her now, he forced himself to take a breath. Much like that first kiss she'd pressed onto his lips, their initial sexual encounter didn't really count because he hadn't known that he'd been touching Mystery. And she hadn't felt the way he would make her body *his*.

He intended to change that.

"Do you know any of your limits, hard or soft?"

A relieved smile flitted across her face. "I told Heath you were responsible and would ask. He wouldn't listen to me. Instead, he suggested you'd whip me until I bled or make me sleep with a stranger . . ." She shook her head, her aversion to either of those possibilities clear. "Just no."

"I don't know where the hell he heard that, but rest easy. Neither of those are in my wheelhouse. In fact, I'd go so far to say they're a hard limit for me."

The relief in her expression deepened. "He said he saw those things during an undercover mission in London."

He raised a brow. "Not in a club with Dominion's reputation. Thorpe has strict rules and an even more stringent membership screening. Everything that happens here is both consensual and well supervised. Whatever Heath saw must have been in a private hard-core club. I like rough play now and then, but nothing like that."

She seemed to sigh with relief. "Good."

"So, any boundaries I need to respect? A soft limit is something that both scares and intrigues you. You're not sure you want to . . . but you're not sure you don't."

"I like bondage. I mean, I like the idea of it." She blushed pro-fusely. "I've never done it, but the thought of it turns me on."

"I like it, too. A lot. We'll definitely go there. What else?"

"The spanking was nice. Not so much the first smack, but the rest . . ." She gave him a dreamy smile, and he held in a chuckle. "I've seen a video with a Dom wielding a soft flogger on his sub's butt. That looked interesting. But I don't know how I feel about anal sex or exhibitionism or so many other things."

Because she'd never tried them out. If he had his way, they'd eliminate whoever threatened her, then he'd spend however long it took to become exactly the Dom and lover she needed.

"Floggers are fine," he said, then gave her a slow smile. "Anal? I love the hell out of it, but it's not for everyone. Exhibitionism doesn't appeal to me much, but I'm not against it, either. At the end of the day, I'm the kind of Dom who prefers to do one thing above all: get in your head and own you."

A visible tremor went through her body. Yeah, she wanted what he could give her. She sought the physical surrender, but she ached to yield her soul even more.

"You can do that, can't you?" Her voice shook as if the possibility aroused her terribly.

"Oh, little girl . . . I can do it so fast, you won't know what hit you or how to stop it, and you won't care because you'll have given every thought, along with your aching pussy, to me."

As he watched her breath catch again, her nipples bead tighter, Axel repressed a smile. The girl liked a dirty mouth. He'd give her that, too.

"I have a few other rules," he began, running a fingertip between her luscious breasts before cupping the weight of one in his palm and caressing it with his thumb.

She almost threw herself against his body, then seemed to remember he'd told her to assume this position and sat on her heels again. "Yes, Axel."

"You don't come until you're given permission. But unless I say otherwise, don't hold back your sighs, whimpers, pleas, or screams. They're mine, and I want them all."

"Yes, Axel." She shifted her hips from one side to the other.

Clearly, Mystery had a bad little habit of trying to ease her desire whenever she pleased.

He gripped her shoulders. "Hold still and stop trying to make your pussy throb less."

Instantly, she complied, but she bit her lip as if the ache was too overwhelming to ignore.

He stroked his fingers across her cheek, then wrapped them around her nape. "You think you're aroused and want me to fuck you now?" When she nodded, he smiled. "Just wait. I'll make you beg—with your mouth, those nervous hands you're wringing, your wide eyes. You'll offer yourself to me with your words, your pouting nipples, your spread legs. When you really know what it's like to need me to fuck you and you've begged sweetly, *then* I'll make you scream."

Mystery closed her eyes and dragged in a ragged breath. "I know you will. I think I've always known that."

Just like on some basic, elemental level, Axel had always known that she would not only torque up his desire but drive his Dominance to new heights and fascinate him completely.

"More beautiful honesty. Excellent."

She sent him a placid smile. It pleased her to please him. What would please him more was to have her naked. He could tell her to strip, but he wanted to unwrap her like a special gift.

Taking her braid in hand, he eased the elastic band from the ends and combed his fingers through her damp tresses. They spilled everywhere around her shoulders, brushed her waist, with soft curls that shined under the golden light from the ceiling fixture. Then he lifted the T-shirt from her curves. The stretchy knit skimmed her waist and caught on her heavy breasts.

As he pulled it over her head, she sat, spine straight, watching him raptly. Damn it, she wore another one of those frilly bras that short-circuited his brain completely. Her nipples were barely contained by the half cups. Only the upward curve of scalloped lace concealed them at all. They poked at the fabric, a deep rosy brown that had his mouth watering.

"You always have the sexiest lingerie," he breathed as he lifted her breast in his palm and dipped his thumb under the edge of the lace.

Her nipple jumped to even stiffer attention. "I like how feminine I feel when I wear it. And I like your reaction to it."

"That bra and panties I hand washed for you at the ghost town? As soon as I took them from the water and set them on the towel rack, I had to jack off. I knew if I didn't, I'd picture you wearing them and you'd be flat on your back with your legs spread for me."

Mystery closed her eyes. She fucking glowed with arousal. She wanted this, wanted him . . .

As badly as he yearned to pounce on her, Axel couldn't. He had to take her slowly, introduce her to some of the kinks he'd like to share with her, convince her without words that she'd be satisfied long, well, and often.

He reached behind her and unclasped the bra. Her breasts bounced free. Damn, he wanted those nipples in his mouth, wanted to know if a bite of pain would excite her.

"Up on your knees," he demanded.

Swallowing hard, she raised her butt from her heels. Her body strained toward him. Even her nipples pointed straight at him. Axel couldn't wait to give her everything she craved.

He wrapped his big hands around her torso. She looked so small comparatively. So soft and submissive. Spreading his legs wider to make room in between, he lifted her closer. Then he bent and kissed her lips, her jaw, dragging his mouth down her neck, then the swell of one breast.

"Offer them to me," he rasped out. "Lift them to me."

Her breath caught as she obeyed, cupping her mounds in her palms. They spilled over her smaller hands, but she brought the stiff tips closer to his mouth, and that's all he needed.

He latched onto one, sucking it deep and hard, giving it a little pinch with his teeth.

Mystery yelped, and Axel waited a breath, a heartbeat, then . . . There came that moan he wanted. From the startled note it held, he suspected the nip of pain had awakened her nipples with sensations she'd never felt.

She wrapped her hands around his head and held him close to her breast. He hadn't given her permission to touch him. He enjoyed her urgency and the closeness for a moment. Someday, he'd make love to Mystery softly and let her touch him at will. Today wasn't that day. Everything inside screamed not only to dominate but to claim her, to bind her to him with pleasure. Because he still didn't know if she would truly want him when the real world came calling again, when her father found out and the tabloids questioned why she was with a man who came from the backwoods, hadn't finished college, and often liked guns more than people. But maybe, if he gave Mystery more pleasure than she could manage, when the dust settled with whoever pursued her, none of that would matter.

Winding his grip around her wrist, he pulled her hands from his scalp and drilled her with a chastising stare. "I told you to offer them to me. Don't stop until I say otherwise."

She licked her lips, then lifted her breasts to him again. "Sorry. Yes, Axel."

Untrained, yes. But so beautifully compliant. He brushed a thumb down her still-wet tip, watching it bob and perk for him. He pinched it, teased it with the hint of his nail . . . and took in her pleading cry for more.

He held in a smile and shifted to her other nipple, stabbing the air and waiting for attention. Against his tongue, it puckered. Her breast swelled. Like a sweet sub, she kept presenting herself for his feasting. She offered. She welcomed. Yes, he'd told her to, but she could have safeworded out. Instead, she looked all too breathless and happy to comply.

He gave her a harder bite with his teeth while holding the other between his thumb and forefinger, squeezing and sliding the pad over her sensitive nub. She gasped, jolted. Barely a moment later, she gave him a long, low moan deep from her throat.

"You're processing the bite faster," he murmured with satisfaction. "So fucking pretty."

"I understand it better now. Having just a little edge is . . . lovely."

Yes, she was a sub to the core, and pride rolled through Axel. He fully intended to teach her about her body and flirt with her boundaries—then ease her past any that merely held her back.

"Mmm. Knowing you feel that way only makes me harder." He let out a rough sigh. "Stand and take off your shoes."

He helped her to her feet, then watched as she kicked off her flip-flops. He eased her pants the rest of the way down her thighs. As she stepped out of them, he cast her shoes aside and placed a soft, lingering kiss on the pad of her pussy.

"This is mine," he insisted in a soft, growled tone, brushing his knuckles across the smooth flesh just over her clit. "Isn't it?"

"Yes, Axel," she rushed to say.

"You know that. Good. I'm still going to prove that to you. Get on the bed. In the middle. Legs spread."

She made her way along the side of the bed, hips swaying, gorgeous ass on display, before crawling on the mattress. She glanced back at him—not in confusion or indecision. Her stare was all come-hither.

He chuckled. "Oh, you're inviting trouble now. I'm so going to fuck you, princess."

She rolled to her back and arched, breasts upthrust as she spread her legs. "Promise?"

Axel sauntered over and sat on the side of the bed, next to her. "You just keep tempting the devil. See what it gets you."

Mystery didn't reply, just watched him grab her wrists and lift them over her head. Since this used to be Thorpe's bedroom and he'd combed every inch of the place when Joaquin had been protecting Bailey here, Axel knew damn well all the kink features built in.

He hit a button, and out popped a pair of leather, sheepskin-lined cuffs from behind a panel. The chains holding them together rattled. She gasped.

He smiled as he buckled one around each wrist. "Tug on those."

She did, testing the restriction of her movement gently at first. Then she jerked a little harder. The more she thrashed against her bonds and realized she wasn't going anywhere, the shallower her breathing became. Her eyes rolled shut. Bliss transformed her face.

Axel's cock jerked so fucking hard he wondered if all the blood in his body had flooded south.

She moaned, tossing her head, seemingly lost in the pleasure of the binds themselves. What a damn pretty sight . . . But he couldn't let her get too far into her own head. He still had more to give her.

After he watched her for a long moment, he cupped her face in his hands. "Stop. Look at me." He waited for her to comply, then delved down into her slightly unfocused hazel eyes. "You're well and truly bound. Unless you say your safe word, you're not going anywhere until I release you."

Mystery whimpered and bucked her hips. Jesus, the girl loved being restrained. The pressure around her wrists would be a constant reminder that he was with her. At least that's how some subs described the sensation. For them, the cuffs served mentally as nonstop attention from their Dom, snug enough to feel like some sort of affection. Clearly, the bindings tripped an emotional trigger inside her.

Axel was damn grateful. He could think of a hundred ways to restrain her. But he'd start simple for now. He didn't know how much longer he could wait to feel her around him.

"Remember, no orgasms without permission."

"Yes, Axel." She said the words, but the begging tone told him she was already desperate and asking for one.

Not even close yet, princess . . .

"Don't forget. I want all your pleas, whimpers, groans, and screams. Be as loud as you need to. I'll drink every sound in." While hearing her would excite the hell out of Axel, it would also serve notice to her bodyguard and would-be lover in the bedroom next door that any hope he might have of making Mystery his was dead.

"Yes, Axel."

"Good. Now spread nice and wide for me. I want to see every bit of that pussy that's *mine*."

* * *

MYSTERY sucked in a sharp breath. Axel seemed to know exactly what to say to ratchet her arousal up yet another notch.

She slid her feet apart across the mattress, her toes unconsciously flexing, heels digging in at the thought of Axel keeping her captive here and just staring to his cock's content. Maybe she should have felt self-conscious or exposed or ashamed by how badly she wanted him, but no. She simply felt ready to combust.

"Pretty." He complimented her, dragging his palm up her calf, the outside of her thigh, her hip, then finally back to her breasts, his thumbs and fingers making a quick, ruthless vise around her nipples. When she cried out, he released her and eased back, scooting down the bed to hover over her sex. "I want to inspect this pussy. Open to me."

Mystery moaned and spread her thighs even wider, beyond eager to give him everything he demanded, anything that would make him want her tomorrow and the next day. And the next . . .

"You like being commanded in bed," Axel murmured, his voice low and thick. "We're going to get along great." He parted her folds with his thumbs, then drew in a long breath. "You smell so good. That night in the ghost town? I could smell you then, too. Drove me out of my fucking mind."

"Everything about you made me want you," she admitted breathlessly. "Everything. Your knowledge of the landscape, your kindness, your protectiveness . . . your sexiness. I remember thinking that, until you, I'd never met a *man*."

His ego probably puffed up at her words. His chest certainly did. Despite the hot need rolling through her veins, the sight warmed her heart.

"That's good to hear," he murmured. "I admit, I never quite figured if you wanted me because you had a bad case of hero worship or whether you saw beyond that."

"I did think you were my hero, but it's more. It always has been. It's like . . . we're in sync."

"We click," he agreed. "To me, you're gorgeous." He turned his attention back to her aching sex. "In every way. I knew when we met that you were a survivor. Despite your dad's wealth and fame, you're not spoiled or difficult. You're sunny and sweet and a little bit naughty. And look at you now, so ripe and rosy and pouting for attention."

Mystery struggled against her bonds. She didn't want out of them. Oddly, they made her feel secure, like she was anchored to him in some way and he'd never let her fall. But everything inside her yearned to invite him in deeper. Never in her life had she felt this need to give herself to a man. Her sexual past had consisted far more of pretty boys who didn't know much about giving an orgasm, much less getting in her head and fulfilling her fantasies. As with everything else, Axel was a whole new breed.

Since she couldn't tempt him with her actions, she fell back on words. "Spreading my legs for you is so arousing. Your stare almost feels like a touch. I remember every moment in your bed earlier today, the way you tasted me. I want you to take all of me. I'm dying to give you everything you want. I don't know how to make that happen or what to do or—"

"Sweetest sub," he praised. "You were stunning, but having you spread out for me this way"—he skated his thumb over her clit, making her jump and moan with desire—"I'm humbled. And I don't think I've ever wanted inside anyone as fucking much as I want you now."

She smiled. "You always know just what to say."

"I say what's on my mind. And right now, that's all about this."

Axel leaned in, peered closely at her pussy. The thought of him looking at her so intently made her need and squirm. And when he pulled her even farther apart with his thumbs, then leaned in closer, she lifted to him.

"Normally, I'd think you meant to coerce me to put my mouth on you. But you're giving yourself to me, aren't you?"

"Yes," she whispered. "I don't know how you sometimes read my mind, but I love that."

He placed the softest, almost chaste kiss right on her clit. That aroused her nearly as much as a hard pull. Without a word, he told her that he treasured her flesh, worshipped it. She melted.

"I loved getting my mouth on you this afternoon. And ever since I figured out who was in my bed, I've been desperate to feel your mouth on me." Axel crawled his way up her body. "Suck my cock, princess."

Mystery's heart stopped. God, she'd love to taste him, get her lips around that salty, manly, sizeable cock.

As he unzipped his pants and shoved his garments down to his hips, his erection sprang free. The length was impressive, but the girth . . . *Holy crap!* No wonder she'd felt so tightly stretched when he'd worked his way inside her. A tingle zapped her from head to toe at the thought of feeling it again.

Eagerly, she opened her mouth to him. He braced his big palm on the wall above the headboard and used the other to feed the huge head past her willing lips. She had to open wide and worried fleetingly that she didn't have enough experience to please him. But when her lips closed around him, they both groaned together. She stopped worrying.

"Jesus, princess. Yes. Deeper."

She strained her neck up, wanting to take more of him on her tongue. His flavor was clean and masculine. She smelled his natural musk wafting up, giving her an olfactory buzz that made her dizzy and wet. Well, wetter.

He pressed his hips forward, and his cock sank nearly to her throat. She tried to open even wider.

"So good," he praised, lifting her by the back of the head and cradling her neck in his hand.

Now she was immobile, at his mercy. Between his cuffs, his hold, and his big body, he controlled every move she made. She couldn't imagine anything turning her on more.

"I'm going to fuck that pretty mouth," he groaned.

Her stare tangled with his. The blue of his eyes had gone hot, electric. She whimpered out her need.

Axel drew back a few inches, then slowly pushed in again, deeper than before. The tip of her nose almost touched his belly. She wanted to work her head from side to side, suck more of him in, try to take every inch he had. But he had the control and he eased out of her mouth again. A deep, rumbling groan escaped from his chest. "Use your tongue."

In answer, she swirled it around the swelling head still perched past her lips. She licked over the pinnacle, found the sensitive spot just under his ridge, then licked the shaft in desperation.

"That's it. Oh, princess . . ." He fucked his way into her mouth again, establishing a brisk, soft rhythm. His eyes closed. His head dropped forward and ecstasy transformed his face.

For long moments, she simply tasted him, pleasured him. She'd never known how badly she longed to please a lover until Axel. Mystery suspected he could teach her a lot of things about her body and her sexuality. He'd already taught her so much about life.

"Damn . . . yes. You keep swiping the head with that wicked tongue, and it's killing me."

It thrilled Mystery to know that she could dismantle such a big bad man.

When he thrust in again, he plunged deeper still and nudged her throat. She did her best not to panic. She breathed through her nose, as one of her girlfriends who loved giving head had instructed, and relaxed her muscles there. Finally, the tip of her nose brushed his abdomen. She wrapped her lips around the base of his cock and sucked deep.

"Shit. Fuck. Son of a bitch!" He yanked from her mouth and dragged in deep, steadying breaths, clearly trying to bring himself under control.

Mystery couldn't help it. The devil sitting on her shoulder

prodded her, and his cock was just there in front of her, wet and purple and swollen. She peeked her tongue out and licked him like an ice cream cone.

His eyes flared open wide, gaze fixed on her, instantly sharp and predatory and just the slightest bit disapproving. "Trying to steal my control again?"

"No." *Maybe a little.* "I missed your flavor."

"But you wanted to take what I didn't intend to give you. You didn't have permission to drive me over the edge, but you still tried."

"I . . . didn't—"

"Think before you lie. Orgasm depravation is a terrible punishment. I can drive you so close to the edge again and again, then deny you for hours. Hell, I can do it for days. If you want to come again anytime soon, you'd better be honest."

Mystery didn't doubt him for a minute. He probably would drive her body to a clawing, aching need and suspend her there for as long as he pleased. He could likely control her body and her reactions, along with himself—in every way. That stirred her desire like mad.

"I wasn't trying to drive you to orgasm," she answered honestly. "But if I had, I would have liked it. I wanted to make you feel good, whether that was a little or a lot."

"I'll have to remember you're a giver." He smiled down at her as he released her neck, then brushed his fingers across her cheek, over her jaw. "You need that, don't you?"

She nodded frantically. "Yes, Axel."

Despite the fact that she ached and clenched and wriggled in need, Mystery still wanted to give Axel whatever would please him. Somewhere in her rational head, she realized that it sounded kind of backward to put her own pleasure on hold, especially since the guys she'd slept with in the past had been of the mind that everyone was responsible for getting their own orgasms during sex. Again, Axel was totally different.

He scrambled off the bed, kicking off his pants as he went, then tore into the drawer of the nightstand, fumbling around until he found an unopened box. He ripped into it, tearing off the entire side of the cardboard to grab one of the foil squares. With his teeth, he yanked off the top of the packet, then rolled the condom down his stiff length as if his life depended on it.

Less than a heartbeat later, he lowered himself on top of her, elbows on either side of her head, and took her lips with his, using them to spread her mouth wide for his kiss. He invited himself inside, his tongue delving, capturing. He invaded her everywhere, and she felt saturated by his scent, consumed by his passion.

Mystery arched up to him, trying to get closer. She was beyond realizing that Axel stirred and excited her unlike any other man. That train had left the station years ago. But somehow, every time he touched her, he reminded her all over again.

As he pushed his fingers into her hair, he gripped the strands in his fist, tilting her head to deepen the kiss. At the same time, he probed her aching sex with his erection, a rhythmic seeking against her slick tissue until he found the spot he sought and began a relentless press forward.

The slide in felt a little easier than it had this afternoon, despite her lingering soreness. As he surged forward, she stretched around his girth, working to accommodate him and losing herself in the delicious burn. He filled her completely. Her flesh stung and tingled as he withdrew slightly and surged deeper—over and over.

Every ruthless thrust should have been uncomfortable, but instead the feel of him forcing her to take every inch had euphoria clouding her head like a drug. She welcomed it—and him—wholeheartedly.

With a whimper, she tilted her hips up in offering. He slid his hands under her ass and gripped tightly. Every fingertip pressed into the flesh of her backside, and he used his strength to yank her onto his cock as if he couldn't wait another second for her to take him all the way to the hilt. He tossed his head back with a low, rumbling groan.

The force of his next drive into her had her gasping with a pleasure-pain she'd never felt. She wanted to hold him in her arms, but they were bound. She wanted to throw her legs around him, but he held her exactly where he wanted her and unleashed a hard, pounding rhythm that had her whimpering, then moaning, then calling his name.

Every thrust of his cock rubbed against sensitive tissue along the front wall of her sex. He doubled the tingles with every lunge inside her as his pelvis rubbed her clit. The sensations climbed. She pressed her fingernails into her palms, tossed her head back, and keened.

Mystery felt herself spinning away, the absolute pleasure overtaking her body, her brain. She tightened on him, throwing her whole body and heart into his kiss as black spots danced behind her eyes.

"You want to come?" he growled. "For me? Right now?"

"Yes. Please . . ." She nodded frantically. "Yes!"

He ramped up his hard surges into her body, the headboard pounding the wall every time he slammed inside her. Above her, his eyes had gone a sexy shade of midnight blue. He stared at her intently, knowing he held the power to grant her orgasm . . . or take it away. She waited, breath held, dissolving for him.

"Beg me more. I'm not convinced you want it enough yet."

Chapter Eleven

He'd barely finished speaking when he drove deep in her pussy again, setting off a chain reaction of tingles. Climax was right there, just waiting for him to give her that perfect touch. Axel withheld it, studying her, watching, waiting.

Mystery quivered around his cock, her flesh constricting tightly. With a low groan, he plunged harder, shoved his way deeper. Sweat beaded at his temples. Moisture coated the bulges of his shoulders. She felt as if he'd stretched the muscles of her inner thighs to their breaking point and knew she'd be sore as hell in a few hours. But she didn't care. She just wanted more.

"Please . . ." she cried out. "I need it. I need you, Axel. I can't take much more."

"That's a little better. I might let you. Sooner, if you're louder."

Louder? Did he want her to shout the building down? She jerked against the restraints and writhed as much as his big body on top of her allowed. "I don't know what to do or say. It's overwhelming and I'm desperate. What else do you want to hear? Please . . ."

"You're getting there. Let me see if I can help you along." Axel hesitated and flung himself off the bed, rummaging around in the nightstand again.

"What are you doing?" Didn't he know she was on fire over here?

"Looking for just the right thing to blow your mind. Here we go." The smile that crossed his square, so-male face made her heart skip a few beats. It dripped sin, promised to push her.

"Hurry," she breathed. "Pretty please. I really need to—"

"Oh, you will." He palmed something and shut the drawer, then shoved whatever had been in his hand under the pillow. "Turn over." He helped her onto her stomach, the chain holding her cuffs together crossing near their hook in the wall. "On your hands and knees."

As he clasped her hips and helped her up, Mystery adjusted herself on the mattress. His stare heated her back. She felt so vulnerable as he grabbed the item from under the pillow, hiding it in his palm again, then positioned himself behind her, planting his knees between hers and spreading them wider.

"You ever been taken from behind?"

Mystery searched her memory, but he'd fried it. "Maybe once or twice. I don't remember."

"So you don't know if you liked it?"

"Well, sex in general never wowed me before you."

"That's beautifully honest. I definitely want to make sure you continue to feel that way, princess."

She heard what sounded like a plastic cap popping open, followed by a squishy noise. He closed the top in place again, and she felt a gentle plop as he tossed the object across the bed. Something drizzled along the small of her back, liquid and slightly warm before it trickled down into the crease between her cheeks.

With a yelp, Mystery raised her ass and tried to lean her torso forward and send the liquid running in the other direction and off the sheets.

Axel wrapped his arm around her waist and pulled her back up. "Don't move."

Her rational brain wanted to argue that they were going to make a mess, but the commanding note in his tone silenced her. She closed her eyes, refocused, breathed.

"Good. The way you understood me instantly and complied turns me the fuck on."

Mystery sincerely hoped that meant that he intended to fit his wide cock against her empty, weeping opening and fill her until he released her to orgasm. If not, she wasn't above begging him again.

For now, she settled for wriggling her hips in what she hoped was an enticing sway.

He palmed one of her cheeks, chuckling. "Believe me, I'm fully aware of your gorgeous ass right in front of me. I could stare at it all day."

Please don't just look. Do something!

"But at the moment, I'd rather fuck you more and hear how well you can beg."

What more did he want her to say? She'd blurted her feelings and added more than one please. She'd told him that she was desperate for the pleasure. What else could she give him?

He answered that question quickly, bending over her body and feeding his cock inside her again. This time, he slid in slowly, easing one molasses inch at a time into her clenching pussy.

"That's it," he crooned. "It's so good."

As he filled her to the hilt, she sucked in a sharp breath. In this position, he felt even bigger, plumbed even farther inside her. His size overwhelmed her, the stretch even more of a burn.

Axel pulled back, nearly withdrawing from her until he surged inside again, a little harder, a little faster. He repeated the process a few times, picking up the tempo and the drive with every thrust.

Mystery closed her eyes and drank the sensations in. She'd loved having him on top of her, but in this position, she felt taken, like his to use at will. Somehow he also made her feel as if he needed her more than he wanted her, and every thrust, grunt, and groan told her he wanted her with a desperation that blindsided and shocked her.

"Axel . . ."

"Yeah, princess. Tell me."

"Oh, god," she panted. "Every time you enter me, you rub something inside me way deep."

"I do." His voice sounded rough, like gravel. "I feel every fucking inch of you."

To prove his point, he sank all the way in again, his balls gently slapping her slick folds, then he gyrated against her spot, prodding, poking, driving her out of her damn mind.

"Yes. There. Oh, right there. That's . . ." She couldn't manage more than a groan.

"Oh, yeah. I know it's right there. You're closing around me. So tight. So fucking sweet. But I need more. I need to touch all of you."

Mystery couldn't fathom what he meant until he brushed his fingertips across the small of her back, spreading the moisture he'd poured onto her skin earlier all around. It was some sort of oil. She could feel it lubricating her now, running into the crevice between her cheeks, pooling around her back entrance.

His thumb joined the fray, sweeping up and down that fissure before circling the opening no one had ever touched.

When she clenched, Axel pried his fingers into the shadowy cleft of her ass and pulled the two halves apart. "Mine." He growled the word, an animalistic sound from the depths of his chest. "All of you. Mine."

The part of her brain that functioned now realized how caveman and possessive he sounded. The woman inside her approved. Her pussy suddenly pulsed. She tossed her hips back at him as he thrust, helping him spear her even more completely.

When he dredged that spot again and he inserted his thumb in her back opening, the sparks lighting up her sex converged with the new ones he'd just introduced. Climax sat right there, so damn close she could just cry for it. One more teeny-tiny sensation would send her tumbling into an abyss unlike anything else. Her vision closed up.

"Axel. Oh . . . my . . ." She couldn't even form the rest of the sentence. Instead, she tossed her head back and wailed. Her voice sounded high-pitched and desperate and rife with the pain of unfulfilled need. She clawed the sheets, sucked in a breath, and thrashed on his cock.

He withdrew so slowly, Mystery swore she would lose every shred of sanity. But when he hurtled his way back in, tunneling past each sensitive spot, she screamed at the top of her lungs.

"Please. Fuck. Me. Yes . . ." She gasped in a breath. "Now. I need it! So . . . good."

"So fucking good," he agreed. "Come for me!"

He plunged inside her again, urgent and fierce, his thumb sliding all the way inside her ass. The sensations coiled just behind her clit. The tingles, the heaviness, the desperate ache all melded together in a dizzy, crazy, sublime euphoria that tightened and gathered before exploding through her limbs, lacing every vein, utterly filling her. Arching to him and clawing at the bed, she screamed, the sound shrill and loud and lasting seemingly forever. So did her orgasm.

God, she never felt anything remotely like this climax that turned her body inside out, dismantled her brain, destroyed her defenses.

When her breath ran out, the ecstasy still pulsed and twitched inside her, battering her like the tide against the rocks of the shore—constantly and without mercy. Mystery had only thought she and Axel had shared combustive sex earlier today. Now? Holy crap, would she even be the same woman after this mind-bending bliss?

Behind her, Axel's grip tightened. He swelled even more inside her, scraping her sensitive flesh once more and prodding a spot that had her crying out again. The headboard banged the wall harder, faster.

And behind her, he leaned over her body and breathed into her ear. "Oh . . . Fuck me, princess." He groaned, the sound vibrating through her oversensitive body. "I'm coming!"

She gave him a warbled little moan as he picked up the speed of his thrusts, bit into her neck, then snarled out his satisfaction in long, plowing strokes. She spiked into another sharp peak.

Timeless moments later, she tumbled down into a soft cloud of satisfaction. Except for the sound of their harsh panting, silence prevailed. The headboard stilled. Axel stopped. Mystery melted into the mattress, her arms and legs giving out under her.

He went down with her, collapsing on top of her in a heap of limbs as he petted her hip absently, as if silently apologizing for crushing her underneath him.

"What happened?" She really didn't know. Her body still pulsed, pinged, and glowed. But right now, she absolutely didn't have a brain.

"Holy fuck." He groaned as he raised himself off her smaller body and let out an exhausted breath. "That was mind-blowing."

Understatement of all time. That had been more than sex, more than two people exchanging pleasure. They'd flowed together, melded, fused somehow. Mystery hadn't ever been in love. She'd always known she had a crush—maybe more—on Axel, but she'd never imagined that she'd fallen for him completely and irrevocably.

That probably explained why she'd never been able to muster more than passing interest for another guy and why she'd so often avoided sex or emotional intimacies. When men had wanted to get to know her, she'd suggested loud clubs and public settings to make that impossible. She'd appreciated having company and often gravitated to dates who would make her laugh. At the time, she'd thought she merely liked guys with a sense of humor. Now she suspected it was because they hadn't been serious about her, either.

How had less than an hour in bed with a man she hadn't seen in years been the most revealing, intimate exchange of her entire life?

Mystery didn't have answers, and emotions she'd been stomping down and burying bubbled to her surface. She burst into tears—and not dainty little sniffling cries. Of course not. These were giant, loud blubbering sobs. The total embarrassment only made her cry harder.

Axel eased out of her well-used body and rolled to her side, taking her in his arms. "It's all right, princess. I'm here. I know. It was big. Powerful. Look at me."

She squeezed her eyes shut, fighting him. He'd only see the love in her eyes. He'd see how badly she wanted to do things that had likely never crossed his mind, like wearing his ring and having his babies and going into debt for a dream house together. Lord, she was so pathetic.

He caressed her back, big sweeps of his palm comforting her and promising more. "Look at me."

Mystery tried to school her features and crack one eye open at him. Understanding lit his blue eyes. Sweat dampened his hair, and he looked spent. But happy. A smile broke out across his face. She answered in kind, even as tears ran down her cheeks.

"I've got you," he vowed. "Hold on to me."

She sniffled and pressed her face to his chest, absorbing his strength and the sense of belonging to him. He kissed the top of her head, rubbed absently at her back. Mystery allowed herself to sink into the lethargy, the sated peace.

"You surprised by how good we are together?" he asked.

Her lids fluttered shut as she fitted herself even more tightly against his big chest. "Yes . . . but mostly no."

She felt him smile above her, and he held her closer. "I'm not surprised much, either."

"It's weird. I don't know you fantastically well, but I feel like I know you deep down, if that makes any sense."

"It does. I understood you from the beginning."

He had, she realized. "Exactly."

Axel stroked her hair, and Mystery floated in a bubble of peace, liberally laced with happiness. They'd found something wonderful. Maybe it was chemistry. Maybe it had been love at first sight . . . delayed by six and a half years. She wasn't sure. But she knew that she couldn't wait to find out what happened next. It sucked that someone felt compelled to chase and threaten her, but that had brought them together—twice. Things happened for a reason, at least to her way of thinking. Maybe all this grief was meant to be because she and Axel were meant to be.

One step at a time.

"Anything hurt? Sore?" he murmured.

"Beside the obvious?" she winced, then laughed. "Not sure how well I'll be walking tomorrow, but at least I'll be smiling."

"I'm hoping so. I'm also hoping that tomorrow I'll be inside that sweet pussy again. Maybe even sooner."

Even if she was tender, that sounded great to her. "I won't complain."

He laughed, then eased off the bed. Mystery lay in a dreamy haze, staring at the ceiling, wearing what was probably a stupid smile. And she didn't care.

She heard the shower in the adjoining bathroom cut on. A spray of water hit the tile. He flipped on a harsh overhead light, dimmed it to something soft, then prowled toward her in all his big, masculine glory, minus the condom. He looked so amazing naked that she could barely remember her name.

When he reached her side, Axel uncuffed her before he wrapped an arm around her waist. Sluggishly, Mystery got to her feet and let him lead her to the bathroom. Steam now fogged the edges of the mirror, and heat rose from the sleekly tiled shower big enough for five. He opened the heavy glass door, and she entered the stall, moaning as soon as the warm spray hit her chest. Axel slipped in behind her, wrapping his arms around her waist and kissing her shoulder.

"If you don't force me to stop touching you, I may not be responsible for what happens next," he warned.

"Force you?" She giggled at him. "How would I ever do that? And why?

Axel would never cross a line with any woman. Mystery knew that personally. He'd make damn sure he had consent before he touched her. She was just so euphoric that he'd finally chosen her.

From a nearby soap dish, he grabbed a bar and lathered it in his big hands. "Hold up your hair."

She did as he asked, and he rewarded her, gliding his wide, soapy palms over her shoulders, back, hips. He bent to wash her feet, her legs, her ass, all the while kneading and rubbing at any knots of tension.

Mystery moaned. Was Axel just the perfect man? Hmm, no one was absolutely perfect. But he was perfect for *her*. Vaguely, she wondered what she'd tell her father about them when they talked next. He'd known years ago that she had a crush on Axel. She wondered if her dad would be surprised that nothing had changed.

"By the way, any worries that my father would care where you came from? Empty. Now, if you let him, he might ask you how to make his films about soldiers and war more realistic, but he's already got a soft spot for you because you saved me once."

"Rinse," he demanded softly, not commenting.

She did as he'd bid. "It's true. You know, he set up a college fund for Alvarez's son. He paid for the extras the government didn't provide for the burials of both your friends who died that day."

"He tried to give me an obscene amount of money, too." He grimaced. "I turned it down."

Mystery knew it would sound crazy to most, and few men would have made that choice. But that summed up Axel. Her heart constricted. Oh, yeah. This was love. It had come hard, felt sappy and drugging—and she loved every minute.

She turned and stood on her tiptoes to kiss him. "If I'm happy, he's happy."

He paused, then began soaping his wide, bulging chest. She followed his movements with her hungry stare. It seemed impossible that she could want him again when she felt this wrung out and more than a little sore. How could she ache to feel him inside her again already?

After he worked a good lather onto his torso, arms, and neck, Axel set the soap aside. That devil on her shoulder started riding her again, and she picked up the white bar. Once she'd soaped up her hands, she reached down and cupped his balls, then began working her way up.

Almost instantly, his cock rose to attention, the shaft filling, the head rising. Mystery watched in fascination, a shiver running through her as Axel groaned.

"Princess, you're inviting trouble."

"What a shame," she teased, batting her lashes his way.

He drilled his gaze down at her, his blue eyes turning hot and dark. He braced one palm on the wall just above her head, caging her in the corner of the shower. But he didn't stop her from stroking his cock in long, slow drags.

His jaw tightened. His breathing turned rough. "I don't recommend this now."

She swiped her thumb across the sensitive head, delighting when he hissed in a breath through his teeth and stiffened even more in her hand. "Why is that?"

"Because I'm about to push you against that cold tile wall while I shove my cock inside your pussy and ride you hard. And I don't have a condom."

Mystery didn't hate the idea of playing with fire—at all. She sidled up to him and rubbed herself against his length, still gripping and stroking him. "Just a little more. Just for a moment."

Clearly, he hadn't expected her assent. Heath's voice rang in her head again, telling her that she didn't know Axel that well, but she blocked it out. Her bodyguard was wrong. *He* was the one who didn't know Axel. He didn't understand. Her heart did.

For a long moment, Axel stood frozen, simply letting her undulate against him, touch him at will. "You're trying to tempt me, princess."

She peered up at him with a smile. "Is it working? It didn't the first time I tried in that little ghost town, but I think—"

He snorted. "Oh, it worked then, too. One more of those fuck-me stares, and I probably would have worked my way inside you and never stopped."

"Really?" She blinked at him.

"Oh, yeah. I would have hated myself for it if I had."

"And now?" She licked her lips and dragged her fingers up the long length of his shaft again in a slow tease. "I'm not a girl anymore. I'm a woman who needs you."

His breath turned choppier. His shoulders tightened. A flush crawled up his face. "You understand you could get pregnant."

"Not the right time of the month. Besides . . . would it be the worst thing in the world?"

Axel gripped her wrist, stilling her stroking hand instantly. He came closer, crowding her even more. His chest flattened her breasts. His intent stare dug into her. "Be sure."

Mystery froze. He would really do it, knowing the risks? Axel wasn't the sort of man to walk away from his own child or the woman who had birthed it. "Is there some other reason I shouldn't want you naturally?"

He gave a sharp jerk of his head. "I'm clean."

She lifted on tiptoe and kissed his jaw. "I'm hungry for you."

Axel sawed in a long breath, on the fence, his fist tightening just a bit on her wrist. "Oh, I want you so bad."

The words had barely cleared his lips when he had her against the wall, her back stinging with the chill of the tile, and her legs in the crook of his elbows. His cock probed her swollen opening, and he sank in to the hilt in one vicious stroke.

Excitement seized her breath, made her heart race. Then he hit that sensitive place deep in her pussy. "Axel!"

His head fell back with a massive groan. "Oh, fuck. Yes. You have such a tight pussy, princess. I'm going to take it. It's mine, and I want to mark it."

Mystery couldn't catch her breath. "Now."

He pumped inside her, watching her breasts jiggle every time he slammed deep. A sense of being taken and owned steamrolled her, and it turned her on more than she'd ever imagined. Yes, she'd wanted to be closer to Axel. Her heart cried out for him. But her body certainly wanted its fair share of him, too.

When he dragged his length down her sensitive channel, then shoved back in again, she clawed his shoulders.

He rammed her, pummeling deep, baring his teeth and staring straight into her eyes. "That's it . . . Feel. Every. Inch. Of. Me." He punctuated each word with another thrust.

His strength, the force of every upward surge, ricocheted through her body. She cried out, her pleas echoing off the tile.

Her nerve endings were already so sensitive, so stimulated—yet miraculously ready for more. The scrape of his cock pushing up through her swollen tissue delivered tingles. As he withdrew, he left behind a terrible ache. Time slipped away, disappearing like the water down the drain. Mystery simply let herself feel as he worked, grunting and flexing, to deliver the orgasm brewing right behind her clit.

She tightened on his cock, locked her arms around his neck, stared into his eyes and swore she saw the future coming together. She'd missed him every day since Death Valley. She didn't ever want to miss him again.

"Axel!" Her breath hitched. She whimpered.

He readjusted, grabbing her by the ass, then using every rippling muscle in his arms, chest, and shoulders, lifting her up his cock, then impaling her again, thrusting at the end of the stroke to reach that damn spot that reacted to the feel of him deep.

With a scream, she splintered in his arms, shattering into little pieces around him.

Axel barely gave her time to catch her breath. Pressing his forehead into hers, he clenched his jaw and jackhammered into her like a madman, the lightning speed and pure power he put into every stroke dazzling her until she saw stars. Mystery reclined her head against the tile, closed her eyes, and tumbled into bright, tingling pleasure again.

Her body was still aglow when he withdrew and set her on her feet. She blinked, head dizzy, as she watched Axel take himself in hand and stroke his cock roughly. Soon, he clenched his teeth and stared at her with blue eyes that burned into her. With one look, he wanted her to know that, even if he wasn't coming inside her, he considered her his. Then he sprayed across her belly with a low groan.

As he panted and recovered, the waterfall from the showerhead pelted his torso. She stood against the wall, protected from the deluge, and felt the most primal urge to touch his seed, rub it into her skin.

When she tested the need by grazing her fingertips over her stomach, he drew closer and grabbed her wrist, then flattened her palm into the warm, thick liquid and worked it. "That's it. I want you to smell like me."

Her breath caught. The idea of carrying his scent all night long didn't merely arouse her again, but made her heart thump. It sounded odd and maybe even a little taboo, she realized, wanting to wear the product of someone's passion. On the other hand, she couldn't deny that she liked the idea of belonging to Axel in every way he would let her.

A tiny part of her heart wished that he'd wanted to come inside her and see if nature blessed them, but she understood why he hadn't. They juggled so much right now—a stalker, a burgeoning relationship. She was supposed to be back in the UK next week. She lived there . . . and he'd still be here. What if she'd conceived? Yeah, she didn't have an answer. She'd better start using her brain and stop letting her heart and hormones run the show.

He cupped her face and dropped a little kiss on her lips. "I'm always going to take care of you first."

His expression told her that he would have loved to take her up on her offer, but duty compelled him to be responsible.

No way could she be upset with him for that. "You always have. Thank you." *I love you.*

He smiled and reached for a towel. Mystery air dried while she tried to repair her hopelessly half-drowned hair. Within a few minutes, they'd dressed, and she felt more than a little wicked knowing that Axel's very essence had seeped into her skin.

As he opened the bedroom door and led her into the hall, he rested his protective hand at the small of her back. "I think Callie stashed something sugary and fattening in the fridge."

Sugary sounded great about now. Once inside, they pulled out plates and forks and a massive piece of turtle cheesecake. With an indulgent grin, Axel took a bite and watched her devour half of it in less than a minute.

"That good?" he teased. "I couldn't tell."

She stuck her tongue out at him. "If you don't stop running off your mouth, I'm going to eat all this alone. You won't get any."

"I've gotten what I wanted." He leaned closer and grabbed the arms of her chair, sliding her and the furniture closer to him. "I might want more of that."

A flush raced to Mystery's cheeks. Every moment with him just seemed easy and natural. They came from totally different worlds, and yet it was as if they'd been made for one another.

"I might give it to you." She bit her lip.

Axel sent her a grin that showed off his dimples. "No 'might' about it. I plan to take you again . . . and again, until you beg me to stop. We'll see if I have any mercy then."

* * *

THEY ate in silence until most of the piece was demolished. Then Axel stood and started a pot of coffee. Mystery fell in beside him, washing off their plate, finding coffee cups and creamer. Then they waited together, and a sense of peace settled over him. Being with this woman was so simple, like breathing.

Not taking her up on her invitation to come inside her had been one of the most difficult things he'd ever done. And if he kept thinking about it, he'd pull her pants down, lay her across the kitchen table, fuck her senseless—and change his mind.

"I'm surprised your father let you come to the States without him," he remarked. "He's incredibly protective. And after what happened to you as a teenager, it's no wonder."

"The only way he'd let me make this trip 'solo' was with Heath. He wanted to send a whole team of people with me, but I argued that Aunt Gail lives in the middle of nowhere. It's not like the paparazzi hang out there. And we'd certainly see any intruders coming a mile away. After World War Three, he finally relented."

"I'm glad you came and your dad compromised."

"I didn't think he was going to." She sighed. "And it sounds terrible, but whenever he's in between girlfriends, he's cranky."

Axel laughed, refraining from pointing out that most men were when they weren't getting any. "I'm sure he'd appreciate that observation. What was it like growing up with Marshall Mullins as a single father? Was he strict? Absent? Difficult?"

She shrugged. "All of the above. Of course, he knew I was always being watched. But after my mother's death, he definitely hovered more, which only got worse after my abduction. It hasn't let up since. As a kid, I missed my mom a lot. I think he did, too. But I have to admit, the house was more peaceful after she passed. They fought all the time."

"About your dad's love life?" Axel asked but he felt sure he knew the answer.

"Totally. He wasn't even discreet about it half the time. At first, I guess he thought I was too young to understand why there were so many pictures of him out on the town with other women. I was about seven when he got slapped with his first paternity suit, but he wasn't the father. I'm sure that was just luck, though."

"Did your mom take the cheating hard?"

"Absolutely. When she'd had too much wine, she'd clutch their wedding album to her chest and ask herself what went wrong. I didn't have an answer."

"Of course not. You were a kid."

"And I was angry with my dad. Furious. I spent most of my time with my mom, so I saw how all his cheating tore her apart. I'd never put up with that. I don't know why she did for so many years."

Axel nodded. She shouldn't have to. No woman should. "Do you think she was depressed?"

"Absolutely. She took medication for it. I've asked myself over and over if her depression contributed to her death. But I don't think she committed suicide."

"I suppose she could fall off a cliff by herself, but she didn't leave a note or give any indication she was ending it. In fact, hadn't she contacted a divorce lawyer earlier that week?"

Mystery nodded. "She planned to divorce Dad and take him for half of everything. When she told him, he blew a gasket. That fight was epic. I remember hearing them in their bedroom have a shake-the-walls screamfest. They said some incredibly ugly things." Mystery gave a hollow laugh. "My mom reminded him that he'd fucked most anyone in Hollywood who wore a skirt in the last nine years. He didn't really have a reply, except to say she'd made mistakes, too. But she was totally serious about leaving. She'd even contacted a real estate agent about some property back in Kansas. My mom was making plans for a new life, not ending it."

Axel agreed. Some of that had been public knowledge—even her terrible fights with her husband. Circumstantial evidence made Marshall Mullins look like the prime suspect. After all, that divorce would have cost him about ten million dollars. But Axel didn't see the famous director as the murderous type. Granted, he might have hired someone . . . But there were holes in that theory, too, like the lack of a money trail.

"Why was your mother in Angeles National Forest that day?" he asked. If he wanted to get to the bottom of Mystery's kidnapping, he'd have to start here.

"She called it her Zen place. Her dad had apparently taken her there as a kid on a camping trip, and she fell in love. Whenever she was upset or needed to clear her head, she'd drive out there. Sometimes, she'd take me, too. I was in school that day, so she didn't."

"Did you know she'd planned to drive to that spot?"

Mystery shook her head. "My mother was often very solitary. She liked being alone, especially when she felt off-kilter. She would pack up the car and disappear for a few hours. Sometimes more."

How would Marshall Mullins have known exactly where in the forest his wife would be and when? Yes, he could have hired someone to follow her, and there had been lots of speculation that a thug from the Asian mafia he'd hired as a consultant for an upcoming film might have been persuaded to do some wet work for the famous director. But the criminal had wound up facedown in the Pacific a few days later, slaughtered by a rival, so they'd never really know. The only facts in evidence: Marshall and Julia Mullins had come to horrific blows over his cheating one morning, and she had threatened to divorce him. Less than six hours later, she'd been dead. He'd benefitted most from her untimely demise. And somehow, this involved their daughter.

"I know what you're thinking." She looked down at the hands she wrung in her lap, then raised big hazel eyes to him. "My dad didn't do this. He might make a lot of movies about warriors and gritty cops, even that one about the serial killer, but he's a pacifist at heart."

Axel frowned. The man who'd sat across a table from him and watched as he and the squad had planned Mystery's rescue had been all for blood if it brought her home. Axel didn't burst her bubble. But he also didn't believe Marshall Mullins had hired someone to kill his wife.

He shrugged. "We'll figure it out. It's time we put your mother to rest and gave you back your safety. Getting there might get bumpy, though."

"I just don't understand why the photo says I'd be safe in England."

"I don't know that we're meant to understand a lot of things about this right now. Once we unravel everything, it will make sense."

A sudden knock behind them made Axel tense. He whirled around in his seat, blocking Mystery from the door with his body. He fully expected to see Heath, ready to brawl now that he'd heard her in pleasure with another man. *Bring it.* Axel itched for a fight.

Instead, he found Zeb, one of his fellow Dominants and Dungeon Monitors, standing in the doorway, looking deeply concerned. "We've got a . . . situation. You need to check this out pronto."

Chapter Twelve

AXEL'S chattiness evaporated in an instant. "Go back to your room and lock the door. You should be safe. I'll find out what's going on and come back for you."

He didn't give her a chance to argue or the opportunity to follow. Before Mystery even rose from her chair, he'd left the room.

With a frown, she looked into the open doorway, then sighed as she jogged back down the hall. If someone had broken into the club and was wreaking havoc, wouldn't alarms have gone off or something?

As she reached the main hallway leading from the back door to the club's main floor, Mystery didn't see anything out of place. She resisted ducking into her room and locking herself in. If something dangerous was happening, how would she know it and escape?

For a few minutes, she paced the hallway, torn between following Axel's demands and tiptoeing around to see what the devil was going on. She didn't like the jerky beat of her heart and the sick worry knotting her belly. What was taking Axel so long? Had he been hurt defending her? They'd been so careful putting out a cover story that she was leaving the country, both to the hotel staff and Twitter. So how the hell could anyone have found her here?

She was still wringing her hands in indecision when Heath came storming toward her, wearing a furious scowl that made her cringe inside.

When he spotted her, his frown deepened to a full glower of disapproval. He grabbed her arm. "What did that man do to you?"

She didn't play dumb or pretend she didn't know what he meant. "You heard us."

"How could I possibly avoid it?" he drilled sharply. "You haven't seen him in forever, and suddenly you decide to—"

"Heath, I appreciate your concern, but it's really none of your business. My father sent you along to keep me safe, not to guard my chastity. I'm not having this argument with you."

He paused, worked his jaw, looking as if he waded through his words carefully. But he didn't let up or let go of her arm. "Did it ever occur to you that you might not be able to trust him? That someone you *can* trust is standing right in front of you?"

Mystery reared back. Was he talking strictly about her safety or had he drifted into romantic territory? Heath had never given her a reason to think of him as anything other than a protective uncle . . . who just happened to be a badass. Had she misread the situation all along?

"What are you saying?"

"You've seen your 'hero' at his best and built him up in your mind. Mystery, you've just given him every part of you, especially your trust. And your body." And he looked as if that disturbed him. "But you've never seen him as just a man with all the other flaws you're terribly familiar with."

"Meaning?" she snapped. "He'd never hurt me."

Heath cursed and looked upward, seemingly for divine intervention. Then he shook his head at her. "You can be the most bloody stubborn woman . . . Come with me."

He dragged her down the hall toward Thorpe's office. He held his finger over his lips to signal her silence.

As they reached the threshold, Heath held out a hand to stop her, and pointed to the far side of the room. Thinking that he must be losing his mind, Mystery shrugged and peeked around the corner. What she saw made her heart stop completely.

Axel sat with his back to the door in a chair, his shoulders eclipsing the backrest. A small woman cuddled in his lap, wrapped up in his big arms. He held her as if no one in the world was more important to him than her.

"How do you feel about that, Sweet Pea?" he asked softly, intently.

Sweet Pea? Who was she? He didn't have a sister that she knew of. Was she a friend? Or his lover?

Mystery's blood went cold.

"I'm willing to do whatever you want." She blinked big brown eyes at him, looking very comfortable in his arms. "I want you to be happy."

He caressed the woman's cheek. "I want you happy, too."

She curled small fingers over his broad shoulder and squeezed. "You've done your best to make me happy for the last two years. I . . . don't have words for how wonderful you are. Your devotion has meant so much to me. I've been so lucky to have you."

Every word out of the woman's mouth was a stab in Mystery's heart. She'd been thinking about love and forever with Axel. She had basically invited him to get her pregnant because she'd been stupidly envisioning what a beautiful family the three of them would make and how happy they could be sharing their tomorrows. With him, she'd feel protected and loved. In return, she would adore and satisfy him.

Now the wretched, crushing humiliation ripping her heart from her chest reminded her of the devastating lesson her mother had learned at her father's hands: Men always strayed.

No, Axel hadn't promised her anything or committed to any sort of future. Mystery had been the one to make naïve assumptions.

But never again. Obviously, he'd been committed to this woman he called Sweet Pea for two years—how had her private investigator missed that?—and Axel had cheated. Mystery was the "other woman" in this scenario, and she felt used.

"It's been my pleasure and privilege." Axel pulled the woman closer and laid a soft kiss on her forehead.

Their exchange lacked passion, but all that told Mystery was that, while he cared for his girlfriend too much to let her go . . . he slaked his lust with other women. Typical. That had always been her father's approach to relationships, too.

Mystery couldn't breathe. She felt dizzy and sick to her stomach. And so fucking betrayed, though she probably had no right to. She shoved back hot tears stabbing her eyes and threatening to spill.

"Have you seen enough?" Heath murmured in her ear.

She didn't even want to speak right now. And she certainly appreciated that Heath didn't say "I told you so" at that moment. He certainly could have, and she would have deserved it.

Why had she thought she'd truly known Axel after so little time together? Mystery shook her head. That was the last time she'd let her hopes and stupid romantic fantasies get the better of her. Heath had been right about her idealizing Axel. She had to stop thinking like a girl and become a woman.

She had to save herself.

Heath curled a gentle hand around her arm and led her back down the hall. She was grateful she didn't have to witness the affection passing between he and the petite brunette anymore. And when they reached Heath's bedroom, Mystery was even more relieved that she didn't have to look at the rumpled bed she'd shared with Axel and smell the sex that undoubtedly still hung in the air. She couldn't have managed that without falling to her knees and sobbing.

"I'm assuming you want nothing more to do with the man?" he asked gently.

The thought of never seeing him again choked her, tore at her heart. But she'd done without him for over six years. She'd manage for the rest of her life somehow because she'd never be the victim her mother had been. "Nothing."

"Pack up anything you've unpacked. Give me . . . ten minutes. I'll have you out of here."

As he turned to leave, she grabbed his arm. "Thank you."

Heath glanced at her hand on him, then at her face. "Anything for you."

* * *

AXEL turned suddenly in his chair, looking into the hall behind him. The hair stood on the back of his neck. He would have sworn he'd heard someone back there. But he saw nothing.

Forcing himself to relax, he directed his attention back to Sweet Pea. "So you're ready to meet Stone?"

"Why does he want to meet me?" she asked, her insecurities all over her small heart-shaped face.

Sometimes, he forgot that, despite her often multicolored hair, her rocker-chick clothing, and her bright tattoo that held a meaning only the two of them understood, she still gripped tightly to her insecurities. She'd come a long way after surviving so much. But like the winged bird she'd inked onto her shoulder, the time had come for her to fly away. Stone may or may not be the man for her, but she was ready to embrace someone else to help her along with the next part of her journey through life.

"He didn't tell me. You'll have to ask him. But I made it clear that he's to respect you and your boundaries," Axel promised.

She nodded, the hair she'd pulled back in a simple ponytail today colored a surprisingly sedate chestnut brown with a few hints of fuchsia streaks. Her long lashes brushed her cheeks as she paused for a moment to gather herself.

Finally, she opened her eyes and regarded him again. "Okay."

More than one Dom over the years had asked about the club's

sweet little receptionist, but she hadn't wanted to come out of her shell. Axel had been suspecting for a while that she was ready for more than he could give her. Her agreeing to meet anyone was a huge step forward.

He hugged her tight. "I'm proud of you. He's waiting. I'll introduce you."

With the little receptionist in his arms, Axel stood, then set Sweet Pea on her seriously high heels. She still only reached the middle of his chest. "I'm scared."

"I'm always here if you need an ear. You know Thorpe is, too."

"I appreciate the offer." She nodded pensively. "But you're with Mystery now. You don't need me."

He frowned. "Misty, you don't have to leave my protection because I've found someone. We'll have to change a few things about our relationship, but I don't want you jumping into any arrangement with another man just because you think I won't be here for you anymore."

She smiled softly. "Axel, you've been so wonderful. I've often wished that I could have been healed enough to love you like you deserve. And that I could be the sort of woman you'd love forever. But we weren't meant to be. You've done more for me than I'm sure you were prepared to when Thorpe asked you to help me along, and you've definitely given me more than you'll ever understand." She teared up. "I'll miss you."

"Sweet Pea . . ." He held her close. "I'm not shoving you out the door and into the cold."

"I'm showing myself out." Tears splashed down her cheeks. "I've worn out my welcome. It's time for you to give your whole self to one woman. That's never going to be me. And it's all right. If she loves you like you deserve—and it sounded earlier like she does—then I'm so happy for you."

Axel looked away with a wry grin. He'd intended for Heath to overhear them, but he hadn't thought Sweet Pea might come to the club early looking for him. When Stone had shown up and asked for her, Zeb had turned protective older brother and fetched Axel from the kitchen. But maybe this was for the best. Maybe the time had come for both he and Misty to move on.

Axel's heart swelled. He'd always have a soft spot for her inside his big, rambling chest. He might have done her a favor by working with her on her ability to trust and communicate her feelings, but she'd taught him more than a little about honesty and letting go of fears, too. All of his brothers were still single, as was his father, and Axel didn't kid himself. All that had so much to do with his mother's abandonment. Trust didn't come easily for him, but Sweet Pea had helped kick-start his healing. He wasn't there yet, but he had high hopes.

He cupped her face, her small bones swallowed by his big palms, and laid a soft, chaste kiss on her lips. For a long breath, he gave her his kindness and adoration. It flowed bittersweet between their lips and hearts as they said their final good-bye as lovers.

More than ready for his future, he broke away and led her toward the dungeon, hoping that he'd be introducing her to a special man who would take her in hand and make her whole.

* * *

MYSTERY raced around the bedroom she and Axel had shared an hour ago. She tried not to look at the bed as she packed up her toiletries, tossed on some clean clothes, zipped up her bags, then waited.

Maybe she was being hasty. She should at least ask Axel about what she'd seen. There must be some rational explanation, right?

For him cuddling another woman and whispering endearments? How often had her mother said she wished she'd listened to her gut about her father's alibis, rather than his slick words? On the other hand, Axel wasn't her father. Daddy liked attention—needed it. Axel stood quiet and watchful. He didn't mind solitude. He wasn't for show, didn't care about flash . . .

But what man turned down sex when a pretty skank in a short skirt offered it? Axel and her father might not be cut from the same cloth, but they were both men with dicks. Maybe that was the only similarity that mattered.

Pacing and chewing on a ragged nail, she waited for Axel to return. She'd ask him about the woman she'd seen him with and his relationship with her. She'd listen and try to make an unemotional judgment. After all, despite the sex they'd had today, he'd never promised her an exclusive relationship.

But what kind of man jumped from the most amazing sex with her—twice—to put another woman on his lap minutes later?

Mystery crossed the bedroom again. Damn, she could talk herself in circles all night.

Bottom line: She had to ask Axel, listen, then do what was best for her, depending on whether he set off her bullshit meter. Heath would want an explanation, and she would give him one but—

Suddenly, the lights flickered, then died. Everything around her went still, black. She stood unmoving, afraid that she'd trip over something in the unfamiliar room. Then slowly, she began feeling her way back to her suitcase near the door.

When she turned the knob and eased into the hallway, a hand suddenly gripped her arm, pulling her against a hard body. Before she could even gasp, he covered her mouth with his palm. Adrenaline surged. Terror spiked. Had whoever left the picture in her hotel room somehow found her?

"We're leaving via the back door now. Stay quiet."

Heath. Mystery heaved a giant sigh of relief. "We should talk about this before we run off. Maybe I'm being hasty."

"Would you really give him more chances to crush your heart? What would your mother say about that?"

To run like hell if she had any suspicion at all that Axel had cheated. "I know."

Heath released her, then brushed past her. She heard a vague grunt as he lifted her admittedly heavy suitcase. "Wrap your hand around my arm and follow."

"But what if I'm safer with him around, too?" she murmured.

"You've let the pleasure cloud your thinking. I've kept you safe all these years. I'm still more than capable. Follow me. We have to hurry. It won't take Axel much longer to figure out that I've simply tripped the breaker."

Mystery hesitated, so torn. She sensed Heath's impatience.

"I told you at the onset that Axel was a player," he pointed out. "It took him less than fifteen minutes to find another woman to seduce."

"He didn't make me any promises," she pointed out.

"But don't you deserve them?"

She sighed. Yes, she did. Her mother had often said that she felt as if she'd accepted feeling like second best because she'd lacked the confidence and temerity to leave. Mystery didn't want to be a victim of her own weakness.

Heath sighed with impatience. "Axel knows where you're heading. If he truly wants you and cares, he'll come after you. If not, then you'll know. But we must leave now."

What he said made a lot of sense. Besides, some time away from Axel and all of his trappings would allow her the space to get her head together and figure out her next step. He wouldn't be thrilled with her departure, especially since this wasn't the first time today she'd run out on him. But she needed some solitude to process.

"All right."

As Mystery allowed Heath to lead her to the back door, a voice inside her kept shouting that she was making a big mistake. Before she could question her decision again, the back door slammed shut behind her.

Mystery hesitated, fighting every instinct to pound on it until someone let her in, until she could see Axel again so they could work their differences out.

"Look forward, not back," Heath encouraged, tugging her along.

No choice now . . . The door through which they'd just exited was locked.

Heath led her across the lot, then hustled her into the town car and pulled away. They sped into the inky night, and Mystery prayed that Axel would come for her. Otherwise, she worried that she'd not only be fending off bad guys but fighting a broken heart.

Chapter Thirteen

AXEL fidgeted in the seat of his rented sedan parked on a rise of the dirt road and behind the tree line, out of sight from Mystery's aunt's farm. For the hundredth time since Mystery had taken off—again—he wondered what the fuck had happened. One minute he'd been sharing mind-blowing sex and turtle cheesecake with the woman he felt himself falling hard and fast for. The next minute, he'd been preparing Sweet Pea to meet Stone before suddenly being plunged into darkness. Once he and Zeb discovered that someone had tampered with the electrical panel and the two of them had restored the lighting, Axel had gone on a frantic search for Mystery.

He'd known in less than sixty seconds that she was gone. Since her personal items and suitcase were absent, too, he didn't think anyone had taken her from the club against her will. But Heath was missing, too. Axel had no doubt the Brit had planned their escape. The question was, had he dragged Mystery out or had she left with the other man of her own free will?

Axel felt as if someone had gutted his insides with a chainsaw. What if he never saw her again? What if he'd failed to protect her from a man she'd mistakenly trusted? Or, Axel wondered, what if she'd scratched her itch for him and simply moved on?

Apprehension brewed in his belly.

The minute he'd realized that Heath, Mystery, and her luggage had all escaped out the back door, he'd hopped on his bike and sped like a wild man down the streets, onto I-35. Mystery wanted to visit her aunt, and Axel suspected the pair would head to Marion, Kansas, about an hour west of Emporia, where the woman lived. But the duo's head start had been too big, and Axel hadn't been able to track them down.

Thanks to Javier and Xander Santiago's plane, he'd instead jetted north and arranged a car so he could reach the middle-of-nowhere farm quickly. That left him plenty of time to worry that his hunch about Mystery's destination wasn't right and to call Joaquin to have him gather some essential facts about her aunt Gail—and her bodyguard, Heath.

The aunt's story checked out. Gail Leedy was a spinster, born and raised in Marion. She'd worked as a nurse for a local doctor for the past twenty years. After a failed attempt at Hollywood fame with her sister, she'd returned to Kansas and taken up residence in the farmhouse that had once belonged to her parents, though she'd sold off the land more than a decade ago. Deeply involved in her church, she sang in the choir and organized the bake sale for their annual Sunday school fund-raiser. She sounded like a lovely lady, and Axel would have simply walked up to the woman's door and introduced himself, then waited for her niece. But Mystery's aunt hadn't been home when he'd arrived. At that point, he'd tracked down Marshall Mullins and explained that his darling daughter had run off. The famous director had blown a gasket, then launched into a tirade about Mystery's safety. They'd both tried to call her and come up empty, so Mullins had promised to ring Aunt Gail and let her know that she should make up another guest room.

Axel had been satisfied on that score but he still wanted dirt about Heath Powell, like, yesterday. Not knowing exactly who had Mystery at his mercy made Axel itchy.

Right on cue, his phone buzzed in the console of his rented sedan. Joaquin called, according to the display.

"What you got for me, man?" Axel asked, skipping the typical greeting as he continued to scan the dirt road for any sign of headlights in the dark.

"A lot, and none of it very good."

"Fuck." Why didn't that surprise him? Axel sighed. "Lay it on me."

"I'll start with your buddy, Heath Powell. Naturally, most of the good information about him is classified. MI5 won't confirm his employment, but I called Sean Mackenzie"—Joaquin spoke of the former FBI agent who had recently married Callie—"and Hunter Edgington. The intelligence community can be small. Lots of people know lots of others. It didn't take long for them to tap into their individual sources and come back with similar stories."

"After I hear this, am I going to want to kill him?"

"You might. But you might also want to give him a hardy slap on the back. Tough call."

Axel had a hard time picturing that. At the moment, the murder scenario sounded far more plausible. "What did you find?"

"Heath Powell and a team he'd been assigned to warned of Islamic extremists planning something in the Underground system before the July 2005 attacks. Their theory was dismissed. After the incident materialized, the agency backtracked and offered him a promotion. He stayed a few more years, thwarted a few more terrorist plots, then someone shot his wife in broad daylight in a London market. The murder had the earmarks of a public retaliation for putting a douchebag—they've never proven exactly who—behind bars. After that Powell resigned, and a few key criminals wound up gruesomely dead over the next few months. No one pursued their deaths too hard, but whoever took them out was a real pro, so you do the math. Powell then took a few odd bodyguarding jobs, sometimes for the sort of lowlifes and thugs he'd once hunted down. Then Marshall Mullins jetted to London with his young, still-traumatized daughter and hired Powell almost immediately. By all accounts, the guy has been Mystery's devoted shadow since."

Axel gripped the phone, his thoughts racing. Yeah, he didn't like what he heard. But he had to compartmentalize his worry and pray that son of a bitch was too devoted to Mystery to kill her. He understood why she trusted her bodyguard, but Axel would bet she had no idea the Brit had gotten in bed with the enemy for a paycheck and more than likely had committed cold-blooded murder.

"Thanks for the info," Axel grumbled.

"Don't thank me yet. Now we come to the worse news. I did some digging about Julia Mullins's killing and talked to the detective originally assigned to her case. He's retired now. Once we established that I wasn't a pesky reporter looking for a scoop or a college student hoping to write a paper that would blow this whole Hollywood drama open again, he admitted that the sheriff's department hid a few things from the media."

That happened more often than not, so Axel wasn't surprised. "And he was willing to tell you about it?"

"Not at first. But we shot the shit over the phone for a while. I had to stretch the truth a little and say that I was helping to protect Mystery while she's on U.S. soil."

"If you get me information, then you are, as far as I'm concerned."

"Well, he hemmed and hawed a bit, checked out my credentials. I guess he'd met Caleb Edgington in the past and finally decided anyone working with or for my stepfather was okay."

"And?"

"At first, he thought Julia Mullins jumped. The trajectory of the body over the cliff suggested some force behind her fall, rather than a suicide leap, though. And Julia's actions just before her death didn't match up."

"Like calling a divorce lawyer and planning a move to Kansas?"

"Yeah. You knew about that?"

"Mystery told me earlier," Axel supplied. "I don't think she knows much else, though."

"The body placement also ruled out an unintentional fall, which left them thinking murder. But the sheriff couldn't positively place either of their only two suspects at the crime scene with her. So the case went unsolved. For some reason, the sheriff didn't publicly classify her death as a homicide."

"Why the hell not?" Axel demanded.

"To cool speculation in the press maybe. The detective I spoke to said they were under a lot of pressure to figure out what had happened. Calling it a murder would only have turned up the heat."

That sheriff had done Julia Mullins and her loved ones a really crappy disservice, in Axel's opinion. "So that's it?"

"Not exactly. Fast-forward about four months," Joaquin went on. "Campers in the valley below took some last-minute pictures before heading out, hours before anyone knew there'd even been a death. They finally got the film developed in their camera—remember, this was before everyone had a digital camera—and they spotted something interesting. I'm sending it to you now."

Within a minute, Axel's phone dinged with a text message. He put Joaquin on speaker and opened the message. Mountains, some snowcapped, filled the landscape, dotted with a thick forest of trees. The shot was panoramic and showed the majesty of the area. Then something to the left of the shot caught his attention. He peered more closely and expanded the view on his phone. But the old picture pixilated the more he tried to zoom in. Still, two things looked very clear: The date and time stamp on the photo coincided with Julia Mullins's murder and on the mountain in which she'd met her doom stood not one figure—but two.

"I see a man and a woman on the mountain in the left side of the background," Axel pointed out. "She's definitely Julia Mullins. That's probably the last picture of her alive."

"Exactly."

"Who's that man standing with her?" Though the snapshot only showed the back of a man wearing a navy blue suit, Axel already knew that couldn't be Mystery's father. "The guy in the photo is too short and has too much gray in his hair to be Marshall Mullins."

The man in the photo also wasn't Heath Powell. He would have been too young at the time of the murder, and school records put him squarely in the UK at the time of Julia Mullins's death. Axel had checked.

"He's also too tall to be Akio Miharu, the Asian Mafia enforcer Mullins hired to consult on a movie and, according to rumor, to kill his wife. With their only two suspects most likely eliminated, the sheriff had nothing else to go on. The quality of the photo isn't fantastic, and the negative is long gone, so we can't improve the clarity."

Which meant that using anything fancy, like recognition software, was out of the question. "So she was definitely murdered, and we have a new suspect we can't identify."

"Pretty much. The sketchy notes here indicate that the detective asked Mullins if he recognized the man with his wife. He claims he didn't."

"Why didn't they ever release this photo to the press? Get it on the news and see if anyone could identify him?"

"Isn't that a good question?" Joaquin asked cynically.

"What about records of people entering and leaving the park? Are any kept so we can cross-reference whoever entered that day with anyone Julia Mullins knew?"

"You need a parking pass for some locations within the forest, but nothing if visitors stay on the roads maintained by Los Angeles County. As far as I can tell, no one checked for a record of the parking passes issued that day."

That was damn fishy. Axel sighed heavily as another question crossed his mind: If Mullins knew his wife had been murdered, why hadn't he told his daughter that fact? Granted, Mystery would have been a child at the time, but he hadn't come clean since she'd grown up. Axel suspected he'd have to break the news to her. He wished to hell the director would hurry up and make the connection between his wife's murder and his daughter's abduction. If Mullins did, he might try harder to help solve the case, which could end the danger to Mystery once and for all.

"And sixteen years later, I wonder if those records even exist anymore. That sucks," Axel growled.

"Big, hairy monkey balls, yes. And the detective had nothing else useful in the file, so that's all I've got."

"I'll have to run this photo past Mystery . . ." Once he caught up to her again and paddled her ass a glowing shade of red. "I'll ask her aunt, too. Maybe one of them will recognize this guy."

"I hope so. Otherwise, this is another dead end."

No shit. "Thanks for the update. Let me know if you find anything else."

Joaquin paused. "Logan and I are prepared to back you up, man. Just say the word. Hunter can't get away with Kata due any day, but since Bailey is already busy with rehearsals because she won the lead in that ballet this summer, I'm free. Logan and I will come out there and help."

The offer surprised him, especially since he and Joaquin weren't really pals. "That's damn nice of y'all."

"Well, it might also be avoidance," Joaquin admitted. "We inherited Caleb's team of operatives when he gave us his business—a halfdozen psycho misfits. One guy is a former army sniper. He won't even let us call him by name. He insists we call him One-Mile, an homage to his longest kill shot. I'd ten times rather deal with your shit than mine."

Axel forced a laugh. "I might take you up on it. Once I get the lay of the land here, I'll let you know."

They rang off, and Axel resumed waiting for Heath to deliver Mystery to her aunt. He only hoped that his gut was right—that Heath wanted her for himself more than he wanted to kill her.

To pass the time so he didn't go insane with worry, he picked up his phone again and texted Sweet Pea. How did the meeting with Stone go? Sorry I couldn't stay. Did Zeb watch over you?

She wrote back almost immediately. Yes. I like Stone. We talked a lot. He wants to see me again and he's going to talk to you.

How do you feel about that? he asked quickly. But he knew Sweet Pea well.

She hesitated, then tapped back. I don't know. A little excited and scared.

She wasn't ready for a Dom she barely knew. Hell, Axel didn't even know if Stone was actually in the lifestyle. Jack Cole vouched for the guy professionally, but that wouldn't cut it in a dungeon with a sub as fragile as Misty.

We'll talk when I get back. Be safe. Call if you need me.

She sent him a winking face and a heart emoticon. Take care of your girl.

With a grimace, Axel tucked his phone away. He didn't bother trying to call "his girl" again. If Mystery hadn't answered the first fifty times, she probably wouldn't answer now. Would she answer tomorrow? Next week? Ever? If Heath hadn't nabbed her with dangerous intentions in mind . . . then what? Axel frowned. Had her post-coital glow worn off because he didn't mean a damn thing to her, and he'd been too busy falling for her to notice? He had a lot of practice with sex . . . and not much with relationships.

This mental jaunt down Maudlin Street bored the shit out of him, so he trekked off this beaten path and glanced at the time. If they'd come straight here, she and Heath should be driving up any minute. Then? He expected fireworks.

Wouldn't his presence here shock the shit out of Mystery? She might not want him around forever, but he'd damn well make her explain that to his face before he let her go. No way would he sit around morosely and wonder why she left him, not after the way Dad had when his mother had taken off for a new life.

Finally, twin lights bobbed up and down the dirt road, coming toward Axel at a careful clip. He held his breath, beyond relieved that Heath had delivered her as promised. If the Brit had wanted her dead, he'd had her alone for nearly seven hours. The man could have snuffed her out and dumped the body anywhere along the road.

At least he knew Heath wanted her alive. As much as Axel didn't like the other man, he had to rule him out as a suspect in Mystery's death threat, damn it. He'd love a reason to pound the asshole's face.

As the lumbering black vehicle headed closer to the little farmhouse in the distance, Axel made sure the headlights were off, started his rental, then pulled forward to block the road. No way would Mystery have another chance to escape without a conversation.

Finally, Heath parked in front of the house, just in the circle of the cheery light from the front porch. He helped her from the car, and she stretched before making her way to the little porch, complete with a rocking chair. Even at a distance, Axel could see Mystery slumping her shoulders and bowing her head, exhaustion evident in every line of her body.

Heath took her by the elbow toward the porch as Aunt Gail opened the door. Axel shut off the engine and exited the rental. He locked it manually so it didn't beep and shut the door softly, grateful the spring breeze muffled the sound.

Mystery hugged her aunt, a tall, thin woman in her fifties with ashy blond hair in a bob and wearing a blue bathrobe. Axel jogged down the lane toward them.

Heath heard him first and turned, gun in his hand. He cursed when Axel stepped into the porch light's glow. "Oh, bloody hell. You're here? Why did you follow her?"

"Did you think I wouldn't?" Axel shot back.

Out of his peripheral vision, he saw Mystery pull from her aunt's arms and turn his way. Her eyes widened when she caught sight of him.

"You." Axel pointed at her. "We're going to talk. Now."

"She has nothing to say to you," Heath answered for her. "Didn't her leaving you indicate that she's had enough?"

"Who is this man?" Aunt Gail asked nervously. "Should I call the police?"

"That would be brilliant." Heath smiled.

"I'm Axel Dillon, ma'am. Mr. Mullins called you about me."

"Of course." She smiled. "Please come in. I hope everyone is hungry. I made cookies."

Heath cursed.

The woman's gesture was a kind one but Axel actually agreed with the Brit just now. Fuck the cookies. "I'm sure they're delicious, and I'll be happy to eat one after I've spoken to your niece."

"You came here?" Mystery sounded shocked.

"Of course." Had she thought he'd simply stay in Dallas with his thumb up his ass and not try to figure out what the fuck had happened between them?

"You came for me?" She looked on the verge of tears, but he couldn't tell if they were happy or sad.

Was she asking if he'd followed her all this way because she was touched by his gesture? Or did she think he was delusional for imagining they had a relationship that didn't exist?

"You called her father?" Heath barked, his tone accusing. "I suppose that explains why he tried to call me."

Why wouldn't this asshole just shut up, Axel wondered. "Mullins wants me with his daughter. I don't shirk my responsibilities."

Mystery gasped. "Responsibility? Is that what—"

"Do you normally barge your way into a paycheck?" Heath demanded, stepping between Axel and Mystery, his stance protective.

He wanted to wring the guy's neck. Mullins wasn't paying him; Axel was just concerned for her. "Do you normally behave like a fidiot?"

"Oh, dear. It's a good thing I don't live close to my neighbors." The older woman looked nervous.

Mystery reached back and absently patted the older woman's hand. "I'll handle this."

"No," Heath assured. "I will. Fidiot, am I?"

Axel nodded. "When someone threatens a target, why would you imagine it's a good idea to take off and leave the one in danger with less protection?" Axel demanded.

"It is when one of my protectors is a cheating douchebag!" Mystery yelled at him, fists clenched, then headed toward the front door.

"Cheating?" As he charged after her, stepping onto the porch, the truth hit him. Somehow, Mystery had seen or heard him with Misty. He grabbed her arm. "You've got it wrong, princess. Sweet Pea and I are friends."

She jerked her arm free. "So you cuddle all your friends on your lap and whisper words of devotion to them? Right, and I was born yesterday. I suppose you're going to tell me next that you've never had sex with her."

Axel gritted his teeth. The truth was only going to make everything exponentially shittier, but he refused to lie. "No. I have—more than once. Our relationship is complicated but it's also over. If you'll tell me why the hell you ran off yet again, then listen to me, I'll explain everything."

She turned her back on him and reached for the front door handle. "Save your lies. After growing up with my dad, I won't have anything to do with a philandering prick."

"Yeah?" He grabbed her around the waist and yanked her back against him. "After growing up *without* my mom, I'm not interested in an unreliable flake."

Mystery looked taken aback, as if the thought that she might have hurt him hadn't occurred to her. "Oh."

Axel gritted his teeth. How did she not grasp that taking off on him twice in less than twelve hours had been hurtful? "Now that we're done exposing all our inner wounds or whatever, let's talk in private."

Heath shook his head. "Leave her alone."

"She doesn't need you to speak for her," Axel spit out.

"Stop it!" Mystery snapped. "Both of you."

"I would—if he'd stop the verbal equivalent of lifting his hind leg on you," Axel muttered.

Heath rolled his eyes. "Coming from you, that's rich. Barmy wanker."

This asshole really crawled up his back, but Axel refused to keep giving the man so much of his energy. He had to focus on Mystery and figure out if they could have more than an inexplicable connection and great sex. Snipping at her bodyguard wasn't going to win him any gold stars.

"Axel, I don't want to talk about it. I'm tired."

At nearly four in the morning, he wasn't surprised. "I am, too. But we need this."

"What's the point? If you want someone else—"

"I don't," he insisted. "I'm willing to believe we're just having a misunderstanding we can clear up quickly. Aren't you even curious to hear what I have to say?"

"No." She hesitated, then sighed. "All right."

Relief pouring through him, Axel took Mystery's hand. Her small fingers curled around him, and he clutched her warm palm to his.

He regarded her aunt. "It's nice to meet you, ma'am. Sorry to come in arguing. We've got some things to settle if I'm going to protect her. Can we talk somewhere private?"

"Anywhere downstairs, I suppose. I didn't expect you so late, young lady, and I'm going back to bed."

"I'm sorry. I called you earlier to let you know," Mystery explained. "Did Bible study run long?"

The woman shook her head. "Errands in Emporia, then a late dinner with some old school friends. Sorry I missed your call. Make yourselves at home. This old broad can't stay awake another minute. See you in the morning."

The trio wished her a good night, and the older woman disappeared up the stairs. On the second floor, a door slammed. No one spoke into the silence. Axel feared it would be a long night.

* * *

THE moment only grew more awkward as time dragged on. Mystery darted into the cozy white and mint-green kitchen. A pewter cross hung above the stove. Not much had changed since she was a kid. She remembered coming here with her mom every summer. The year she'd passed away, they'd visited during spring break. Mystery remembered the snow and being amazed that the white stuff could fall so close to April. That was the first time she'd ever played in a winter wonderland. She and her mom had been sledding, then shared a big mug of hot chocolate afterward.

The ghost of that memory lingered in the air, though now the space would be haunted by a new presence she didn't think she'd ever forget: Axel.

He entered the kitchen after her, Heath hot on his heels. God, these two needed to back the hell down and stop arguing. Since they weren't going to do that all by themselves, she had to put her foot down.

"Are you both on your man period or something?" she challenged.

They glared at her, neither deigning to acknowledge her remark.

"No? Then Heath, will you please give Axel and me a few minutes? If you want to go to bed, I'm sure my aunt left some pillows and blankets on the living room sofa or she made up the guest room upstairs. First door on the left."

He looked ready to hit something and let out a frustrated breath. "I'll secure the perimeter."

Without another word, he let himself out the back door, and it rattled behind him.

Exhaustion weighing down her every limb, Mystery turned to

look at Axel. He'd curled one hand into a fist, and to say he seemed tense would be a gross understatement.

Mystery sighed, bracing herself for a battle. Honestly, she wasn't even sure why he'd come. For her or out of a sense of duty to her father?

She spied the kettle on the stove. Craving a warm cup of tea, she grabbed a box of teabags from the cabinet, then turned to him. "Want some?"

"No, thanks." He sat in one of the small kitchen chairs, upholstered in vinyl with a leaf-and-grape pattern that had been outdated for twenty years. "Listen, Mystery, I am not sleeping with Sweet Pea."

"By your own admission, you've taken her to bed before, so . . ." The thought of him with the little pixie of a brunette stabbed Mystery's chest like a machete. She had to stop seeing them together in her head and torturing herself. "You know what? It doesn't matter."

"The hell it doesn't! Will you just listen?"

God, she'd heard her parents have this argument a hundred times when she was a kid. Her father had always denied any wrongdoing and he'd always been full of shit. Mystery wanted to believe Axel, but she didn't want to be gullible, either. How could she be rational when she was so freaking tired? Still, she loved him and had for years. For that reason alone, she would listen this once. If his speech smelled like BS, she'd figure out how to move on without him.

"Fine. If you weren't seducing her last night, then what were you doing? She's a pretty girl. So I doubt you two were playing a rousing game of checkers."

"We weren't playing checkers, but we weren't fucking, either. Our relationship isn't about that."

Of course. She was "just a friend" or "just a coworker" or whatever convenient role Axel could fit her into, the way Mystery's father always had when conning her mother. Now, she faced the stove, determined not to let Axel see her cry. She'd already shed too many tears over him. Her mother had cried too much for her father, and

Mystery didn't want to repeat the pattern. Maybe she should cut her losses now . . . but her stubborn heart didn't want to give up.

Axel made his way to her, cupping her hips in his big hands and pulling her against him. The feel of his wide, solid chest at her back comforted her against her will. He felt like a safe haven. She felt as if she belonged to him. What was wrong with her?

Pulling a mug from the cabinet, Mystery tried to sniffle quietly, but nothing made it past him.

"Shh, princess. Here's the truth about me and Misty. That's her name, by the way. I am *not* in love with her. I never have been. She's not in love with me, either."

At that, Mystery nearly rolled her eyes. Attractive, smart, funny, protective, damn good in bed . . . "You don't owe me anything, so you don't have to come up with an excuse. You have a girlfriend. I barged into your life and threw myself at you. I wish you hadn't taken me up on the stupid offer if you were in a relationship, but it's done. I won't be the other woman, so I'd appreciate it if you stopped touching me."

"You're not the other woman because Misty is not my girlfriend. She never has been." Axel wrapped his arms around her waist and held her close.

It was all Mystery could do not to snort. She'd bet Misty didn't view the situation the way Axel did. In fact, it would probably be news to her that she wasn't his girlfriend.

"And I'm not going to stop touching you," he vowed, tugging her away from the stove. "Come here."

As he pulled her back to the table and tried to settle her on his lap, Mystery balked, jumping to her feet again. "I said I'd listen, but I won't crawl on your lap like she did. Whatever you have to say, you can do it without your hands or your dick."

Gritting his teeth, he let her up, then kicked one of the other chairs from under the table. "Then sit. And I want you to fucking listen."

Mystery started to tell him that he wasn't the boss of her, but he was used to being in charge in bed . . . and probably out of it, too. A part of her wanted to believe that he wouldn't bother to talk it out with her if she meant nothing to him beyond a piece of ass. But who knew?

She backed into the chair and crossed her arms over her chest. "What?"

"I'm trying to have a conversation with you, face-to-face, the way adults do. You're making that damn hard when you're pouting."

"Well, excuse the hell out of me for being shocked that you could fuck me twice in the last few hours, then look awfully comfortable with another woman on your lap. Do you know how stupid that made me feel? How manipulated and used?"

"And you didn't use me when you picked me up in the bar to scratch your itch? By your own admission, you had zero intention of coming clean with me about your identity or talking to me again."

"We discussed this. I never meant to hurt you. I apologized."

"But I genuinely listened and tried to see your side of the story. Could you extend me the same courtesy?"

His question pricked her with guilt. He had listened. She just kept butting in and sounding like a jealous shrew. "Fine. I'm all ears. What's with you two?"

"In a nutshell, without divulging Misty's secrets. She came to Thorpe's club a few years ago in a very fragile state. She'd been through a lot. She needed a friend, an ear, a Dominant to give her some boundaries and foundation. In short, she needed someone she could count on. But every once in a while, she craved a man to hold her. Because Misty trusted me most and Thorpe asked me to take her under my wing, I did it."

Mystery didn't understand. "So . . . you're saying you just gave her a pity fuck when she wanted it?"

"What I did for her wasn't about sex. I love Misty. But like I said, I'm not *in love* with her."

"Meaning, you don't love her enough to be monogamous." She rolled her eyes. "What kind of semantics is that?"

"You're making snap decisions based on your past experiences, and none of that has anything to do with *me*. What you're thinking is wrong. Misty and I have never had an exclusive relationship. I was her Dominant, not her boyfriend. I made her feel safe by checking her locks, installing a security system for her, helping her pick out a dog, and giving her someone to call at three a.m. if she thought she heard something out of place at her apartment. I gave her an ear whenever nightmares overwhelmed her or whenever some dirtbag hit on her too hard and scared the crap out of her. I gave her a pal when she wanted to see a movie or didn't want to spend a holiday alone. Just like I gave her a spanking when she was too bottled up to cry and I gave her sex when she was desperate to feel like a 'normal' woman. Because it was my role as her Dominant, I gave her whatever she needed. Sometimes that was a firm 'no' when she reached for that third cosmo. Sometimes that was a long, slow fuck by the lake. I learned her well and took care of her even better because I cared. I wasn't attached to anyone else, and I'm happier when I'm needed. It was a win-win for us both."

Mystery gaped at him. She wasn't even sure how to process his words. "It sounds like you were pretty devoted for not being her boyfriend."

"It's hard to explain the concept of Dominant and protector to people who apply the terms through their vanilla filter. I dated other people. She encouraged me to because we weren't romantically involved. Emotionally, yeah. But not hearts and flowers. More like . . . friends with benefits, but the friendship far outweighed the sex." He leaned forward, elbows on his knees. "To be honest, Misty would only break down once or twice a year and ask for sex. Only then would she give herself voluntarily."

Frowning, Mystery digested Axel's words. Pity smothered her anger. "She was raped."

He held up his hands. "Her secrets are her own. I care about you, Mystery, and I want to save whatever *us* we might have, but I can't betray her confidence. It wouldn't be fair."

In a way, she respected him more for it. Yeah, it infuriated her and made her feel a bit like she was on the outside looking in. On the other hand, he stayed true to his friends and his principles. Mystery didn't exactly understand this relationship he'd shared with Misty. But she also didn't imagine Axel would be trying so hard to explain their odd, romantically platonic relationship if she wasn't important to him.

She bit her lip, still trying to wrap her head around everything he'd said. "So she's your submissive?"

"Not anymore. What you saw tonight was Misty and me moving on. Despite the fact that she's not ready to be alone, she realized I could no longer be her Dominant in every way. She broke it off so I would be free to go after the woman who could make me happy. You."

His words stunned her. Sizzled through her. Flattened her. Her cautious side told her not to leap too quickly at his pretty words. The rest of her jumped at them. "Is that why you came up to my aunt's house?"

"Of course." He searched her face. "Why else would I pull all kinds of strings to borrow a jet to reach you before you could slip through my fingers again?"

"I'm not just . . . a responsibility?"

"Fuck no. Why would you think that?"

Mystery ducked her head, wringing her hands. "Well, you told Heath that you came because my father wanted you here and—"

"Princess, I'm telling your bodyguard what I think he'll actually hear because I don't owe him the truth. You deserve to know what I'm thinking and how I feel, so here I am. I hope like hell you're understanding me."

She was, and hope welled inside her. Mystery didn't want to be that naïve girl who believed everything the man she was crazy over told her, but she also didn't want to be the cynic who let a good thing slip away because she was too jaded to believe. "I was excited you'd come here. Relieved."

"Because you didn't want to be alone with Heath? Did he hurt you?"

"No. He never would." She bit her lip, oddly nervous, but if Axel was being so honest, she had to try, too. "I was glad you'd traveled up here because I figured if you did, I must mean something to you."

He gave her a slow smile. "You could say that. When I realized you were gone, I fucking panicked. I'm just glad I found you and that you're all right."

His phone buzzed. He stared at the screen, then shook his head.

"Something wrong?"

"Misty. She can't sleep and wants to know if I 'got my girl yet.' See?" He flashed her the phone.

Mystery read their last few messages, then wished like hell she hadn't accused him of cheating. Now she felt somewhere between chastened and regretful. "She's worried about you."

He answered the woman quickly, and Mystery wished she knew what he'd said, but he tucked his phone away. "I might have been her protector, but she's pretty protective, too."

"Are you sad she won't be there for you anymore?"

The kettle whistled on the stove, and before she could get to her feet, Axel made his way to it, poured the water, rummaged around for the honey and a spoon, then brought it to her. "Be careful. It's hot."

When he set the mug in front of her, their eyes met. She nodded solemnly, drowning in his deep blue stare. "Thanks."

As she sat, he paused to collect his words. "We'll always be friends. She can confide in me any time, and until she finds her One, I expect her to. Like any friend, if I see her floundering without someone to talk to, I'll step in because I'm worried about her. But we didn't 'break up.' We never had that sort of relationship to start with. But Misty wants more than I can give her."

Of course she did. Mystery understood very well wanting more of Axel. "So she does want a boyfriend?"

He shook his head. "She wants a sadist. That's not who I am."

Mystery reared back, blinking at him. On the one hand, his admission relieved her. She didn't have any interest in a man who yearned to give her pain. But . . . "Why would she want that?"

"I don't think you're a masochist, so you may not completely get it. But she enjoys the pain. It becomes its own pleasure. And in some cases, a masochist is able to release their internal pain with someone who torments them physically. It's as if they can only process one agony at a time, so they have to let go of the one inside them. For some, like Misty, it's really cathartic."

"And you did that for her? You spanked or flogged or—"

"Sometimes. If she got really bottled up, I'd call in a sadist friend of mine from Houston and let him spend a few hours with her. She always seemed profoundly happy afterward."

Mystery had a million questions. Had Axel minded watching another man give her pain? Had Misty slept with this other man, and had it bothered Axel? In fact, his whole arrangement with the woman boggled her mind. But the truth was, he didn't seem upset about separating from Misty. Nor did he seem jealous that she might find someone else, only concerned that she'd find the right sort of someone. And Axel had been incredibly direct. The truth was, he could have told her that his thing with Misty was none of her business.

She sipped her tea and gathered her words. "You're right. I don't really get it. It might be selfish to say, but I'm glad you're not with her anymore."

"It's for the best because we both want something else." He dragged her chair closer. "After last night, I already knew I had to change my relationship with Sweet Pea. I couldn't pull the emotional rug out from under her, but I also realized I couldn't have sex with her anymore, not even for her sake. Not when I want you so much."

Against her will, happiness flooded Mystery. She sat back in her chair, trying to sort everything out logically. Her mother might have called her foolishly trusting. Maybe Axel would hurt her in the end. On the other hand, she'd never know what could be if she didn't give them a chance. She didn't want to look back with regrets and wonder *what if* she'd really tried to believe in them? Right now, he must have a million doubts about her since she kept running out on him. The first time, he'd somewhat taken in stride. This last time, when she and Heath had fled Dominion? Mystery got the feeling she hadn't begun to pay for that yet.

"Thank you for explaining. I overreacted when I saw you two. And I know you and I probably aren't going anywhere, right? You live in Dallas and I live in London and—"

"Let's cut the shit. I don't know exactly what's happening between us, but don't sell us short. I want you. I don't want it to end. I suspect I'm falling hard and fast—"

"I'm in love with you," she blurted. As long as Axel was putting his cards on the table, she should, too. "I think I always have been. Seeing you with Misty . . . I freaked. I'm sorry. I guess I hit a sore spot with your mom and all by running off, but that wasn't my intention."

"I'll be honest. That isn't my only hang-up, but that's my biggest."

Mystery frowned. "She walked out on a husband and four boys? Just left?"

"Yeah. Said she was going to the grocery store. She drove into town, cleaned out our bank account, took our only car, and drove off. Last I heard, she'd shacked up with some guy in New Orleans."

God, he must have been confused, sad, angry, lost. "You could track her down now and ask why."

Axel shook his head, his frown telling her that he held in an emotional torment that haunted him. "I know why. She wanted more out of life than cooking and cleaning and working shifts at

Walmart as a checker. She wanted adventure and money, not another fifteen years with the guy who'd knocked her up in high school. She'd been a baby having babies, and she'd come to the point in her life where she wanted something totally different than us."

Her heart ached for him. She reached for Axel's hand and squeezed it. "That had to be tough on you. How old were you?"

"Eight." He didn't state that her abandonment had hurt, but the stoic protector in front of her couldn't keep the pain off his face.

Mystery slid out of her chair and climbed onto his lap. "You deserved more. She didn't stay around to see what an incredible man you've become, and it's her loss. You amazed me the day we met. You keep doing it every minute I'm with you."

"Why do you keep leaving me, then?"

He asked the question so quietly, and it ripped her in two. She'd never imagined this big badass could look so vulnerable, and Mystery hated the fact that she'd put doubt in his heart.

"Look at us, both kind of lost in our own insecurities. You're thinking I'm going to run out on you because it's what your mother did. I'm thinking I'm not interesting or pretty enough, and a guy like you could get any woman he wanted, so of course you'd want women other than me. I'm just waiting, like my mom did, for you to cheat on me, even though we never committed to anything."

"Bullshit. Maybe not with words, but what happened at Dominion felt pretty damn serious to me. You can't look me in the eye and tell me that was just sex."

Mystery shook her head. "That's why seeing you with Misty crushed me. I'm afraid and I don't want to wind up like my mom, you know?"

Axel held her close. "I do know. I don't want to become a bitter, lonely alcoholic like my dad. So here it is: Giving you up after your rescue was something I had to do, not something I wanted to do. Giving you up now is something I won't do without a damn good reason. I'm pretty sure it won't be long before I'm telling you that I've fallen in love with you, too."

Her insides went warm and gooey at his words. Just like everything else about him, his straightforward honesty amazed her. No game playing. No fronting. Just his unvarnished truth.

She smiled at him. "I'd like that."

Axel brought her closer and gripped her face in his big hands. "But if you leave me again, I'll be done. It's not a threat, but an honest reality. I know myself and my limitations. I'm willing to stash my concerns now because we've had extenuating circumstances. But we've talked, so from here on out . . . If you run off, I'll know it's because you wanted and meant to. Are we clear?"

A bolt of fear struck to the bottom of her heart. Then she dismissed it as foolish. As much as she adored Axel, why would she intentionally leave him again? "I'm not going anywhere. We'll figure out where and how we can be together later."

"I'm never going to fit into that whole Hollywood scene."

She scoffed at him. "Neither do I. Why do you think I've retreated into books? Why I didn't protest the move to London, despite the mostly dreary weather and terrible food?"

He heaved a breath. "I don't have much—"

"Stop there. Without my dad, I don't, either. He buys me nice things when we have to appear in public because my image affects his. If I showed up in something I bought three years ago at Debenhams, the press would write about it."

"De what?"

She laughed. "It's a department store in London. Decent stuff, but nothing designer. Dad won't have it if we have to walk a red carpet. The rest of the time, I live pretty normally."

He raised a tawny brow at her. "The TMZ shit?"

"Only happens in the States. Frankly, I didn't expect anyone to even care that I was back in the country. But I guess having a renowned director for a father, a mother who died an infamous death, and being dramatically rescued from a kidnapper only to become a recluse makes me interesting to these people, huh?"

"I'm sure." He shrugged. "Look, I don't have all the answers, but I know I don't want to let you go again, Mystery."

A warm glow suffused her. She smiled at him with her heart in her eyes. "I don't want to let you go, either."

Axel gave her a slow nod. "Good. The man in me is satisfied that we're on the same page and talking. I like it."

Mystery had a feeling she knew where he was going with this, and her heart tripped, then speeded up. Her breasts turned heavy. Her pussy began to ache. "But the Dom in you?"

He sent her a dark smile. "Is itching to punish you, princess. Go upstairs and wait for me, naked and kneeling by the door."

Chapter Fourteen

AXEL watched the sway of Mystery's hips as she sashayed out of the kitchen. The room was small and frilly and dated, but somehow welcoming. He'd also bet it was well stocked. If Gail Leedy liked baking, then she'd have drawers full of pervertables. Axel wished like hell that he'd brought a toy bag, but he'd only managed to throw a few necessities in his duffel before the Santiagos' plane had been fueled and ready. He didn't like being unprepared, but he'd figure out how to adapt, improvise, and overcome.

Quickly, he found a wooden spoon, a few clothespins, a plastic container of rice, and a cutting board. He bypassed the twine probably used for things like tying turkey legs together. That stuff was tough on human circulation, and he wanted Mystery tightly but safely bound for what he had in mind.

Just as he perched the smaller items on the block of wood to take upstairs, he heard the back door creak open and slam shut. Axel cursed under his breath. Heath. Talk about bad fucking timing.

When the other man stormed in the kitchen, he didn't look like the fresh air had improved his mood. Axel wished the asshole would give he and Mystery some breathing room.

Heath glanced at the bundle in his hands and cursed. "Are you joking, fuckwit? You're going to paddle her with a wooden spoon like a naughty little girl for protecting her heart before you could crush it."

Axel raised a brow. "And you helped her right out Dominion's door, didn't you?"

"She was upset," he defended.

"She was vulnerable," Axel growled in his face. "You took advantage of that because you're dying to stick your cock in her and fuck her into next week. But Mystery is mine now. Get used to it. I intend to keep it that way."

Heath ground his teeth together. "I shouldn't be surprised you assume I have the most lascivious motive possible. I care about that girl—"

"That makes two of us."

"I would lay down my life for her," Heath argued.

"I did that when I barely knew her. I'd do it again. Are you trying to convince me that you're not interested in having sex with her?"

"My personal feelings are none of your concern. Mystery's safety and happiness are what I'm paid to upkeep, and frankly, I've given you too much latitude."

"You haven't given me shit except a hard time," Axel argued. "Mystery and I talked through our problems just now and we know where we're heading. I think I can make her happy. I have no intention of leaving, straying, or hurting her. You still got a problem with me?"

"And your girlfriend?" he challenged.

"Not my girlfriend. I already hashed this out with Mystery."

"You truly have feelings for her?"

Axel was fucking tired of this guy being in his way all the time. "More than I can even express. I will never let anything happen to her as long as there's a breath in my body."

Heath sighed. "I need to talk to her."

"Not going to happen right now. She's waiting for me."

"And everything in your hands?" He glanced at the items Axel had been balancing on the cutting board.

"What's your point?"

Heath shook his head. "Forget it. We can argue later over Mystery's love life. While I was walking about the farm, I started sorting through this tangle of events. There's something about this setup I don't like. The hairs on the back of my neck are standing up. Besides the three of us and Mystery's aunt, who else knows we're here?"

"My boss, Mitchell Thorpe, and the Santiago brothers. I think that's it, and they would never tell anyone or put Mystery in danger. What about your stops on the drive along the way?"

"I concealed her with a baseball cap and some sunglasses in case people recognized her, but no one even glanced her way, and we did our best to stop a few miles from the freeway, at small establishments without many security cameras. I think we were safe."

"So what's making your hair stand up?" Axel asked. Because he had a few concerns that chafed him, too.

"First, we still don't know who broke into her room and left the photo inside."

True, and Stone was no doubt way busier with Sweet Pea than hacking into the hotel's security recordings. He'd also probably crashed at the club last night, then had a five-hour drive home. With a grimace, Axel pulled his phone from his pocket and texted Stone. Right away, he got back a promise of information "soon." What if that wasn't soon enough?

Firing off another text to remind him that a life hung in the balance, he pocketed the device again. "I'll give him another two hours before I bug the shit out of him."

And Axel had to admit again that if Heath were guilty, he probably wouldn't be pursuing that security footage from the hotel. If the film caught him sneaking into her room, his jig would be up. Sure, the stiff

Brit could have paid someone to put the picture there, like the maid who usually provided turndown service or a maintenance worker. He'd be too slick to leave a trail leading back to him.

With a shake of his head, he filed that fact away until Stone came back with the film. "Something else bothering you about her stalker?"

"Everything. But what troubles me most is that he's in control right now."

Now Heath was speaking his language. "Agreed. I know Mystery wants to visit her aunt, but we're cornered here. I'm not sure how the hell we solve her mother's murder that took place in Southern California sixteen years ago while we're stuck in rural Kansas."

"Divide and conquer?"

As much as Axel would love to get Heath far away from Mystery, he shook his head. "It won't be long until whoever's terrorizing her realizes she didn't hop a plane back to London. I'll bet we've got twenty-four hours—tops—before this dirtbag gets suspicious. Where's the first place he'll come looking for her?"

"Here," Heath answered grimly, gripping his chin. "Bloody hell. So both of us need to stay here for her protection, it seems."

"If you want to go investigate, I could call some buddies—"

"I can't leave her side," the Brit insisted. "Her father paid me to stay with her. I made a solemn vow that I wouldn't let anything happen to her on my watch."

Knowing what he knew about Heath now, Axel supposed the guy's insistence had something to do with his wife's murder. He couldn't fault the Brit for that. "Totally get it. That means we're cornered here. Nifty."

"Indeed. With no new leads to follow." Heath sighed.

Well, not exactly . . . Axel weighed how much he could trust Heath versus his need to solve this case. Figuring out who had killed Julia Mullins and might want Mystery dead trumped everything.

"I got something fresh about an hour ago."

That perked the Brit up. "Really? Enlighten me."

Axel set his pervertables down on the counter and whipped out his phone again, then brought up the picture Joaquin had sent him. "Julia Mullins at the place of her death, less than an hour prior. She wasn't alone."

Powell peered at the picture. "Who is the man with her?"

"No idea."

"He doesn't look familiar to me, either."

That wasn't great news. It also wasn't unexpected. "I definitely plan to ask Aunt Gail in the morning if she knows who her sister might have been close to back then. But . . ." Axel grimaced. "I'm torn about showing it to Mystery. She might have information."

"She also might start a one-woman crusade to catch her mother's killer."

"Exactly."

Heath shrugged. "Well, I think we show her. Then we'll have to contain Mystery and do our best to solve this murder before the killer comes looking for her."

And she deserved the truth. Axel agreed. "I don't see any other plan."

"I don't, either. Damn it all." He rubbed at his dark eyes with his thumb and forefinger. "I'm fucking exhausted."

"We all are. Go to bed. We'll tackle this after we've all slept." Axel reached for his makeshift sex toys.

"You're not going to leave her be tonight?"

Axel shook his head. "If I thought that was best for her, I would. She needs reassurance that I want her above all else. It's the truth, so it shouldn't be hard to persuade her. Then I'll make sure she gets a good night's sleep. I have a feeling it's going to be a rough day tomorrow. You taking the parlor down here or the guest room upstairs, across the hall?"

Powell raised a dark brow. "Where will you be?"

"Right beside her." At least he would be if all went according to plan.

The bodyguard dragged in a breath. "I'll stay downstairs and keep watch. God knows the last thing I want to hear again is her screaming for you."

"Does that bother you because you're in love with her?"

"We'll talk later." Heath headed for the exit without answering, then turned to glance at the implements in Axel's hands. "Be careful of the wooden spoon. It can leave nasty welts."

"You know that from personal experience?" Somehow, that didn't surprise Axel much.

The other man didn't answer, just left in near silence, despite the fact that the hardwood floor creaked with nearly every step.

Once he'd gone and shut the double doors down the hall, Axel headed out of the kitchen, all but tiptoeing up the narrow stairs. Despite its dubious "character," the old house was homey. He liked it here. When he'd been a kid growing up in a run-down double-wide with three brothers and an alcoholic father, he'd imagined that home looked a lot like this. He loved his place now, and was damn proud of it. But it had never felt like a place to stay forever. It had never felt like a place to share love. And now he was getting sappy as fuck.

With a stupid smile, he reached the top of the stairs, passing a big, decorative cross on the wall flanked by pictures of well-known televangelists Oral Roberts, Jerry Falwell, Peter Grace, and a few others Axel couldn't identify. Mystery's aunt clearly believed in her preachers.

Turning away with a shrug, he cracked open the first door on the right. Mystery knelt there, waiting, head bowed, naked and pale in the moonlight.

As he set the cutting board and other goodies on the nearby dresser, his breath caught. "Princess . . ."

"Axel."

He crouched down to her and lifted her chin. She blinked, her eyes opening, focusing on him. They stared at each other in silence. Mystery reached into his chest and tugged on his heart. The uncertainty in her hazel eyes got to him, the yearning for love, the crash of desire all struck resonating notes inside him.

"You're so beautiful."

"I'm not." She tried to drop her gaze.

He gripped her chin, refusing to let her. "You are, and I won't hear arguments otherwise. Understand?"

A little smile tipped the corners of her lips. "Yes, Axel."

"Hmm, when you go submissive that sweet voice of yours wraps around my cock." He held out a hand to her. "Stand."

Mystery allowed him to help her to her feet and looked around the room, a bit lost, like she wasn't sure what to do next.

"Relax," he instructed. "I'll let you know what I want. You tell me if you can't handle something. Easy breezy. Just us being us together in whatever way feels good, yeah?"

She nodded and released a breath, along with visible stress. "Yeah."

"Good. Bend over the side of the bed for me. Stretch your arms up, head to one side. Plant your feet apart."

She moved slowly, as if she tried to picture the pose in her head. After a long moment, she arranged herself exactly as he'd instructed, then looked to him for reassurance.

Axel gave it readily. "That's it. What's your safe word?"

"Red."

"Good." He bent over the bed, getting down to eye level with her. "This punishment is as much for you as it is for me. I need to know that you understand that running from me without communicating isn't acceptable. If something bothers you, we talk. Vice versa. I also need to make it crystal clear that as long as you're in danger, you don't leave half your protection to lick your wounds."

"I know it was stupid," she admitted. "I was upset. I jumped to conclusions—"

"Understandable, given what your mom went through. I'm not punishing you for thinking it or wondering or worrying. I need to be clear about that. This is all about you leaving without talking to me. We could have cleared this up with a conversation. Now it's going to take a whole lot more."

Mystery nodded. "I'm sorry. By the time Heath cut the lights and we left out the back, I was having second thoughts. Once we got outside and the door locked behind us, it was too late."

Axel stroked her soft curls. "I'm glad to know you were already reconsidering before you'd even gone. Want to tell me why you didn't call me or answer your phone during the drive? Even your dad tried to call."

She winced. "Shit. Oh, he's going to be worried. And mad."

"He wasn't the only one. You'd better get used to having another overprotective male in your life."

"Yeah . . . I think I left my phone back at Dominion. Damn it."

And Axel doubted Heath would have been in a hurry to lend her his phone so she could call the competition. *Shithead.* "I'll find out in a few hours."

"Thanks." She obviously sensed the end of the conversation and stiffened.

He petted her back, fingers gliding down her spine. "Deep breath. In." He waited until she complied. "Out. Good . . . Close your eyes."

Mystery did exactly as he bid, her lashes fluttering shut. "Now?"

"Clear your head and focus on me. Don't open your eyes. Latch onto my voice. I'm here."

She nodded, but before he could correct her, she murmured, "Yes, Axel."

Blowing out a breath, he centered himself and retrieved the wooden spoon from the dresser. He rested his palm on the small of her back as he leaned over her beautiful supine curves and bent to press his lips to her ear. "You're going to be very quiet. No matter what, don't make a sound. I don't think you want your aunt to know that I'm punishing you."

"No," she muttered, sounding so regretful.

Axel understood the submissive need to please and the inherent sadness when she knew she hadn't. "And then we'll put this behind us, right?"

"I hope so." Her voice nearly broke.

"Shh, we will. Count with me."

Before she could question what he meant, Axel stood tall and flipped on the little lamp on the nightstand. With a glance back, he ensured the door to the bedroom was closed. He noticed that Mystery had already shut the curtains. They were completely, blessedly alone.

He raised his arm over her ass, hovering a moment to judge her posture, take in her tender, unblemished skin. He wasn't much of a sadist, but he did love the idea of leaving his marks on her—something she could remember him by every time she sat, something he'd recall when she stripped for him again. But he also refused to lose sight of the fact that she was a novice and he couldn't frighten her away.

With one last brush of his fingers across the sweet curve of her ass, he lowered the spoon with the other hand—a quick sting before he jerked up again.

"One," she breathed out.

He struck the fleshy part of her butt again, this time a bit harder, gratified to see the first blush of red spreading across her skin.

"Two." She squeezed her eyes shut more tightly.

She looked beautiful spread across the bed, at his mercy, but the slow pace drove him fucking mad. He had to change this up.

"Mystery, you've done well so far. You don't have to count anymore."

At his words, she utterly relaxed, the tension draining from her face, her body, as she let out a long breath.

So she thought they were done? Not even close.

Axel pulled his phone from his pocket and scrolled to his playlist. Immediately, the sounds of Nirvana filled the room. Though he kept the volume low, the beat remained steady, something he could zone in to. *Perfect.*

Matching the pace of the music, he took the spoon in hand again and began whacking her butt in a soft, stinging rhythm. Under his tempered torment, Mystery tensed, grabbed the quilt in her fist, and gasped.

He leaned over her again, taking her long tresses in his grip and urging her up until his lips brushed her ear. "Not a single noise or I add more."

She nodded frantically, at least as much as his hold allowed. He tested her immediately, standing tall again and whacking her with the spoon. More red bloomed across her ass. He'd nearly covered the width of her backside. The lovely shade of her freshly spanked skin made his cock jerk, and he desperately wanted to cast the spoon aside and lay siege to her bare ass with his palm, but that would make too much noise and wake her aunt. Damn it. The moment he got her alone and naked . . . Axel smiled. Such a beautiful backside needed attention, and he'd give her plenty.

The music segued into a mellower Evanescence tune, and he adjusted the rhythm. He'd lost count. He'd bet she had, too, especially as he watched her body slowly melt into the mattress. Her fists unclenched around the quilt. Her eyes slid shut. Her breathing evened out. Her cheeks began to glow with his ministrations.

Axel smiled. She'd fly off into subspace for him someday. This little torment had merely refocused and calmed her—exactly what she'd needed.

As the song shifted from verse to chorus, Axel set the spoon aside and crawled on the bed over her, rubbing one palm over her heated butt. "How are you feeling?"

"My skin is hot. I feel so alive. It might sound odd but I'm more relaxed. My head is . . ."

"Quieter?" he prompted.

"Yeah." Her lashes fluttered open, her face glowing. "That's it."

Could he want her any more than he did now? Axel didn't think so. But he wanted to give her an experience that would allow her to put herself entirely in his hands and prove she could trust him. But this was still punishment.

He grabbed the container of rice off the dresser, spread it over the cutting board, and hid the rest of the pervertables. "Stand and face me."

He waited until she did, then glanced down at the floor. "Kneel on the cutting board."

She frowned. "Why is it covered in rice?"

"So you'll remember that running off without telling me what's troubling you is unacceptable."

Mystery shrugged, as if assuring herself that rice was plenty benign. Axel merely smiled. She'd find out otherwise quickly enough.

He held out a hand to help her down since he hadn't found a wide cutting board and kneeling with grace was something completely new to her. On her way down, Mystery glanced up at him, those sultry hazel eyes wide open in thanks.

The second her knees hit the cutting board covered with the hard pellets, she sucked in a breath. Her eyes widened in shock. "What the hell?"

"It's punishment."

She nearly choked. "The cruel and unusual kind. The rice digs into your skin. Holy crap!"

"Quiet," he reminded softly, striking his open palm with the wooden spoon to drive his point home.

"You sure you're not a sadist?" she hissed.

"No." But he definitely intended to give her an experience she wouldn't soon forget. To do that, he needed a few more implements. After a glance around the room, he had an idea or two.

"Stand."

Relief crossed her face, and when he held out his hand to help her up, she placed her fingers in his palm. "Thank you."

"You're welcome. Now come over here." He pointed to the other side of the cutting board, facing away from the bedroom door. Once she'd complied, Axel brushed a hand from her nape to the base of her spine, petting her softly. "Kneel again."

"Are you kidding me?"

He leaned in with his most intimidating glower and grabbed her chin until they stood nose to nose. "Do I look like I'm kidding?"

Mystery hesitated a long moment, and he wondered what thoughts spun around her head. "What happens if I use my safe word?"

"Then I know you're unable or unwilling to submit. I'll back off and leave you alone for the rest of the night."

She bit her lip, and Axel wanted to take the plump red flesh between his own teeth and give her a playful nip. Hell, he wanted to fuck her into next week, but if all went well now, that would follow.

Finally, she held out her hand to him. As soon as he balanced her, she knelt on the cutting board again, hissing as her knees bore her weight on the little white hard granules.

"Wow, that's uncomfortable."

"That's why it's punishment." Axel watched for a moment as she winced and tried to shift her weight, then he decided to throw her a bone. "You know . . . the more you move, the more uncomfortable it is."

"Staying still is no picnic, either," she complained. "It's like kneeling on glass."

Normally, Axel wouldn't put up with backtalk and bitching. But she'd endured a lot today, and he had to admit he found her adorable, no matter what she did.

"It's not supposed to feel like feathers," he shot back, casting his gaze around in search of a few extras he needed. "Does anyone sleep in this room?"

"No. Aunt Gail lives alone. It used to be my mom's room when she was a teenager, but it's all been redone. I think my aunt uses it now as storage and an occasional craft room."

Which explained the sewing machine, the bolts of fabric, and the shelves of plastic bins filled with stuff he couldn't possibly explain.

"Anything in the closet?"

Mystery shook her head. "I think she uses it to store her off-season clothes. Why?"

Axel didn't answer, just prowled to the closet—and found exactly what he needed. He grabbed everything that might prove useful, then curled them in his fist and wrapped them around his hand.

He turned back to Mystery. "Rise and kneel on the bed, facing the window, away from me."

She turned to stare at the items curled around his fingers, then met his stare. That one glance of her hazel eyes sizzled down his spine and settled in his cock. Weirdly enough, something a lot like happiness took up residence in his chest, too. Then she brushed the residual rice from her knees and gave in to his demands. Axel gobbled up the sight of her lush breasts and thighs before she spun around to give him the visual of her lean spine, graceful hips, and rosy ass.

For years, he'd been stationary, living in Dallas, taking care of Sweet Pea, working for Thorpe. He enjoyed his life and liked knowing he did right by his friends, but he'd never been too close to anyone, never allowed himself to really latch on, much less fall in love. He didn't want to be that sad sack hugging his bottle of gin on Christmas day, trying to forget that he had four hungry mouths to feed and no helpmate to cook, love, or keep him warm at night.

In a flash of clarity, the truth hit him like a two-by-four in the face. He'd drifted into Dominance not only because he enjoyed giving women what they needed but to control his interactions with them. After all, if he kept a tight leash on everything, he couldn't lose his heart, his hope, or his future, right?

This one woman had shown him that was just an illusion. She'd knocked his world on end with one pickup line. She'd made him crave her like an addict after a single afternoon fix. She'd dug her way into his heart in one late-night rave. Or maybe what he felt had been years in the making. Whatever.

Mystery Mullins was in his heart for the rest of his fucking life, and he couldn't control a damn thing about it.

"You want to know what I'm going to do to you?" he murmured against her neck as he stepped up, blanketing her back, and set all the items in his hand on the mattress beside her.

"Yes, Axel."

"Steal your control." He shouldn't be alone in that. "Put your hands behind your back." Instantly, she complied, clasping her fingers together just above the sweet curve of her ass. He set her hands side by side, then wrapped an ugly green and tan scarf he'd found in the closet around her wrists, knotting it off. "Can you get out of that?"

She wiggled her hands and tried to work her way free. "No."

"Comfortable?"

"It doesn't hurt."

"Move your fingers," he demanded.

She did as he bid. "I'm fine."

"I'll be watching. If they turn numb, you stop me immediately. Is that clear?"

"Yes, Axel," she breathed.

Almost as if she felt the submissive urge, she released the tension from her shoulders and bowed her head. Did she have any idea what the fuck that did to him? After everything they'd been through since she'd picked him up in that bar, to see her trust in him made his cock ache and his heart flip. A spanking wouldn't stop her from being the one woman he couldn't forget, and he didn't want to change her.

He wanted to devour her.

"If this hurts or pushes the limits of your ability to endure, say 'yellow.' You got it?"

"I understand."

He uncoiled one of the belts he found in the closet, a thin shiny yellow number that would provide just enough give but still be plenty secure. He buckled it around her forearms, pulling it a bit tighter. Her shoulders lifted, and Axel had no doubt that if he stood in front of her, he'd have seen those beautiful breasts thrust out for his greedy stare.

"Too tight? Am I straining your shoulders?"

"No." Her voice sounded even more soft and thready than before.

He adjusted himself in his jeans, aching to take them off. And he would. It better be really damn soon or he'd combust.

"Good."

And because he couldn't help himself, he moved the long fall of her dark curls over one shoulder and pressed his lips to the curve of her neck. She smelled like wanton woman. The musk of her pussy combined with the sweetness of her skin to waft into something so intoxicating, Axel had no idea how the hell he was going to keep himself from pouncing on her in the next two minutes. The urge to not only take her, fill her and give her pleasure, but claim her rode him hard.

He nipped her gently with his teeth, scraping over her skin so she couldn't possibly forget that he touched her. He listened to her moan and smiled in masculine satisfaction.

"Not a sound," he warned, then took the wide tail of the next belt and gave her hip a little warning snap—just enough to get her attention.

Mystery wriggled and pressed her thighs together, sending him a frantic nod.

"None of that, either," he growled in her ear, reaching around her to tuck a hand between her thighs. "Spread your legs apart."

She hesitated, writhed a bit more, then finally complied.

"A bit faster next time, princess." He slid another scarf, this one a pink paisley, over her eyes, doubling the long strip around her head to ensure she couldn't see through the delicate silk. He flashed a hand in front of her face. She didn't flinch. "Anything?"

"No. What are you doing to me?"

"Making you give yourself completely. Want out?"

She took a moment to answer. "I probably should because I have no idea how you and I are going to work this out from different countries, with different lives, but . . . no."

Yeah, he didn't have the answers she sought, but right now, he didn't give a shit about logistics. According to her, she loved him. His feelings were damn strong, too. As far as he was concerned, this woman settled him, intrigued him, made him want to take a chance with his heart for the very first time.

"Good."

The quiet of the house wrapped around them, solemn, almost reverent. He circled her body, heard her swallow down nerves, listened to her deep breathing.

He cupped her cheek, grazing his fingers down the soft skin there. She tilted her face, nestling into his touch. Mystery giving herself to him nearly fucking undid his restraint.

Axel grabbed the next belt in the stack, a thick black number that belonged with a stylish coat. Soft leather covered the hard boning underneath, absolutely ideal for his purposes.

As she sat back on her heels, he shoved the belt under her knee and jostled it down to her shin, almost to her ankle. Then he buckled it high on her thigh, securing her bent leg together.

"Is that uncomfortable? Your feet numb or your knee hurt?"

"Why are you tying my leg bent?"

"Answer the question."

"No, I'm fine. I just don't understand—"

"This is where trust comes into play, princess." Since she didn't have any physical difficulty with the right leg, he moved onto the left, securing it with a similar belt in red.

As soon as Axel finished, he stepped back and admired his handiwork. Bound for him, trembling, hair hanging over one shoulder and flirting with her nipple, legs spread to show her bare pussy, Mystery looked like his kink fantasy come true. But he suspected she was much more—the dream his heart had been too afraid to wish for.

The fact she couldn't touch him in return right now completely turned him on. Yes, he liked it when she put her soft fingers on him, stroked his body, and wrapped them around his cock. But in this moment, he was totally in control. He owned her.

Axel swallowed down a lump of lust. But the damn blood rushed south anyway, jetting into his cock, leaving him light-headed.

Just one thing missing . . . He crossed the room, toward the pile of pervertables.

"Axel?" Her voice shook.

He plucked up two clothespins with a wicked grin, then hustled back to her side. "Right here," he assured. "I didn't go far. I never will."

When he cupped her breast, she gave a breathy little jump, then settled again with an embarrassed smile. He brushed his thumb over the dark berry of her nipple, fascinated with the way it engorged and tightened, the tip lengthening, the areola bunching. His mouth watered.

Axel bent to her and suckled one of her succulent nipples, taking a long pull on her sensitive flesh before he swiped his tongue over the nub. Her body twitched, her shoulders jerked, as if she wanted to reach out and touch him, cup him closer. But all trussed up, she couldn't do anything more than allow him to do his worst.

With a stinging little nip of his teeth, he withdrew from that nipple to direct his attention to the other. As he took the neglected one onto his tongue, he groped around for the first of the clothespins. He licked gently at the hard nub in his mouth, moaning low at the feel of her hardening around his lips, even as he pressed the clothespin open and slowly closed it around the first nipple he'd prepared.

Instantly, she sucked in a hissing breath between clenched teeth. The sound eventually turned ragged and breathy, becoming a whimper.

"Quiet," he reminded. "Breathe."

"It hurts."

"Give it a minute," he crooned, then resumed toying with her unadorned nipple. When he was satisfied it, too, was ready, he grabbed the other clothespin and applied it. "Breathe through it. Wait for it . . ."

Soon, the makeshift clamps did their job, trapping the blood in her swollen nipples. Suddenly, her little whimpers turned to startled gasps, one after the other. She thrust her nipples at him.

Axel dragged his lips in the warm, musky valley between her breasts. "What do you feel?"

"It hurt at first." She breathed out, as if trying to empty her lungs enough to suck in a whole breath. "Then it tapered to a sweet stinging. It was as if all the nerve endings in my body rushed to my nipples and . . ." She didn't finish the sentence, just gave a plaintive sigh. "My entire body is on fire."

Because she liked a little bite and loved being restrained. Because he'd fucked with her body and her head, making her wonder and feel and ache.

Damn it, he intended to punish her, leave her needing and begging for a while so she'd know what it felt like to wonder where he was and what he intended to do. But the sight of her turning rosy and arching closer, dragging in choppy breaths just couldn't wait.

He ripped off his shirt and shucked everything below his waist in record time, then grabbed a condom and tossed it on the mattress before launching himself on the little bed, wincing when the box springs protested. The squeaking might wake up Aunt Gail but being this close to Mystery, he was beyond giving a fuck about that.

Once he settled himself in the middle of the bed, he reached for her, wrapping his hands around her middle. When he lifted her, Mystery yelped.

"What are you doing?" she whispered feverishly.

He held her suspended above his body. "I won't drop you."

"I know. But this feels so . . . weird." She tried to flail but could only move her torso.

He held her, biceps and forearms bunching and working, as he stabilized her. "Stop. Be still. You're in my hands. Give yourself over to me."

"But if I fall—"

"Will I let you?" He zipped the question at her.

She stopped fidgeting, relaxed, sighed. "No."

"No," he assured as he lowered her to straddle his thighs. Then he took her cheeks in his hands, brushing stray tresses from her face and breasts. "I'm not going to do anything but make you come so hard, you'll want to scream the walls down."

Her breath caught, turned jagged. She nodded. "Okay."

Smiling at her, Axel leaned in and captured her mouth. This. Right here. He belonged in whatever space she inhabited, with his mouth on hers, tasting her, being one with her. Every time he touched her just reinforced his belief.

He groaned as he nudged her lips apart and surged inside her mouth. He circled her tongue with his own, stroking, caressing, teasing, pulling back, then plunging deep again.

Exactly like he planned to do with his cock.

Axel brushed his fingertips over the clothespins dangling from her nipples, jostling them on her sensitive flesh. Instantly, she gasped with the shock of sensation.

"You're so beautifully restrained and totally at my mercy, aren't you?"

She nodded. "Yes, Axel."

The thin syllables went straight to his cock. "Are you wet?"

"Yes," she answered even more quickly.

"Do you ache for me?" He caressed her thighs, his thumbs rubbing so close to her cunt.

"Yes. Help me."

Mystery sounded downright desperate, and that's exactly the way Axel wanted her.

"Do you want me to touch you?" he taunted, dragging his knuckles up the pad of her pussy before trailing his fingertips down, nearly to her clit.

"Please. Now," she pleaded. "Yes."

"I like your enthusiasm, but . . ." He stopped just shy of probing her wet folds and withdrew his touch.

She mewled in protest. "Axel!"

He nipped her earlobe in warning. "If you can't be quiet, I can't touch you anymore."

"I will," she promised. "Just don't leave me like this."

"I have something in mind."

Mystery sent him a frustrated grunt but didn't protest otherwise. He took her silence as assent and smiled at her. She couldn't see him, but if she could, she'd know she should worry.

Axel gripped her around the waist and lifted her again. As she gasped and tried to flail a bit once more, he leaned back on the pillows and held her above him.

"Mystery . . ." His voice lashed the air between them in warning.

Instantly, she stilled and fell silent. She bowed her head, looking somewhere between chagrined and beautifully submissive.

"Good. Remember to be quiet."

Leaving her to ponder his meaning, Axel lowered Mystery on

top of him, settling her thighs on either side of his head. He raised his face to her pussy and raked his tongue through her wet folds.

"Axel!" she squealed, a high-pitched cry full of sensual panic and need.

In answer, he devoured her clit, flicking it with the tip of his tongue, then laving the sensitive bud with the flat. He reveled in the way she squirmed on top of him, looking for either control or relief. He didn't allow either. Instead, he gripped her hips in his hands and eliminated her ability to move. Mystery might be sitting on top of him, but Axel wanted to make sure she didn't have any illusion that she held the power. He set the pace. He provided the sensations he chose to give her. He alone determined when she orgasmed . . . or if.

When he clamped his fingers around her hips, restraining them as fully as the rest of her body, she panted and struggled harder.

He dug his fingers into her flesh and withdrew his mouth from her cunt. "Are you giving yourself over to me? Or fighting for what you think you want?"

Mystery let her head roll back on her shoulders and sucked in a breath. "Fighting. I don't know how to just give myself up."

"You're going to learn, princess. Whether we're talking about pleasure or danger, I'm always going to do what's best for you. But you have to let me. Relax. Let your mind go and give your will to me."

She gnawed on her lip again, her entire body strung tightly. Finally, she dragged in a couple of long breaths and let them out in controlled exhalations. Then she nodded. "I'll try."

"Just surrender."

Above him, she relaxed her thighs and forced her breathing to even out.

She gave in.

With his dick aching and his patience running out, he lifted her back over his face and surged up, latching onto her pussy again, tormenting her clit with his tongue.

This time, Mystery didn't fight against his rhythm or silently demand more. She put herself in his hands, quiet, still. As he raked through her folds and nipped the sensitive bud of her nerves with his teeth, her body tensed. She spread her legs wider, gave more of herself, allowed him to control her utterly.

Her breathing picked up speed, and he watched the rosy flush cover her skin. Against his tongue, her folds engorged. Her clit turned harder than stone.

"You're close, princess."

"So close," she breathed.

"Have you been good enough to earn this climax?" he taunted.

"I've tried. Please . . ."

On the one hand, Axel really hoped that she'd learned that fighting him and insisting on doing everything her way wouldn't get her what she wanted. So maybe she'd think twice before she picked up and left without talking to him again. At least he hoped so, because he was damn desperate to get inside her.

Shit, he needed to tamp down this impatience. Axel didn't remember a woman ever stealing past his control so easily or thoroughly, and he'd have to be diligent in the future so she didn't figure out that she could wrap him around her finger with that pretty pussy. But that was a worry for later.

Right now, he wanted to taste her essence on his tongue.

"Quiet." He released her hips and pinched the clothespins around her nipples open. "Come for me."

A breathy sigh turned into an almost animal whine as Mystery tensed and shuddered on top of him. Using his fingers, he twisted and toyed with her sensitive nipples. As the blood rushed back into the tips, her entire body jolted. He laved her swollen pussy through the long, trembling climax, relishing the way she opened her mouth in a long, silent scream and opened to him completely.

As her clit slowly softened, her body sagged. Axel petted her with his tongue, sinking beyond her clit, to the tight opening he hoped to invade soon. He scooped her against his mouth, then prodded her clit with the tip once more.

Mystery shivered and let out a little moan. "I'm so . . . Ohmigod."

"Sensitive?" he asked against her pussy.

"Uh huh." She nodded, squirming.

He loved reducing her to nearly incoherent syllables. Later, when he didn't need to be inside her so damn badly, he'd do it again for the sheer joy of watching her melt in his arms. Now, he needed more.

Axel settled her thighs back on his torso and eased her torso down until her breasts rested against his chest, until she buried her face in his neck and glided kisses across his jaw, jacking up his desire even more. He felt around the mattress for his condom. He couldn't see his cock past her body draped over his, warm and damp and welcoming, but he could sure as hell feel his aching erection as he tore the foil apart with his teeth and wrapped his arms around her to sheathe himself.

As if she finally caught on to what he had in mind, she paused, her body still. "Axel?"

"Do you trust me?"

"Yes." She didn't hesitate.

"Do you want me?"

"Always." Mystery sounded even more certain.

"Then let me take you the way I want. I need that. I need you."

* * *

AXEL'S words made her bite back a gasp. What the hell could he possibly do to her when she was all trussed up, hands and arms bound together behind her back, legs bent and restrained, her heels nearly digging into her ass.

But Mystery had no doubt he would show her exactly what he had in mind. Even though her shoulders ached a bit, she knew she'd love whatever he did to her.

"I'm all yours," she murmured.

He lifted her into the air. Though she couldn't see, his sheer strength in raising her off the bed from something near a supine position amazed her.

"Princess . . ." He began lowering her again—and she felt the head of his cock prod her hungry opening, now gaping with the need for him to fill her.

As he shoved her down on his cock, he lifted his hips, rising beneath her to plant his erection deep, as if embedding himself in the place he considered home.

"Fuck," he hissed. "This is mine. You're mine. You're always going to be mine."

His growled words sparked need inside her, even as his stiff length tunneled deeper, tripping across every nerve ending. Mystery tossed her head back, lacing her fingers together behind her back because she had nothing else to hold on to. He controlled everything. She could do nothing more than allow him to fuck her. And she drowned in the experience.

"Yes," she whispered. "Yours. I think I always have been."

"Then take what I give you." He pounded inside her, withdrew, and thrust up again relentlessly. "All of me. Every inch. Everything I have."

His possessive insistence lit something inside her. No way could she keep any emotional walls or barriers up between them. Whatever happened tomorrow, she was all in right now—so deep Mystery felt sure she'd never escape. She was totally at peace with that realization.

Under her, he continued to lift her up his cock as he tilted his hips into the mattress, then lunged up as he yanked her down again, plunging deeper inside her than ever. The slow rhythm incinerated her. His harsh breathing. Her pounding heart. The squeaking mattress. Every thrust into her scraped the head of his cock against her most sensitive spots, over and over, until she felt dizzy and breathless and ready to scream.

"Oh, fuck . . ." He sounded hoarse, as if someone had ripped the words from his chest. "So good. That's it. That's . . . Fuck!"

His pace picked up, relentless and totally beyond her control. He took her at will and played her body like an instrument he'd learned well. Sleep, danger, duty—none of it mattered in the face of her desire for this man.

He strained to get deeper inside her, and Mystery felt the trembling of his body under her own. Her sensitive flesh burned with need as he impaled her again, filling her so full she stretched wide to accommodate his girth. He managed to stimulate every bit of her channel with each frenzied push up and rapid retreat back. She tightened around him as climax coiled low in her belly, groaning softly into the rise of bliss.

"Axel . . ." She wanted to reach out and touch him, steady herself, grab onto him and never let go. But as he had from the first moment they'd met, he held her safely in his grip and he would take care of her.

"Come for me, princess. Let yourself go and give everything to me."

No way she could refuse that.

With his next stroke, the gathering sensations inside her converged. Blood rushed. Her heart roared. Her entire body felt alive as he swelled inside her. He groaned, possessing her deeper than ever. And in one dazzling moment, she released the entire torrent of need into his keeping. The sensations ripped through her body and seized her heart, melting and remolding her. Changing her.

From this moment on, she belonged to Axel. Even if he didn't want her tomorrow, Mystery knew she'd be in love with him forever.

Chapter Fifteen

AXEL woke a few hours later to sun slanting through the windows, a chill in the air nipping at his nose, and Mystery curled around him trustingly in sleep.

He glanced around the bed and found all the scarves and belts he'd used to restrain her last night, and the pleasure had been beyond intense. Something more like cataclysmic. Moving. Life-altering.

Wouldn't Thorpe be saying "I told you so" now? Yep, and Axel didn't mind at all. He simply held Mystery close against him, reveling in the warmth of her sleep-soft body.

The buzzing of his phone on the nightstand startled him, and he frowned, wondering what the hell time it was. The sun looked high in the sky and he'd slept half the morning away. *Shit.*

He plucked the phone off the nightstand, extricating himself from Mystery, and sat up, staring at the device.

Seeing the name on the display, he pressed the button to accept the call instantly. "Stone. What do you have for me?"

"Oh, you finally answer the phone, Sleeping Beauty?"

Axel didn't ask what Stone meant. He'd bet that if he looked through the record of his missed calls, he'd find more than a few. "It was a really late night getting here and making sure we were secure enough to turn in. Did you sort through the footage leading up to Mystery's hotel room?"

"Yep. I got nothing usable for you. Whoever did it knew they were being filmed. They wore a hat with a wide brim and a trench coat, along with sunglasses, a wig . . . the works. The only thing I can tell you is that whoever left the picture is female. She entered through a service door at the back of the hotel and exited the same way, walking out of the courtyard, onto the street. No vehicle or license plate to trace. I can't tell under the layers of shit how old the woman is or discern any of her facial features. She's got her hands in her pockets, so I can't see any identifying marks or jewelry. The camera angle hid her shoes. I'm guessing she's a hotel employee or an actress looking for a few extra bucks, but no way of knowing for sure."

"Sounds like a dead fucking end."

"It's looking that way, too. Since I had a little extra time this morning, I called the hotel manager. He's spoken with the staff on duty then. No one remembers seeing her. So she either blended in or timed it well."

"Fuck," Axel muttered, not wanting to wake Mystery. "Any idea whose key card the woman used to access the hotel room?"

"The housekeeping manager—a man—reported his master card missing from his desk about two hours before anyone let themselves into Mystery's room. He left about forty-five minutes before that photo appeared in her room. There's footage of him driving out of the employee lot and everything."

"So . . . nothing."

"Nope. Sorry."

"Thanks for trying, man."

"No worries." Stone hesitated, and Axel knew exactly where this conversation was headed. "I'd like to talk to you about Misty."

"She told me last night that you wanted to talk. I'm not opposed, and technically she's no longer my submissive, but if you're serious, I'd really appreciate it if you'd have a chat with Thorpe about your intentions. I'll be back in a few days, then we can sit down and work everything out."

Stone heaved an impatient sigh. Obviously, he didn't like it but he didn't have much choice. "Sure."

"It's for her benefit. She's skittish."

"I know. It's the only reason I didn't tell you to blow it out your ass. Because if you wanted to stand between me and Misty, well . . . the twenty-two months I spent in prison for my fun white-collar crime taught me two things: That Uncle Sam has no sense of humor, and how to kill a man with my bare hands."

Axel rolled his eyes. He did not have time for Stone's posturing now. If the dude wanted to impress upon him how much he wanted Sweet Pea, message received.

"I'll call you when I'm back at Dominion." And before Stone could answer, Axel hung up.

Then he placed a call to Callie. The woman answered on the first ring. "Hey, Axel. All okay? How's Mystery?"

"Sleeping," he murmured. "Do you happen to know if she left her phone behind?"

"Actually, I found it on the floor of Thorpe's old bedroom last night. I stashed it in his office. Do you want me to send it somewhere?"

Axel didn't think they could afford to stay at this remote house for more than twenty-four hours before the bad guys—whoever they were—closed in. Even if Callie overnighted the device, he doubted they'd be spending that much time on this farm. "No. Just tuck it away. I'll take care of everything else."

"Will do."

"You all right? You don't sound like your usual chipper self this morning," he asked with concern. "Morning sickness still bothering you?"

"More like morning, noon, and night sickness. Ugh. I'll be so glad to get past my first trimester. I'm praying it gets better."

"I hope so, but I'm sure Thorpe and Sean are spoiling you silly."

"Completely."

Axel heard the sigh in her voice and smiled. Callie deserved happiness. So did Thorpe, for that matter. And Sean seemed like a good guy, so if those two made her happy, then he was thrilled for them.

"Good deal. Talk to you later."

"Bye!"

They rang off, and Axel eased from the bed and shoved on his jeans. He hit the head down the hall and brushed his teeth, then jogged down the stairs for some coffee.

In the kitchen, he spotted Heath sitting alone at the table with an iPad and a cup of brew he'd probably pushed aside some time ago.

"Morning," he said, banging around the cabinets for a cup.

"Your four a.m. rendezvous was only slightly quieter than last night at Dominion. Can't you two keep it down?" He sounded somewhere between sour and pissed off.

"We tried." Axel shrugged. "Protecting your delicate ears wasn't my number one priority. Where's Mystery's aunt?"

"She ran to pick up her dry cleaning and hit the post office to mail off some bills before her big mission trip."

"Makes sense. You working on something?"

Heath sent him a noisy huff, then glanced down at the tablet's screen. "Because I dislike loose ends, I reached out to see if I could get a record of everyone who requested a parking pass in Angeles National Forest the day Julia Mullins died. The typical request takes six weeks to process. They'll 'rush' it and give me an answer within two."

"That's useless," Axel quipped. "Like the security footage from the hotel."

He filled Heath in on Stone's findings, sipping coffee and trying to figure out how the hell to solve this long-unsolved murder.

"So we've got nothing," he summarized, sending the former MI5 agent a speculative glance. "If you were playing amateur sleuth, who's your best suspect?"

"Well, until you showed me that snapshot on your phone, I would have suspected some slighted paramour of Mr. Mullins. Certainly, some starlet or another would have liked to cast herself in the role of wife to the famous widower."

"Good point. I guess the man on the mountain with Mystery's mother could be hired muscle. But if that's the case, why is he wearing a perfectly pressed business suit to commit murder?"

"It wouldn't be my first choice of wardrobe for the occasion." Heath shook his head. "That white shirt would show every speck of blood. Black is much better for concealing nasty stains."

"Yep." Axel had no doubt they both knew that from experience. "So the police report isn't going to give us anything new. All the follow-ups we have are dead ends. Mystery has told us everything we know. Have you ever asked Mullins about his wife's murder?"

"I tried once. He made it clear that anything to do with her death was a very closed subject."

A grieving man wanting to lick his wounds in private? Or something more? Yes, the famous director had been ruled out as a suspect, and he apparently hadn't hired the Asian Mafia enforcer he'd known to commit the murder. That wasn't to say, however, that he hadn't found another capable assassin.

"Have you tried to follow any sort of money trail from Mullins's accounts around the time of the murder?"

"No. I don't have any notion if he's the sort of fellow who would want his wife dead, but I can't imagine he'd want any harm to come to his daughter. He loves her."

"That's my sense, too," Axel agreed. "I think we're going to have to talk to Mullins, his daughter, and her aunt today."

"I'm not hopeful we'll figure out much, but I'm afraid we've got nothing else." Heath kicked back in his chair, set the tablet aside, and chugged his coffee. "But for pity's sake, could you put a shirt on first?"

With a chuckle, Axel took his sweet time rising to his feet. He enjoyed a moment of towering over the other man before he trudged upstairs. In the bedroom, he found Mystery stretching, her completely naked body visible to his hungry stare, opening her eyes to the world.

He sat on the edge of the bed and cradled her breast, sweeping down her abdomen to pet her pussy before he leaned in to kiss her forehead. "Morning, princess."

"Morning." She winced. "If you have any wicked ideas, you should know I'm awfully sore right now."

"And you should probably get used to that state around me." He winked. "But you're in luck this morning. I'm here for a shirt because Heath doesn't like the way I'm dressed. When you're up and ready, come downstairs. We'll rustle up some breakfast, then we have to talk about who might want to hurt you and why."

She nodded at him solemnly. As Axel brushed a lingering kiss on her lips, he realized this wouldn't be easy on her. "All right."

Reliving both her mother's death and her own kidnapping would be traumatic enough. Forcing her to look at everyone in her life as a potential suspect on top of that? Absolutely both shitty and heartbreaking.

"We'll be downstairs."

With that, he left her in privacy and shuffled back downstairs, tugging his T-shirt over his head. In the kitchen again, he watched Heath pace the room in about three steps in any given direction, each of his long strides eating up ground.

"Better?" Axel held out his arms. Not that he really cared for Heath's opinion. As long as the asswipe shut up about his attire, that would be great.

"Much. I think we need to talk to Mullins, try showing him this picture your friend procured once more and see if we jog his memory."

Since he still had to reassure the man that Mystery was fine and had merely misplaced her phone, he could mark two things off his to-do list with one call. Axel nodded. "Go for it."

Heath yanked out his cell and punched a few buttons, then enabled the speakerphone.

Mullins answered quick. "Heath, anything wrong?"

"Not per se. Mystery and I left Dallas last night and are now at her aunt's home. We've tried to hoodwink whoever is after her by announcing that she'll be returning to London on Twitter. We think that will buy us at least today to solve as much of this riddle as possible. If we can't piece it together by then, she'll probably have to fly home."

"I'd rather have her here, anyway. Fly her home ASAP."

"As you know, we've tried. Mystery will fight us all on that. We can safely hold her here today, then we'll get her home."

The director sighed noisily, obviously not liking the situation.

"Hi, Mullins. Axel here. I'm sure you've been trying to call your daughter. She accidentally left her phone at my place. A friend of mine is keeping it safe for her."

Mystery's father paused. "Your place. I can track her phone, you know. I know exactly where her phone is."

Fuck. Axel had hoped her father was low-tech and he wouldn't have to explain Dominion to his girlfriend's father. "It's actually my place of employment. I took her there last night because it's secure, but she had other ideas."

"And insisted we reach her aunt right away," Heath filled in.

Axel shot the other man a shocked stare. Why would the Brit help him out? Or maybe he'd told the white lie to keep the director off Mystery's back. Either way, it worked in his favor.

"That girl needs to stop being so damn impulsive . . ." Mullins sighed. "So you work there, huh? Do you play there, too?"

Though Axel would prefer to tell Mullins that his sex life was none of the man's business, if he wanted to be in Mystery's future, lying to her father wouldn't get him far. "Yes."

The man sucked in a breath. "Does Mystery know?"

Translation: Have you played with her? *Fuck, fuck, fuck.* He'd never really dealt with overprotective fathers before. "Yes. Sir, with all due respect, she's a grown woman."

"But she's always going to be my daughter. How does she feel about your kink?"

"She's not protesting. Look, I didn't once touch her in the desert when I rescued her. She was too young and emotionally rattled. Now, everything between us is completely consensual—"

"I know you didn't touch Mystery back then. She was actually crushed you hadn't."

Axel couldn't help but smile. "She's made me see the error of my ways since she returned to the States."

"I don't want to know what you two do, but if she's happier, then I'm glad for her."

Letting out a pent-up breath, Axel sagged into his chair. Thank fuck the man didn't want to kill him. "I'll do my best to always make her happy. But we'll have to talk about that after we've dealt with the danger to her. Sir, Heath and I genuinely believe that whoever's threatening her now had something to do with your wife's murder."

Mullins hesitated. "Julia's passing was never definitively ruled a homicide."

"But you know it was," Axel shot back. "A friend of mine spoke to the detective in charge of the investigation when your wife died. He showed me the picture from the hikers."

"Photos can be doctored," Mullins pointed out. "I'm not convinced those people didn't tamper with the photo to sell it to the *Enquirer* or *Star* or some other rag that would have paid them a fortune, regardless of whether it was real. Everyone wanted a piece of that story."

"The hikers never sold that picture to anyone," Axel reasoned.

Mullins scoffed. "I'm not giving them a medal for their restraint."

Marshall was a brilliant director and a protective father, but the man was more than a tad convinced the world revolved around him.

"If they'd simply wanted money for their picture and to ride your coattails for their fifteen minutes of fame, wouldn't they have doctored the image to make the man on the mountain with your wife look like you? Or someone you knew?"

A long pause followed. "That would be most obvious, but—"

"Then let's pretend for a minute that the picture is real. You haven't seen the image in . . . what? Over fifteen years?"

"No," he admitted.

"I'll send it to you again from my phone." Axel texted the snapshot to him. "Just look at it one more time and tell me if you recognize the man with your wife at all."

He heard a little ding on the other end of the line, and a few tense moments passed. "No. I have no idea who he is." A pause ensued, followed by Mullins's distressed sigh. "God, even seeing Julia in a grainy image like this is . . . It's so hard. I loved that woman. I wasn't a good husband. I know it. But she gave me the most precious gift ever."

At that moment, Mystery skipped down the stairs and raced to the kitchen. "Hi, Dad."

"Mystery. How are you, kiddo?" he sounded wistful.

"Fine. Heath and I drove most of the night, so I slept in. But I'm good now."

"Excellent."

Axel noticed cynically that the man didn't ask his daughter how she felt about the newfound kink in her sex life.

"So . . ." Mullins went on. "How's your aunt Gail?"

"I only saw her briefly last night, but she seems well. Nothing much has changed here."

"I know that would have made your mother smile."

"Yeah. It's nice to be here again."

A million questions swirled through Axel's brain. He wanted to ask the man about his wife's death, but he didn't want to be the one to break the truth about the murder to Mystery. Unfortunately, waiting for the right moment cost time, and that was a luxury they didn't have.

He took a deep breath and glanced at Mystery. She looked refreshed and beautiful, despite being sleep tossed and wearing yesterday's clothes. "Have a seat. I called your dad to discuss the day your mother died."

* * *

MYSTERY blinked, then sat slowly. She'd give anything not to rehash one of the worst days of her life, but she knew how necessary it was. "You mean the day she was murdered?"

"You knew that?" her father asked.

"I suspected. You never said anything, but . . ." She choked. Her voice broke.

"I just wanted to protect you, kiddo," her father protested.

"I know." And she did. Her mom's death had devastated him, too. She didn't understand why he couldn't have loved her enough to be faithful. It was irrelevant now. "But the press was all too happy to report what they thought happened, and the murder scenario just made more sense."

Axel squeezed her hand and sighed. "I'm so damn glad I don't have to be the one to explain that she was murdered and rip your world apart. This is a photo taken by random hikers just before your mother died. Does this man look at all familiar?"

Axel showed her the picture, doing his best to zoom in on the two people on the hilltop in the distance.

"I can only see his back. Maybe if I had a face . . ."

"Do you remember your mother knowing anyone with that height, build, and hair color? He's probably around six feet, medium build. In this picture, he looks more gray than not."

"Nothing." She shook her head. Then a distant memory spun

through her head, and she laughed at it. "Well . . . The only person I can think of is this guy who came to one of my dance recitals. I was maybe five or six. When I ran offstage, my mom introduced me to him. He was wearing a suit a lot like this and was graying, too. She called him Peter."

"Was he the dad of one of the other kids?"

"Probably." She shrugged. "It only jumped out at me because Mom seemed really nervous, and they were having this very intent conversation until I reached them. Then they were suddenly all smiles." She winced. "The guy's stare was kind of creepy. I remember hiding behind my mother and wanting him to leave."

"Did you ever see him again?" her father asked.

"No."

"Do you remember anything else? Any detail?" Axel leaned in, face intent.

"I don't even know why I brought it up. Three years passed between that incident and my mom's death. I never saw the guy again. They're probably totally unrelated."

"You're probably right." Axel palmed her crown.

She felt so fortunate to have him here and sent him a faint smile. "I just wish I could help more. I've told you what I know about the day she died. Mom and Dad fought about divorce that morning."

"We never meant for you to hear." Her father sounded contrite.

"Dad, the whole house could hear."

"Shit," he cursed. "We really thought you were asleep."

"No," Mystery admitted softly. "Mom had been in my room about ten minutes before you two started arguing. I woke to the sounds of her crying."

"I'm sorry, sweetheart." She could almost hear her father's heartbreak on the other end of the line.

"And I'm sorry to ask either of you to relive it, but the information can only help." Axel laced his fingers through hers—his silent way of telling her he supported her. "You've told me what you know, so I'd like to ask your dad what else he recalls now."

That made sense. She'd been nothing more than a kid. Her dad would know more.

"I remember more than I'd like to." Her dad sighed. "I came in that morning about three. I'd been out with . . . some people I was working with on a film."

"Oh, just stop lying already." Mystery gave him a frustrated huff. "You were screwing that blonde you were directing in the action/thriller flick you'd been working on, and Mom found out."

"Yes." Her father hesitated. "And she was pregnant."

Mystery gasped, feeling as if someone had punched her in the stomach, and closed her eyes. As if this conversation wasn't awful enough, the new revelations coming out now made it downright horrifying.

"Was she worth it? Were any of those slutbags you took to bed worth destroying your family?" The anger just poured out. Mystery heard it but couldn't seem to stop it. It wasn't as if her father had cheated on her . . . yet it had always felt as if he'd betrayed her, too, not just her mom. For years, Mystery had pretended she didn't know. She'd never confronted her dad because his love life didn't matter now that her mom was gone. But deep down, it mattered to her. His wandering dick had ripped apart a marriage, stained her childhood, maybe even somehow cut short her mother's life. The resulting scars had nearly caused her to walk out on Axel forever.

"No," he choked out.

Small consolation now. It didn't really make a dent in her rage. Even if anger didn't solve anything now, she couldn't seem to stop feeling it. "So because your whore was pregnant, you asked Mom for the divorce?"

"No!" He was quick to correct her. "She found out somehow and told me that she'd called a lawyer. She wanted to leave. The sex meant nothing to me but a conquest and some fleeting pleasure, but your mother didn't see it that way."

No, her mom had seen it as a stab in the heart. Mystery did, too. It had made her wary and a bit cynical of relationships, and that wasn't who she wanted to be.

"I loved her," her father swore. "Too much to let her leave. But she asked me for a divorce. Worse, she wanted to take you with her back to Kansas. So we fought. We didn't resolve anything. I lost my temper and left. That was the last time I saw your mother alive."

"And the blonde's baby?" Mystery snapped. "You just left that child to be raised by a single mother?"

"You think that's the sort of father I am?"

The hurt in his voice ripped through her. Regret followed. As a father, he'd never been anything but attentive and doting. "Sorry. That was unfair. You're a great dad."

"Thinking I would soon be a father again, I'd prepared a financial settlement for both the actress and the child, along with a visitation agreement. Then . . ." He sighed. "The baby came out Asian."

Beside her, Axel reared back at that information. Mystery certainly felt her own jaw drop. "So that wasn't your baby."

"No. I had every reason to think I'd fathered that child. I admit it. But finding out I hadn't was a guilty relief." He sighed. "I fucked up. Believe me, I know. Your mother loved that forest, but I don't think she would have been there the day she died if she hadn't been seeking calm."

Mystery had thought the same thing herself. But her dad was beating himself up, and she didn't see the point of heaping more guilt on him now.

"Can you tell us anything else you recall about that day, Mr. Mullins?" Heath cut in. "Anything stand out? Anything unusual?"

"It's not every day your wife asks you for a divorce then dies, so I'd say the whole day was unusual."

Axel cleared his throat. "Let's walk through the events and see if we can find any clue the sheriff overlooked. We don't know who this man in the picture is, so we need some suspects, and maybe your wife's behavior will give us some direction."

Her father let out a rough breath. "I must have done this fifty times for the police, but I'll try again. Um . . . I came in late. Julia was asleep—or pretending to be. I crashed and woke up about six when she slipped out of bed to wake Mystery for school. Julia wasn't trying hard to be quiet. She was itching for a fight, and when she returned from Mystery's room, I could tell she'd been crying. We argued. She told me she knew about my latest mistress being pregnant and she wanted a divorce. She'd hired a lawyer and wanted to move back to Kansas. I told her that if she took Mystery from me, I wouldn't give her a dime of alimony. We screamed at each other. We'd already been to counseling, and I didn't see the point of going back." He hesitated there. "I'm not sure if any of that is helpful."

"When did you first notice your wife was missing?" Axel asked.

"The school called to say that Julia hadn't picked up Mystery. She never missed that time with our daughter. Nannies took care of her when we traveled or attended evening events, but Julia did her best to revolve her schedule around picking Mystery up and having a little girl time before homework, bath, and bed. So when the teacher called, I knew something was deeply wrong."

"Keep going," Axel encouraged. "Tell me everything else that happened."

"I left the set and picked Mystery up. I called the police, but of course there was nothing they could do for twenty-four hours. I couldn't wait that long, so I came home and started looking through Julia's things to see if I could find any clues. I called her friends, her sister, even her yoga studio. All I could see was that most of her belongings were packed. She'd bought two plane tickets to Kansas City, departing the next day, and she and some of her personal effects were gone."

Mystery remembered that day—the panic, the fear, the uncertainty. She'd gone to bed knowing deep in her heart that the worst had happened. Her mother would never have abandoned her, and her heart went out to Axel. Yes, they'd both lost mothers, but hers had been taken. His had just walked out as if he didn't matter. Yet despite the fact that Mystery had left him last night, he sat beside her, comforting her.

He'd proven it the day they'd met and he kept proving it all over again—Axel was a man of strength, integrity, conviction. It hadn't been fair to assume he had the same roving eye as her father and accuse him. Thank goodness he understood that she had difficulty with trust and had given her a great deal of patience.

"Personal items?" Axel asked.

"Her purse, her car, her laptop."

Beside her, Axel stiffened, then turned to Heath, who suddenly scrambled to scroll through his tablet. She leaned over to read whatever he acted so desperate to retrieve. What the hell was going on?

The police report, she realized a moment later. They had an electronic copy of it.

They intended to do everything possible to figure out this cold case, and Mystery didn't have any illusions why. They were doing it to save her.

Even as the realization humbled her, warmth spread to every corner of her body. She was beyond lucky to have them both in her corner. She felt even luckier that Axel cared enough to forgive all her stupid, rash actions over the past eighteen hours. And Heath . . . Mystery hated to think of a man as strong and wonderful, who'd already survived such shock and grief, not finding a happy ending for himself.

"Where did you get that police report?" she asked the pair of them.

"The sheriff's department," Axel answered grimly, then he addressed Heath. "Do you see it? Anywhere?"

He scrolled up, then back down, his dark eyes and big fingers moving over the screen. "I don't."

Mystery didn't understand at all. "What? What are you two all agitated about?"

"Did you find something?" her dad asked over the line.

"Your wife's laptop," Axel finally answered. "The police found her car and her purse, both intact. There's no record of them recovering a laptop at the scene. For that matter, why did she take it way out there? There wasn't an electrical outlet for dozens of miles."

"At that time, the battery life on those machines was next to nothing," her father added. "I never thought about it. With so much else going on and the investigation, my grief, Mystery's upset . . . I never pursued that."

"What did your wife keep on that laptop?" Heath asked.

"I don't really know." He sighed, and Mystery heard her dad's strain. "She asked for one. She almost never asked me for anything for herself, so I had an assistant find the best money could buy at the time and . . ."

He'd hoped it would make him feel less guilty. Mystery could hear that subtext in his unfinished sentence. "You never saw her type on it? She never told you about anything she was working on?"

"She e-mailed. She'd joined one of those sites where you kept up with your old classmates. We didn't talk much about it."

Mystery would bet they hadn't talked about a lot of things, and that's how their marriage had fallen apart. Her father hadn't felt connected enough to his bride to be faithful, and she'd been unable to truly express her sadness and resentment until she'd had enough.

"I remember asking her once what she did with the laptop," Mystery added. "She said she was keeping a journal."

"Like a diary?" Axel asked, frowning.

"Yeah." She nodded. "That's how she described it."

"Did she know something that could have gotten her killed?" Heath asked.

"Well . . ." Her father hesitated.

Trepidation iced through Mystery's veins. Had her mom stumbled across dangerous information that had provoked someone to silence her for good? But what? Mom's past hadn't been shady. She hadn't worked on films anymore or rubbed elbows with politicians.

"If Julia knew as much about all my affairs as she did the one she confronted me about, then she knew about my relationship with the wife of a powerful, dangerous man," her father admitted. "Actually, it's possible she knew a lot of secrets. I can't say more than that. I'm heading into a conference call. Kiddo, stay near Heath and Axel. The fact they're with you is the only reason I haven't boarded a plane and rushed to the States myself. I love you. Be careful where you dig. Stay safe."

Then her father hung up.

As if sensing her distress, Axel curled his arm around her. Mystery melted into his side. What wouldn't her dad admit? Was he keeping quiet because he worried it would get her killed if he told her?

"Breakfast, anyone? I'm starving. I'll cook," Heath offered into the sudden silence.

She appreciated his attempt to lighten the mood but suspected it had far more to do with distracting her so she didn't ask tough questions about her mother's murder. With new information coming to light, she wished she'd jumped in with both feet and solved the woman's killing sooner, rather than following her father's advice and moving on, tucking all those terrible memories away in a box marked "painful" and letting it gather dust.

This trip to the States had been about more than experiencing Axel so she could get him out of her system. Instead, she felt as if she'd finally come into her own and figured out what she wanted. Now she just had to execute it.

"He knows something he's not telling us," she murmured.

Axel and Heath exchanged glances. They didn't really know or like each other, yet they had some silent communication. Mystery didn't comprehend precisely what that look said, but she got the gist.

That she was right.

"I'll try talking to him in a bit," Heath offered. "You know, man to man. He may have felt as if he'd already said too much in front of his little girl."

By discussing all the sleazy bimbos in his life willing to cash in on their morals to either sleep with someone famous or land a role? Too bad. "Give me your phone. I'll talk to him."

"Princess." Axel turned her to face him. "You're the one he's protecting. He loves you. He's not going to divulge more to you. Seriously. Let us handle it."

As much as she hated it, Mystery suspected they were right. It pissed her off again to be left out of the big-boy penis club or whatever the hell they had going on. "Fine. I'll have my hands on the items my mother saved for me this afternoon. Maybe I'll find something helpful there."

"Don't be upset. We're in this together," Axel assured.

In her head, she knew that. In her heart . . . emotion tangled up. Disappointment that she hadn't spent more of her adulthood solving this tragedy in her life, impatience to get started now that she'd seen the error of her ways, frustration that the man she loved was sheltering her more than she wanted—even if she knew he meant well.

"I'll make breakfast," she offered. "You two keep trying to figure out what we're missing in this crazy puzzle."

Mystery whipped up pancake batter and heated a pan of bacon, humming and swaying her hips to a chipper little tune. She could feel both men staring at her.

"Stop looking at her ass," Axel grumbled.

"I'm her bodyguard. I'm guarding her body." Heath bristled.

"You're full of shit."

"And I can hear you both. Shut up." Mystery shook her head. "Don't we have enough drama going on?"

Thankfully, that quieted them. She set warm plates in front of everyone a few minutes later, the smells of warm syrup and fried bacon filling the air.

Everyone ate in silence, scarfing down their breakfast. Mystery let her thoughts drift away to the coming day and whatever personal effects her mother might have left here in Kansas for her. Why hadn't her aunt simply mailed them? Or left them with her father? Why so much secrecy? Asking Axel and Heath would be pointless; they knew nothing. Likely, that was true of her dad, too. She'd just have to be patient a bit longer.

Once everyone finished shoveling away their food, she stacked the dishes in the sink. Then her aunt drove up with a big bundle of clothes hanging in plastic wrap. With the hangers, the garments were taller than her, and she had to hold them high above her head not to drag them across the dirt road.

Axel jumped to his feet and ran outside to help the woman. She smiled. Being from Tennessee, he had that southern gentleman thing down. Or maybe he was just that sort of man.

Heath rose and darted across the kitchen, cupping her shoulder. "Are you all right?"

Was her life perfect? No, but she was doing all right at the moment. Maybe better than all right since she and Axel might have some sort of future—provided they could figure out who wanted to end hers. "Why wouldn't I be?"

"You were upset when we left Dallas."

"Axel explained that. It's fine." She had to believe that he cared enough about her to tell her the truth.

He nodded slowly, not as if he agreed but like he gathered his words carefully. "The conversation we had before breakfast can't have been easy. All the talk of your father's adultery must have unnerved you, too."

"Damn it." She turned and glared at him. "I don't need you trying to stir up my insecurities."

He held up both hands to ward off her tirade. "I understand. I just want to ensure you're thinking properly."

"I'm not stupid."

Heath swept his fingertips down her cheek. "No, you're vulnerable. And I don't want him to take advantage of you."

Mystery didn't want to open her mouth, didn't want to court trouble, but after years of ignoring her mother's murder, she knew better than to hope her problems would simply vanish. "Are you in love with me?"

He didn't hesitate. "Yes."

She closed her eyes. "Heath, I . . ."

"Don't say it." He shook his head, his dark eyes looking so damn sad. "I already know. I simply want you to be sure before you give him your heart."

It was too late for that, but she didn't want to dig the knife any deeper into his. "I appreciate your concern."

"I'll be here as long as you need me. And if you ever want more than my friendship . . ." He cupped her other shoulder and brushed a kiss against her ear before he whispered, "It's yours."

Chapter Sixteen

As Axel entered the kitchen with the bundle from the dry cleaners, Heath stepped away from Mystery. Something had passed between them—and Axel didn't like it one bit.

"Don't." He shook his head at the Brit in warning.

"We've talked. It's up to her." Heath held up his hands. "I haven't touched her."

This was the source of Axel's mistrust—Mystery herself. Heath would keep her safe. And if she ever decided that she wanted a different man in her life, he'd be there waiting.

The crowbar of insecurity split open Axel's composure. He forced himself to put a mental bandage on it. She'd said she loved him. She'd given him not just her body, but her trust. Her surrender.

Axel forced himself to breathe out and hung the dry cleaning in the closet near the front door before he returned to the kitchen. "Keep it that way."

Her aunt bustled in, carrying a little package and glancing at her watch. "I called the attorney's office. He confirmed that he'll see us at three today. Can you be ready?"

"Attorney?" Mystery asked.

"You didn't know?" Aunt Gail frowned, then rushed to the stove to make a cup of tea. "The effects your mother left behind are with an attorney she hired in Emporia. He was instructed to keep them safe until you turned eighteen or you retrieved them."

Those words clearly confused Mystery. They stumped Axel, too.

"So she didn't just leave some jewelry or photos here with you?"

"Some, yes. And I've gathered them all for you and put them in your room. It's not much, but the bulk of what she left, she gave to this attorney to hold in trust. I was supposed to give you this before you saw him." The older woman held out the package.

With a frown, Mystery opened it, then sent her aunt a puzzled stare. "A key?"

That's exactly what it was, and it looked as if it belonged to a safe-deposit box. Axel didn't like any of this.

The woman shrugged. "I only did what she asked me to. Frankly, that last visit you two made over spring break, just before her death . . . It was a flurry of confusing activity. Every time I asked her why she left something with me or wanted to keep items with an attorney, she simply said she was leaving you the gift she couldn't give you as a child. At the time, I had no idea what my sister meant."

"Ma'am, did you think she had any idea someone would murder her?" Axel asked.

"Murder?" The woman reared back, her faded blue eyes startled. She pressed a veiny hand to her chest. "Oh, dear. I didn't . . . I thought she fell. I always imagined she had some premonition of her death and left me these items for you because of it. But you think she was intentionally killed?"

The older woman looked near tears, and Axel could imagine how difficult it would be to hear that a beloved sibling hadn't simply had a tragic accident, but someone had snuffed out their life. "I'm sorry if you didn't know. The police never officially ruled it a homicide, but we have every reason to believe it was." He explained the positioning of Julia Mullins's body at the bottom of the cliff. "We can also place someone at the crime scene with her less than an hour before her death." He whipped out his phone and showed her the picture. "How close were you and your sister before her death? Do you recognize this man?"

Gail blinked and stared in openmouthed shock. "I . . . Oh, goodness. This is all so much." She fanned her face with a delicate hand. "I'd steeled myself to visit her attorney and see the items she'd left with him. That's already like suffering her death again. But this news is terrible."

"I know." Mystery hugged her aunt. "Do you have any idea who the man in the picture is?"

"Well, no. I hadn't been out to California since I gave up on my silly Hollywood dreams and moved home. Your mother stayed behind to marry your father and—" She sighed. "I'm afraid I didn't know everyone in her life. We weren't terribly close after I moved home."

"So this man is not familiar?" Axel directed her back to the photo.

"No. And she didn't confide much to me about who or what was in her life before she died. The only thing I know is that she'd been discussing leaving your father and moving home. I applauded her decision. I know you love your father, but he was hardly a faithful husband."

"He wasn't," she agreed. "And I know how much that hurt her."

"Of course. She loved that man, and he devastated her over and over. I was helping her find a home here. We'd planned to enroll you in school here before the fall term started. Honestly, those last few weeks of Julia's life were the most I'd talked to her in ten years."

"You mentioned confusing activity when she was here last," Axel reminded her. "Can you tell me more specifically what you mean?"

"Well, Julia was quite secretive. She didn't say a lot to me, really. During the day, we'd take Mystery on day trips and look around the countryside for potential places she could move. At night, after she'd tucked Mystery in, she'd drag out that dratted laptop and tap away. I asked her what she was working on, but . . . she didn't tell me much."

A shock wave zipped through Axel. That laptop of hers, the missing one. Whatever Julia Mullins was typing on it could well be at the heart of her murder. He glanced over at Heath. Yeah, they might not agree on who got to claim Mystery, but they both knew instantly this was important.

"Can you recall anything she did tell you?" Heath asked.

"If you know anything about my mother's murder, please. Even a small speck of information would be helpful. I think whoever's behind her death means to kill me, too."

"Kill you?" The woman looked positively petrified. "Oh, my. Oh, dear." She fanned herself again. "Are you sure?"

"Very," Axel answered. "So anything you can tell us is helpful."

The woman sank into a chair at the kitchen table, empty mug forgotten. "Well, she seemed withdrawn and wouldn't answer questions. The only thing she said that I remember is that she expected your father would take forever to give her a single cent from the divorce. So she knew that money would be an issue when she left him."

Mystery frowned. "She was wrong about that. My dad said he'd give her money as long as she didn't move me back to Kansas."

Gail shrugged. "When she came to visit the month before she died, Julia was certain Marshall would cut her off, so she was determined to make her own money. She told me she'd been writing a . . . memoir or something. She intended to sell it and had a publisher interested. When I pointed out that she was hardly a famous woman after a few small roles in movies and TV, she huffed at me and admitted that she wasn't the focus of the book."

Marshall Mullins had been. His wife had intended to blow the doors wide open on his extracurricular love life. She'd been writing a tell-all book. Axel swore under his breath. Across the top of Mystery's head, he noticed that Heath did the same.

Time to question her father again. He definitely knew more than
he was letting on, and he'd press the famous bastard hard—without
Mystery listening to inhibit his tongue—until he got some damn
answers.

Seeming to read his mind, Mystery gaped. "But Daddy didn't kill
her. I know he didn't."

"He doesn't look like the man in that photo," Axel conceded.
"But certainly there are plenty of douchebags willing to kill a de-
fenseless woman for a few dollars."

"Yeah, but . . ." Mystery shook her head. "My mom asked for the
divorce, not him. He was upset when she demanded they split."

"Maybe then he snapped," Gail supplied. "It happens. I watch
the ID TV channel all the time, and you see the shows about these
crimes of passion that—"

"With all due respect, we're just speculating now," Axel cut in.
"Your sister could have written things in that book that upset any
number of people."

"Indeed," Heath agreed. "Mr. Mullins said something about the
wife of a very dangerous man. Maybe that man found out about the
affair. Maybe some other woman didn't want her secret fling with
Mullins exposed, so she made sure his wife's accusations could never
be printed."

"Maybe." Mystery frowned. "But who else knew she was writing
this book? Not my dad."

"She would have tried to hide it, I'm sure. It's not like she'd have
wanted him to know that she intended to blow the lid on his sex life
wide open," Axel pointed out.

She scoffed. "All anyone had to do was read the tabloids. Dad
didn't try very hard to hide who he was sleeping with on any given day."

"That may be true, but your mom could give far more accurate
information, not tabloid speculation. And maybe she'd found out
about some lover of your father's who'd go to any length to keep
their cheating out of the rags."

"The way they hounded him relentlessly, I can't see the paparazzi missing even one of his girlfriends. But I guess it's possible."

"Whatever your mother knew may have gotten her killed." Axel reached for her hand. "We have to keep digging and figure this out."

"Yes." Gail looked flustered. "Yes, of course. I think . . . I need a few minutes to myself to process everything. My poor sister." She stood and looked as if she fought tears. "If we're going to reach the lawyer's office by three, we should leave here shortly before two, but there's a café in Emporia. It's one of my favorites. If we leave in the next hour, I'd like to have lunch there. It was one of Julia's favorites, too."

No way and no reason Axel could say no to that. "Of course. We'll be ready to leave about noon."

"I'll bring you some of those cookies I baked last night and my homemade lemonade to tide you over." Aunt Gail sniffled. "Thank you."

Then she left the room and ran up the stairs, looking distraught.

Mystery's face fell. She looked at him with tears swimming in her big eyes. "What did my mother know that got her killed? It can't be who my father shared a bed with."

Axel agreed with her assessment. "We don't know. The bigger question is how do we get our hands on that manuscript? Can you think of any place she would have stashed a copy?"

"No. We've moved twice since she died. Someone would have found it. If she'd left it with a friend . . ." Her eyes widened as if a thought occurred to her.

It occurred to Axel, too. "She was far more likely to leave it with her sister."

"Or near her. Perhaps that's what the attorney has been safekeeping," Heath mused. "Perhaps that's what the key is for."

She let out a shuddering breath. "I think you're right."

Mystery stood, looking pale. Axel's heart thudded in his chest. He fucking hated to see her worried or in pain or afraid. Right now, his princess looked as if she'd been flattened by all of the above, and it made him want to draw a damn sword and do battle for her—whatever was necessary to help her slay her dragons and find peace again . . . as corny as that sounded.

"Axel," Heath muttered. "We have to discuss this."

He noticed the other man now glided his palm soothingly between Mystery's shoulder blades.

She looked up at Heath. "You think there's danger? Whoever left me the photo at the hotel room could still be watching and have some plan to kill me if I try to claim whatever my mother left with that attorney for me?"

Despite the coiling of danger that made his gut burn, Axel shot Heath a wry stare. "Why couldn't she have been a stupid girl? Sometimes, like now, if she had fewer brain cells, it might set me at ease."

Mystery scoffed but flubbed the sound. It turned into a laugh. "I don't think you'd like me if I was a dumb ass."

"Probably not," Axel admitted, then braced his hand on the small of her back, soothing her with a brush of his palm.

His fingers collided with Heath's, still caressing her. He sent the other man a glare that warned him to back off. And Heath just smiled in a tight, fuck-off sort of way.

As if he didn't have enough fucking problems . . . Besides the emotional aunt and the flaring danger, now he had to put up with a would-be Romeo. Fucking awesome.

"We should get ready to go." Axel ushered Mystery toward the stairs, away from Heath's touch. "I'm assuming you want a shower?"

"Yeah." She swiped a hand over her tired face. "God, I hope I'm ready for this. But it's now or never."

"I'll always do everything I can to keep you safe," Heath vowed across the room.

She turned back to him with a grateful stare, and Axel tried not to take the Brit's head off for expressing concern. He needed to downshift on the resentment. If Mystery had wanted the man, she would have already been in his bed. Because no way would Heath have turned her down. Right now, she needed protection more than jealousy. And he needed to pull his head out of his ass and call Mullins again—out of Mystery's earshot.

"We both will. Let's go."

* * *

IN Emporia, the pace of the traffic was definitely an upswing from Marion, but it still had a small-town feel. Aunt Gail had made everyone a glass of homemade lemonade before they'd started the drive, reminding Mystery so much of visits here with her mom. She was still feeling wistful as they reached the diner.

Most everyone had been quiet during the hour-long drive here. Mystery looked over at Axel. He seemed surprisingly jumpy and a bit impatient, preoccupied—probably with keeping her safe. She appreciated the protector in him as he slid into a booth, her against the wall across the faux wooden table from Heath, Axel beside her, facing Aunt Gail.

This place hadn't changed a bit since she was a kid. Same rust-colored vinyl seats, same dark wooden trim, same aging linoleum, same bubble-bulb fixtures from the seventies. Mystery remembered being here, laughing with her mom. They'd sat on the far side of the room and eaten fried chicken with mashed potatoes, topped it off with ice cream and laughter.

Less than a month later, her mother had been dead.

Today, she might finally find out why. She only hoped she lived to tell the world what had really befallen Julia Mullins.

Mystery folded her hands on the table in front of her.

"You all right?" Heath asked.

She didn't bother lying to him. He knew her too well. So she just smiled, but her heart broke a little for him. Mystery had always suspected that he cared, but love? Everything about her life was a mess right now. Besides all this crap with her mother's death, she now held her bodyguard's feelings in her hands. It would have been so much easier if she could have loved him back. They lived in the same country. He'd never refuse her. They got along fairly well.

But her heart had fixated on Axel long ago, and her chances of getting over him now were nil. She wanted to believe that he was in as deep with her, but he'd merely said he was falling. He hadn't actually said the "L" word to her. Would he ever?

Tucking the thought away, she forced a smile as the waitress handed them each a menu. Honestly, she wasn't hungry, having just had breakfast a few hours ago and knowing that her meeting with the attorney could be anywhere between painful and difficult. But this meant a lot to her aunt, and Mystery enjoyed the memories here. She liked the place.

At least until the perky waitress sidled closer to Axel and sent him a flirty smile. "What can I get you? Fried chicken is our specialty, but I also have some tasty pie."

Mystery rolled her eyes. Did the woman think she was being subtle? "I'll have a glass of iced tea."

"That sounds good, too." Axel didn't seem to pay the woman much attention.

As the waitress jotted down their drink orders, her aunt ordered iced tea, too. Heath shivered and murmured something about sacrilege, then asked for water.

"Sure." The waitress flashed them a megawatt smile, her brassy blond tresses spilling over her shoulders to brush the tops of her full breasts, which she arched and thrust out just a bit in Axel's direction. "Can I get you anything else?"

Aunt Gail looked at her watch. "Give us a few minutes to look over the menu, please."

The waitress, whose nametag read PATRICE, let her gaze linger on Axel again. "Sure."

Mystery sighed. Clearly, she was going to have to get used to women hitting on her man if she and Axel managed to stay alive and work out all their other differences.

He fidgeted in his seat and lifted his head from the menu. Staring at Patrice's swaying ass as she walked away?

The thought really pissed her off, and Mystery took a deep breath. She couldn't convict Axel of cheating because he'd looked around the room. Even if he'd looked for the waitress, maybe he'd thought of something else he'd like to drink.

God, she so didn't want to be like her mom.

"How far is the attorney's office?" she asked her aunt for a distraction.

"About three miles east." She gestured vaguely in the direction. "I'm glad I called to confirm the appointment. I didn't want to mistake the time. I don't always remember everything anymore." She sighed. "C.R.S."

"C.R.S., ma'am?" Axel asked.

Gail flushed. "Can't remember, um . . ." She dropped her voice to the merest whisper. "Shit."

Mystery laughed. This was the Aunt Gail she remembered. A little dotty, a little unexpected, and usually a lot of fun.

After her mother's death, she seemed to have become more solemn and pious. Mystery understood. Julia Mullins's murder had affected them all.

Patrice dropped off everyone's drinks, bustled away, then returned with some cornbread. She took everyone's orders, "accidentally" brushing against Axel's thigh a couple of times. Mystery wished he would put an arm around her or indicate to the forward waitress in some way that he was taken, but he seemed distant. No, distracted.

After Patrice collected their menus with a wink and sashayed off, Heath turned to her aunt. "You're feeling better since we gave you the terrible news about your sister in the kitchen?"

Aunt Gail drew in a thoughtful breath and seemed to contemplate her answer. "It was a shock, but I prayed before we left. In my room, I caught the last few minutes of *Hour of Grace* on TV. I just love Reverend Grace. Do you watch him?"

"I don't think I've heard of him in the UK," Heath deferred politely.

"Is that true?" her aunt asked.

Mystery nodded. "I don't know who he is. A televangelist, I'm guessing."

"You'd say so. He's brilliant. Anyway, part of the sermon I caught was about letting go. You can tell from his stirring words that he's lost deeply in life. He helped me realize that the cause of Julia's death doesn't matter much. Nothing will bring her back. I hate that her last moments were of aggression and fear. But she's with the Lord now, and in a far better place."

While Mystery supposed that was true, it wasn't as cut and dried for her. Maybe because she didn't have Aunt Gail's sort of faith to bolster or calm her. Instead, she just felt angry that she still didn't know who to hate or who to picture taking the mental violence she'd never dish out. But why spoil lunch with this conversation?

Across the table, Heath looked as if he fiercely disagreed with her aunt. She frowned at him in question, and he gave a subtle shake of his head. Mystery made a mental note to ask him later.

"Absolutely," she murmured. "Tell me about your upcoming mission trip to Indonesia."

"Isn't it exciting?" Her aunt smiled, looking far younger than her years. "I'm looking forward to a whole new adventure. There's so much need for medical care in so many third-world countries, so the chance to help vaccinate children and assist mothers give birth safely while spreading the gospel is such a fabulous opportunity."

"Are you just traveling with people from your church?"

"No. It's actually been organized through Reverend Grace's ministry. He's sending ten medical professionals there. We'll assess their needs, their existing equipment, and their reception to the Lord. It's a spiritual reconnaissance trip. I think it's my calling now that I'm retired. I have the time and the will to help these people."

Mystery felt a little ashamed that she'd never had such a selfless need to help strangers on the other side of the world. "It sounds like a great cause. I'm sure they need everything you and the others will bring them."

Her aunt smiled as if an inner peace glowed from within. "Serve the Lord, and you'll never be left wanting again."

Beside her aunt, Heath tapped on his phone, looking distracted. Mystery drank her tea, noticing that Axel fidgeted, glancing around the restaurant. Why were these two so on edge? Yes, she was nervous about seeing what she'd inherited, and maybe she'd be collecting whatever had gotten her mom killed. But after all these years, could whatever secret Julia Mullins had taken to the grave still be that important?

The food arrived moments later, and Patrice set everything down, saving Axel's for last, serving his grilled chicken and veggies with a saucy wink.

Mystery just really wanted to slap the woman. Instead, she forced a smile. "Can I have the ketchup?"

Patrice reached to the next booth over, now empty, and plucked one up, almost slamming it down on the table in front of her. "Anything else?"

Axel shifted his weight in his seat again. "Where's the restroom?"

Clearly glad to be of service, the waitress sent him a sultry smile. "I'm headed that direction myself, sugar. Why don't you follow me?"

"You okay?" Mystery muttered to him as he slid out of the booth.

"Yeah. Quick restroom break. I'll be back."

As he hustled across the café, her aunt reached for her hand. "Let's pray."

Mystery took Aunt Gail's outstretched fingers and bowed her head on cue. She listened with half an ear, utterly distracted today.

"Amen. Dig in, dear," her aunt instructed. "It looks delicious."

It did. Mystery remembered the amazing hamburgers the diner served from her childhood. With gusto, she picked the sandwich up and took a big bite, then moaned. *Heaven.*

Heath picked at his pork chops. His thoughts were turning, she could tell. He always got a little distant when something bothered him. But Mystery had no idea what might have put him in such a mood.

Her aunt seemed not to notice. She waxed poetic about her fried chicken and filled the empty space at the table with chatter about all the things she planned to do in Indonesia. "They have some beautiful coastline, and this Kansas girl is looking forward to just soaking it all in."

"Isn't that a primarily Islamic country?" Heath asked.

She turned to him, looking a bit surprised by his question. "All the more reason for us to travel there. Less than ten percent of the population is Christian, and it's a shame they're missing out on the Lord's blessing."

Mystery plastered on a smile and refrained from pointing out that the people there had religion, just not necessarily hers, mostly because she knew it did matter to her aunt which God these people had chosen to follow. Aunt Gail had always been religious. That cross hanging above the stove had been there for decades. But the one at the top of the stairs with pictures of the TV preachers raking in millions in tax-free cash were new. Mystery hated to be so cynical, but didn't quite grasp how these televangelists could be so gung-ho to minister to the millions they couldn't interact with if a little bit of greed wasn't involved.

Lifting her glass of tea only to realize it was empty, she looked around for Patrice. She was nowhere to be found. *Typical.*

Beside Mystery's burger sat Axel's untouched food. He'd been gone more than a few minutes. Had he gotten sick? Was he okay?

"Excuse me," she said to Heath and her aunt, then filed out of the booth.

Heath nudged Aunt Gail. "I'm afraid I have to follow her. Occupational hazard."

That startled the older woman. "Oh, of course. You know where to find the restrooms?"

Absently, Mystery wished her aunt hadn't shouted that in such a public place, but the woman often talked on the loud side. Thankfully, only a few patrons lingered at nearly two o'clock. "I'm fine."

As they both scooted out and to their feet, Mystery made her way to the back of the restaurant and turned right to enter the hallway that held the bathrooms, Heath right behind her. The lighting in the narrow hallway wasn't spectacular, but she made out two shapes leaning against the wall, entwined.

Axel stood with his back against the dark paneling. And Patrice was draped all over him.

Mystery stopped short, taking in the waitress's mouth on his. Her shirt and bra had been ripped wide open, and now she pressed her bare breasts to his chest. She'd also wrapped one arm around Axel's thick neck while they kissed. The fingers of her free hand tugged at his zipper.

Mystery blinked, stunned. Shocked. Pain hit her chest with a terrible blow. Every inch of her froze over. She gasped.

Suddenly, Axel shoved the waitress off him, arranging his expression to look somewhere between stunned and pissed off.

Oh, he hadn't begun to see pissed off as far as Mystery was concerned.

"What the hell are you doing?" he asked Patrice.

The waitress bit her lip and fastened her bra. "Oops, is that your girlfriend who caught us? You were right; we should have gone in the break room across the hall and locked the door."

"What the fuck are you're talking about?" Axel demanded, setting Patrice farther away.

Mystery wondered how often her dad had said similar words to her mom. How often had he made her question her judgment, feel paranoid for being suspicious, or deflected the situation to make it sound like her fault, not his.

She wasn't going to fall into that trap, not when she'd seen Axel with another woman—again—less than twenty-four hours after the last fiasco.

"You fucking bastard," she growled.

Axel stepped toward her, his face imploring. "Take a deep breath. Think rationally. It's not what you're imagining, princess."

"Of course it's not. It never is."

"Seriously. She crawled on me less than two seconds before you came around the corner. I didn't touch her. I had nothing to do with it."

"Stop! Just stop." She threw up a hand to ward him off, icy betrayal chilling her bloodstream that otherwise sizzled with fury and scorn. "Don't come near me. And don't you dare touch me."

"I guess she's sensitive?" Patrice muttered. "I had no idea . . ."

"Shut up," Mystery snarled. "I guess I shouldn't be surprised by this little quickie fling but somehow I am. Two can play that game."

Without warning, she turned and collided with Heath's substantial body, then wrapped her arms around his neck and slanted her lips over his. He stiffened in shock—then began devouring her lips with his own like a starving man needing sustenance.

Mystery pulled away, dazed and out of breath. She didn't feel vindicated or even happily spiteful. Instead, everything she'd done felt terribly wrong. She didn't want Heath, and it wasn't fair to use him to make Axel angry or lead him on. But she was so damn angry . . .

"Are you fucking serious?" Axel demanded. "That's really how you're going to play this?"

No. She wasn't. No matter how she felt about Axel, she couldn't be unfair to Heath. He'd done nothing but be a faithful protector and friend for six years.

She backed away and sent her bodyguard an apologetic glance.

His dark eyes held hurt and censure that promised a long discussion later. A blade of shame struck her deep.

Curling her arms around herself, Mystery turned to Axel again to find him tucking in his shirt and righting his pants. The sight infuriated and hurt her all over again. New tears stung her eyes like acid.

"I believed you were different," she sobbed, wishing she could hold it back. "I believed it when you told me you were just friends with Sweet Pea. I let myself trust you. I fell in love with you. I'm such an idiot."

Mystery stumbled away. She had to get out of here, away from him, before she broke down and succumbed to the urge to ask if there was any way she'd mistaken what she'd seen and whether Patrice really had been the aggressor, taking Axel by surprise.

But it was time to accept that no man was perfect, even the one who had once saved her life and starred as the hero of all her fantasies. At the end of the day, he was just a man, like her father, who was a fabulous director, friend, coworker, and dad. But he couldn't be perfect at everything, and he happened to be a lousy mate. Axel had so many amazing qualities, she could have put up with some faults. Why did his have to be that he was a cheating asshole?

The question ripped her insides apart, and all she kept seeing in her mind was the waitress's lips against his, her hands at his zipper.

"Let's go." Heath shot Axel a look of disbelief and disgust, then wrapped his arm around her.

Her aunt stood stock-still, looking too shocked to even breathe. "Oh, my . . . You poor girl."

Mystery let the two of them tuck her between them and lead her away from the darkened hallway and the terrible nightmare unfolding.

"Don't you leave, Mystery." Axel came after her, his heavy footfalls resounding on the old flooring. "Don't you walk out on me before we've talked."

More tears stabbed her eyes. She covered her face in her hands. Yes, she'd promised they would talk things out from now on. He'd spanked her for leaving once before . . . then made love to her so masterfully. No, he'd fucked her body and her head all at once, and she didn't owe him a damn thing.

Why would he bother cheating? Did he simply have a wandering eye? Did he get a thrill out of indulging in a little something on the side? Or had he viewed her as nothing more than a path to fame or a meal ticket? Maybe she'd never been remotely relevant to him at all.

The thought only made her sob more. And when Heath shoved her toward the exit, pausing only long enough to throw some bills on the table for their meal, Mystery didn't fight him.

"If you do this, you know how I'll take it," Axel shouted after her.

Yes, if she walked out on him now, they would be done forever. He'd warned her. But what did they have to save? If he couldn't love just her, then they had absolutely nothing.

Heath pushed the door open and gave her a nudge. She resisted for a moment, then turned to look at Axel one last time. He looked big, agitated, so damn masculine. And blurry. More tears spilled and scalded her cheeks.

Maybe they'd always been doomed. If everything happened for a reason, maybe this had transpired because she'd needed to see the real him to grow up, move on. Maybe she'd witnessed this so she could finally fall out of love with him.

"Go to hell!" she shouted.

Then she ran out the door, tumbled into the car, and refused to look back.

Chapter Seventeen

THAT motherfucker, Heath Powell, drove Mystery away before Axel could say more than a handful of words to her. He heard the last of the spinning tires and watched the black car disappear down the street. His guts fell somewhere around his toes and his heart broke open wide.

Why the fuck was he just now grasping the fact that he'd fallen completely in love with Mystery Mullins? Not that his stupid ass realization did him any good now.

Hell, she'd blindsided him. One minute the sex had been so hot she'd nearly melted him, but his need for more than her body had been something new. Axel hadn't known how to interpret it. He'd never felt anything like that. So he'd avoided labeling it.

Wasn't that biting him in the ass now? Maybe if he'd realized his feelings sooner, he could have simply told her he loved her and they could have avoided this stupid misunderstanding at the café. Instead, she'd seen him "cheating" and overreacted. But Axel kind of understood because when he'd seen her kiss Heath, he'd felt some weird red haze jack up his temper. Then she'd threatened to leave, and he'd totally overreacted, too.

So rather than holding her close, he got to watch Mystery skid out of the parking lot with the man she'd locked lips with behind the wheel. Axel tried to imagine spending his life without her. He couldn't. He didn't want to.

So what now? Chase after her like a damn puppy? Axel sighed at the picture that painted. But wasn't that better than spending the rest of his life with his insides crushed and feeling as if he were missing the other half of his soul?

Put like that, the dog scenario sounded way better.

But would that be the end of it? Would she run out on him yet again because she wasn't capable of the death-do-us-part, forever sort of love? He didn't want to be gloom and doom, but for the third time in twenty-fours, she'd left him cold. How was he supposed to get over that?

Axel stood with his hands on his hips, gaping at the street, though the town car was long gone from view. He had no ride back to his rental at the farm. He'd have to find one, then wait for Mystery and her aunt to return so he could talk some sense into her. He'd figure out why he'd suddenly felt a pressing need to pee yet again and apologize for not taking the waitress's overtures seriously until it was too late. If that didn't work, if Mystery wouldn't talk to him . . . he'd have to figure out what fucking tactic to take next, because he couldn't give up. That only led to the bottom of a bottle and decades of misery.

"What just happened?" a woman asked behind him.

He turned to find Patrice looking brutally confused and grabbed her arm. "You tell me. Why the hell did you climb all over me uninvited?"

Grimacing, she yanked her arm free and removed the elastic band securing her blond tresses in a ponytail. "I was hired to. I'm an actress. Someone contacted my agent and paid my travel expenses out to this one-pony town to pull a practical joke on you."

Axel heard her words—and she might as well have been speaking a foreign language. "What?"

"Yeah. I'm from L.A. My agent just told me that someone important wanted me to play a joke on one of his friends. I got your picture and some instructions . . ." She shrugged. "I'm so sorry. I really had no idea it would screw up everything between you and your girlfriend."

Who the hell would do that? And why? Axel's thoughts raced. Someone wanted him separated from Mystery and had figured out that she'd stomp away if she believed he couldn't keep his pants zipped. He could only see two possible motives: Either someone didn't like his relationship with Mystery—Heath came to mind—or someone dangerous wanted her to be minus a protector who would lay down his life to save hers.

"How much?" he demanded.

"What?"

"Money. How much were you paid to do this?"

"Ten grand, plus travel expenses," she admitted. "I feel terrible. I really am sorry."

Too late for that. "Call your agent and ask him who hired you."

"I asked before I took the gig. He wouldn't tell me, but I needed the money to make rent. The only condition was anonymity. Sal told me that whoever hired me swore you'd know who it was."

So Heath was toying with him . . . or the killer was. Axel did some quick mental math. Could Heath come up with ten grand plus travel expenses in less than twenty-four hours? Since Joaquin had already given him the guy's bank balance before Patrice had been hired, Axel knew the answer was no. Heath had investments, but none he could get his hands on right away.

Since he didn't think Heath wanted to kill Mystery, this stunt probably had nothing to do with her love life and everything to do with the reason for her mother's murder. That made Heath the last line of Mystery's defense against the psycho hunting her.

Axel groaned. Yeah, he'd said that he wouldn't come after Mystery if she left him again. But he couldn't stay away. The circumstances had been extenuating, and someone had set them up to fail. He intended to make sure they didn't succeed, especially if her life was on the line.

"Shit," Axel cursed, feeling behind the eight ball. He had to talk to Heath, ensure the Brit knew something was up and the killer was likely planning to make his move.

Who wanted Mystery dead? Who, among her friends or family, had the money and connections to hire this actress at the last minute? Gail Leedy had chosen the restaurant, which cast suspicion on her, but the woman didn't have any money to hire someone. Axel had seen her bank balance, too. After selling off the land around her farm for a pittance to a neighbor about ten years ago, she'd lived on it and her salary from the medical clinic, saving a modest amount in an IRA. She donated more money to religious organizations each month than to the upkeep of her own home. And why would the pious older woman want her niece dead?

Axel sighed. He didn't have time for a fucking puzzle. He had to get to Mystery pronto, but he had no car and didn't know the name of her attorney's office.

Beside him, Patrice—if that was even her name—hovered, looking utterly contrite.

He turned to her. "Did you meet the café's manager or owner before you started this farce?"

"A waitress." She nodded quickly, as if finally glad she could be of assistance. "I'm actually taking Betty's shift today. She's waiting in the employee break room to take over again."

"Ask her to come out here. I need to talk to her. Tell her it's a matter of life and death." At least Axel suspected it was.

"S-sure." Patrice darted off.

Yanking his phone from his belt, Axel scrolled through his contacts until he found Heath's number. It rang once . . . twice . . . a third time—then rolled to voice mail.

He swore as the last of the Brit's clipped greeting played. "Mystery is in danger. I have a bad feeling that once she gets her hands on whatever her mother left for her, all hell will break loose. Call me as soon as you get this. If I can figure out where you're going, I'll head in that direction."

Axel ended the call, then someone tapped him on the shoulder. He turned to find Patrice standing there with a salty older woman whose hair was a very unlikely shade of red. She was sixty-five if she was a day. She chomped on a piece of gum, looking at him as if she'd seen and done it all and now it bored her terribly.

"Betty?" he asked her.

"That's me. What you need?" She smiled. "Back in my day, I would have done just about anything to help a hunk like you."

Nice, but they didn't have time for memory lane now. He cleared his throat. "My girlfriend has gone to an attorney's office to deal with the last provisions of a will. I'm told the office is about three miles east of here. Any idea whose office I should be looking for?"

She nodded as if he'd asked an easy question. "Sure. You want Press and Osborne. I'll give you the address, but you head down the main drag . . ."

Axel took note as the woman gave him directions, committing cross streets and the name of the building in which the offices were located to memory.

"Thank you. Can either of you give me a ride there or tell me where to find a taxi?"

"I gotta start my shift. Dinner rush starts here about five, and we're still a mess from lunch." She sent Patrice an accusing stare.

The blonde held up her hands, stare incredulous. "I'm an actress, not a waitress."

"And a slob, too. You can get out as soon as you pay me the two hundred dollars for giving you my shift."

Patrice rolled her eyes and extracted a wad of bills from a pocket in her little skirt. She shoved a handful of bills into Betty's palm. "If I never come here again, I'll be thrilled."

Ditto for him, Axel thought.

"You got a car?" he asked the actress.

"No. I have a shuttle coming to my hotel at five to take me to the airport. The hotel is only a few blocks, so I walked."

Frustration crawled over Axel like a million stinging ants. "Can either of you tell me how to find a fucking taxi in this town before my girlfriend dies?"

At that, Betty scrambled to attention. "Yeah. Should I call the police?"

For a crime that hadn't actually happened yet? The cops wouldn't do a damn bit of good until it was too late. "I can do that. Just get me a taxi."

As Betty darted away to do his bidding, Axel stabbed at the screen of his phone again. He only knew one person who had money to burn, contacts in Hollywood, and secrets to keep. He intended to get the son of a bitch on the phone now.

Finally, he pressed the button to engage the call.

"Hello?" Marshall Mullins answered almost instantly.

"I'll skip the 'how-the-fuck-could-you' speech and get right to asking where she is."

"What are you talking about?"

"Well, your plan to send me an actress to play the role of waitress slash nympho worked damn well, and now Mystery is convinced I'm a cheating scum." *Like you.* "She's run off with Heath and her aunt and left me behind at some craptastic diner while the secrets you've been holding in are breathing down her neck. But I guess you planned it like that."

"Why would I do that?" he asked incredulously. "I've wanted you to stay with my daughter since the danger started. You and Heath are the only two I trust with her safety."

"The taxi will be here in a few," Betty whispered in his other ear. "Good luck."

When Axel turned to nod at her, he noticed that the jaded woman's face had softened. "Thanks."

He stepped outside to await his ride and turned his focus on Mullins again. "Did you have anything to do with your wife's murder? Did you pay someone to off her? Who's going to rub Mystery out here in Kansas? You'll have an even better alibi this time, by the way, being over a thousand miles away. Smart thinking."

"You're way the hell out of line, Dillon," Mullins roared. "I didn't kill Julia. I didn't have her killed, either. I would never harm a hair on Mystery's head. Why else would I send her to the States with protection if I wanted her dead?"

"You tell me. You're keeping a shitload of secrets, and it's putting her in danger. So you start talking and tell me whatever you've kept quiet. If you don't and something terrible happens to the woman I love, so help me, I will hunt you down. One day when you least expect it, you will find me beside you in an alley and I'll have even less mercy for you than you did for your wife and daughter. You have no idea how painful I'll make your death or how much I'll relish it."

"Whoa!" Mullins choked. "What's happened? Why don't you start at the beginning?"

"I don't have time. If you're serious about keeping Mystery safe, prove it by telling me what the fuck you're hiding from her and the rest of the world."

Her father sighed. "Let me see if I can get ahold of Heath and have him skip this appointment with the attorney and take her to a safe location."

"I tried to call him already. No answer."

"Frankly, I don't think you're his favorite person, so he may not answer you. Hang on."

"All right, but if you double-cross me . . . I've warned you."

The director let out a rough breath. "You did. I swear, my only concern is Mystery's safety. I'll be right back with you."

Axel squirmed in his seat. Damn it, he needed to pee again, and he had no idea why. He didn't have time to deal with this shit.

The minute seemed to take ten years before Mullins clicked back over and let out a panicked groan. "Heath isn't answering me, either. You think something is wrong?"

Axel could almost guarantee it was. "Tell me whose secret you're keeping or what you're protecting. It may help me save her life. Because I can't think of any other way to help her right now."

Mullins gave him a shaky sigh. "All right, but I kept this to myself purely for Mystery's protection. I never wanted anything to touch her, and I never dreamed that it could become her worst nightmare. What I'm about to say can never leak out to the public. And it can't ever reach her ears."

"Go ahead. I'm listening . . ."

* * *

IN the passenger's seat, Mystery curled her knees against her chest, heels clinging to the corner of the seat, and lowered her head. She didn't want anyone to see her cry. Her aunt would only tell her to rely on God. Maybe that would be a comfort to the woman, but Mystery couldn't manage spiritual just now. And she had no right to ask Heath for anything after she'd tried to use him to make Axel feel as wretched as she did.

What had she been thinking? Nothing, clearly. She'd let emotion take over like an idiot. Normally, she'd scoff at people who couldn't keep their crap together. In fact, Mystery couldn't remember a time since that spat with Axel at the hotel in the ghost town when she'd been worked up enough to lose all sense of logic. But now . . . she knew how being completely shocked and emotional screwed with her head.

She'd lashed out at Axel for hurting her, and it definitely hadn't been her proudest moment. In fact, she'd really like to forget it, go back to the wee hours of the morning when she'd been cozied up

with Axel in bed, feeling so loved and secure. She knew that unleash-
ing her temper, as she'd done after Axel's rejection in Cerro Gordo,
solved nothing. She also knew how much running out would hurt
Axel. But she'd done it anyway. Now she had to face that fact, like
life, head-on.

"I'm sorry, Heath."

He nodded slowly, then glanced into the rearview mirror at her
aunt in the backseat. "Where to?"

"Drive down this road about two miles. Three blocks up, take a
left. It's the second building on your right."

"Very good," he said to her aunt as they stopped at a light. He
stared straight ahead, as if he refused to look at Mystery.

She winced. She'd hurt his feelings. Somehow, she had to make
amends.

"Kissing you in that situation was wrong and unfair," she whispered. "If I could take it back, I—"

"But you can't," he cut in softly. "And you would never have
kissed me voluntarily if you hadn't been trying to hurt Axel."

Mystery wanted to say something that would soothe Heath, but
he wasn't wrong, and lying would only make matters worse. "I'm
sorry."

"This trip has made me realize that I've been an idiot. When
your father first hired me, you were a lovely girl, and I was a grieving
widower. I didn't see you as a woman. But as I got to know you, I
enjoyed your company, your wit and smile, the way you slowly came
out of your shell. I liked that you needed me, confided in me, persuaded me to emerge from my self-imposed exile. I didn't realize
until I saw you with Axel how completely I'd fallen in love with you.
I've been blind all this time. Now I can't unsee what's in my heart."

Mystery peered over at him, eyes willing and wishing she could
comfort him, even as she acknowledged that she was the problem.
And that made her feel awful. "I care for you. I really do."

"But today proved that I'll never be more than a substitute for you. Even if you never see Axel again, you love him. I could probably take advantage of your vulnerability and coax you into some sort of relationship for a few days, a few weeks, maybe even forever. But you'll never truly be mine, and I must break away from this unhealthy connection and start living again."

A bolt of shock struck her square in the chest. "What are you saying?"

"As soon as I have you back safely in London and delivered to your father, I'll be resigning. If he's interested in hiring another bodyguard for you, I can recommend several who would be excellent. But I cannot stay."

She didn't deserve to indulge in a pity party, but she couldn't seem to not make herself the guest of honor. How had she managed to screw up everything so catastrophically so quickly? How did she pull herself out of it?

Suck it up, cupcake. Tomorrow, she could be on her way back to the UK. She'd sort through whatever her mom had left her, along with the mess she'd made of her life, and figure out what to do next. Right now, she just had to get through this meeting.

Mystery sniffled and rifled in the glove box for some tissues, using them to dab her eyes. "I understand. I never meant to hurt you."

He answered with a manly grunt and focused unwaveringly on the road ahead. Finally, they reached the attorney's office and parked. After checking her face—her eyes were a puffy nightmare, but at least she hadn't been wearing mascara—Mystery dug some lipstick out of her purse and applied it.

"Are you all right?" her aunt asked, clucking like a mother hen.

"I'll be fine. What floor?" Mystery asked more to change the subject than because she really cared.

"Fourth." Aunt Gail smiled and patted her hand.

As Heath exited the car, he looked around cautiously, taking note of the street, passersby, other cars, any open windows. Mystery knew the drill. He went through the rundown in his head anytime they were in public.

"Do you still have the key I gave you?"

Mystery nodded at her aunt. "In my purse. I'm ready."

"Are you?" Heath asked.

No, but she'd run out of time. She'd dragged her feet in claiming her mother's belongings at eighteen, telling herself that her friends and future were more important than a bunch of her mom's junk from the past. The truth was, she hadn't really wanted to sift through the contents and have to deal with the aftermath of what she found. Then she'd moved to London, so the excuses had been easy. When would she ever get to Emporia, Kansas, again, right? But in order to pursue what she'd been feeling for Axel, she'd had to give her father a plausible excuse, and retrieving her mother's effects had slipped off her tongue. Now that her relationship with Axel was in shambles, Mystery wished she could snuggle in front of the fire in her flat back home with her laptop, her characters, and a glass of wine, far away from the uncertainty and danger.

"Sure," she murmured.

In front of the elevator a sign affixed to a dangling red chain hanging between two stanchions read OUT OF ORDER. Aunt Gail groaned as they made their way up the stairs, huffing and puffing hard by the third flight. En route, they passed a dentist's office, a tutoring facility, and quite a few suites under refurbishment.

When they reached the fourth floor, Heath opened the door and peeked out. Once he deemed the empty space safe, he waved them out of the stairwell.

Mystery stepped through, checking the open landing with faux trees and nondescript dark-wood and beige chairs. The short pile carpeting in an uninspiring shade of oatmeal and the wall sconces with brass accents looked tired and out of date.

Whatever. She just wanted this over with. She was concerned that whoever had left the threatening picture in her hotel room in

Dallas would be lying in wait for her here. Mystery would love to believe that, somehow, she'd lost the psycho's trail and could just search her mother's belongings in peace, but a tingling at the back of her neck told her otherwise. And after all the drama of the day, she absolutely didn't need more.

Inside the office's faux frosted-glass double doors, a fortysomething receptionist looked up from her gossip magazine, barely concealing irritation at the interruption, and buzzed Mr. Osborne. Two minutes later, she ushered them to the back, past a coffee station, a dark office, then to the end of the hall. The placard on the door read NELSON OSBORNE.

A man pushing sixty rose to his average height, wearing his gray suit well as he stood and greeted them with a jaunty wave. The movement didn't ruffle his artificially dark hair, sprayed into place just so.

"Come on in." He stuck out his hand. "Welcome. I'm Nelson."

"Hi. I'm Julia Mullins's daughter, Mystery." They shook hands, then she turned to the others. "This is my mother's sister, Gail Leedy."

"I think we met years ago," Osborne said.

"I believe so," her aunt said placidly, then scooted to the far side of the desk to take one of the two guest chairs.

"And this is my . . . friend Heath." Mystery hesitated to admit he was a bodyguard. To some, it sounded either paranoid or pretentious. And if Osborne or anyone in his office was somehow in on the plot to kill her, she didn't want to tip off the fact that she'd come armed with protection.

But Heath gave himself away when he nodded sharply, cased the office, then took up sentry by the door. *So inconspicuous . . .* Mystery sighed.

Osborne sat again. "You look so much like your mother. It's uncanny. She was a beautiful woman, too. I was so sorry to hear about her sudden and terrible passing."

Mystery really didn't want to rehash it now. She felt as if she'd reached the drama quotient lately, and she'd grieve her mother's death again on its anniversary next Tuesday. "Thank you. As you know, I've come for her effects."

He nodded. "We'll have a few papers to sign, but let's claim your mother's belongings, then you can acknowledge receipt and whatnot. You have your key?"

"I do." She nodded, wondering where Mom's safe-deposit box was located. This office didn't look like a secure facility, and she couldn't imagine where the attorney would keep such things properly locked up.

"We'll be heading to the bank across the street. I've given them a copy of your mother's death certificate and prepared the other necessary paperwork. Your aunt, as executor of her will, provided testament that you are now the exclusive box holder and, therefore, the only person who can open it. As long as you have a photo ID, we should sail through the process." Osborne rose from his seat.

Mystery followed suit. While keeping her mother's possessions at the bank made more sense, she wished Osborne could have simply had them waiting for her. Legally, she knew that wasn't possible, but she was anxious to have this behind her and return safely to the farm so she could lick her wounds in private. And she had to admit that she hoped she'd see Axel if he came back for his duffel and rental car. No idea what she'd say to him. She didn't know how to reconcile so many red flags that pointed to him being a cheater with the hero she'd first fallen for. Had she gotten it all wrong today? Even if she had, she didn't think he'd tolerate the fact that she'd told him off and walked out.

"I'll follow you over there," Mystery murmured.

"Very good." Osborne stepped around his desk and sent a wary glance Heath's way. "Whenever you're ready . . ."

Aunt Gail fidgeted in her seat. "Goodness, I'd rather not have to walk up and down the stairs again. Your elevator is out of order, and I'm afraid I'm not recovered from the last hike. May I stay here?"

Osborne looked around his fastidious office. Not a single sheet of paper cluttered his massive mahogany desk. He ensured all his filing cabinets were locked and closed his laptop, which likely needed a password to access. "Of course. Forgive me, but I'm required to be cautious with other people's sensitive legal issues."

"Of course." Gail smiled in relief. "May I help myself to coffee?"

"Please do."

Mystery followed Osborne out the door, down the stairs, and to the bank. It was a sterile environment that tried to look friendly, with posters of people supposedly happy about taking out loans. Or maybe she was just feeling cynical right now because she was miserable thinking about Axel, not to mention worried that someone would try to kill her.

Within moments, a female bank employee in gray pants and a blue sweater had given her a form to sign and checked her ID. Everyone followed the woman with the flowing brown curls into the room with the safe-deposit boxes, passing row after row of the drawers in different sizes. Toward the back, the bank's officer produced her key. Mystery fished the other from her purse. Together, they opened the dual locks and withdrew the box from its slot to place it on the lone table in the adjacent room.

"I'll leave you to look through the contents. When you're done, let me know." The young woman gave her a bland smile, did a double take as she discreetly checked out Heath, then melted away.

Osborne stepped back. "Would you prefer for me to stay or go?"

"I think I'd like to do this alone," she murmured, both because it was true and because she wasn't sure she could trust him. "Thanks for understanding."

"Of course." He turned away and headed out of the vault.

"I won't leave you unprotected. Don't ask that of me." Heath crossed his beefy arms over his chest.

"I wouldn't." Mystery shook her head. "I want you here."

She kind of wished Axel was here, too, but refused to dwell on what wasn't and might never be again. Then she took a deep breath, wondering if she could ever really be ready to face whatever her mom had safeguarded for her, shut the door to the private room, and lifted the box's lid.

Inside, she found some jewelry, including some diamond earrings that had once belonged to her maternal grandmother. Julia had worn them on her wedding day, and they'd become a gift, as Mystery had heard the story. She also found a gorgeous cross made of rose and yellow gold entwined with lovely flourishes and embellishments. The center sparkled with a diamond that had to be at least a carat. Where had that come from? She didn't remember her mom wearing it.

Mystery also found what looked like some letters to her mom from her dad. Instantly, she recognized her father's handwriting on the yellowed envelopes. Based on the postmark of the first few, they had been written during their courtship and the early days of their marriage.

Despite their ill-fated union, these notes had been valuable to her mother. Mystery already knew that her father kept some from his late wife locked in his desk, along with a collection of her pictures. They'd loved each other completely and passionately once. Why had her father never tried to be a better husband? They'd both been human, filled with insecurity and capable of stupid mistakes. Had her mother somehow failed to understand that?

Tears sprang to her eyes, and Mystery sniffed them away. Now wasn't the time to get philosophical. She had to carry on.

She didn't see anything else at the bottom of the box. So odd . . . It didn't seem possible that these few pieces of jewelry or the dozen love notes would really be worth killing or dying for.

"That's it?" Heath looked over her shoulder. He sounded as puzzled as she felt.

"I guess."

Mystery lifted the earrings out of the box, wondering what her mother had been thinking when she'd placed them here for the last time. Had she known she'd never wear them again?

Swallowing back a lump of grief and loss, she tucked the diamond drops in her ears and closed her eyes. The earrings weren't heavy. In fact, she barely felt them, but wearing the gorgeous glittery things made her feel somehow closer to her mom.

She touched the cross with a reverent finger, tracing the lines, before picking it up and fastening it around her neck. The cross fell just below the hollow of her throat and felt shockingly cold against her skin. Then again, the necklace had been sitting untouched by human warmth for sixteen years.

"Let me look." Heath took her by the shoulders and turned her to face him, studying her with intent, dark eyes that missed nothing. "It's brilliant, but it isn't you."

"The earrings or the cross?"

"The cross. It's too ornate compared to your usual jewelry. The earrings look perfect, simple but elegant."

Mystery didn't have a mirror so she couldn't comment. Heath was probably right, but she wanted to wear the cross. It made her feel as if death, along with nearly a decade and a half, didn't separate her from her mom.

She lifted the stack of notes to open the first one and peek at the contents. As she did, she noticed something totally new underneath.

A little electronic disc of some sort, small and almost square. The kind capable of holding a tell-all book that might have gotten her mother killed?

Mystery's blood turned to ice.

Heath took the disc from her numb fingers. "It's an SD card. We need to read this quickly and decide on our best course of action."

She knew that, even if everything inside her violently disagreed. "How?"

"My laptop is in the car. It will read this disc."

Just like that, he'd open his trunk, and inside two minutes she would be reading whatever secrets her mother had kept until the day she died. Was she really ready for this?

Did she have a choice?

"I'll read on the drive back to Aunt Gail's farm," she murmured.

He gave her back a soothing pat. She may have insulted or upset him at the café today, but he'd put all that aside to comfort her because she needed it. Mystery wished she could have loved him in return. Heath would be a devoted protector and lover. He could be serious or funny. He was highly intelligent and had a great sense of adventure. Unfortunately, kissing him hadn't given her a fraction of the giddy, heart-beating thrill that simply being in the same room with Axel did.

She shoved the letters and the SD card in her purse, leaving the jewelry on. She signaled to the bank manager that she was done. Once the empty safe-deposit box was locked up, she signed the paperwork necessary to terminate the box, then left with Heath and Osborne, the attorney mentioning just a few more papers she needed to sign in his office.

A warm breeze brushed her face and the late afternoon sun blinded her as she walked between them back to the office building. The attorney led the way, while Heath watched her back. Heart pumping, Mystery kept vigilant, almost expecting someone to jump out at her and demand she turn over her mother's effects.

Inside the office building again, the air was almost too still. The carpenters renovating the empty suites on the lower floors were either packing up for the day or already gone.

Finally, they reached the fourth floor and Osborne's office again. Inside, they found Aunt Gail reading a paperback she'd likely pulled from her purse, and sipping coffee. She'd poured several other cups and left them on the corner of the desk.

As soon as they entered, she jumped out of her seat. "Were you successful?"

Mystery didn't really want to talk about it, but of course her aunt wanted to know what her only sister had left behind before her death. "Yeah. I found letters and jewelry." She showed off the earrings and the cross. "And some other stuff. We'll look at it more carefully in the car."

"Excellent. Coffee?" Aunt Gail asked her.

"Sure." Mystery didn't actually want any, but as evidenced by the cookies and lemonade, the woman liked to feed others. She didn't want to refuse, so she set it on the desk in front of her.

"No, thank you," Osborne murmured as he retrieved some papers in a folder. "At my age, caffeine past noon keeps me awake half the night."

"Luckily, I haven't run into that yet." Her aunt took another sip. "I sleep like a baby. Heath?" She all but pressed the cup into his hand. "It's really delicious. I noticed you drank nearly a whole pot this morning. You'll appreciate this brew." She turned to the attorney. "What sort of beans are these, Mr. Osborne?"

He smiled almost smugly. "It took me over a decade to find the perfect coffee. It's a Kona-Colombian blend. I have it specially roasted in Mexico, but it's about the best coffee I've ever tasted."

"Wonderful." Her aunt all but moaned around the lip of her Styrofoam cup, then turned to Heath. "Cream or sugar?"

"Black is fine." He sniffed the brew, then sipped it. "It's strong, the way I like it."

Her aunt smiled, then settled back into her chair, shoving the book in her purse as Mystery and Osborne got down to business.

Several conversations and a handful of forms later, she stood and shook the attorney's hand. Her aunt did the same. Heath nodded. As Mystery looked his way, she noticed he was slow to push away from the wall.

"Are you all right?" she asked.

"Sure."

He looked pale. His lids drooped tiredly. His mouth looked a bit slack. Mystery didn't think he felt all right. But she knew the stubborn man. He could have a limb hanging off or be dying of a hemorrhagic fever and he'd still insist that he felt fine.

With a sigh at his stubbornness, they made their way out the office. Heath stopped at the receptionist's desk. "Can you show me where to find your loo?"

At the slur of his words, Mystery frowned and wrapped a hand around his arm.

The woman barely peeked over her magazine to send him a confused stare. Then she narrowed her eyes at him. "Loo? I've never heard it called that, but no way am I lifting my skirt for a total stranger—I don't care how hot you are—and showing you my—"

"He means the bathroom," Mystery clarified for the clueless receptionist.

She had the good grace to turn pink. "Sorry. Across the hall, to the right of the elevator. Second door."

Heath nodded. "Thanks."

When he tripped over his own two feet heading across the open space, Mystery tugged on his arm. "Are you sure you're all right?"

His expression looked a tad unfocused until he blinked and spent some effort focusing on her. "I'll be all right. The jet lag and lack of sleep lately just have me a bit knackered."

While his answer made sense, his words sounded even more slurred than before. Mystery didn't like it.

"You want more coffee?" she asked.

"No. I'll step in there and splash some cold water on my face."

"We'll wait in the car," her aunt said, tottering on her feet. "I'm afraid I find myself a bit dizzy, too."

As the woman put a hand to her head, Mystery watched them both, wondering if someone had slipped something in their coffee. After all, she and Mr. Osborne had been the only ones not to drink it.

With a nod, Heath shoved the car keys in her hand, then pushed into the restroom, not quite steady on his feet. As she watched him with a concerned frown, her aunt nearly lost her balance while standing perfectly still. Mystery cursed. She didn't want to leave either of them alone.

Axel would really have come in handy right now, a voice whispered in her head. Yes, he would, but she needed him for far more than helping her ailing traveling party. Her heart needed him. As soon as Heath reached the car, she'd return to the café and hunt her man down. They had to talk. She just couldn't believe that today's lunch was the end of them. It couldn't be. Mystery didn't think she could live without him. She didn't really want to try.

Was this why her mother had taken so long to work up the gumption to leave her father? Had she known it was in her best interest but she just hadn't been able to break away from the charismatic man she'd fallen for?

Disquieted by the parallel between her life and her mom's, she turned to Aunt Gail, firmly focusing on the present. "I'll help you to the car."

The older woman gave her a shaky nod, then grabbed her arm to steady herself. "Thank you."

"One second." Mystery leaned her aunt against the railing, then pressed against the door to the men's room. "I'll be back to help you as soon as I can."

She heard water splashing, heard him grunt out an answer. He didn't sound good, and she wondered what the hell was going on.

As Mystery raced back to her aunt's side, foreboding gonged through her belly. Everyone around her today seemed afflicted by some ailment. Had someone concocted a ploy to get her alone? But who could have tampered with Axel's bladder, as well as Heath's and Aunt Gail's equilibrium? She would have suspected the attorney, but he hadn't been at the café. She'd love to blame Patrice, but shouldn't any drug the skanky waitress put in their food have taken effect within thirty minutes?

Thankfully, Mystery guided her aunt down the stairs, and she seemed to recover a bit with the exertion. Outside, the brisk wind in her face revived her a bit, too.

She helped Aunt Gail around to the passenger's door and opened it for her. "There you go. Get settled, and I'll be back with Heath in a moment."

"I don't think so." The older woman reached into her purse with a tight smile. When she withdrew her hand, she pointed a small gun right a Mystery's heart. "Give me the keys and get in. Where you're going, Heath will only be in my way."

Chapter Eighteen

W HEN the taxi rolled up to the attorney's building, Axel didn't see Heath's car parked along the street or in the adjoining lot. He cursed. He'd waited nearly twenty minutes for the shuffling old driver to show up in the first place. Thanks to the delay, he had no idea where to find Mystery, Heath, or her aunt now.

He pulled out his phone again and tried to dial the bodyguard. Nothing.

"Can you wait here? I'll be back in five minutes."

Axel didn't even hang around for the taxi driver to acknowledge him. In less than an instant, he slammed the door and ran into the building, pausing to look at the directory to find the attorney before he darted up the stairs, taking two at a time until he reached the lawyer's office.

At his approach, the receptionist sighed as she lowered her magazine, then blinked, gave him a once-over, and smiled sweet as pie. Axel didn't have time for her games.

"Mystery Mullins and her party, how long ago did they leave?"

The fortyish woman with her teased highlights gaped at him. "Just a few minutes."

"Did they say where they were headed?

She shook her head. "Not to me. Wait one second." She picked up the office phone and presumably called Mystery's mother's attorney. A moment later, she hung up. "Ms. Mullins didn't say anything to Mr. Osborne, either. The man with her asked me for the loo. That's British for the restroom." She acted as if the knowledge made her superior. "I directed him across the hall, and they left."

Another freaking dead end, damn it. But Axel could stand to hit the head again, so he jogged in the direction the receptionist had gestured. As he walked in, he spotted Heath coming out of a stall, looking paler than a sheet.

"You're here. Thank God. What the hell happened to you?" Axel asked.

"I think I was drugged. It was the coffee in the lawyer's office." He grimaced. "I nearly passed out, then realized what had happened. I made myself vomit. It's still in my system, but I don't think I absorbed all of the sedative."

Maybe not, but he still looked damn weak. With a grudging sigh, Axel tugged down his zipper and used the urinal. "Where's Mystery?"

"Why do you care?" Heath shot back. "You all but shagged that waitress at the café. Did you finish that, get bored, and decide to follow Mystery again?"

"No. Fuck off. The waitress admitted that she's an actress and was paid to come on to me."

Surprise rolled across Heath's face, then suspicion took over again. "Why should I believe you? Why should Mystery?"

"If I have to lie to a woman to keep her, then I don't deserve her. Seriously, someone staged the whole scene with Patrice at the café to separate me from Mystery. I'd suspect good ol' Aunt Gail, but she has no money."

Heath frowned. "If she intended to sell her sister's secrets, she may have borrowed the funds against her forthcoming payday. Or perhaps she's blackmailed someone into murdering Mystery."

Axel hadn't considered that previously—and didn't want to now. "Where are Mystery and Gail?"

"They should be waiting in the car."

"Where is it parked?" He hoped like hell he simply hadn't seen where Heath had parked it.

"Out front."

As he raised his zipper, foreboding rolled through his gut. "Not anymore. It's gone."

Heath's eyes flared wide as he soaped his hands in the sink. "I can't think of a single reason they'd move the car elsewhere. We weren't in a no-parking zone."

Quickly, Axel washed up, too. "Then she's in danger. I'm beginning to suspect that her aunt sold her out."

After a considering pause, Heath nodded. "She made coffee for everyone while we were at the bank. She was the only one who could have doctored the brew."

"I'm convinced she gave me something that's made me need to pee every ten damn minutes, probably in that lemonade I drank as we left the farm."

"It's possible she's been waiting all these years for Mystery to claim her mother's articles so she could gain control of whatever bloody secrets Mrs. Mullins held."

"Or she may be guiltier than that. Maybe she's looking to cover up her own crimes," Axel grated out.

Together, they pushed out of the bathroom, Heath wearing a frown. They hit the stairs and began running down. So many possibilities. So little time to save the woman he loved.

"We have to find them. Any idea where to start?"

Heath still looked weak, like he wanted to puke again, but he sucked in a breath and grinned. "She's got my key fob." He reached for his phone. "I'm forever losing my keys, so I made sure I can track them."

* * *

WITH her free hand, Aunt Gail snatched Heath's keys from Mystery and shoved them in her purse. The woman was all business as she fished out a pair of handcuffs and, with an awkward one-handed maneuver, used them to restrain her niece to the car door.

Mystery would have fought back, but the barrel of the firearm hovered barely a foot away from her face.

Her aunt wore a ladylike little smile as she clicked the cuffs into place. "You couldn't have been polite and simply drank your coffee. It contained a little something to keep you compliant. After so many years as a nurse, I know my controlled substances. I had a lovely Schedule Four waiting in your coffee, but you had to be difficult." She heaved a sigh of annoyance. "Stay put."

When her aunt would have shut the door, Mystery worked her way past the shock and stuck her foot out to block her. "No. Stop! What are you doing?"

Her aunt thrust the gun closer to her face, then glanced at her watch. "Shut up. I'll explain on the drive. We're running late."

"For what?"

Aunt Gail just kicked her leg out of the way, her practical shoes surprisingly mean, then shut the door and bustled behind the car. The older woman climbed into the driver's seat and started the engine, pulling out of the parking lot sedately, as if refusing to attract attention. "I had a car like this once, a nice big sedan. My father gave it to me as an engagement present."

Engagement? Mystery thought her aunt had never been married—not that it mattered right now. Figuring out what the heck was going on and escaping did.

"Where are we going?" she demanded. "You can't shoot me. I'm your niece. You're—"

"Prepared to do what I must," she snapped. "You've asked questions, and I'm trying to explain, so pay attention.

"When my engagement fell apart, I decided to move to Hollywood and try my hand at acting. I'd been in a few school plays. I could sing and dance reasonably well. I'd been told I was pretty. So I saved some money and packed my bags. Julia had graduated from high school the year before and didn't want to live on the farm any more than I did." Aunt Gail gave a long-suffering sigh. "Why I let her wheedle her way into driving to California with me, I'll never know."

"I'd appreciate it if you stopped pointing the gun at me and let me go." Mystery could barely concentrate on her aunt's words. Her stare locked with the semiautomatic in the older woman's hand, nestled against her torso.

"Quiet! You're just like your mother. You think you're special and deserve more than everyone else. You want everyone to cater to you. You're certainly a whore, like her. I heard you and that . . . man early this morning. But the fact that you're a promiscuous slut doesn't surprise me at all."

Was this woman even the same Aunt Gail she'd known all her life? She seemed unhinged and bitter, not to mention violent.

"What do you want? The things I picked up from my mother's safe-deposit box?" Mystery offered. "I'll give them to you. You can let me go."

"That's not for me to decide. I'm telling you what you want to know, jezebel. What I've been dying to tell you. Now close your mouth and listen." She cleared her throat, obviously incensed. "When Julia and I reached Hollywood, we both found agents quickly and started auditioning. Julia landed a few roles, nothing major. She was wholly unremarkable but somehow managed to catch your father's eye. I'd met Marshall first at a party and we dated a bit. Then he hired my sister for a bit part. That was the last movie he made before that silly action film that launched him wide." She scoffed as she stopped at a red light. "Next thing I knew, he and Julia were an item. I couldn't believe when he proposed to her."

Mystery blinked. Her aunt's words registered but . . . She'd had no idea that Gail had ever dated her father. She also knew her father too well. "You had sex with my dad?"

"Yes and no." She giggled, then sobered. "You keep interrupting. Stop that!" She waved the gun again.

The thought that her father had taken her aunt to bed before marrying her mom made her ill. *Yeah, what about after?*

Honestly, if they'd continued screwing after his wedding to her mother, Mystery didn't want to know.

"None of this should have surprised me. Julia had always been the devil's mistress. Everyone thought she was so beautiful and sultry—like you. She seduced your father into forgetting I existed. But after they married, his career took off. It wasn't long before your mother heard rumors of his infidelity." Her aunt sneered, then sped away when the light turned green, heading toward the edge of town. "She said she needed spiritual solace, and she sought it from a man of God, one of the most esteemed I've ever had the honor of meeting. But could she respect his pious service to the Lord? No, not your mother. She lured him like a serpent in the garden, coaxing him to eat the forbidden fruit. She coerced him to immorality and rendered him temporarily wicked. From that unholy alliance, you were conceived."

"What?" Mystery breathed but she couldn't possibly have heard that right. No way had Aunt Gail just told her that Marshall Mullins wasn't her biological father.

"So you didn't know." She smiled with malicious glee, picking up speed as they approached the outskirts of the downtown area. "I don't even think you suspected. Julia hid the truth from Marshall and gave you that silly name to disarm his suspicions."

Mystery wondered how she could ever live with this secret. If, by some miracle, she didn't die today, what would she tell her dad?

"As the years went on, Julia began insisting that she intended to divorce her husband," her aunt continued. "She told me that she intended to write a tell-all book, telling *all*." She scoffed. "I applauded her desire to drag Marshall through the mud. He deserved it, always thinking with his instrument of lust. But your mother could not be allowed to shame and stain such a beacon of light—of God himself—because Satan's mistress had weakened him in one terrible moment. She had to be silenced."

Mystery gaped at her aunt, a million thoughts racing through her brain so quickly she couldn't grasp onto or give voice to just one. The implications just zoomed through her head. She blinked, gaped, jaw hanging as her aunt pulled up to an abandoned building with a rusty metal ladder leading up to the roof and a FOR RENT sign inside its lone, dark-tinted window. The rest of the building had been boarded up. On one side, she saw a dirt lot where someone's antique shop had been torn down and the rubble remained. On the other side sat shabby storage facilities. Why would Aunt Gail bring her here?

"You had something to do with my mother's murder?" Mystery finally voiced the thought that had been buzzing the fastest and loudest in her head.

"Everything. Your biological father can't have his life's work destroyed by one stupid whore. He's destined for much greater things, and when I told him about Julia's plans, we worked together to send my sister to the light. He assures me I've helped him achieve God's will and that she's at peace now."

Mystery stared, blinked, shook her head. It occurred to her that she had to get over her shock and fight back, but Gail just kept dropping bombshells, one after the other. "I—I don't understand. She was your only sister."

"Who spread her legs often to tempt men to sin." Gail scoffed. "She'd stepped off the righteous path long ago. I insisted that she be blessed just before her death, and the blessed man assures me that she was. So we can rest easy that we saved the reputation of a man of God and my sister's soul the morning she went to heaven."

Every word out of her mouth sounded twisted, and Mystery cringed. "My biological father was the man in that picture snapped by the hikers just before Mom's death? He killed her?"

"You're missing the point; he sent her to God, who is glorious and will forgive all. He will remake her soul into something worthy."

And Aunt Gail sounded one hundred percent whackadoodle crazy.

As they pulled around to the back of the building, Mystery spotted another sleek black car empty and waiting. Someone else was here. It was finally hitting her that her aunt meant her harm and may have called for some help.

"After Julia was gone, things were lovely and quiet. Then you turned eighteen and were legally able to collect your mother's effects. You didn't seem to want them at first, so all was well. But then you mentioned coming to get them during your second semester of college and . . . something had to be done."

Mystery absolutely didn't recall that, but she always got sentimental about her mother and their last trip to Kansas before her death. Maybe she had mentioned it. "Something?"

"Your abduction and the DNA test. Did you remember someone taking your blood?"

Shock drilled through her composure. "That's why?"

"We had to know for certain that you were the out-of-wedlock spawn of sin. And you were. But Marshall had you rescued before you could be eliminated."

Eliminated? "You and my biological father—who is he?—planned to kill me?"

Gail looked her way as if speaking to a simpleton. "We didn't silence Julia only to have this secret revealed by a silly girl. Thankfully, the abduction seemed to put some fear into you. Then you moved to the UK and seemed to lose all interest in anything associated with your 'misfortune' or your mother. We breathed easier, at least until you insisted on coming back to the States. And you know the rest." Her aunt waved her away. "I drove to Dallas and left you the picture in your hotel room, hoping you would take the hint and leave the country again. But you proved stubborn, like your mother.

You brought the one Neanderthal, Heath, with you. Thankfully, drugging his coffee took care of him. But the other one, the man you fornicated with in my house . . . Getting rid of him was fun. I overheard you two talking in my kitchen. Poor little girl scarred by her cheating 'daddy.'" She sneered. "And him, all damaged by his mother's abandonment." She rolled her eyes. "It was pitifully easy to orchestrate your breakup. My messiah, the man who gave his seed for you, knew just how to hire an actress capable of causing a fight between you two. I slipped a diuretic in Axel's lemonade, and when he went to the restroom, she moved in. Then you saw what you expected and walked out on him. It was perfect. Of course, I suspect Axel may already be looking for you. He's not one who will give up easily, so let's hurry inside, shall we?"

So Axel hadn't given in to a moment's lust in the café and betrayed her? He hadn't come on to that waitress? Mystery tried to piece it all together in her head. The details slipped through her fingers, but the big picture was frightfully clear. Her aunt had conspired with her mother's lover—her biological father—to split her apart from Axel and Heath. Her aunt had gone to so much effort to get her alone because she'd be more vulnerable. Mystery wondered what the hell she was going to do now.

No phone, no ally, no friends in this town, no police nearby. The only person perhaps capable of finding her was Axel, and he'd sworn that if she walked out on him he'd consider them done forever.

Still, some part of her hoped, wanted to have faith—not in the warped version of God her aunt had clutched to her bitter, dried-up heart and twisted to fill the emptiness inside, but in the love that she and Axel had shared, however briefly.

"I won't go in that building."

"You will," her aunt insisted, grabbing Mystery's purse from the floorboard. "If you refuse, I will shoot you right here."

It sucked, and Mystery was terrified, shocked, and beyond furious. But right now, cuffed to the car door, she didn't see any way to escape. She'd have to watch for opportunities. After all, her aunt was older, presumably not as strong. If she played this right, she might be able to overpower the woman on the way to the door and scream for help. "Looks like I don't have a choice."

Gail sent her an acid smile. "Exactly. Now, it's time you met your true father."

Chapter Nineteen

THIS far out of town, the only signs of life near the abandoned building were the weeds growing up through the cracks in the sidewalk. Her aunt walked with the gun pressed to Mystery's spine straight up to the ominous dark door. She would have screamed for help if anyone was around to hear. Scrambling for other options, Mystery decided to take her chances and tackle her aunt on the sidewalk in public.

Suddenly, the door opened from the inside.

Clutching her purse, Mystery blinked, her eyes adjusting to the interior darkness, focused on a black shadow in front of her. Slowly, the shadow sharpened into a man with gray hair sporting hints of brown and pale blue eyes. His pale skin looked oddly smooth, given the fact he must be in his early fifties, and he wore a plastically kind smile that showed a row of even white teeth. She knew that face.

"Peter Grace?"

"The great Reverend Peter Grace," Gail corrected, her tone superior. "He's as close to God as you'll ever see on this Earth."

The picture of the man at the top of her aunt's stairs, along with the chatter about him today, only reinforced her notion that Gail was one of his biggest fans.

"Yes. Isn't she devoted?" He sent her an empty smile as he tugged Mystery inside.

Her aunt followed, and slammed the door shut, locking it behind her. Mystery watched, her heart sinking. She was trapped in an abandoned building with a gun, a crazy bitch, and a man capable of committing murder.

She blew out a nervous breath, praying they just wanted her mother's possessions. "What are you after? The SD card my mother left in the safe-deposit box? You can have it. I'm not sure I want to know what it says and I don't care. To me, Marshall Mullins will always be my father."

"I'm glad we're on the same page. I would prefer for the world to believe that as well." He adjusted his tie, his stare almost wistful. "You do look so much like your mother."

"She's a sinner, too. Fornicator!" her aunt broke in.

Reverend Grace rested a well-manicured hand on Gail's. "We'll show her the Lord."

That seemed to soothe the woman.

Mystery tensed. Did they mean they meant to kill her? "Look, I don't want anything except to walk out this door alive. I'll sign anything you want to have drawn up stating that you and I are of no relation and I have no intention of ever suing you for any reason. I will never speak of this and—"

"That's a lovely gesture," he assured. "I'm afraid it's not that simple. You see, loose ends have, over the decades, proven to be a problem. Too many still dangle, especially now that whatever your mother wrote has been unlocked. I need to clean everything up. Otherwise, a really intrepid reporter or detective will uncover my sin. And what would my millions of followers think if they learned their favorite man of God had a 'love child' while his own wife was expecting baby number three? Jimmy Swaggart's infamous 'I have sinned' speech was useless then, just as it would be now. No, I have to eradicate all lingering traces. Even your middle name is a clue."

Grace. A wave of dizzy shock swept over Mystery. Her mother had given her his surname for her middle name. As a tribute to Reverend Grace? Or as a taunt at her father? "I'll change it. I'll go to court and make it whatever you want."

He sent her a faintly regretful smile. "I'm afraid that won't work. The change of name would still be a matter of public record, and therefore, a clue."

Was he saying his only alternative was to kill her? Mystery swallowed hard and started looking around the empty, cavernous room for anything she might use as a weapon or any exit she hadn't spotted from the street.

"I've ensured the room is empty and all the doors are locked." Reverend Grace snapped his fingers. "Eyes on me."

Mystery wasn't simply going to take his word for it, but it sounded as if he'd planned two steps ahead of her and done all he could to prevent her escape. "You don't have to kill me to keep your secret. I'm just—"

"Give me the SD card you found in her safe-deposit box." He stepped closer, avoiding all negotiation with her. "And I'll need that cross from around your neck."

Automatically, she lifted her hand to her chest to cover it. "What?"

She didn't love the piece, but her mother had left it to her. She couldn't imagine why he wanted something that had mostly sentimental value. Sure, it was worth something, but Peter Grace had millions—tax free. He didn't need to steal her mom's cross.

"I inscribed our initials on the back and gave that to her. Once, she was my . . . special follower. She came to me for spiritual guidance after her new, troubled marriage was falling apart due to Mullins's infidelity. I counseled her for several months and encouraged her to bring him in for couple's therapy, so I could show him God's way. He refused. Apparently, they saw a secular marriage counselor.

I applauded them for getting any sort of help until Julia realized Mullins had lain with the very woman they'd hired to help them resolve their troubles. She found out while her husband was out of the country filming a movie. She came to me in a state—confused and angry and wanting revenge. She tempted me, and Satan can sneak up on a man when he's not always vigilant." He sighed. "It wasn't my finest moment. I've suffered for my sin ever since."

Mystery just stared. In his custom suit, Italian loafers, and perfect manicure, Peter Grace didn't look like he'd suffered a bit. Nor would he suffer in killing his illegitimate daughter.

She had to figure out how to get out of here. She couldn't take on both Reverend Grace and her aunt at once. Somehow, she'd have to eliminate them one at a time. Maybe she was grasping at straws, but she had nothing better now.

Slowly, Mystery removed the cross from around her neck. Knowing she'd received it from the reverend who'd blamed her mother for his own lust, just like an utter creep, made Mystery's skin crawl. Once she'd unclasped it, she handed the piece of jewelry to him. "All yours."

He took it in his palm, looking way too placid for someone about to commit murder. "Thank you for your cooperation." He tucked the cross into his pocket. "Now the SD card. Have you read anything on it?"

"Not a word. We haven't had time since retrieving it from the bank." She wished now they'd had time to grab Heath's computer from the trunk of the car so she'd know what secrets her mother held sacred, but she'd gladly trade the knowledge for her life.

"Excellent." He nodded. "The good news is, not only will destroying this file help me, but Mullins, too. If this is the same text I read on Julia's computer after her sad death, many of that man's secrets will never see the light of day. So this debacle will at least end happily for a few."

Just not for her, if he got his way.

Mystery tried to focus moment by moment as she reached into her purse for the SD card. She knew exactly what pocket she'd secured it in but pretended otherwise to buy herself time to look for anything that could be used as a weapon. She found a hairbrush, lipstick, wallet, breath mints . . . but nothing sharp or blunt.

"Hurry up," her aunt demanded. "Give the card to me."

"Or I'm afraid we'll be forced to shoot," Reverend Grace added.

Since he'd pushed the mother of one of his children off a cliff to her death, she believed him.

With shaking hands, she started to do as he bid, then realized that once she gave him the disc, she was disposable. He would kill her and not think twice. He might also kill her if she played dumb, but her odds were better if she stalled.

"I can't find it," she lied.

"How can that be?" her aunt cried. "You said you had it. Did you already lose it, you terrible spawn of sin?"

Mystery looked at Gail again. Had the woman felt this way about her during every childhood visit? Every craft project they'd done together? Every cookie they'd baked? The thought saddened her, almost defeated her. But Mystery knew she couldn't dwell on that. The woman under Gail's façade was petty, small-minded, and fanatical. This "pious" woman believed she was a soldier of God and would rejoice in her own niece's death.

"Maybe it fell out of my purse," Mystery suggested with a shrug, secretly scooping it between her fingers while pretending to scour the insides of the bag.

"Give that to me," her aunt snapped, gripping the leather straps and giving them a good tug.

As her aunt seized the bag, Mystery managed to catch the disc in her palm. Instantly, she shoved her hand in her pocket like it was a nervous habit. That wasn't the best hiding place for the card, but stashing it bought her more time. Maybe by then Heath would find her. She'd love to think that Axel would come looking for her, too, but . . . *Don't go there. One second at a time. Deal with heartache tomorrow.*

Still, she wished she could go back in time to the moment she'd seen Axel with the waitress—the actress—and handle everything differently. She had to stop knee-jerking and seeing everything through her mom's filter. She had to start using her own head.

If she lived through this ordeal, Mystery swore that's exactly what she'd do.

Gail dumped the purse upside down, and the contents splattered all over the floor. The woman knelt, setting the gun at her feet, then sifted through everything, prying into her belongings and either throwing or shoving them away when the invasive search proved fruitless.

Mystery couldn't reach the firearm without reaching across her aunt's body, and either the crazy bitch or the psycho would kill her for it. Still, she had to try.

As she tried to inch toward it, Gail picked the bag up by its bottom and shook vigorously. With a frustrated grunt when nothing new fell out, she tossed the purse across the room and retrieved the gun.

"Before we left the car, you said the disc was in here." Her aunt sent her an accusing stare, pointing the ominous barrel of the weapon at her.

"I thought it was," Mystery lied, shrugging. "Maybe it fell out in the car or on the walk over here. Or maybe . . ." She pretended horror. "At Osborne's office. I don't know."

Her aunt huffed, then looked at Reverend Grace. "I told you she's a foolish jezebel, like her mother."

He raised a brow at Mystery, then knelt to retrieve the letters she'd retrieved from her mom's safe-deposit box. He opened one of the love notes and scanned. "Jealousy is such a destructive emotion. Your mother resented every female who flirted with her husband. He is a man easily led by lust—a weak man she should never have fallen in love with—but Julia allowed that jealousy to drive a wedge between them that never healed." He turned to Aunt Gail. "It's the same jealousy that allowed hate to fester in the older sister for the younger."

Gail blinked at him in shock. "Jealous? I had no reason to feel a moment's envy for Julia."

When Mystery realized her aunt's hand wavered at the accusation, she piled more on. "You totally did. You resented that she horned in on your 'adventure' to Hollywood. You were pissed off that she got a bit part in a movie and some TV roles when you never even received a callback. You especially hated that my father"—she sneered at Reverend Grace—"tossed you out of his bed because he preferred my mother. And he *married* her. He may not be perfect, but you wanted Marshall Mullins. And he loved her."

With wide, furious eyes, Gail curled her finger around the trigger of the gun and steadied her stance. "Give me the word, Reverend."

"Not yet. I think your niece knows exactly where that disc is, and I think I know exactly how to make her give it to me." The minister sauntered closer to Gail.

What he lacked in style, he made up for with a calm, knowledgeable charisma that probably spoke to his lost and confused followers who desperately sought a leader in their daily lives—like her aunt. How gullible a mark she must have been for him.

"Did you sleep with Gail, too?" Mystery blurted.

"Of course not!" her aunt gasped out.

Reverend Grace shook his head. "No. You will never believe me when I say that Julia was the only woman with whom I strayed from my marriage. I truly do strive to build a Christian empire God would be proud of and live by His teachings. Occasionally . . . unfortunate situations present themselves, and I'm still paying for my most terrible sin: you." He sent her a tight little smile. "Julia really was the prettier sister."

Mystery could barely take in all the craziness dripping from that speech, but the verbal slap across her aunt's face came through loud and clear.

He reached for Gail's hand, the one currently gripping the gun, and wrapped his fingers around hers. As he did, a shaft of sunlight leaked through the ceiling, and Mystery saw then that he wore flesh-colored latex gloves. He gripped the weapon firmly over her hand and raised the weapon. As he raised it to Gail's temple, he entwined his finger with hers, smiling into her gaping expression. "You really have been a good soldier."

Then he pulled the trigger.

Mystery gasped so loudly, the sound reverberated through the entire building. She shook as she watched her aunt collapse to the ground, her brains sprayed across the tile floor. Blood splattered everywhere. Gail's eyes were still open.

"Do I have your attention now?" he asked, retrieving the gun from her aunt's limp hand.

She jerked her gaze away from the corpse and over to the supposed man of God who'd pulled the trigger as if doing nothing more out of the ordinary than starting a car or opening a window.

"Yeah." She gave him a jerky nod.

"Excellent. Poor, distraught woman simply couldn't handle the stress of seeing all the personal effects her sister left behind and that drove her to kill herself . . ." He affected a sad pout.

Mystery wanted to choke. "How can you treat people as if they're expendable?"

"The lives of the lowly many simply aren't worth those of the exalted few."

Her jaw dropped. "Like you?"

"Precisely. Now, let's search your pockets. If that proves unsuccessful, I'll have to retrace your steps and . . ." Wearing a bland expression that probably soothed his gullible followers, he tsked at her, indicating that it wouldn't end well for her.

That scared the hell out of Mystery.

A siren wailed in the distance, and she prayed that Heath had noticed her missing or someone had heard the gunshots and called for help. A rattling at the front door sounded through the eerie still next, as if someone gave it a few good tugs, then realized it was locked tight.

Reverend Grace's gaze zipped to the door. "I'd hoped to have the peace of knowing you further before . . . But I need the disc more. Let's get down to business and not dwell on unpleasantries. Turn out your pants pockets."

Once she did, he'd know that she'd plotted and lied. He'd pull the trigger. He'd spew her brains all over the floor, too.

Mystery cut her stare to her aunt's lifeless body, surrounded by a thick pool of her coppery blood. The smell nearly made her wretch. She started shaking again. *Think fast. Now!*

If she could lure him closer to her, she might be able to swipe the gun from him. Or if he came at her like an attacker, she could fight him off. After feeling so helpless in that shack with nothing but sand and shrieking wind around her, then having Axel rescue her and insist that she learn to defend herself, Mystery had.

"Make me." She shoved her fists on her hips for effect, praying it needled him.

Instead, he just looked weary—and pointed the gun at her. "Do it or I pull the trigger."

She swallowed as she stared down the barrel. Her father—the one who mattered—would suffer a huge blow if she didn't make it out alive. Mystery wanted to live to explain the truth about her mother's murder to him. She wanted to live long enough to apologize to Axel and tell him that she loved him. She wanted to have his children and grow old and . . . For any of that to happen, she had to be smart.

"No, you won't, because if I don't have it in my pocket, I'm the only person who knows exactly which path I walked all day. Gail could have helped you, but you were hasty and impatient and you murdered someone who idolized you." What would his followers say about that? Mystery wanted to taunt him with that but if she did, he'd probably only kill her sooner. She was definitely a loose end he wouldn't leave dangling.

The wail of the siren came closer. Something rattled at the side of the building, a noise of metal scraping wood. Mystery couldn't place it but she prayed it was someone trying to help her get free and live.

Reverend Grace lowered the gun from her head, aiming for her thigh. "I'm running out of time, I fear. I'll wound you. It will hurt, but you'll still be able to help me retrace your path to find the disc. Now hurry and turn your pockets out or you'll learn that God has far more mercy than I do."

"And if you get your hands on the disc, you'll kill me." She shrugged. "You're not getting out of here, you know. Someone is on the other side of the wall, looking for a way to save me."

A trickle of sweat ran from his temple down to his cheek. "You're right. You'll make a much better hostage." Without warning, he grabbed her arm and smacked her on the side of the head with the gun in his hand. Pain exploded through her skull. She gasped, feeling dazed. She stumbled. Her world nearly went black.

Reverend Grace used the opportunity to jerk her back against his chest. He gave a vicious yank on her hair—and wedged the barrel of the gun to her ribs. Then he shoved his left hand in the empty pocket of her jeans and turned it inside out.

When nothing emerged, he heaved a frustrated sigh. "Don't move."

He leaned away, switched the gun to his left hand, and fumbled a bit. Despite her head throbbing and the nausea churning in her stomach, Mystery knew she had to act. Because if he put his hand into her right pocket, it would be game over for her.

Summoning her balance and strength, she raised her foot and stomped on his toes. He hopped on one foot behind her with a nasty curse.

In the same moment, the siren screamed ever closer. Her head throbbed. Something landed on the roof of the building with a thud. A metallic creaking filled the room. She whirled around, looking for the source of the sound.

Instead, Reverend Grace got right in her face. "Bitch! I mourned Julia. It saddened me to kill Gail. You? I'll enjoy."

Then he pointed the gun directly at her head, mere inches away.

He would do it, Mystery knew. She wasn't ready to die, and she didn't want to hurt her father—not this sperm donor, but the one who'd actually raised her. Marshall Mullins would grieve terribly. For that, she was sorry. She knew Heath would feel guilty that he'd failed to save her, just as he'd been unable to save his wife. And Axel . . . the selfish part of her hoped that he'd mourn her, but then she shut that down. What she really wanted to know before she died was whether he loved her. But it would be better for him if he didn't. He could easily move on with his life, maybe make peace with his mother, find someone he could love, and live happily ever after.

She'd be lying, though, if she said she didn't want to be the woman next to him in that vision. She had one opportunity to make that happen before this "devout" piece of trash in her face pulled the trigger.

"I'll make it look as if your distraught aunt shot you before turning the gun on herself. What a terrible shame." He gave her a cruel sneer.

"How are you going to get out of here without being seen? We're surrounded."

He looked around the building, the sweat rolling down the side of his face a bit faster. "I'll think of something. I always do. I have the Lord on my side."

The only thing he had was flat fucking craziness.

"Now give me the disc. Turn out your damn pocket!"

Mystery shoved her hand into her pocket, pretending she needed to widen her stance in order to dig deeper. Her head was still swimming, and dizziness began to overtake her. She dragged in a deep breath of air. The smell of blood made her stomach turn once more, and she almost lost her lunch, bucking and heaving.

"No fucking way. Empty your pocket now!" he screamed.

The sirens now sounded right outside the door. Another noise on the roof snagged her attention. His finger tightened around the trigger.

It was now or never.

She gathered all her strength—and kicked him in the balls.

With a cry, he dropped the gun, sending it clattering across the tile to the back of the room as he clutched his genitals with a terrible groan. "Cunt."

"Asshole," she tossed over her shoulder as she ran for the door. Safety and freedom awaited her out there if she could just get the door open.

Heart racing, every muscle trembling, she struggled to retain her balance and reach the front entrance of the building. She barely held her nausea at bay as she gripped the knob of the dead bolt and turned it. But when she tried to push the door open, it wouldn't budge.

Mystery whimpered. She tried not to panic as she sucked back her tears and forced herself to focus, turning the knob in the other direction.

Behind her, she heard footsteps and whirled to find Reverend Grace recovered and ready to pull the trigger again. "That card is in your pocket or you wouldn't be fighting me so hard. I'm going to blow your brains all over this fucking door and take that card. I'll preserve my legacy. You'll be nothing but a fading headline and dust. Good-bye."

As she heard the door's dead bolt finally retract, Axel suddenly appeared from the shadows in the cavernous room behind the psycho. He had his weapon drawn and gripped firmly in his beefy hands, his face fierce, his stance all warrior.

Relief swept through Mystery. Her knees almost went out from under her. "Axel."

He didn't look her way.

"Put the gun down," he demanded of Reverend Grace. "Or I'll kill you before you can twitch, you scum-sucking motherfucker."

He didn't turn to face Axel. "Her first."

As the televangelist moved to pull the trigger, the door in front of her whooshed open, and Heath filled up the portal. His eyes went cold as he shoved her down toward the ground. Suddenly, gunfire echoed all around her. Her head hit the metallic doorframe. Pain ripped through her skull. She fell, crumpling on her side, and saw Axel sprinting toward her with worry and fear all over his face. Heath loomed above her.

"Are you all right?" one of them shouted.

"You came," she managed to eke out. "I saved it. Right pocket."

Then everything went black.

Chapter Twenty

MYSTERY woke in the hospital to the sounds of a man murmuring softly.

"She suffered a mild concussion, but she'll be fine with rest. We've treated her other various abrasions and contusions. She required two stitches in her scalp from a blow to the side of the head. With a gun, according to the police report. But she'll recover fully soon. All in all, she's a lucky woman."

"Oh, thank goodness." Worry tightened that familiar voice. Though it wavered a bit, Mystery would have recognized it anywhere.

"Dad," she managed to croak out as she struggled to open her eyes.

The sounds of scuffling came next, and she felt a strong hand grip hers with such care. "Mystery, my baby girl."

"Excuse me, sir. This is the first time the patient has been conscious since the ambulance brought her in. You'll have to let me examine her first."

Her father squeezed her hand and reluctantly let go. Mystery wasn't ready to release his familiar comfort yet and tried to reach out for him again, but her arm seemed to weigh a thousand pounds.

With the lure of sleep trying to pull her back under, she simply couldn't lift it.

The doctor moved closer. He smelled like antiseptic and latex. When he touched her cheek, he felt cool but gentle.

"Can you open your eyes, Ms. Mullins?"

Mystery summoned her strength and lifted her lashes. Everything in her view looked fuzzy at first. She focused from the blur of white all around her to the flashing lights of the monitors keeping track of her vital signs. The doctor wore blue scrubs. Beyond him, she saw the Oscar-winning director she'd always called her father. He looked haggard and frantic. No matter what the press thought, that fame didn't shield him from normal human emotions and concerns. She froze. Did he know the truth about her parentage yet?

The doctor checked a few more vitals, read her chart, and asked questions. Yes, her head still hurt. Yes, she knew her name and what had happened in the abandoned building. Yesterday? Had she been unconscious for a whole day?

"Sedated," said the doctor, a kind man in his forties with brown eyes and a calm demeanor. "You don't remember coming to the hospital?"

She shook her head.

"It's not uncommon to have lapses in memory with concussions. Your CAT scans look otherwise normal, and I'd like to monitor you one more day. But I think you'll be able to leave here tomorrow."

Mystery thanked him in a croaky voice. The man she'd always considered her father shook his hand, then rushed to her side as the doctor left.

"You had me so worried," he said, his voice breaking.

"When did you get here?" It was good to see him, but he looked as if he hadn't slept in days. He'd clearly raked his fingers through his shaggy salt-and-pepper hair a lot.

"A few hours ago. I spoke to a nurse on the phone, then I saw

Heath and Axel, followed by the police. I'm just now reaching your side."

Her stomach tightened. "So you know everything?"

He didn't pretend to misunderstand. His face softened. "I've always known. Not who Julia had the affair with, but that you weren't mine biologically. It simply wasn't possible."

Her eyes watered, and it immediately made her head hurt worse. "You never told me?"

He brushed the tear from the corner of her eye. "Your mother and I intended to when you were older. After she died, I meant to. I knew I should. But I never considered you any less than my daughter. I guess . . . a part of me worried that, if you knew the truth, you would."

"Never." Her voice sounded more like a squeak as her eyes filled again. "You're my father and you always will be."

Past her IV and all the electrodes for the monitors, her dad hugged her as tightly as he dared. "I worried about you so much, kiddo. If it hadn't been for Heath and Axel, I don't know what would have happened."

As he choked on his words, Mystery absorbed all his worry and pain. She cupped his face, wincing as the tape over her IV pinched her skin. "I was *thisclose* to escaping by myself, but yeah, they got me out safely. I'm going to be fine."

She wanted to ask where they were, but her father jumped in. "I thanked Heath with enough money to live well for a couple of years. He, um . . . gave me his notice, effective immediately. He passed on a recommendation for a few capable colleagues but—"

"I knew he was going to quit." She winced.

God, she would miss Heath so much. He'd been a part of her everyday life for over six years. But it wasn't fair of her to cling onto him when she couldn't cling back. He deserved the chance to make a life with a woman who could devote herself utterly to him. Maybe he'd find a nice British woman with some cats who taught primary school and would give him a few children. Mystery couldn't picture him settling down again, but stranger things had happened.

"Did he finally admit that he loves you or did you figure it out?" her father asked.

"You knew?" Mystery blinked.

"I've known for a while."

"I suspected, so I asked. I don't feel the same way." And she felt terrible about kissing him the way she had. She'd like to apologize to him again, but at this point, it would soothe her more than help him. "Has he already returned to London?"

"Not just yet." Her father grimaced. "In saving you, he took a bullet. A nick in the forearm, really, but he's just come out of surgery, so I think he'll be here at least a few days. The good news is, Peter Grace is dead. Heath and Axel both landed a headshot, one in front, one in back. Wasn't much left. The cross he gave your mother is part of the police evidence, but will eventually be returned to you. But the SD card you retrieved from your mother's safe-deposit box mysteriously vanished." He sent her an expression of mock innocence. "Regardless, the press has already run with the story that he killed both your mother and your aunt, so it's a huge scandal. His religious fiefdom is done."

"Do the press know . . . why that bastard murdered them and tried to kill me?" *Do they know I'm not your daughter by blood?* She couldn't bring herself to voice the question.

"No," he murmured. "The police have refused to comment about Grace's motive or the particulars."

Mystery breathed a sigh of relief. "Were they able to discern the events from the scene of the crime?"

"Based on the evidence and statements from Heath and Axel, yes. They've pieced together enough so they should be able to close the case, once you give a statement and corroborate their accounts. Then we'll deal with the press. So far, they're speculating wildly about Grace's motives, but they haven't come anywhere near the truth. I'll leave that up to you. Of course, Heath and Axel know, but I'll never tell anyone if you'd rather keep that a secret between us."

Mystery turned that notion and its consequences over in her head as much as her weariness allowed. But really, it didn't matter who'd donated the sperm that had created her. What mattered was she'd become the woman she was today in large part because of this flawed, artistic, infuriating, incredibly loving father in front of her. "It's our secret."

He smiled at her, his eyes tearing up. "I love you."

"I love you, too, Dad. I wish you could be happy someday, find that one woman who could really complete you, even if that sounds cheesy to you and—"

"It's doesn't, and I'm damn tired of being lonely." He raked his hand through his hair again and forced a laugh. "I'm fifty-two, I drive a red sports car, and date women half my age. I'm a fucking walking cliché. I need to figure out what's missing or broken inside me and fix it. Believe it or not, I'd like to be married again, maybe even have another baby. Who knows?" He shrugged. "I actually started seeing a therapist last month. It's . . . good so far. We'll see. I'm a work in progress."

She cracked a smile. "That's true. Sometimes I don't know whether to call you a piece of work or a work of art, but you're a wonderful father and I couldn't have asked for better."

"You've made me so proud, kiddo. I know if your mom could see the woman you've become, she'd smile and tell you how much she loves you. You were her everything."

"I know, and I still miss her."

"I do, too. I wish I had a second chance to tell her so many things, but I can't take back the words I never said. Hell, if I had her in my life again, I'd do so many things differently. I can only say that I've learned and grown since then. I hope she's forgiven me."

"You know Mom. She didn't have the ugliness in her to stay

angry or hate. She probably wished she could understand why you strayed, but I'm sure she forgave you."

"I'm working on understanding, too, so when I find the right woman, it won't happen again."

Silence lulled between them for a long moment, and Mystery couldn't help but think about all that had happened in two short days . . . and wonder what came next. She knew someone to whom she owed a huge apology.

"So, you've seen Axel? Is he all right?" A horrifying thought occurred to her. "Did he get hurt, too?"

"No," her father rushed to assure her. "He's fine. He's been fielding the press and spending time at your bedside, from what I understand. You love him."

Her father's words gave her hope. "I never stopped. Spending the last few days with him just made my love that much deeper. I feel terrible about the things I believed and said at that crappy café. I should have stopped to think . . . to realize the sort of man he is and not—"

Mystery broke off when she realized that her father probably had no idea what she was talking about.

He laughed. "I'm sure he'll be happy to hear that. I believe he said something about an apology as well. But I'll leave that to you two." Her father released her and eased back toward the wall.

Then Axel filled her vision, and for a moment, she was struck speechless. He looked so vital and masculine in a dark blue shirt that showed off his broad shoulders and bulging chest. He carried himself with a quiet confidence that still made her melt. For the second time in her life, he'd rescued her from a life-or-death situation. He'd always be her hero. Now she simply hoped that he wanted her to make him her man.

"Marshall." He stuck out his hand to her father, and they shook. "Press conference handled. I hate those flesh-eating bastards, but your PR firm helped a great deal. They're waiting for you."

"I'm grateful for everything. I know it's absolutely none of my business, but I think you're wonderful for my daughter. You'd make a great son-in-law, too." He grabbed something from his pocket and winked. "I brought that item you asked for."

As Axel took whatever her father held, Mystery tried not to gape. Her dad had *not* just said that. She bit back a groan, vowing to clobber her father later.

With an apologetic grimace, her father slid across the floor and kissed her forehead again. "I'll see you in a bit. Once I'm gone, say what you need to. And be happy."

"Bye, Dad." She put just enough bite in her voice to reinforce the fact that she'd have words for him later.

Pressing her lips together, she watched him clap Axel's arm again and leave the room.

Then Mystery didn't know what to say. The old her might have feigned sleep to avoid the embarrassment and potential rejection. She wasn't that girl anymore.

"Hi."

"Hi," he answered, the syllable a low rumble from his big chest as he shoved the something her father had brought in his pocket. His voice had always melted her, and today was no exception.

"I'm sorry if he embarrassed you." Mystery wanted to cringe almost as much as she wanted to know what her father had given him.

"Not at all. I need to talk to you." He sounded beyond serious. His square face and blue eyes had gone solemn.

She swallowed. "First, I have to say a couple of things, if you'll let me."

He gestured to her. "Ladies first."

Mystery nodded, took a deep breath, gathered her courage—and jumped off the proverbial cliff. "First, you rescued me again, and I'm grateful. Thank you so very much." She shook her head, hating that she teared up and her head felt as if it were splitting open and she probably looked as appealing as the bottom of a shoe. But he was listening. Nothing else mattered. "Words are totally inadequate to thank you for all you've done for me. I'm better for knowing you, Axel. You were the first person who told me I could accomplish anything I wanted in life. You taught me to climb a mountain—literally. After you rescued me the first time, I started climbing them alone figuratively because I finally believed I could. After you opened my eyes, I learned to defend myself, I published books, I embraced life. I learned to do almost everything, except to live without you. I just couldn't do that."

He reached behind him with that huge wingspan and dragged the rolling chair over to her bedside, then thumbed the tears from her eyes. "Princess—"

"Let me finish, okay?"

"Sure." He brushed the hair from her face, caressing her head in a slow, soothing motion.

"Before you saved me this time, you taught me what sex felt like and how wonderful being adored feels. And I screwed up everything. I think deep down I was always that scared nineteen-year-old who wanted your affection and never believed I'd have it. I'm sorry I ran out on you. I'm sorry I didn't believe you at the café or listen to you or . . ." She drew in a shuddering breath. "Do anything that proves how much I love you. I made mistakes. I'll always make them. But these last few days with you have taught me that if I want forever, I have to fight for it. So I'm asking you for another chance. Let me get things right this time. I'll never leave you again."

He eased closer and swallowed. "You've taught me a few things, too. You know, I really didn't know what the hell listening to my heart felt like until you. I was a soldier. I knew order and rules and discipline. You, Mystery, burst into my life and gave me lovely chaos. I saw the world through new eyes. Every moment with you has been an adventure. I could do with a bit less adrenaline going forward." He smiled softly at her, his blue eyes so tender she teared up all over again. "But until you, I never believed I'd have anyone to call my own."

"Axel . . ." She wanted to get out of this damn hospital bed and hug him. Frustration that she couldn't welled up.

"I'm sorry I lost my temper after lunch and let you go. And you'll never know how badly nearly losing you yesterday scared the hell out of me. After that son of a bitch nearly shot you, I ran across the room and scooped you up in my arms." His face tightened, as did his grip on her hand. His eyes swam with tears. "I knew I couldn't live without you another moment. And I knew I loved you. Well, I knew it when you left the café, and like an idiot, I'd failed more than once to see the other half of my soul right in front of me. Never again. You're mine."

His expression, the warm glow of his blue eyes, told her that he meant every word. Her heart nearly burst. A huge smile broke across her face. "And you're mine."

He leaned in and kissed her so gently it made her chest tighten and her heart soar. "I knew how to fight for forever, but I didn't know how to embrace it . . . until you. So what do you want to do next, princess? Obviously, you need to marry me." He gripped her hand tighter. "And we'll have to decide where to live. I've never been to London, but I'm not opposed—"

"Say that again?" Mystery couldn't possibly have heard that right.

"I'll move to London with you." He grinned at her.

"Actually, I'd like to stay here, but repeat the part you said just prior."

He sighed heavily, then pressed another kiss to her lips. "I can't slip anything past you, can I? All right. Marry me."

"You're sure? We've really only known one another for a few days." She played devil's advocate. "Are you certain?"

"Yep." He grinned broadly, showing off his dimples. "I don't have to think twice. When you know, you just know. In fact, I'm so sure that when I called your dad to tell him everything that had happened, I asked him for permission to marry you. I wanted to propose to you with an engagement ring but I wanted it to be special, like you. Meaningful. The most meaningful thing I could think of was your mother's wedding ring."

He extracted it from his pocket and held it up, his big fingers around the thin band holding up the winking diamond solitaire. Mystery gasped, touched all the way down to the bottom of her heart. Mom couldn't be with her, but with this ring, Axel both gave her the promise of a future and something like her mother's spirit and blessing.

Tears stung her eyes, rolled down her cheeks.

"We can have a new wedding band made to match. Or if you want something that's all yours, that's fine. I want you to have whatever—"

"This is perfect. Ohmigod, I love that you thought of this," she sobbed out, losing herself in his eyes. "I've always known you were the one for me. I swear I'll do my best to be the most loving, trusting, supportive wife ever, but I'm not perfect and I may slip up—"

"I might, too. Listen, I took your advice and tracked down my mom this morning. Turns out she regrets leaving the family more than anything and didn't think any of us would ever speak to her again. She's sad and lonely and broken, just like my dad and brothers. Just like I would have been without you. We're going to keep talking, but the whole thing made me realize that I masked my isolation well by taking care of everyone around me, especially Sweet Pea. But no one ever touched my heart until you. We're not perfect people, but I think we're perfect for each other. Isn't that what's important?"

Happiness broke through her headache, the fog of her sedatives, her exhaustion, insecurities, and trembling desperation.

"Yes." Mystery met him halfway for a reverent kiss. She pressed her lips to his for a long, lingering heartbeat. "With my whole heart, yes. Nothing is more important than how perfect we are together. I will very happily marry you, you wonderful man." She cupped his face; she couldn't touch him enough, couldn't think of anything she wanted more than to see him in her arms, across her kitchen table, smiling in the car, holding her and their children. She couldn't think of anyone else she wanted to share a future with.

"Oh, thank God." Axel sounded like he'd been genuinely worried about her answer. "And you want to stay in Dallas?"

"I think so. It's hotter than hell, and I may change my mind come August, but yes. I'm an American girl at heart. I can write anywhere, but this is your home."

"You're an amazing woman. I'm so lucky you said yes."

Mystery smiled, then rolled her eyes. "How could you doubt my answer? Come on, I've thrown myself at you since almost the moment I met you. At the ghost town . . ."

He groaned. "I wanted so badly to throw you against the wall and fuck you blind."

Mystery smiled. "I wanted you to, but you were right. Now that I've felt how connected we are when we make love, I couldn't have handled the emotion then."

He dragged in a shuddering breath. "I don't know if I could have even handled it. But when you picked me up at that little beer dive the other day? Oh, princess, the things I wanted to do to you. You know, I've only scratched the surface."

He hissed through his teeth, a sound sizzling with need. Every cell in her body pinged with life. "Is that right? Well, then . . . I really wish we could go somewhere more private and . . ."

"Talk?" He echoed the words he'd said to her in the bar the afternoon that had changed both their lives. The heated grin he paired with that deep, dark syllable had her shivering. Conversation was the last thing on his mind.

"No." She shook her head and sent him a saucy, come-hither stare. "To fuck. Would you be interested?"

As she traced a random pattern across his jaw and over the rapidly beating pulse at his neck, he sucked in a breath. "Every day. I love you, princess."

"My hero." She sighed, smiling at him with her whole heart. "I love you, too."

Don't miss the next book in Shayla Black's
New York Times bestselling Wicked Lovers series

Yours to Protect

Coming soon from Berkley Books

Now, turn the page for a sneak preview of the next
Perfect Gentlemen novel from *New York Times*
bestselling authors Shayla Black and Lexi Blake

Seduction in Session

Coming Winter 2016 from Berkley Books

I DON'T really need a bodyguard." Lara Armstrong took a sip of her chai tea and sat back, staring out the coffeehouse window. Everywhere she looked, people bustled by, their briefcases in hand, cell phones pressed to their ears. They were lawyers and politicians, along with their aides, and anyone else who thought they were important in the political spectrum. Soon, one of those people hustling about would be the man designated to throw himself in front of a bullet for her.

Connor. No last name. Or maybe that was his last name and he hadn't given her his first name. She wasn't sure. She only knew that enigmatic Connor had commanded she meet him here at three thirty. Did he realize how bad traffic was going to get?

"Look, someone knows what you've been doing, L, and that means you need a bodyguard." Her best friend, Kiki, traded a look with the only male at the table.

Tom sat forward, his hands around his nonfat latte as though he needed the warmth. "I don't know. I kind of agree with Lara."

Kiki rolled her dark eyes. "You always agree with Lara. You even agreed with her when she broke off your engagement. You're a doormat."

"I'm helpful and practical." He frowned. "Look, she's only received a couple of e-mails, and it wasn't as if the sender attached a bomb or anything. The contents simply stated that they 'know.' Know what? That could mean anything."

Lara sighed and lowered her voice. Only a couple of people in the world knew what she did for a living, and she meant to keep it that way. "He knows I run CS."

Capitol Scandals, DC's most fun and informative news site. Oh, most people called it a horrid tabloid rag that aimed to ruin the lives and reputations of politicians and bigwigs, but Lara liked her description better. And she never ran a piece that wasn't true or aimed at someone who didn't deserve it. Well, she never ran a serious piece that she couldn't verify. She didn't personally know the size of the current president's penis, though several confidential informants had used the words *extra extra large*.

"Shit." Tom's thin lips flattened further, and she knew she was in for a lecture. Unlike Kiki, who often wrote articles for CS, Tom thought the site was a horrible idea. "I told you something bad would come of this. You can't expose the people you do and expect to get away with it. I thought someone had realized you spearheaded the effort to remove vending machines from public schools or something."

"Those vending machines never sell anything but processed foods. Kids should have healthier options in school," she began.

Tom shook his head. "People don't like it when you take away their sodas, L. They get crabby. Still, I was fairly certain no one would actually kill you over that. Running a tabloid that ruins high-powered careers? That might be a little different."

Kiki nodded. "Exactly. Have you told your father?"

Lara winced. Her father knew about Capitol Scandals. He'd been very supportive when it had been a little site that reported on things like environmental bills and ran essays on the Lilly Ledbetter Act. When she'd changed to the current iteration of the site, she knew she'd tested him. He'd called screaming when she'd run a not-so-glowing story about one of his closest allies. She'd detailed just how much money the congressman had spent on hookers outside his district while those actually working in his district had lamented about a drastic downturn in income.

She'd been perfectly right to publish the story since the congressman had been running on a platform to bring new jobs and opportunities to his constituency. All the while, he'd been making deals with businessmen to send jobs offshore to Korea. So it really was a true-life metaphor for all that was wrong in politics.

Shortly after she'd published the story, the late-night circuit had picked it up. While the comedians and hosts had laughed about the hookers, their viewers had also heard the very true news about backdoor deals, too. Lara had learned early on that she had to catch the public's attention if she wanted to do any good in the world. And she wouldn't do that with a protest or a well-crafted op-ed piece.

"I'm not telling my dad. He already blackmails me. If he found out that someone else knows and is sending me semi-threatening e-mails, he would likely force me to move in with him or something. It would be awful."

It wasn't as if she didn't love her father. Her parents were amazing people. She couldn't think of another man in the world who would support her the way her dad did. He'd been angry when he'd learned about CS, but he hadn't outed her. And given that he was a senator from the great state of Virginia, he probably should have. Instead, he'd forced her to accept an apartment in a swanky part of town. She could never have afforded her DuPont Circle condo on her own. She'd wanted a little loft in a more real part of town, but her parents had been insistent.

Luckily, she'd never had to decide whether or not to run a story about her father. He was madly in love with her mom and he played things straight. Lara had never gotten a tip about him taking bribes or selling out his constituents. When she'd started Capitol Scandals, she'd realized a surprising majority of politicians were acting in the public's best interests—even if you didn't agree with their beliefs, they were following their own convictions. It was just that rancid ten percent who really screwed things up for everyone else.

She'd created Capitol Scandals to call them out.

"Maybe you should move back in with him. He has serious security." Kiki set down her mocha. "Not just a doorman named Moe who sleeps on the job."

"Moe has a serious case of narcolepsy. You shouldn't judge." She shook her head. "Besides, I can't risk working at Dad's place for two reasons: One, I don't know who's watching him. I've long thought the CIA, the NSA, or DARPA listens in on all elected officials."

Tom coughed but it sounded suspiciously like *paranoid*.

She ignored him because she knew paranoia could be a lifesaver. "And two, if anyone ever learns my secret and outs me, I want my parents to have plausible deniability."

"I don't think they'd care. They would stand by you," Kiki said.

Bringing trouble down on them was her only real fear. Well, that and global climate change. She fought for what she believed in, but she loved her parents, too. She didn't want to cause her dad issues.

"I have a plan," Tom said, getting serious again. "Hear me out. You close down the site for a while and come stay with me. I have a second bedroom. I can watch out for you. I am a Krav Maga god. We'll hang, and the heat will die down. Then you can go back to fighting the good fight."

She loved Tom, but she wasn't going there again. There was a reason she'd broken off their engagement. There was also the fact that Niall thought she needed someone to watch out for her.

Niall. Her heart did a little shudder as she thought about him. Since he ran a small site that called for transparency in California politics, he'd come to her a confidential informant. Nothing he'd sent her had actually panned out, but that wasn't so surprising.

Ninety percent of her leads were dead ends. But Niall had come to mean more to her than just a source. Over the course of the month, she'd come to view him as something of a soul mate.

"No," she said with a sigh. "I need to meet this bodyguard. I'll talk to him and see what he thinks. He's supposed to be a professional. He can give me advice."

"He can give you protection," Kiki argued. She was dressed in her normal Bohemian garb: a peasant blouse and a flowy skirt. She somehow managed to make it sexy. "You have to take this seriously. Whoever sent you that threat knew your personal e-mail."

"But there wasn't anything specific about the threat," Tom argued, then turned to Kiki. "In fact, I'm not even sure it was a threat. Maybe we're freaking out about nothing. What are the real odds that someone's put this all together? There are rumors everywhere about who runs CS, and not a one of them mentions you, Lara."

She wasn't sure that was true. What else could someone know about her? She was Senator Armstrong's vegan hippie daughter, whom everyone in the Republican party knew not to put on camera because she would use the opportunity to talk about policy as she saw it.

There really wasn't anything else about her that would be considered even slightly gossip-worthy. Good grades in the right schools. A degree in political science that would probably lead to law school when she found the time someday. She'd broken her engagement an acceptable amount of time before the wedding. She hadn't even dated in the two years since she and Tom had broken up. Capitol Scandals was the sum of her "nefarious" existence. She'd put everything she had into it, and she was finally scenting something big.

Could this new threat have anything to do with the anonymous stranger who claimed to know what really happened to Maddox Crawford? He'd hinted that if she figured out the truth, the trail would lead to something much bigger.

She merely needed to find a woman named Natalia Kuilikov. Just find one Russian immigrant, and the yellow brick road would open up and take her straight to Oz.

Lara found it interesting that her first big case and her first death threat had come so close together.

"I don't know that there's no threat, but simply figuring out who I am doesn't mean someone intends to kill me. I might have over-stated that," she admitted.

"To your Internet guy?" Kiki wasn't Niall's biggest fan. She might have mentioned on more than one occasion that he was likely a middle-aged creep looking for some online hookup. "He's the one you told, even before you told me. Before you told Tom. I hate to say it, but you seem to have some stake in the guy, and that's why you're listening to him."

"Maybe you should listen to the people who have been with you for years. What do we know about this Niall guy? Next to nothing. You can't just let this random dude start to dictate your life." Tom hopped off his barstool. He straightened his V-neck tee. "I've got to run. We have oral arguments on the McNally case tomorrow. Lara, call me if you need me. You know I'm always here for you." He walked away.

Tom clerked for an appellate judge, so he was always talking about oral arguments and drafting opinions. She had to admit, watching Tom was one of the reasons she hadn't given in to her parents' pressure and gone to law school. He was endlessly writing other people's opinions. She wanted to make up her own mind.

"Holy jeez." Kiki's eyes went wide as she stared beyond the door through which Tom had exited moments ago. "I think my mouth just watered. I finally understand what that means."

"What?" Lara turned and caught sight of a man in jeans and a T-shirt. He stood right outside the coffeehouse, his cell phone against his ear.

His shoulders were so wide they almost spanned the window. He had to be six and a half feet tall, and his T-shirt molded to every muscle and sinew of his lean strength.

He turned slightly, his profile coming into view. Lara realized then that *mouthwatering* was really just an elevated term. *Drooling* was more accurate. The man was stunning. His jaw looked perfectly square, though the lines of his face were far too angular to be beautiful. His dark blond hair was cut in an almost military style, accentuating his features. Manly. Handsome. Sexy.

His lips suddenly curled up in the hottest smirk she'd ever seen.

Caveman. Alpha male. Probably straight off some military base. She could appreciate him on an aesthetic level, but she preferred her men a little more civilized. "He's very nice looking, Kiki."

Kiki groaned. "Nice looking? There is nothing 'nice' about him. He's dirty. He's bad. And you can't dare call him a boy because he's all man."

Lara adjusted her glasses. "I like Niall more."

Niall had perfect surfer hair and the sweetest face.

"You've never met Niall."

She shrugged. "Niall is more my type."

"And by that you mean a thousand miles away and unobtainable. Safe." Kiki slapped the table. "Damn it, it's time you got laid. How long has it been?"

"Not long." She put her head down and mumbled. "Two years."

Kiki gasped. "You haven't slept with anyone since Tom? Oh my god. I never imagined it was this bad. I thought you just didn't want to talk about it."

"I talk to you about everything and you didn't think I would mention a couple of one-night stands somewhere in there?" Her eyes trailed back to Caveman Hottie. He really was amazing to gawk at. The slightest hint of a beard spread across his jaw. Though he'd probably shaved this morning, his masculinity wouldn't be denied.

"It's a muscle, you know. You have to use it to keep it healthy. I think your vajayjay has atrophied. That's why you can't think straight about this death threat stuff."

"It's not a muscle," Lara argued. But it probably had atrophied . . . and maybe grown a few cobwebs because she hadn't even played around down there herself in the longest time. She hadn't had time. Even in her head she sounded prim, like she was already collecting cats and preparing for old-maid-dom.

She had a sudden vision of that caveman putting his hands on her. Big hands. They wouldn't be soft. When he touched her, she would be able to feel every callous and rough edge of his skin. He would have working hands, hands that had built things and pro-tected people. He wouldn't ask her what she wanted. No, he wouldn't hesitate to give her what he thought she needed.

"Um, do you want to borrow my sweater?" Kiki's question forced her out of her daydream.

"No. Why?" Lara turned, not wanting to get caught staring.

"Yours is really thin and your nipples are giving this group a show," she pointed out.

Lara crossed her arms over her ridiculously erect nipples. "Guess I was a little cold."

Kiki gave her a skeptical glare. "How about we go and introduce ourselves to the hottie and see if we can buy him a coffee. Or better yet, we could take him to the bar next door, get him tipsy, and have our wicked way with him."

"Our?"

"There's a reason I'm known as Kinky Kiki, hon." She grinned, looking back at the caveman. "I'll go talk to him and you can join us after you interview the bodyguard." She glanced down at her watch. "He's late."

Lara checked her phone. Sure enough, she was supposed to have met the mysterious Connor five minutes ago. She'd gotten here early enough to have a cup of tea, but then she'd actually been instructed to meet him . . . outside.

Oh, god. Lara nearly fell off her seat. There was only one person standing outside the coffeehouse.

That glorious hunk of man.

"Kiki?" she squeaked.

Her friend settled a designer bag over her shoulder. Lara had tried to convince her to buy a purse from some Nepalese women's organization that supported indigenous children, but Kiki had replied that when Louis Vuitton supported them, she would, too. "Yes?"

"I think that's my bodyguard."

About the Author

Shayla Black is the *New York Times* and *USA Today* bestselling author of more than forty sizzling contemporary, erotic, paranormal, and historical romances produced via traditional, small press, independent, and audio publishing. She lives in Texas with her husband, munchkin, and one very spoiled cat. In her "free" time, she enjoys watching reality TV, reading, and listening to an eclectic blend of music.

Shayla's books have been translated in about a dozen languages. She has also received or been nominated for the Passionate Plume, the Holt Medallion, Colorado Romance Writers Award of Excellence, and the National Readers Choice Award. RT BOOKclub has twice nominated her for Best Erotic Romance of the Year, and also awarded her several Top Picks and a KISS Hero Award.

A writing risk-taker, Shayla enjoys tackling writing challenges with every new book. Find Shayla at ShaylaBlack.com or visit her Shayla Black-Author Facebook page.